T0265644

DEATH PACT

Also by Matt Hilton

The Grey and Villere thrillers

BLOOD TRACKS *
PAINTED SKINS *
RAW WOUNDS *
WORST FEAR *
FALSE MOVE *
ROUGH JUSTICE *
COLLISION COURSE *
BLOOD KIN *
FATAL CONFLICT *
COLD FIRE *

Joe Hunter series

RULES OF HONOUR
RED STRIPES
THE LAWLESS KIND
THE DEVIL'S ANVIL
NO SAFE PLACE
MARKED FOR DEATH
THE FOURTH OPTION

Novels

DARKE
THE GIRL ON SHATTERED ROCK
WILDFIRE
THE GIRL IN THE SMOKE *

* *available from Severn House*

DEATH PACT

Matt Hilton

SEVERN
HOUSE

First world edition published in Great Britain and the USA in 2024
by Severn House, an imprint of Canongate Books Ltd,
14 High Street, Edinburgh EH1 1TE.

severnhouse.com

British Library Cataloguing-in-Publication Data
A CIP catalogue record for this title is available from the British Library.

ISBN-13: 978-1-4483-1084-5 (cased)
ISBN-13: 978-1-4483-1085-2 (e-book)

All Severn House titles are printed on acid-free paper.

Typeset by Palimpsest Book Production Ltd., Falkirk, Stirlingshire, Scotland.
Printed and bound in Great Britain by TJ Books, Padstow, Cornwall.

Praise for Matt Hilton

"A superior standalone thriller"
Publisher's Weekly on *The Girl in the Smoke*

"The fight scenes are exceptional"
Library Journal on *Cold Fire*

"Hot conflicts rage in the freezing cold"
Kirkus Reviews on *Cold Fire*

"Just right for the Hammett and Chandler crowd"
Booklist on *Fatal Conflict*

"A riotous action read"
Booklist on *Collision Course*

"Action galore"
Kirkus Reviews on *Collision Course*

"Hilton once again shows he can tell a gripping crime story"
Publishers Weekly on *Rough Justice*

About the author

Matt Hilton worked for 23 years in private security and the police force in Cumbria. He is a 4th Dan blackbelt and coach in Ju-Jitsu. He is the author of thirteen novels in the Joe Hunter series, and ten in the Grey & Villere thrillers.

www.matthiltonbooks.com

ONE

Ohop Island, Washington, USA
1999

'We have kids in here,' Special Agent Milo Turrell hollers.

There are seven children ranging in ages from toddler to adolescent, all huddled in a cell-like room. The eldest is a girl; she'd set herself between the children and Turrell the instant he'd pushed through the door. Through tears and bared teeth, she snarls at him with the ferocity of a wild cat.

'I'm not going to hurt you,' Turrell promises, though he doesn't lower his weapon. The girl hisses again, and rakes the smoke-laden air between them. Turrell retreats a step, placating her with an out-held palm. She slaps at him.

'Can I get a little help in here?' His breathing apparatus muffles Turrell's voice, and it is lost in the calamity going on around him. He snatches a glance over his shoulder, seeking assistance. Through drifting smoke other FBI agents move, racing against the spreading flames to clear the warren of rooms and corridors. Their task is made more difficult because of the reluctance of some of those to leave; some of them resist with violence. Their hands are full, so it's down to Turrell to get the kids to safety. Unfortunately the girl's panic and animosity is spreading among the others. Some wail, others gather their courage to leap to the girl's aid.

'I'm not going to hurt you,' Turrell reiterates, 'I'm a federal agent . . . I'm here to help.'

He can imagine their fear as he hulks in the doorway, dressed in matte black paramilitary fatigues, goggles and gas mask, and toting a submachine gun. They have been taught to fear the authorities, because they are the enemies of their faith. The sudden and violent breaching of their commune will have only cemented the dogma in their young minds.

'We are the Children of Hamor . . .' the girl screeches. 'Leave us!'

'Calm down,' Turrell warns. 'I have to get you out of here. The fire . . .'

'The fire cleanses!' The girl hurtles at him, her hands forming claws. She grasps at his mask, trying to tear it from him so he'll choke in the gathering smoke. With no other option, Turrell backhands her; if he can't save her, he'll concentrate on getting the younger children to freedom. The girl wobbles, and goes to her knees. One of the boys leaps to her side, arms enveloping her protectively; he also snarls in defiance.

Turrell keys his radio and gives his call sign. 'Is anyone listening? I've a group of kids here, and need assistance getting them out.'

Nobody responds directly to him; everyone is dealing with their own emergencies as the breaching of the doors has helped fan the flames and they are spreading fast, fed by accelerants deliberately spilled by its occupants throughout the commune. It's down to him to save the kids or he may as well walk away now.

'OK!' he barks. 'Listen up. I'm here to get you to safety. Now you' – he directs his words at the boy protecting the trouble-making girl – 'help her. The rest of you, get up, and follow me out of here.'

None of them moves.

Turrell shakes his head in dismay. The smoke is thickening. Already some of the kids are beginning to wheeze.

Another boy stands, slightly older than the first but still pre-teens. He looks pained, but the grimace on his face isn't from hatred, more hopefulness. He pulls up some of the other smaller kids, then reaches to place a hand on the other boy's shoulder. 'Come on, Will, we have to trust him,' he says, 'we have to get the little ones out.'

The boy blinks up at Turrell, and Turrell nods his gratitude.

'You're in charge of them, sport,' Turrell tells him. 'What say we get them outta here together, huh?'

The boy nods, and urges the smaller children forward. One diminutive boy wails in terror, and scurries deeper into the back corner, and the older boy reaches and lifts him from the floor. What the hell? Turrell momentarily baulks at the amount of blood seeping through the older boy's cotton shirt. When he turns, with the toddler in his arms, the boy grimaces in pain, but he moves to follow the others. The kid he'd referred to as Will also urges the older girl to join them, but she shakes her head in vehemence and in a second she's out of the door and flees, screaming, towards where the smoke is thickest.

'Cassandra! Come back!' Will starts, as if he's about to chase her, but Turrell grabs him, and pushes him in the opposite direction. 'That way!' he snaps. 'You can't help her, so get the little ones out before the whole place goes up!'

Will checks with the bloody boy, who nods reassurance at him. Will gathers the three smaller children around him, and trots forward. Turrell reports the situation into his mike, while he follows sharply after them. He is watchful, because the adolescent girl isn't the only person prepared to give up their life or take others with them this day. Except his gaze keeps returning to the blood seeping from the boy's wounds: what torment had the poor kid gone through at the hands of his supposed religious leaders?

He hears shots fired. Distantly something explodes, followed by screams and angry shouts. The kids react with fear, crouching down, but he yells at them to keep moving. The smoke is thicker, and hot with the proximity of the fire. They exit a corridor into a larger room. At the far end flames dance up the walls and scorch the ceiling; noxious smoke billows in waves through the room towards them, but not soon enough to conceal what hangs in plain sight.

'Don't look, don't look,' Turrell commands. 'That window over there, get to the window. Hurry!'

As the group of children scuttle to where he indicates, Turrell ignores his own command, and stares for a second too long at the corpses hanging from a flaming crossbeam. He knows that, as briefly as he's looked, it will be a long time before he shakes the grotesque image from his mind. He is an Operation Desert Storm veteran, and had witnessed some terrible sights during a tank battle at Medina Ridge, but there is nothing like the human form flayed of its skin to induce nightmares.

He turns after the kids, thinking that religion has played no part in the monstrous killings; these are the actions of demented minds. The blood soaking the boy's shirt hints that the breaching of the commune hasn't come a second too soon for him. All of these children, Turrell fears, were next to be strung up and peeled of their hides. Suddenly he wishes one of the freaks responsible for murdering their own would show their faces, because he'll gladly replace the horrific images in his mind's eye with the sight of one of them lying dead at his feet.

The kids all gather under the window, coughing and spluttering. Beyond it, the expansive grounds of the commune are filled with drifting smoke, but moving through them like wraiths, FBI agents marshal other survivors, and possibly captives, to safety. There is a danger that he might add to the intensity of the fire raging beyond them, but Turrell has no recourse: he bellows at the kids to stand aside, then beats at the window with the stock of his gun. Glass shatters and tinkles outside. Before he can begin assisting the kids out, Turrell knocks more shards from the frame. This time, without his instruction, the two older boys begin helping the little ones out of the broken window. Turrell looks back once; the hanging corpses are hidden from view by the smoke now racing for egress through the opening, and around him sparks rain. Turrell again keys his mike, and is grateful when he hears affirmative responses, and spots colleagues rushing to the kids' assistance. Will clambers out, and the bloody boy hands the toddler to him. Turrell moves in, and gives the final boy a leg up, helping him out; now that it is only his life in peril, the boy's strength has failed him, and he gets hung up on the frame. Little wonder, considering the amount of blood he's lost.

'Jump,' Turrell tells him. 'Just do it. Help's coming.'

The boy meets Turrell's gaze through the lenses of his goggles. He nods his thanks at the FBI agent, before his mouth drops open in warning. As the boy falls outside, Turrell twists around, but is too late.

He is hot inside his coveralls, but the knife slipping into his lower back is like a sliver of ice. He spins, only for the blade to plunge into him once more, again just below his anti-ballistic vest, and knocks aside the figure that's launched on him out of the smoke. It is a woman, her eyes insanely wide, froth ejecting from the corners of her mouth as she screams in fury. She is soot-streaked, and the hair on one side of her head has been scorched down to stubble, and the shoulder of her plain grey dress has been burned away, displaying reddened flesh beneath. The woman is crazed with pain, but also blood lust. She stabs again at Turrell, and finds his groin. He strikes her with the barrel of his submachine gun, forces her backwards, but she attacks again, shrieking.

Turrell fires, a second after he hears the bloody boy's shout: 'No, Mum, he's trying to save us . . . don't!'

The woman either doesn't hear the plea or she doesn't care. She jams the blade into the gap under Turrell's helmet, finding the narrow space between his protective ski mask and the top of his vest. It sinks to the hilt in his neck in the same moment his 10-mm round blows a hole through her chest. They both sink down as smoke rolls over them, and the last thing Turrell hears is the boy again crying out in admonishment of his mom.

TWO

**Cowley Dale Farm, Peak District, UK
2022**

'What the hell am I looking at? Is that a donkey's head?' Detective Inspector Ray Logan wonders aloud.

Deadpan, Detective Sergeant Kylie McMahon says, 'Ass.'

Logan glances sharply at her, but she isn't being sarcastic, only stating a fact. He nods at her correction: the selection of the particular type of draught animal might be pertinent to their investigation. If this were a case of animal cruelty it would be bad enough, but it isn't only an ass that's been decapitated.

Logan puffs out his cheeks and shakes his head softly. He stands in silence in the pre-dawn chill of winter. He isn't often lost for words, but the alternative is to swear in disbelief at the sheer lunacy of what greets him at the remote farm. Beside him DS McMahon also stares; although this isn't her first viewing of the crime scene, it hadn't lost any of its horror through familiarity.

Finally the detectives turn and look at one another, and their expressions show they're both troubled.

'Does it feel as if we just walked into a Dennis Wheatley story to you?' Logan asks.

'Who?' McMahon is stuck to uttering monosyllabic responses.

'Before your time, I suppose.' Logan's in his mid-fifties, McMahon almost twenty years his junior. With nearly a quarter of a century of police work behind him, he's witnessed some disturbing crimes, but nothing along these lines. He gestures at the victim. 'You don't normally see stuff like this outside of a horror movie.'

McMahon swallows. Even single words fail her now.

Before entering the crime scene, McMahon had handed gloves and overshoes to Logan. Now, putting them on, he hasn't proceeded beyond the front door of the barn yet, from where he's limited to a partial view of the victims. Painted on the wall adjacent to the door is a large symbol, indecipherable to him, *weird*. It is currently being photographed and logged by a crime scene investigator: its presence gives validity to Logan's nod to a horror movie. He enters the barn tentatively. The Crime Scene Investigation team has marked out a safe approach route – it is necessary to protect the scene's forensic integrity, but also to avoid hazards as the barn is almost filled to capacity with rusting agricultural implements. Logan follows the DS within the ancient redbrick barn, taking the circuitous route marked out with blue and white tape, and arc lights to illuminate their passage.

'Be careful here, you don't want to scratch yourself, boss,' says McMahon, the most vocal he's heard her since his arrival. She directs him around the spokes of a threshing machine; they are long and sharp, discoloured with corrosion. Logan takes care navigating around them: he can't recall when he'd last had a tetanus booster, and with his aversion to needles didn't fancy one now. Taking care to negotiate the cluttered interior, it isn't until he's standing less than ten feet away from the victim that he gets his first clear look. His throat seals tight for a moment. Nothing could have prepared him for the monstrosity he stares at. Beside him, McMahon has fallen silent again, caught between revulsion and perhaps a little awe.

A naked man is seated on an old oak barrel, with other similar containers stacked around him so that he appears to be at the centre of a large, rustic throne. His forearms rest on smaller barrels, held in place by thick copper wire that has cut into the skin. His modesty is protected because his ankles are similarly bound with wire, nipping his knees together around another barrel wedged between them. Blood has sheeted down his abdomen from the raw mess of his chest from where most of the skin has been excised, and also from the stump of his neck. The ass's head has been perched atop the victim's shoulders, looking huge by comparison, and very uncanny.

Michelle Stanley, the crime scene manager, sidles up to Logan. She is dressed in white Tyvek coveralls, goggles and respirator, and is indistinguishable from the others in her team working around the victim but for her diminutive stature. She jostles aside her facemask and goggles. Her mouth is set lopsided as she looks up at him. 'This is a first for me, Ray,' she says.

'You aren't kidding. Are there any leads you can give me yet, Shelly?'

'You might be looking for a demented Shakespeare fan.' Her off-centre smirk doesn't reset.

Logan gets the reference. She is hinting that the victim has been posed to resemble Nick Bottom, the weaver turned half-man, half-donkey by the mischievous fairy, Puck. 'A Midsummer Night's Dream,' he intones. 'Nah, this is more like a bloody nightmare.'

The CSI manager appraises the victim. 'I think it's easy to assume that the body's been posed for dramatic effect. You might be wondering about the head . . . the human one, that is.'

'Taken as a trophy?'

'No. It's in the barrel between his knees. It's still in situ until the coroner arrives and pronounces the victim dead.'

Stanley's announcement sounds ludicrous under the circumstances, but procedure is procedure. 'What about the rest of the ass? Was it killed here too, or are we looking for a second crime scene?'

'The carcass is out the back in its paddock. This wasn't set up on a whim. There was some planning that went into the arrangement of the body; I believe the victim was brought to this specific location because the killer knew there was an ass here and wanted to involve it in the tableau. I'm no pathologist, Ray, but the blood flow from the wounds tells me he was murdered where he was seated . . . but only after the flesh was excised from his chest.'

'He was still alive when that happened? Jesus . . .'

'That's nothing. Note the blood spatter pattern.' Stanley indicates red droplets on some of the nearby machinery, before widening her gestures to take in a large swathe around the corpse. 'That's arterial spray. His decapitation began while his heart was still pumping.'

Logan swallows hard.

This was not his first murder investigation, but the other times they'd been easily solved – an incident of domestic violence gone to extremes, a fistfight where one combatant was woefully outclassed by his opponent so chose to pick up a weapon, and a hit and run; all three cases had later been downgraded to two counts of manslaughter and one of causing death by dangerous driving. Some inspectors might pray for a case to test their detection skills and ingenuity, but Logan was never that ambitious: if he wanted more creative murders to deal with, he would have stayed in Manchester, instead of accepting a transfer to a rural patch in the Peak District. He is happier when investigating low-level crime – thefts of quad bikes, diesel and sheep – not this level of . . . *psychopathy*. He has no other description for what has gone on at this farm than these were the actions of a depraved and sadistic mind. It is the type of case that could make or break careers, and being unenthusiastic about promotion he could guess what would become of him. It is a relief to him that he's only here as the night duty inspector and will be handing over the case after his preliminary inspection.

He follows Stanley and DS McMahon outside: he's seen enough already to tell he wants no further part of the investigation, but he must check out where the ass was slain. Stanley directs them around the semi-derelict barn and they approach the paddock via a path from an adjacent field. In the dull glow preceding dawn, Logan spots the hump steaming in the chilly air at the centre of the paddock, and feels no desire to get any closer. A uniformed constable stands at the rear of the barn, protecting the scene until Stanley's team extend their examination into the field. Logan halts. 'Are there any footprints leading from the carcass to the barn?'

'Yes,' says Stanley.

'Then it's best we don't disturb the scene any more than we need to.' From the edge of the field he can see enough to make a preliminary report, and what he can't make out, Stanley can

fill in for him. 'The footprints . . . how confident are you that
you can lift an identifiable cast of the footwear?'

'Reasonably confident,' she replies. 'And if not from the field,
there's the bloody footprints inside: on cursory inspection I made
out three different distinct tracks, and there are other partial prints.'

Logan nods. That more than one person was involved in the
murder comes as no surprise: it is far too elaborate a scenario
for any individual to have managed alone. And, if he discounts
the inclusion of the slaughtered ass, it fits the pattern of the two
previous murders that have already shocked the nation in the
preceding month . . . right down to the strange symbols depicted
in the victims' blood near their corpses.

'OK. That's all I need for now. This one's definitely for the
NCA taskforce. Let's go.' Logan jerks his head for the others to
back away.

He catches a glimpse of disapproval from DS McMahon before
she lowers her head and trudges after him. Her continued lack
of verbosity is clear to him then; she desperately wants to be
included in the investigation, but knows her boss wants no part
of it. Tough. She isn't eighteen months away from retirement on
a full pension the same as he is. She craves a big case, while
he's happier plodding through his final months as a copper with
no drama. He takes out his mobile phone: it's time to throw this
case further up the line.

THREE

Kershope Forest, Northern England

*N*ate Freeman shot Jenny Onatade's husband a fraction of
a second too late. By then the large kitchen knife had
plunged through the soft tissue of her neck, and arterial
spray painted the floor. Lifeless, her husband dropped and splayed
out; Jenny crumpled to her knees, clutching in horror at the
awful gash in her throat. Her eyes were wide in disbelief, but
they dimmed as she flopped forward. She lacked the strength to
cover her wound, and another spurt of blood speckled Freeman's

*boots as he rushed towards her. His priority was to check that
the threat was neutralized, and the knife out of reach, despite
his urgency to help Jenny.*

*Her drunken, abusive husband would trouble nobody ever
again. The single bullet from Freeman's carbine had taken a
chunk the size of a golf ball out of his skull. Freeman still kicked
the knife aside. By then others were racing to help Jenny, but it
was too late: she was as dead as her husband. The bottom fell
out of Freeman's stomach. Where Jenny lay, her head was tilted
to one side, her mouth hanging open. Freeman averted his face,
unable to meet her flat gaze because of the condemnation in it.*
Why had he hesitated when he had a clear shot?

His hands are hot and slick, blisters forming, but Nate Freeman
doesn't relent. Despite the coolness of a December afternoon,
sweat rolls off his forehead and down his back, soaking his shirt.
He swings and chops, swings and chops, the axe scattering chunks
of wood high in the air. With each arc of the axe he exhales
sharper, louder, until he hacks furiously at the final few inches
tethering one end of the log to the other. It gives with a final
crack, and the two sections thud on the dirt track. Freeman
stumbles back, gasping for air, black spots swimming in his
vision, but they aren't enough to block out the memory of Jenny
Onatade's awful death. He screws his eyelids tight, bends over
and rests the axe head in the dirt, using its handle as a crutch.
His palms throb, his muscles shiver and his lungs ache for oxygen.
He's deliberately making the task more difficult than necessary:
the pain is penance, and he welcomes it.

It's over two years since he failed to save Jenny from her
abusive husband, but his guilt has only grown more acute. Usually
tough, honest labour helps clear his mind, but it isn't working
today. Hers wasn't his first experience of violent death, but it
has acted as a trigger to bring memories of worse slaughter to
the fore. Because of what he'd witnessed before, he has dedicated
himself to saving innocents, and yet when Jenny needed him
he'd frozen, only for an instant, but that was the difference
between life and death for her.

Freeman opens his eyes, stares at the splintered log. He props
the axe against the wheel arch of his battered Land Rover
Defender, and returns to work, shaking the sting out of his hands.

He wrestles the cut end of the tree off the cycle trail, before turning his attention to hewing the remainder into manageable logs. If he can't shake the memories, he'll at least cloud them with fatigue; maybe he'll get some untroubled sleep when he returns to his home on the bank of Kershope Burn, the bolthole he'd fled to after Jenny died. An IPCC investigation into the shooting cleared him of any wrongdoing, but it has failed to soothe his conscience, and he's exchanged his M5 carbine and the streets of London for an axe and forest trails.

The sun is lowering in the west, throwing orange fire on the treetops overhead, and deep shadows around Freeman. He halts, shaking droplets of sweat off his nose, and reaches for a bottle of water in the Defender's cab. He chugs down half a litre in one go, before capping the bottle. Exhaustion hangs like a sodden blanket round his shoulders, and his legs feel as heavy as the logs he's manhandled off the trail. This is his desired result. Finally he feels able to load up his tools, and follow the trail home. His forearms burn, the hairs prickling as he steers the 4x4 down tracks designed for mountain bikes. He has negotiated this and the other biking and hiking trails so often that he's intimate with each dip and hump in the packed dirt, and he ensures he hits each one: more punishment, but this time to keep his attention on making it home safely rather than dwelling on past failures.

His house, a converted youth hostel, is surrounded by unruly woodland in opposition to the managed forest he works in. A small pond sits in a boggy hollow between the house and Kershope Burn, the small river that marks the England–Scotland border in this remote part of northern Cumbria. On the Scottish side of the burn, the wild terrain sweeps in a steady rise to another managed forest. The treetops have lost their fiery nimbus before he parks his Defender alongside the house, and are now a bulwark of darkness against the horizon. As he steps from his car, an icy breeze plucks at him, chilling the sweat in his clothing. He shivers, grabs his rucksack and heads inside without another glance at his surroundings.

Before he makes it to the kitchen, his Wi-Fi kicks in and his mobile begins pinging as it loads his missed messages. All he wants is a warm shower, and to collapse on his easy chair in front of the TV. It is a benefit of working in the deeper woods, a mobile phone black spot even these days, where he can escape the outside world, and he sometimes regrets installing a broadband connection at home. A nightly ritual is to go through his un-solicited spam messages, deleting and consigning them to the trash bin: rarely is a message of any importance, unless it's work-related. He sets down his rucksack and fishes out his bait box and flask, and the half-empty bottle of water, before digging in his pocket and pulling out his phone. Five emails and four text messages await his attention: he deliberately avoids social media. Only one email is worth looking at – it's a request from his employers, the Forestry Commission, to investigate and clean up a fly-tipping event on his patch. The other emails he bins unread, then turns his attention to his texts. All four are from Jim Powell, a fellow woodland warden he occasionally works alongside on heavier jobs. These days, Powell is the nearest thing to an acquaintance Freeman has, though he's positive Powell thinks of them as being best pals. He's been trying to get Freeman to socialize with him for months, usually by text messages asking him to join him at a nearby village pub. He always declines, but it doesn't stop Powell asking again; he's persistent.

The texts aren't invitations to a drink though. Powell has sent the same message four times over the last two hours.

STICK THE NEWS ON. THAT SCAR ON YOUR BACK MIGHT NEED EXPLAINING, MATE.

FOUR

When planning a night in front of the TV screen, it was with some mindless programme playing in the back-ground while Freeman dozes. He's gone into self-imposed exile to escape the media and avoids watching newscasts for that reason. He is burying his head, because the world continues to revolve with all its inherent evil playing out around him, but he prefers ignorance to reality. He can't dodge every-thing, of course; even though he mostly works alone, he still interacts with other colleagues and members of the public on occasion. In this day and age, everyone has an opinion about everything, so he has been drawn into conversations he neither cared about nor wanted to be included in. One conversation with Jim Powell had been too uncomfortable. Freeman avoids undressing in front of others, but Powell had caught sight of the scars on his back when he'd unexpectedly dropped by the house and found Freeman working shirtless in his garden. Freeman had swiftly pulled on a sweatshirt, and lied that the scars were the result of a motorcycling accident in his youth: Powell hadn't bought the explanation, but hadn't pressed, understanding his scarring was a troubling subject for his friend. However, Powell had studied the scars long enough to decide there was nothing random about them, however weirdly shaped.

It's probably psychosomatic, but the scar tissue on his back prickles as Freeman aims the remote at his TV. He shrugs to loosen his damp shirt, holding off from pressing the power button. Sometimes it's difficult to apportion the tone of voice to a text message, but there's a definite hint of accusation in Powell's words. With some trepidation he flicks through the channels until he finds a newsfeed. Whatever Powell had alluded to, he has got no idea, because the story currently on screen concentrates on the usual political shenanigans surrounding Parliament. Freeman watches for a few seconds, taking in nothing, before he resumes unpacking his rucksack. He is swilling his flask out at the kitchen sink when the newsreader's words impinge on him and send another qualm of discomfort up his back: instantly he feels icy and the skin on his scalp shrinks. Weak-kneed, he leans against the doorframe between his kitchen and living room, fearful of slumping down, and stares in dismay at the TV screen.

The news has returned to its leading story. It isn't the fact that police investigating a series of murders have discovered a third victim, it is that they've finally admitted the victims have been subjected to some kind of ritualistic torture that shocks him. Ordinarily investigators play down the savagery of murders, keeping pertinent aspects of the case out of the public eye so that they can separate the loonies and fantasists from genuine suspects when they invariably claim responsibility. However, it appears someone has leaked video footage of the latest crime scene online, and the wider media outlets have jumped on the story's graphic and almost theatrical content. Freeman watches in disbelief as the camera sweeps by solemn-faced uniformed officers and alights on a brick wall. The picture zooms in, juddering slightly before being brought into focus, and a symbol daubed on it is brought into horrible clarity: the colour has dulled to a reddish brown, but Freeman doesn't require the newsreader to tell him it was painted in blood. This is no simple cross or squiggles but one so intricate that it would've taken time to paint: it has dripped in places, but is whole enough to see that the artist knew his subject well. Freeman is only one of a very few people who might recognize the symbol – though Powell too must have an uncanny memory for detail – because it's identical to the one sliced into his back when he was a child. Feeling his gorge rise, he staggers to and then sinks down in his easy chair in front of the TV, still in a state of abject disbelief. Unconsciously, his hand creeps over his mouth and he exhales a single word into his hot palm.

'Covenant.'

FIVE

Greater Manchester Police Headquarters

Kylie McMahon adjusts her clothing as she trots up the steps, feeling overdressed in a heavy overcoat and trouser suit. She's dressed to impress, to display her professionalism, but now thinks she's gone over the top. The Burberry wool and cashmere overcoat is possibly the most expensive garment in her wardrobe, except she'd purchased it from a charity shop in Oldham for ten pounds, and it has been designed for a woman larger than her: she feels swamped, and seriously considers returning to her car and dumping it out of sight in the boot. It's too late for that, because she's already been spotted, and the detective waiting to greet her already has his hand outstretched in greeting. He is a tall man, with steel grey hair and eyes to match, and, to Kylie's relief, is also wearing a heavy overcoat that skims his knees. The difference is that his fits perfectly, defining his slim, but broad-shouldered silhouette. Mentally shrugging away her concern for her appearance, Kylie continues towards where he waits outside the main entrance of Greater Manchester Police Headquarters.

'Detective Sergeant Kylie McMahon,' she announces as she shakes the man's hand.

'Yes. I recognize you from your brief appearance on the evening news.' His gaze settles momentarily on the spray of freckles across the bridge of her nose, before moving up to her green eyes. His gaze holds as long as his grip on her hand, a fraction longer than expected.

Kylie brushes back a lock of red hair, self-conscious in another way under his scrutiny. Jesus, she'd looked a state when the camera crew had cornered her for a sound bite earlier, and she is glad she'd found an opportunity to freshen up since. She hopes she's scrubbed up satisfactorily, despite wearing a dead woman's coat. He seems satisfied with her.

The man smiles. 'I'm DCI Grant Openshaw, Metropolitan Police.'

'Yes, sir.' She has recognized the detective chief inspector. His image had filled the TV screens for much longer than hers had when he'd delivered a statement from these very steps to the press earlier. Then again, he is rather more photogenic than Kylie personally feels. 'You didn't have to wait outside for me, sir.'

'I didn't. I was clearing my head before going inside and spotted you parking your car. It would've been rude of me to enter when I knew you were joining us.' He holds out an arm, indicating the doors. 'Are you ready? I'll show you up.'

Kylie smiles, and moves past him, but immediately inside she waits, deferring to his rank over his chivalrous gesture.

Kylie has rarely visited GMPHQ, a huge oblong of glass and steel that doesn't look out of place in what is effectively a business park two miles outside of Manchester. The building had only been opened in recent years, and still retains the atmosphere of a new build: everything echoes. DCI Openshaw's rubber soles suck at the floor as he approaches a reception desk and flashes his warrant card. He'd been in and out of the HQ on a number of occasions already, and so is generally recognized. The young woman manning the desk purses her lips at Kylie, and she too fishes out her warrant card and gives her name and rank. She's made to sign in and given a visitor's badge. Throughout, Openshaw waits for her, and she finally turns with a brief apology, but he only offers another smile and indicates a bank of lifts. 'We've taken over an office on the top floor. I don't know about you, but I'd prefer to avoid the stairs if possible.'

'Of course, sir.'

He taps his left leg, and winks. 'You'll have to excuse my dodgy knee. An old war wound that still troubles me when it rains.'

She's unsure if he's joking or not; for one, it is frosty outside, the evening sky clear. Second, he looks fit and healthy as he strides for the elevator, his overcoat flaring behind him. She's forced to trot to keep up. His is the pace expected of a Met DCI, where life is much faster than on her sleepy rural patch. In the few minutes she's been in his company, she's decided Openshaw is both energetic and inspiring, two qualities that her boss DI Ray Logan lacks. But she's thankful in a way that Logan's so lazy, otherwise she wouldn't be the one drafted in to assist the National Crime Agency taskforce. She'd almost burst with delight when he'd earlier delegated the task of CISO – crime investigation support officer – to her as his representative, despite his own smug satisfaction that he'd got one over on her. She'd bet that Logan's bubble had since popped, after he was left behind to weather the butt-reaming from their superintendent over the leaked crime scene video footage. After their brief inspection of the decapitated ass's carcass in the paddock, they'd returned to the front of the redbrick barn to find a couple of youthful farmhands astride a quad bike, one of them holding up a smartphone. Immediately the youths had taken off, and Kylie had suggested sending a uniformed constable after them to demand they delete the footage, but as usual it was too troublesome a task for Logan, who'd shrugged and said, 'What harm can come from them taking selfies?' Well, they'd only gone and jeopardized the entire case by revealing pertinent information previously kept from the public; Logan now has a hell of a mess to contend with, and in Kylie's opinion it couldn't happen to a more deserving fella.

They ride the lift in silence, Kylie feeling hot under the collar as Openshaw stands so close to her. The ascent is short, the HQ being only six storeys tall, and they exit moments later into a corridor blocked by a secure door. Openshaw presses a button, and looks up at the overhead CCTV camera. They are buzzed inside.

'Have you worked on many murder investigations, Kylie?'

DCI Openshaw's question is unexpected. But she knows what

he's getting at. Usually CISOs seconded to the cross-agency team come with extensive experience in serious crime investigation.

'This is my first,' she admits.

'Not a problem. This case is unique; I doubt anyone in the room has come across anything along these lines before, so don't be intimidated by their supposed expertise. I'd say we're all newbies, so don't be afraid to speak up, or to challenge bull when you hear it.'

'Thanks, sir.'

'For what?'

'For having faith in me.'

'I've no reason not to. I spoke with your DI . . . Ray Logan? He thinks very highly of you.'

'Really?'

'You're surprised?'

'Erm, yes, sir, it's just Ray isn't usually so effusive with his praise.'

Openshaw grins. 'See, I knew you had your BS detector primed. Keep it up, Kylie, and you'll do all right by me.'

He leads the way along the corridor; the institutional blue carpet now muffles his footsteps. They pass doorways to offices deserted this late in the evening. Another double set of doors blocks further passage, and again requires permission to enter. However, they are expected, and a heavyset man in his late fifties holds open the door for them with a hairy arm. He's rolled up his shirtsleeves and loosened his tie, and his grey suit trousers are baggy at the knees: he's obviously worked long hours this day. He only gives a cursory nod at Kylie, before speaking directly to Openshaw. 'I was just about to call you, Grant. We've just received a call from Cumbria Constabulary. They have a bloke up there claiming to know the meaning behind the symbol painted at Cowley Dale Farm.'

Openshaw glances at Kylie, raising an eyebrow in question. She wonders what he's thinking.

'Is there any veracity to his claim?' he asks of the heavyset man.

'He's ex Job, latterly with SCO19. There's a possibility you might even know him.'

'You get a name, Jeff?'

DI Jeff Brady indicates they follow him to his desk. It is one of a dozen identical desks arranged around a room large enough to hold a conference in. There are people seated at most of the desks, police detectives and NCA specialists in other fields, and Kylie searches for a familiar face among them: all are strangers to her. There is another large table surrounded by chairs at the far end of the room, and the wall beyond is largely obscured behind whiteboards decorated with crime scene photographs. Kylie spots Chief Superintendent Cadbury, the designated GMP Gold commander for the latest case. He glances at her once, but it's doubtful if Cadbury recognizes her. Having no intention of attracting his attention, Kylie tucks in alongside Openshaw and follows to Jeff's desk, where he checks a note he'd scrawled on a pad. 'Does the name Nathaniel Freeman ring any bells?'

'Bloody hell!' Openshaw runs his fingers through his hair. 'I know that name, all right. How has he managed to get involved in this mess?'

'Don't know, to be honest. He presented himself at Carlisle nick, but after announcing he had information pertinent to the case in regards the symbols, he demanded he speak in person with you. You got some history with him, Grant?'

Openshaw sucks air through his teeth. 'You might say that. I was his CO when he shot and killed Henry Onatade a couple of years back. You might remember it making the news; the escalation of events following Onatade's fatal shooting started a riot in Hackney.'

'Yeah,' says Jeff. 'I remember. It was a bad show, incited racial tension, right? I mean, why'd it happen? Wasn't Freeman trying to save Onatade's wife from him at the time?'

'The details didn't matter to those who only saw the shooting as another example of cops shooting black people. They needed a target for their anger, and unfortunately for Freeman, he was it. Poor bugger couldn't win; after the riots cooled down, Jenny Onatade's family tried to sue him for causing her death because he didn't stop her husband soon enough. He was never the same man afterwards.'

Kylie has only been in Openshaw's presence for minutes, but the change in his demeanour can't be missed. He's troubled by what has become of an armed officer under his command, and his empathy wins kudos with her: Ray Logan would throw her under a bus and sleep soundly at night.

'Look,' Openshaw says to Kylie, after a glance at his wristwatch, 'I've got to give the chief super an update. How's about I leave you in Jeff's company for a few minutes, and you can decide if you're up for a trip to Carlisle with me?'

'I'm up for it, sir,' she says, perhaps a tad too enthusiastically, which brings back the smile to Openshaw's eyes.

'That's good. The drive up will give us an opportunity to go over the case, and get to know each other better.' He grins. 'Whether or not you like it, DS McMahon, you might be stuck with me for a while.'

SIX

Nuns Moor, Newcastle upon Tyne

K ids are letting off fireworks. They've been at it since September, and there's still no let-up a month after Guy Fawkes's night. The clear night sky's the perfect canvas for the showering sparks, and carries the pops and crackles over the silvered rooftops. It also ensures ice on the ground; rime to be scraped off windscreens. A twisted ankle, if Darren Sykes isn't careful.

He jogs the frost-buckled paving with caution, wary of black ice concealed in the shadows where the wan streetlights don't touch. He's already missed out on the Town Moor run due to a pulled hamstring, and doesn't want to be laid up with another injury. But he's aiming for the Northumberland Coastal Marathon in February and has to get back to form. He loves the coastal route, with its spectacular setting of castles and beaches. To protect the coastal paths, the run is limited to five hundred applicants, so he'd booked his place early and paid upfront. It'd be crap if he lost his space again through a moment's inattentiveness on the slippery pavement.

In the last decade December has become a month of storms, or at least of wet and windy spells, in the north – he blames it on global warming – so the cold snap is a bit of a surprise. It makes things more festive as Darren chugs along, pluming clouds of frigid breath in his wake, adding extra magic to the twinkling

Christmas lights strung on the trees and shrubs of this more affluent area of Newcastle upon Tyne. Here the festive decorations are cheery and invoke a Dickensian image of the season, unlike those in the tacky neighbourhood he calls home. His neighbours deck their halls with cheap tat from pound shops, trying to outdo each other with the most migraine-inducing light displays that must send their smart meters into terminal meltdown. It'll be their chav kids setting off the fireworks, he bets, because who else would be out this late on a school night?

It's approaching ten p.m. Late for a run, but he has to rack up the miles when he can and today has been a long one at work. He's plotted a ten-mile route, enough to be getting on with, and is nearing the three-quarters mark, about to begin the final push for home through Nuns Moor. Traffic is light on Grandstand Road, nonexistent once he hits the footpath through the park. The gravel path isn't as slippery either, shielded from the plummeting temperatures under the trees. He picks up pace, pleased to find he's left the nagging pain in his thigh a few miles behind.

Vandals have attacked the streetlamps along the track. Here the trees hem in the path and, even without foliage, the network of limbs is still enough to throw the route into blackness. The next pool of light is a good hundred metres ahead, and he aims for it, clenching his teeth at a pathological fear of the dark that has haunted him since childhood.

A dimmed torch briefly limns the silhouette of a figure, casting its shadow large against the mist under the trees. Darren falters in his step, uneasy about meeting anyone in the otherwise deserted park. He conjures images of belligerent drug addicts, winos and muggers, who'll drag him down and steal the expensive Nike Zoom running shoes off his feet. It's probably a dog walker, pooper-scooper in hand, searching for where Rover has just done its toilet. Darren keeps going, angling to swerve around the figure so he doesn't get crap on his trainers . . . and one of those bloody fireworks explodes behind his eyes!

Another searing flash wakes him. It's totally different to the first; this is one of red raw agony in his feet. He tries to hiss in pain, but his tongue clogs the back of his throat. His first thought is that he's tripped over, fallen hard and knocked himself senseless. Bloody hell! This is the last thing he needs. Not only one twisted ankle, but both, and . . . what the hell!

Clarity is shocked into him.

He isn't in the park.

He's inside – some kind of echoing space that stinks of perished rubber and rat piss.

Chains looped around his knees and waist suspend him above a floor strewn with junk and broken glass. The open maw of a bucket hovers close to the top of his head.

What in God's name is he doing hanging upside down?

He bucks and twists, the chains clanking at the effort, but they are sunk painfully into his flesh and don't give a millimetre. He grabs at the chains around his waist, and only then realizes he can't: his arms are bound, forced tight to his sides.

'What's going on?' A gag compresses his tongue, muffling his words.

There's movement behind him, and the crunch of feet on the littered floor.

'Help me!' Darren twists as best he can, but can make out only the darkest of shapes. 'Help me please!'

'Shhh . . .'

'Please, you have to get me down—'

Hands grasp him, feeling strange on his bare flesh. They are cold and lifeless.

He is naked! *Oh, dear God in heaven! What's happening to me?*

He bucks in his restraints. Overhead a beam creaks under the strain. He jack-knifes, but is roughly forced down.

'Must I strike you again?' The voice is almost as muffled as his, undeniably deep though, and probably male.

He realizes what happened on Nuns Moor. As he'd swerved to pass the bogus dog-walker, he'd run straight into a trap. A fist, or something harder, had knocked him unconscious and he'd been transported to this derelict building, then stripped and suspended while asleep.

'Why are you doing this to me?' Again his questions are a series of muffled sounds. 'Who . . . who are you?'

'You know who I am, Darren.'

'*I doooon't!*'

'Think back to the pact you once made.' Fingers tap between Darren's shoulder blades. 'That's right, Darren, *the* promise. It's time that I call you on it.'

'*Oh, God, noooo!*'

'Yes.'

His captor says nothing more.

Chains begin ratcheting. Darren's feet remain in place, but the loop around his waist inches up, hauling him towards the horizontal. He strains his abdominal muscles, trying to hold up his torso, but they fail in seconds, and he flops again, head down. His captor nudges the bucket beneath him again.

SEVEN

Northern Divisional Police HQ, Carlisle, Cumbria

Freeman shifts his backside on the bolted-down plastic chair, but is no less uncomfortable than he has been for hours. He leans forward, pushes aside a plastic cup, and folds his arms on the table. He stares at the grain in the blue Formica, regretting presenting himself at Carlisle Police Station but with the knowledge he'd no other option. He hadn't been greeted with professional courtesy as an ex-police officer, but with ill-veiled contempt. To those police officers that checked in on him, he was potentially one of two things – mad or a murder suspect, and neither engendered a civil response. He knows he's become the subject of morbid interest to those working in the station, and that word of his arrival has spread. He's become a veritable zoo exhibit. Seated in an interview room where he can be viewed via a narrow window in the door, patrol officers returning to the station make it their business to peer in at him. He is not, as yet, under arrest, but that'll probably change if he attempts to leave.

After he'd been placed in the interview room – at least this one was reserved for witness interviews and not in the custody suite – a detective called Ronnie Wilson had fetched him some vending machine coffee and told him to give him a shout if he needed anything else. Wilson hasn't shown face since, and an age has passed. The coffee dregs have long since formed a white scum on top, but Freeman has decided to forgo another anyway. If he drinks too much, he'll need to pee, and he doesn't want an escort to ensure he doesn't do a runner. He can't blame anybody for the duration of his wait, because he'd made it clear he'd speak to nobody else but Detective Inspector Grant Openshaw, despite his old commanding officer being stationed more than three hundred miles to the south, and a good six hours' drive away.

He doesn't wear a watch, and doesn't bother checking the clock on the wall, because the last thing he wants is to count down the seconds until Openshaw arrives. Openshaw will arrive when he arrives, and not before, and all the urging for speed won't make a difference. He'd expected a long wait, so doesn't complain. Besides, he spends most of his time alone in the woods, so seclusion doesn't bother him. The worst thing about being seated in a small, airless room devoid of any charm is that his attention is prone to wander, and usually to images imprinted on his mind. The flashbacks are vivid, and painted in shades of crimson and scarlet. Earlier Jenny Onatade's stare of reproof as her life faded to nothing had been the image riding roughshod through his mind's eye, but another fresher image has been juxtaposed alongside her, that of the bloody symbol daubed on the barn wall at the recent murder scene. Nobody but Freeman could know how one related to the other, but each in their way has led his life in a downward spiral to this very moment in time.

The door opens and he glances up. Detective Wilson remains at the threshold. Freeman waits.

'You're in luck, mate. DCI Openshaw was at GMP headquarters when I tracked him down.' Wilson checks the time on the wall clock. 'The M6 should be quiet by now, so he should be here in no time.'

It's a two-and-a-half-hour drive from Manchester to Carlisle, but who knew how long ago Openshaw had received his summons; he doubts Wilson has hurried to share the news.

'Y'know,' Wilson goes on, 'you could've saved us all some time and just told me what you know.'

'I could've,' Freeman agrees, 'but it isn't going to happen. I'll wait for Openshaw.'

'Suit yoursel'.'

'You could've saved us all some time too, detective, and arrested me for withholding evidence in a murder investigation. Why haven't you?'

'Somehow I don't think doing that would've loosened your

tongue.' Wilson nods at the cold coffee dregs. 'Speakin' of loos-
enin' tongues, d'you want another brew?'

'No thanks.'

'Don't blame you. It's not the best.'

'I'm more concerned about you spitting in it before you fetch
it back.'

'Why would I do that?'

Freeman only offers a withering smile. Wilson sniffs, and
returns a sly smile of his own. Yes, he's made up his mind on
which of the two Freeman is . . . a suspect.

'DCI?' Freeman asks.

'You what?'

'You called Openshaw a DCI.'

'That's right.'

'He was only a DI when I knew him before. Stands to reason
he'd get promoted.' Freeman adds no more.

Wilson eyes him a moment longer, then retreats, pulling the
door to until it snicks shut. Freeman leans back, laces his fingers
behind his neck, and closes his eyes. Immediately the images
return, and he sighs, stands, and paces around the room. There
are various crime prevention posters dotted about the walls. They
are all familiar to him, but they take his mind off his memories
for a minute or two. He moves to the door, tempted to try the
handle. Through the narrow pane of glass, he spots a uniformed
copper standing outside: the young man is fresh-faced, his high-
visibility tunic pristine, probably a recent recruit given the onerous
task of keeping an eye on him. He feels no rancour towards the
copper, only pity: he recalls many such dull jobs handed to him
during his own probationary period with the Met. The man catches
Freeman looking. Freeman raises his eyebrows and offers a
conciliatory smile, but he only stares back stonily, practising his
copper's face, but looking as if he needs to take a piss as desperately as Freeman does.

Freeman sits again, toys with the plastic cup, and then dumps
it in a nearby waste bin. He returns to his earlier pose, arms
folded on the table, and this time rests his chin on them. He
stares at the far wall, allowing his gaze to zone out. Around him
the constant hum of a working police station lulls him into a
trance-like doze. The sound of the door sucking open startles
him, and he bolts upright, blinking lucidity back into his gaze.

Having taken no note of the wall clock, he has no idea how much time has passed since he'd met the uniformed copper's eye, but has a sense it has been some minutes. Despite himself, he glances from the red-haired woman in the doorway to the clock – it is approaching one a.m. – then beyond her to the tall, steel-haired man following her into the interview room.

Freeman says nothing, just stands looking at his old boss. Physically Openshaw hasn't changed much in the past two years. Maybe there are extra wrinkles at the corners of his eyes, a few more silver hairs, but Freeman can't say. When they'd worked together in SCO19, the Metropolitan Police's specialist firearms unit, Openshaw had been a good boss, and more importantly a good friend, and it irks Freeman that as they meet gazes there's a hint of suspicion in the DCI's eyes. Then again, what does he expect? Openshaw has been forced to travel for hours to hear what very well may be a confession to three vicious murders.

'Nate,' Openshaw finally says, and extends his hand, 'it's been too long.'

Freeman accepts the handshake. Openshaw's grip is firm and warm. His own palm is still hot; the friction built during his laborious log chopping has caused pressure sores beneath his calluses. Openshaw holds on to his hand while he indicates the woman beside him. 'This is DS Kylie McMahon, Greater Manchester Police.'

Freeman nods at the young woman. She regards him with bright green eyes and her mouth slightly open: judging him. To Openshaw, he says, 'I'd prefer speaking with you alone, boss.'

He has slipped immediately into his old ways, addressing Openshaw with the title. But he can't forget that Openshaw is no longer his commanding officer, and not necessarily a friend: he is a DCI investigating a serial murderer, who for all he knows could be the one whose hand he is holding.

'You should've rung me, Nate, met as old friends, instead of turning up here.' Openshaw indicates the interview room. 'This way, we have to keep things formal. DS McMahon's assisting me as part of an NCA taskforce; anything you say to me is equally valid to her.'

'I appreciate what you're saying, but I had no way of ringing you. After . . . well, after I moved north, I lost contact.' He'd deliberately cut ties, because to forget the past he can't hang on to any reminders of it, and that includes friends and colleagues. Freeman shrugs. He glances again at the DS. She stands with her hands clasped in front of her, waiting for instruction from Openshaw. The DCI doesn't ask her to leave. Freeman shrugs a second time, and waves at the two seats opposite him. Both detectives sit. Freeman settles down again.

'So?' asks Openshaw after a respectable few seconds.

Freeman thumbs towards the door. 'This lot's under the impression I'm here to confess to the killings.'

'And are you, Nate?' Openshaw smiles at the ridiculousness of the question, but his gaze remains steely.

Freeman grunts. 'Aren't you forgetting something?'

DS McMahon sits forward and reminds Freeman that he isn't under arrest, but that the interview will be conducted under caution. It isn't being recorded on audiotape, or video, but she takes from her bag a notebook and pen, and sits poised to take notes. At the end, Freeman knows he'll be asked to verify and sign her notes as a true record of what was said. That's if there isn't a turn of events where DCI Openshaw makes things more official and arrests him.

'Before I say anything, there's something you must see; it'll explain a lot, but also raise more questions.' Freeman stares at Openshaw until he nods. Rising to his feet, Freeman aims an almost embarrassed glimpse again at McMahon. 'I'm going to have to take off my shirt, OK?'

'Fine by me,' McMahon says.

Freeman has to move away from the table, forcing the detectives to swivel on their chairs. McMahon leans past Openshaw. He takes off his jacket and stands with his back to them while he unbuttons his shirt, then throws it back off his shoulders. The material falls midway down the small of his back. Behind him the silence is almost tangible.

Freeman waits. There's the sound of movement, and he turns slightly, to find DS McMahon aiming her phone at him. She snaps a sequence of photos. Freeman jerks back into his shirt and turns to them. He isn't annoyed at her for taking his picture; he's expected as much, and also that Openshaw might call on a crime scene investigator to make an official record of his scarring. However, the scarring is a point of shame to him, and he feels exposed with his shirt off. 'I think you might recognize the symbol?'

Openshaw is momentarily stunned. He pinches the bridge of his nose as he takes stock. Finally he stands too, meeting Freeman eye-to-eye. McMahon studies the images on her phone, before she too stares at Freeman.

'All those years we worked together, I'd no idea . . .' Openshaw shakes his head. Many times they'd been in the same locker room as they'd kitted up for duty, but Freeman knows his boss has never seen him in a state of undress. He only ever showered when he was alone, and wore at least one layer of clothing when in company. 'When did that happen to you? I mean . . . how?'

Freeman shrugs. 'I've carried this scar since I was eleven years old.' He coughs out a laugh. 'It was partially responsible for me joining the police force.'

'Jesus, Nate . . .' Openshaw is still reeling.

'There's stuff about my history you never knew about, Grant.'

'So tell me about it now.' Openshaw flicks a hand at him. 'Without double-checking, I couldn't say for certain if your scars are the same as the symbols we've found but—'

'They're the same. I can assure you of that.'

'They're . . . what? Satanic?'

Freeman grunts. 'No, they only share the same source material as Satanism, but this' – he points over his shoulder – '*this* goes back much further in time than either Satanism or Christianity. You might even say it goes all the way back to the creation of mankind; in fact, before that.'

'How can that be?' Openshaw asks, confused. 'I mean, who was around before mankind?'

'Wait a minute,' DS McMahon interjects, her eyes wide and bright. 'Are you talking about angels?'

Freeman's lips pull into a tight line.

'No way,' McMahon scoffs. 'There's nothing angelic about the cases we are investigating. Whoever did those killings is pure evil.'

'DS McMahon, I don't mean to sound rude,' says Freeman, 'but what exactly do you know about angel lore?'

'I've read my Bible.'

Freeman snorts. 'Then you should be aware that all angels are not goodness and light. In fact, if you'll excuse my language, they're some of the most murderous fuckers you'll ever come across.'

EIGHT

'**B**etter now?' DCI Openshaw asks.

'Yeah. I needed that.' Freeman squeezes out an embarrassed grimace for Kylie McMahon's sake, after he's returned from relieving his aching bladder. He sits down on a plush chair reserved normally for the top brass when policing strategy meetings are conducted at the station. As well as comfy chairs, Openshaw has arranged for fresh coffee, and it's served in real mugs as opposed to disposable plastic cups from the canteen vending machine.

After throwing off her heavy cashmere overcoat, Kylie hands Freeman a steaming cup, before taking a chair opposite. Again she keeps her pocketbook open, her pen ready, but after a gesture from the DCI earlier, hasn't taken down many notes; what Freeman had to say isn't pertinent to the crimes themselves, but possibly to the killer's motivation towards them.

Openshaw's too intrigued to sit; he paces back and forth in front of a large north-facing window that overlooks the nighttime cityscape. 'I can't believe you were kept in that sweat box all those hours, Nate. On behalf of the service, I apologize.'

'I suppose that was my fault,' Nate replies. 'Could have been worse, I could've been held in a cell until you arrived.'

'Yes, there is that.' Openshaw has chosen to move their conversation to somewhere more comfortable than the sterile environment of the interview room. For one, he's made up his mind that Freeman isn't involved in any of the killings, but also that he is a source to be mined of valuable information to point him at the actual killer. Treating him as an asset means extending a level of professional courtesy to the ex-police officer, so he's usurped the vacant chief superintendent's office so they can talk in private and comfort. The night duty inspector had been loath to allow Openshaw access to the office at first, but was trumped in rank, and by a swift reminder that the DCI is liaison to the countrywide NCA taskforce, whom the chief superintendent himself would defer to if he were on site. Openshaw ensures the door is shut tight, and is confident that nobody passing the office will overhear them. He finally hooks a chair with his heel and drags it closer. He sits, forearms on his thighs, leaning towards Freeman. 'Right, let's take up again where you left off, Nate. You were talking about angels.'

Freeman sets aside his coffee on a small table. 'Yeah, and I can tell by your tone you think I'm talking rubbish. You don't have to believe in angels, Grant, only that there are many people in the world that do, and one of them is the murderer.'

'My tone isn't of disbelief, Nate. I'm a bit surprised by the subject matter, but I'm open-minded and want to hear your take on it. How'd you end up with that symbol cut into your back?'

'Before I get to that, it's best I start at the beginning. Like I already said, there's a part of my history you've no idea about.'

'Go on.'

'What do you know of the Covenant of Dead Names?'

Openshaw's silence is telling.

'I'm not surprised,' says Freeman, 'most mentions of the Covenant were hushed up by the FBI. Perhaps you've heard of the Children of Hamor instead?'

Openshaw's eyelids pinch, but he still has no reply. Seated behind his right shoulder, it's Kylie's turn to lean forward, tapping her pen on her knee. 'Weren't they one of those doomsday cults or something? I'm sure I watched a TV documentary about them once; they planned a mass suicide to mark the new millennium, right, something to do with heralding in the second coming of the Messiah?'

'You're partly right, but their second coming had nothing to do with Christ.' Freeman puffs out his cheeks. 'But again, I'm getting ahead of myself. I wasn't called Freeman at birth; my biological parents were actually named Carl and Ellen Walker, kind of hippie-traveller types. Back in the early Nineties, they moved our family to the USA to join a commune on Ohop Island off Washington State, hoping to live off-grid and out from under the influence of governmental and societal rules. They were recruited here in the UK by followers of Weyland Berith, a self-styled angelic avatar; once they arrived at the private island, they soon fell under the spell of his captivating and persuasive leadership. I guess you've got an idea of what went on; think Manson or Koresh and you'll get the gist.'

Kylie nods enthusiastically. 'Didn't things end up like it did at the Branch Davidian commune in Waco, with an FBI raid going spectacularly wrong?'

Freeman reaches for it and cups his mug in both palms, but stares over it at the floor. 'You might say that. Except that the killings began before the FBI could respond, and in the case of Ohop Island, the fire was deliberately started to cover up the crimes once the raid was initiated. I'm ashamed to admit it, but my parents had risen through the ranks to where they were Berith's seconds, his "high priests", for want of a better description, and it's believed that my father, Carl Walker, was the one who lit what he referred to as the "Cleansing Flame". He was personally responsible for the deaths of a dozen people, and also perished in the flames. I watched my mother die too.'

'Another victim of the flames?' Kylie presses.

'No, that would've been too easy for that evil witch.' Freeman swallows down his hatred. Shakes his head. 'I owe mine, and the lives of five more children, to a special agent called Milo Turrell. Singlehanded, he led us through a burning building, and got us to the safety of a window he broke open, only for him to die at the last moment. My mother stabbed him repeatedly with a knife' – Freeman catches Openshaw's eye as he mimes jamming a blade in the side of his own neck – 'the final time, right here.'

Openshaw expels a short gasp of understanding. He glances back at Kylie, then at Freeman again, as if begging permission to offer his conclusion. Freeman nods to go ahead. 'Witnessing something like that must've been horrible to a young child. That's why Jenny Onatade's death affected you so hard, Nate? In that moment you relived what you'd seen your mother do to the agent?'

Freeman sniffs, gives the briefest of nods. 'I fully believe if she'd lived, my mother would've dragged me back into the flames with her, and the other children too if she could've reached them. But as his final act, Turrell shot her dead, and good riddance.' He laughs without humour, his eyes glassy. 'It was because of Turrell's heroics that I later decided to become a cop, to be like him, only I royally fucked up when it came to the pinch, shooting Henry Onatade after it was too late to save his wife. I froze, Grant, despite getting the green light to drop him, and Jenny was stabbed in the neck, the same as Turrell was.'

'Why didn't you tell me this before?'

'Why? The IPCC found me faultless in the shooting, so why complicate matters by admitting I was messed up in the head at the time? It wouldn't have helped my case, or yours, so I said nothing.'

'It might have won you some sympathy from the press, and with the top brass, both of whom gladly allowed you to be the fall guy for the riot that followed.'

Freeman laughs in disbelief. 'If you believe that, Grant, you're not the wise man I always thought.'

Openshaw also laughs. 'Yeah, forgive me the bullshit. I was only trying to make you feel better. That incident lost me a good officer, and it lost you your career.'

'That was my decision, Grant. Besides, I've discovered I prefer to cut down trees rather than people.'

For the past minute Kylie has remained silent while she absorbs Freeman's macabre tale. She's already heard some of the details about Freeman's fall from grace from DI Jeff Brady back at GMPHQ, and also from Openshaw on the drive up to Carlisle, but to hear it from Freeman's mouth is shiver-inducing. She recalls Openshaw's assertion that she should speak up, and to challenge bull when she hears it. Not that she disbelieves Freeman's story, but there's so much he is yet to tell, and if she allows Openshaw to go off on a tangent of pity for him, they'll be hours hearing it. 'Both your parents died in the fire, but if I'm correct then their leader was taken into custody?'

Freeman looks grateful to be back on track. 'Unlike his followers, Weyland Berith wasn't too keen on giving up his life. He was arrested, and later imprisoned. The last I heard he's still on Death Row at Walla Walla State Pen. He should've been given the lethal injection by now, but the current state governor has put a hold on executions while he's in office. That could change after the next election.'

Openshaw looks directly at Kylie, but she's already scribbling down a note to contact their counterparts in the US, to discover what they can about Weyland Berith's current situation: is it possible he still has influence and is directing these murders from his cell? Openshaw returns his attention to Freeman. 'The scar on your back, that was down to Berith?'

'Indirectly. At Berith's command my father did the cutting, or the sealing of the *promise*. It marked me as one of the Children of Hamor, and a sacrifice to Berith.' Again Freeman thumbs over his shoulder. 'This is Berith's seal, and translates as "covenant", as does his name.'

'A covenant is a promise, a pact of sorts?' Kylie asks.

'Yes. It's unclear what exactly his covenant is, but Weyland Berith preached that it was the great duke's promise to ascend once more to his rightful throne, having long ago been sealed into Hell by King Solomon. He taught his followers that he was already the mortal vessel or avatar for the *actual* Berith's angelic spirit, and through the fulfilment of the covenant, they would be one, and achieve immortality.'

'You said Berith's sealed in Hell. You're talking about a demon, surely?'

'Only in the sense that Christianity refers to him; in other beliefs he is referred to as a djinn, but most often as one of the fallen angels, a follower of Lucifer.'

'So this is Satanic after all?'

'Lucifer was the most radiant among God's angels before he rebelled and was cast from Heaven.' Freeman purses his mouth. 'If you prefer to think of Berith in demonic terms, go ahead. But he was still an angel, and has been referred to by other names throughout the ages; Beal and Bolfri, and sometimes Beroth. But it was in the Jewish form, due to his association with Solomon – Berith – that he is most commonly referred to by his followers.'

'It sounds like a fairy story,' Kylie utters, as she jots down the various names for fact-checking later.

'To me it was a horror story,' Freeman states bluntly.

'Sorry. I didn't mean to trivialize your suffering, just that . . . well, it takes some coming to terms with.' She squeezes an apologetic smile, and Freeman shrugs off her concern.

Openshaw raises a finger. 'You mentioned Berith's followers, Nate. Are you hinting somebody could be out there, attempting to finish off what this nutjob started all those years ago? They're trying to fulfil this death pact and unify an angelic spirit with Weyland Berith before it's too late?'

'I couldn't say what's on the killer's mind; all I can say is that I was once promised as a sacrifice, and the other children saved that day were similarly scarred. I'd be interested in hearing the names of the murder victims, and if they too were Children of Hamor.'

'At this moment in time, I can't divulge that to you.' Openshaw's forehead creases. 'Hamor: you've mentioned that name a few times now, but haven't told us what it means.'

'It's simple really. Roughly it translates as "sacrifice", but in ancient Mesopotamian tradition it was specifically the name given to a male ass slaughtered to their deity.'

'An ass!' Kylie grabs Openshaw's shoulder in surprise, and he also gives a grunt of understanding. Freeman watches them both, slightly bemused by their response.

'OK,' says Openshaw after a moment's consideration. 'I'm about to tell you something about the latest murder in the Peak District, but it doesn't go beyond this room. Are we clear on that, Nate?'

'Crystal.'

'The victim was decapitated, and the head of an ass set on his shoulders.'

Freeman expels air. 'Man, that's something I don't want to picture.'

'Yeah,' says Openshaw in mutual morbidity, and with a glance of sympathy for Kylie. 'I only saw photographs and they were bad enough.'

'There's still some debate about the actual meaning of *Hamor*,' Freeman changes the subject, 'with some scholars pointing out that it can also mean "red one"; which I guess also makes some absurd sense, considering the angelic Berith is usually depicted as a crowned warrior dressed in red, so quite literally he's also known as the "Red One".'

Openshaw ruminates for a few seconds, before leaning forward once more. 'Nate, you said there were other children saved that day, and they were all similarly scarred like you were. Do you know of any others that were from here in the UK?'

'Two more of them were Brits. There was a little kid called Darren, and my younger brother, William. Unfortunately, I've no idea what names they go by now. After our parents died in the fire, we were repatriated to England, and all went into care of the social services. I was adopted by Peter and Brenda Freeman, but whatever came of the others, I've no idea. Our old identities were sealed on a court order, and we were given new birth certificates and such to protect us. I've searched for Will for years, but never come close to finding him.' Freeman halts, his stomach sinking. 'You don't think Will could be one of the murderer's victims?'

Openshaw shakes his head. No, that isn't what he's thinking, not at all. His mind has gone to a much darker place.

NINE

University of Newcastle upon Tyne

Her footsteps ring hollowly as Emily Prince meanders through the corridors of one of the research centres presided over by the Faculty of Humanities and Social Science. In the small hours of the morning, Emily largely has the building to herself, but for the occasional appearance of a security guard or cleaner. The facility is housed in one of the original redbrick buildings from when the university was established back in 1834 as a school of medicine and surgery, a creepy old place. Although it has been dressed with the modern accoutrements of a prestigious research-intensive facility, it's a veneer over the centuries-old structure Emily can sense in the dimmest corners and creaking floors. It'd be easy to become spooked if she dwells on the echoing footsteps, as if she is being stalked by an unseen presence lurking in the deepest shadows where the night-lights don't reach. Instead she concentrates on the glowing screen of her tablet, only occasionally glancing up to check her route as she mulls over the meagre information she's discovered.

She is unsure whether she should email across what she's found immediately, or hang on until she's followed up on another lead: she suspects that DI Jeff Brady isn't sitting by his computer waiting specifically for her reply, and has plenty of other things to be getting on with. It will be best to wait until she has something more to offer the detective, although his first request had contained little detail, other than that he was trying to establish the meaning of a donkey-headed man in the most obscure corners of ancient art and culture.

She has found little, to be fair, and what was mostly flagged in her research applied to the character of Bottom in William

Shakespeare's *A Midsummer Night's Dream*, which the DI has
already told her he isn't interested in. Other than that, the most
telling information she's discovered relates to the *Alexamenos
graffito*, a drawing scratched into a plastered wall near the Palatine
Hill in Rome, dated between the first and third centuries. The
vandal had scraped the image of a man worshipping a donkey-
headed crucified 'Jesus', and added Greek words that translated
as 'Alexamenos worships (his) God', believed to be an insult
aimed towards his Christian beliefs. Emily has scanned the image
and accompanying translation, ready to send to the detective, but
feels it simply isn't enough. This is the first time her specialist
knowledge has been called on by the National Crime Agency,
and she doesn't want to spoil her chances of a recall by drawing
a blank on her first commission. Her consultancy fee is not to
be sneezed at, and will help keep her bank account in the black
if it becomes a semi-regular feature. Except, she has to be real-
istic. How many times will the services of a postgraduate social
anthropologist specializing in the impact of occult symbology
on communal groups really be needed?

'Jesus,' she wheezes under her breath, in response to the doubt,
'I'm beginning to sound just like my parents.'

She keys in a code, and is allowed entry to the faculty library.
The lights flick on automatically, so bright she squints and blinks.
It is a sterile environment, unlike regular libraries. For a start
there are very few actual books, most of the records contained
herein being scanned images of the originals kept safe within
acetate shrouds. A concerted undertaking to transfer the countless
thousands of images to a digital format has been underway for
years, but there is still information unavailable on the university's
intranet system. That means the good old-fashioned method of
sifting through catalogues to locate what she is looking for stored
in myriad files housed in boxes on rows of shelves. Joyful!

Before beginning, she sets down her tablet on a desk, and dons
white gloves. No sooner has she pulled them on than a chime
sounds from her tablet. It indicates an incoming request for a
video call from DI Brady. Does she really want to speak face to
face with the detective, looking the way she does? Being called
out in the early hours, she hasn't bothered with make-up, and has
simply yanked back her hair into a ponytail, and pulled on a duffel
coat against the chill over sweat pants and a baggy crew-neck

sweater abandoned in her apartment by her ex-husband. The tablet chimes again. To hell with her appearance, she bets the DI has viewed worse that day.

She swipes to answer, but is thwarted by the thin cotton gloves. She works her fingers free from the right-hand glove before she can swipe again, then jostles to set the tablet upright on its stand. 'Hello, Inspector Brady . . . just give me a sec and I'll be right with you.' She grabs a chair and sits down, fiddling the tablet into position. 'There, that's better, I can see you now.'

For his part the DI sits far too close to the screen. He's worked a long shift by the look of him. His eyes are bloodshot and baggy, and his jowls droop. She can count the individual stubble on his chin, and the longer hairs protruding from his nostrils. Why was she worried about her own appearance?

'Thanks for taking my call, Ms Prince,' he says, and thankfully sits further from his device. 'I wasn't sure if you'd still be awake . . . bloody hell, is it really after four o'clock?'

'I thought your request was urgent enough to work through the night.'

His bushy eyebrows do a little dance. 'Yeah, you and me both.' His head tilts as he studies her. 'It's good to put a face to a voice, but if you don't mind me saying so, you're unlike what I expected.'

Emily chuckles politely. 'You were expecting an older woman dressed in tweeds and wearing bifocals?'

'I'm not sure what I expected. With you being into all that Dan Brown stuff, well, I dunno, maybe . . .'

'A Lara Croft clone?' She smiles to show she's kidding, and gets a blank look in return. He has no idea who she's referring to, so she lets it go. It perhaps isn't the right time to tell him she'd expected someone more dashing too, but with his saggy cheeks and pale colouring she is reminded of Droopy from those old MGM cartoons she'd loved as a child. She taps the side of her head for emphasis. 'I can assure you, you don't have to be a fusty old professor to have it up here.'

He shows the palms of both hands. 'That was never an issue, I assure you. Anyway, the reason for my call . . .'

'I'm afraid I've little to show from my research yet—'

'Oh, I wasn't trying to hurry you along, Ms Prince.'

'Call me Emily. I get all that Miss and Ms stuff all day from the faculty and students; when I'm on my own time, I'm just Emily.'

'That's fine by me. You can call me Jeff, if you want?'

'Well, I would ordinarily, Inspector, but you are still on duty, right?'

'I am,' he says, with a regretful shake of his head, 'and between you and me, I'm unsure when that will change. It's the reason for my call at this ungodly hour. We've received fresh intelligence from DCI Openshaw, who has asked me to pass on the details to you. He thinks you can drop the search for donkey heads, and use your skills on a more important matter. I've put everything in an email for you, and will send it across in a minute or two. It'll explain everything better than I ever could. It's weird stuff, if you ask me.'

'Weird stuff's my bailiwick, Inspector. How's about a hint?' Emily smiles sweetly.

'As part of your field studies, you infiltrated various occult sects and fringe religious groups, didn't you?' He knows she has; it was the prime reason for the NCA selecting her as their go-to expert. 'Does either the "Covenant of Dead Names" or the "Children of Hamor" mean anything to you?'

She sits back, unconsciously scratching behind her left ear.

'I guess they mean nothing, then,' says DI Brady.

'Actually, I'm surprised to hear the Children of Hamor come up. It's a huge coincidence perhaps, but I only learned about that particular group a few weeks ago, after I came across a story on an American news site, reporting the failing health of its leader. Off the top of my head, I can't think of his name . . .'

'Weyland Berith.'

'The very person,' Emily says. 'The report didn't go into much detail, just mentioned he was the leader of a millennium suicide cult, which I found surprising, as I thought I'd studied most of them for my PhD. I'd earmarked the webpage with a view to doing some deeper research, but admit to getting sidetracked. Sounds as if what I initially thought of as a coincidence could actually be serendipity: DCI Openshaw wants me to look into this doomsday sect, does he?'

'He does. He also asked if you'd be prepared to meet with a humint source . . . sorry, that's police speak for an informant . . . and determine if there's anything you can pool your knowledge on to identify a possible suspect in the case.'

'Does this involve a prison visit?' she wonders, guessing her voice conveys her reticence. She isn't about to go into it with

Jeff Brady, but she'd endured a horrible experience once when conducting a prisoner interview, where the inmate had both physically assaulted and sexually molested her before the guards could separate them.

'We could set up the meeting at a place of your convenience, Emily,' DI Brady suggests. 'You've nothing to fear; the person you'll be working with is an ex-police officer and, according to DCI Openshaw, one of the good guys.'

'An ex-*British* police officer?'

'What else? Oh—'

Emily cuts in quickly. 'Don't worry, I wasn't expecting an all-expenses-paid trip to the States, only that it surprises me that a Brit copper could have any knowledge about what went on at a remote island near Seattle all those years ago.'

'It apparently surprised DCI Openshaw too. Anyhow, you won't be travelling too far from home, Emily. The bloke's nearby, just over at Carlisle. Can I get back to the DCI with your reply, or do you need some time to think about it?'

She rubs her mouth with her gloved hand. 'I'd need some time to get cleaned up and what not, but, yeah, it's only just over an hour's drive to Carlisle. I could be there tomorrow morning, if you'd like to get things set up.'

He winks. 'I'll do that, then shoot you across another email to confirm things, OK?' He fiddles with his screen. 'There's the first one I promised you.'

'Thanks, Inspector.' She gives him double thumbs up as her tablet pings with the arrival of his email.

He leans towards the screen again, this time close enough she can make out the pores on the tip of his nose. 'Can I ask you something, Emily? What's with only one white glove?'

'As well as not looking at all like the clichéd academic, it surprises some people to hear I also moonlight as the world's worst Michael Jackson tribute act.' She hits the screen to end the call, even as Brady sits back chortling in amusement.

She also chuckles, but soon sobers. Sitting back in the creaking chair, she covers her face with her hands. Some of the awful detail concerning Weyland Berith is coming back from the brief reading she'd made of the webpage – one of them his penchant for flaying the hides of his followers. 'What the hell have I just got myself into?'

TEN

Haydon Bridge, Northumberland

The South Tyne reflects the pale blue vault of the sky, twinkling with myriad highlights where the shallow water rushes over the cobble-strewn riverbed. There are barely any clouds, only a few insubstantial tufts to the south and north of the river valley. The sun is radiant, but little of its heat reaches Haydon Bridge, a small Northumberland town. Nate Freeman rests his elbows on the parapet wall of a sandstone footbridge connecting the two halves of the small town nestled on opposite banks of the river. A nearby bypass diverts traffic from the town's main street. The morning school run has passed and it's still early for many residents to be out and about. Other than for an occasional dog walker, Freeman has the bridge to himself, and he makes the most of the view and tranquillity. It isn't silent – the rush of traffic on the A69 bypass and the flow of water melds into constant white noise – but isn't harsh on the ear. It lulls him and, for a change, he's able to concentrate on the view. He misses noticing the young woman approaching on the bridge, until the ping of an incoming message to her phone intrudes. He turns his head and regards her, and almost writes her off, as she doesn't look at all like he'd imagined. She is bundled against the chill in an aubergine-coloured quilted jacket, woollen bobble hat, skinny jeans and trainers, and is barely as tall as his shoulder; she lugs a heavy canvas bag over one shoulder. She's pretty, and holds his attention a moment longer than is probably appropriate. He glances away at the water.

'Hello? Are you Mr Freeman?'

He jerks around, and finds the woman standing a few feet away, expectant.

'Uh, yeah, I'm Nate. Are you . . .' He checks beyond her, to the deserted town street, as if she's been sent on ahead by the real Doctor Prince, an assistant perhaps.

'Emily Prince,' she announces, and extends a leather-gloved

hand. She smiles in greeting as he shakes it. She checks out their surroundings. 'You know, I've lived only thirty miles away for years, and never been here before. It's lovely.'

He nods at her summation. These days a number of towns on the main east–west route have been bypassed and almost forgotten, or are ignored, by drivers whizzing past. He'd once been on a train that halted here, before continuing on towards Newcastle. But it is the first time he's had his boots on the ground in the old railway town. He spreads his hands. 'I thought this was central for the two of us,' he explained, 'rather than have you travel all the way to Carlisle.'

'I didn't mind the drive,' she assures him. 'It's nice to get out and about for a change.'

Freeman nods. She must spend a lot of time in classrooms and libraries; fresh air has to be a bonus. To the contrary, most of his days are spent outdoors, but after spending many hours cooped up at Carlisle nick last night, it has only reinforced his desire for open spaces. She checks out the scenery, and shivers in delight, or that is how he perceives it. 'Aren't you freezing, Mr Freeman?'

He shrugs. As usual, after a quick trip home to shower and shave, he's dressed in a thin cotton jacket over a checked shirt and denims. 'I work outside; I'm used to it.'

'Well I'm chittered.' She smiles at her colloquialism. 'How about we go over there and get a drink to warm us up?'

Across the road from the bridge there is a teashop, tacked on to the end of a larger hotel. 'The stuff we've got to speak about might put the locals off their breakfasts,' he cautions.

In the lea of the teashop there are metal tables and chairs set on the footpath. She gestures. 'We can sit there, if you prefer? Still out of earshot, but with a couple of nice, warm lattes to huddle over.'

'OK, Doctor Prince, that'll suit me.'

She leads the way, eager for caffeine and hot milk. Over her shoulder she says, 'Just call me Emily. I'm only a doctor of philosophy, not a real one.'

'Getting a PhD's nothing to sneeze at,' he replies. 'You deserve the honorific. Personally, I've no degrees, no GCSE results to speak of, and left school the first opportunity I got. If I had my time over again, I'd like to have done things differently.'

'I hear you were an armed officer with the Met – that isn't something to be sneezed at either.'

'These days I chop wood for a living. Serves me right for not sticking in at school, eh? To get where you are so young, you must have an admirable study ethic.'

'I'm not as young as I look, and should probably dress more age-appropriate,' she says, self-deprecatingly. Others who'd expected an older woman when they met her possibly challenged her about her age too. Now that he's been in her company for more than a minute, he's decided she isn't in her mid-twenties as he'd first estimated, but a decade older than that: the timbre of her voice is rich, and he likes her gentle Geordie accent. 'Besides,' she goes on, 'my fading youth's no barrier to wisdom, just to common sense.'

She laughs at her own joke as she pulls off her woollen hat and stuffs it in a jacket pocket. She runs her fingers through her dark hair, taking a moment to fix the elastic band holding a tiny ponytail in place. 'Instant facelift,' she grins. 'Unless I keep this pulled back tightly, I look twenty years older.'

Freeman smiles at her daft humour, feeling at ease in her company.

She enters the teashop to order their drinks. He elects for a mug of strong tea. Freeman chooses to sit with his back to the teashop, with a view across the main road and bridge. The chill from the brushed metal chair instantly conducts through the seat of his denim jeans. If Emily is too cold, he really should offer to sit inside with her. However, a quick check over his shoulder shows him that the teashop is half-full of patrons, and he prefers for them not to eavesdrop. Before he's finished his thought, his discomfort disappears as the conduction process goes both ways. Now he is static, and shielded from the gentle breeze, the warmth of the sun plays on his face and hands: Emily should warm up quickly enough.

She returns empty-handed – a server will bring their drinks – and she sets down their order slip on the table. After a brief examination of the seating arrangements, she jostles around a chair so she is perpendicular to him and hangs her shoulder bag over it. She sits to get the benefit of the sunshine. 'So, do you want to wait for our drinks first, or just get started?'

'We should make the most of our time. I've taken the morning off work, but have to get back this afternoon. There's a pile of fly-tipped junk to clear up with my name on it.'

'You said you chop wood these days,' she begins, appraising his lithe build. 'Aren't you a lumberjack?'

'Woodland warden,' he corrects, then with a flash of humour adds, 'but I'm still all right.'

She doesn't get the joke, too young to get the reference. 'What does that entail?'

'Cutting out the dead wood, cleaning up other people's messes.'

'So much the same as when you were a copper?' Her teeth flash.

'You've got it.'

They are both silent. Emily wants to know more about the event that ended his career with the police, and Freeman doesn't want to go into it. He says: 'Grant Openshaw told me you're a social anthropologist. How does that differ from, say, a regular anthropologist?'

'In a nutshell, social anthropologists try to understand how people try to make their lives meaningful within the societies they live in. If you want the party line, or longer explanation, it's the study of how societies are organized, the relationship values and behaviour of that society, and how and why people do what they do within that society.'

Freeman says nothing.

Emily is compelled to fill the silence. 'Studies are based on participant observation over an extended time frame, basically to determine what makes people tick and what motivates them to behave in particular ways. You might wonder how that could be of value in the wider world. You only have to look at some of the giant internet companies, the social networks and search engines, for instance, which use social anthropologists to understand how people interact with technology, and design their product to capitalize on their findings.'

He nods. 'But instead of how our behaviour will affect the products of our future, you personally chose to look back in time?'

'The results of our collective history impact on the social groups we currently live in. Our governments, or more particularly the state bureaucracies that form them, are often built on our societal experiences around key cultural practices and beliefs.

Worldwide, the behaviour of humanity is based on daily life, which in turn is determined largely by marriage, laws and religion in both their positive and negative connotations. Basically, I look to the past to figure out what has led to certain current behaviour, in order to not only understand the motivation behind it but how to manage it.'

Freeman absorbs her words.

Emily also sits silently.

A teenaged female server brings their drinks, and they make polite noises of thanks, waiting for her to leave them in peace.

Once the server bustles back indoors, Freeman finally says: 'So basically we're all products of learned behaviour and that behaviour can then be manipulated to make us act in a particular way?'

Emily huddles over her steaming latte. 'When you say it like that, it all sounds kind of sinister.'

'Perhaps it is.' He shrugs off the subject in its wider context. 'But I think you're right when it comes to secular groups like the Covenant of Dead Names. Erm, you've probably heard of them by a different name, the Children of Hamor.'

'Yes. DCI Openshaw believes that through understanding their social beliefs, their religion, their symbology, it can help determine how to locate any current followers, and the person responsible for the murders he's investigating.'

His tea is black and hot. It doesn't deter him from taking a long gulp. He sets down the mug, leans back in the creaking chair. 'So where do we begin?'

She raises a finger. Juggles around her canvas bag and takes out a tablet and fires it up. She also slides a digital audio recorder to the centre of the table. 'You don't mind me recording our conversation?'

'Will I have to mind my Ps and Qs?'

'I'm broad-minded.' She winks, and he smiles, because he really isn't one for using bad language.

She turns the tablet towards him, and he eyes the photo on the screen. 'DS McMahon sent you that?'

'Yes. This is the symbol that's on your back.'

'It's . . . more vivid than I realized,' he admits. 'I've caught sight of it in reflections, but this is the first time I've seen it square-on in its entirety.'

'You've never tried to photograph it yourself?'

'I'm not into all that "selfie" stuff. To be honest, I've tried to put it out of my mind, to ignore it, but haven't been too successful. I'm ashamed of it, and keep it hidden.'

'I'm surprised you haven't elected to have corrective surgery.'

'When I was a boy there was some talk of skin grafts, but the thought of the procedure terrified me. I'd already been under the knife once, and didn't want to go through it again.'

She exhales. 'DS McMahon said your father was responsible for wounding you.'

'Marking me,' he corrects. 'Sealing the covenant. Promising me in sacrifice to Berith.'

'How did you ever come to terms with your own father doing that to you?'

'I never have.' He stares at her, and decides to be blunt. 'If he hadn't died in the fire, I would've hunted him down by now and killed the bastard.'

ELEVEN

On his return to Kershope Forest, Freeman's mind isn't on his job. He locates where some inconsiderate joiner has dumped the contents out the back of their work van at the edge of a clearing used for recreation and picnics. He's gone prepared, towing a trailer behind his Land Rover. He stacks the junk on to it in a desultory manner. He wants the onerous task to be finished with, but can't stimulate much enthusiasm. The clean-up should have taken less than an hour but it has stretched to almost two, typically through his regular pauses to think without distraction. Unusually his mind isn't on Jenny Onatade's death, it isn't on Berith's sigil either, but primarily on Emily Prince, or – more precisely – her opinion of him.

They'd spent almost two hours together, seated outside the teashop in Haydon Bridge, while they worked through a couple of refills of their drinks and the history of his sad childhood under the rigid ministrations of soulless parents and the domineering presence of Weyland Berith who'd loomed over them all.

Emily allowed him to speak, only interjecting to clarify certain points: it was the most talkative he'd been in years, and his throat ached despite regular gulps of tea. Going over his past was cathartic, and the weight of his memories had lightened when he finally stood up; or the caffeine had gone to his head. They walked to her parked car, and as they shook hands and made their goodbyes, Freeman felt a trickle of regret. Despite the subject matter, he'd enjoyed her company. He'd have happily spent more time with her if not for the siren call of his workload, so it was he who'd called an ending to their meeting.

Emily was easy to be with, and humorous without trying. But his regret isn't at missing an opportunity to get to know her better, he's certain he'd failed to persuade her he isn't some vengeful lunatic almost as dangerous as the murderer they hoped to help catch. Why the hell had he admitted wanting to kill his father if he could? It makes him sound bitter and twisted . . . a nutjob she'd prefer to avoid from there on?

After his frank announcement, he'd watched the tiny, almost imperceptible expressions that danced over her features, fearing she'd make an excuse to leave. He'd tried to laugh off his words, remarking he was only being rhetorical, but hadn't convinced her. It had taken more than the sunlight on her face to warm her up for a while after that. Thankfully, as they went through his story about being saved from certain death by Special Agent Turrell, and the savage attack by his mother, Emily's initial shock had been replaced by sympathy. He'd told her how Turrell's selfless act inspired him to follow a similar path, which led him to joining the Metropolitan Police Force.

'That didn't work out the way I hoped,' he'd admitted, but didn't go into the events that ended his law enforcement career. He was satisfied she'd heard a version of it from Openshaw or McMahon already, and didn't wish to explain his involvement in Jenny's tragic death. She didn't press the issue. Instead she'd purposefully guided the discussion on to the archaic symbology of the Children of Hamor, and how it could be used to identify the murderer. Freeman had been as helpful as possible. By the time he watched her drive away, he felt he'd reassured her he wasn't a total psychopath, only partly one.

Lumbering back and forward, casting junk into the trailer, his thoughts dwell on why it is important Emily doesn't think badly of him. He doesn't normally seek acceptance from anyone; he hides from it as much as he did the bad feelings he'd run from in London. If he discounts his adoptive parents, he holds everyone at arm's length: at a distance they are safer from harm or can't betray him. He isn't a complete hermit; he has enjoyed female company before but never with any strings attached. However, the thought of never seeing Emily again leaves him feeling mildly panicked. He wants her to approve of him, well . . . because he likes her.

The sound of an engine echoes off the trees. The acoustics of the clearing make pinpointing its direction difficult, but a vehicle is approaching. Freeman snatches up the last few pieces of rubbish, and casts them on the trailer. He grabs a rope to tie down the pile, rushing to get away before anyone arrives. He is making the final knot, about to head for the shelter of his Land Rover, when a familiar pickup truck pulls alongside him.

'How's it goin', mate?' Jim Powell grins. With his rosy cheeks and missing teeth, he has the comical face a kid might sketch on a balloon. 'I see the coppers let you go, then?'

'I wasn't expecting to see you here, Jim.'

Powell glances around furtively, as if their employers might be spying on them from the trees. 'I had to come and get the crack, mate. What happened?'

Freeman has lived in the locality long enough to know 'getting the crack' means hearing the details; more so it means 'gossiping'. Wishing he'd never let Powell know he planned on speaking to the police about his scar, Freeman says: 'You expected them to lock me up or something?'

'Nah, 'course not. I know you had nowt to do with some of those murders.' He offers his gap-toothed grin again. 'For two of them I'm your alibi, mate. Can't say the same for the latest one.'

'Better watch out, Jim, or they'll have you in as an accomplice.'

Powell clambers out the pickup, laughing at the absurdity. He nods at the loaded trailer. 'You finished loading? I was gonna give you a hand.'

'More like you were watching from a distance until I finished.'

Powell laughs, closes in on the trailer, and pushes and prods

at the stacked wood. 'There's nowt in there that identifies the
fly-tipper?'

'Nothing.' Freeman hasn't given the issue any thought; it is
the last thing on his mind. 'It's mostly cut ends of wood or the
carcasses of kitchen cupboards. Most of it'll go through the
chipper when I get it back to the depot. If there's anything with
a name or address on it in the rubbish bags, I'll fish it out when
I get there.'

'Just throw the lot in the skip, mate. Why make work for
yourself?' His features grow rigid as he holds up an index finger.
'Don't forget, you're not a copper any more. It's not for you to
track down the culprit; leave it to those getting paid the big bucks
to do that job.'

Freeman also pauses, studying Powell's earnest expression.
Powell isn't simply warning him off trying to find the indiscrimi-
nate litterbug.

'The cops are finished with me for now. I showed them my
scar, told them what I knew about it, and they buggered off back
to Manchester. That's my bit done, as far as I'm concerned.'

'So . . . when do you tell me how you got that scar? And don't
give me that bollocks about falling off your motorbike again.
You weren't into all that Goth shit as a lad, were you?'

Freeman taps the side of his nose. 'I'm sworn to secrecy, pal.'

'Aye, that'll be right.'

'Seriously, Jim, it's "need to know", and anyway, it's better
that you don't.'

'When you say it like that it makes me want to know even
more. C'mon, Nate, tell me some of the juicy stuff.'

Shaking his head, Freeman checks the rope is fully secured,
and walks to his Defender. He pauses at the open door. 'Trust
me, you don't want to hear, not before you've eaten your supper.
You following me back to the depot, or are you finished for the
day?'

Powell raises both hands in surrender. 'I'm done for now,
Nate.' But Powell, Freeman knows, is persistent. 'What d'you
reckon: meet me at the pub later and you can tell me over a pint
or three?'

'I'll see you at work tomorrow.' Freeman steps in the cab, and
drives off.

TWELVE

Greater Manchester Police HQ

DS Kylie McMahon had gone home for a few hours' sleep. Openshaw was booked into a chain hotel only a few hundred metres from GMPHQ. So, after the urgent summons came, Kylie again is last to arrive at headquarters and finds the DCI waiting outside for her. His car is parked illegally at the kerbside, alongside the anti-ram barriers that surround the building.

'We're not going up,' he announces. 'If you've got everything you need, let's go.'

Kylie has forgone her camel coat, this time favouring a light-weight anorak over her trouser suit. She has everything else she needs in a tote bag. She ducks inside the now familiar surroundings of Openshaw's black Audi A6, settling comfortably in the passenger seat as he pulls away.

'Did you get any sleep?' he asks.

'I managed a couple of hours.'

He nods. He'd slept too, but his mussed hair and the shadow on his chin shows he's had little time for anything else since arriving back from their northern trip. 'If I'd known where we were going to end up today, I'd have planned things a little better and stayed handy in Cumbria.'

'How could we predict the next murder would be in Newcastle?'

'You've heard who the latest victim is, right?'

'Darren Sykes,' she says. 'Yeah, his name got me thinking. Nathaniel Freeman mentioned one of the other surviving children was called Darren. Before driving here, I put in a call to social services, to see if our victim was one and the same person.'

'Any joy?'

'Not without a warrant.'

'Get on to Jeff Brady; have him chase up the warrant, and he can coordinate things with them. Tell Jeff it doesn't matter how many official barriers they try to put in our way, he's to kick them over. I want confirmation of Darren Sykes's identity before we get up there. While he's at it, tell him I want the names of all the kids repatriated from that island, and where they are now.'

'Do you think they're all in danger?'

Openshaw frowns over at her.

It was a stupid question.

THIRTEEN

Kershope Forest

'Nate? It's Kylie McMahon. Can you hear me?'

Freeman juggles his phone to his ear, while ramming a length of plank into an industrial-sized wood chipper. The roar of pulverizing wood makes hearing the DS almost impossible. 'Hang on. I'll get somewhere quieter,' he shouts, and marches to where he left his Land Rover after uncoupling the trailer. 'There . . . you can hear me now?'

'Yes. Nate, it's me Kylie. We met last night . . .'

'Yeah. I've no problem with my memory.' He grimaces at the irony of his words. 'Sorry. How can I help you?'

'I'm with DCI Openshaw. Grant,' she adds for clarity. 'We're driving up to Newcastle. Where are you?'

'I'm at work. You want me to come to Newcastle?'

'No. That's not why I'm calling. Listen, Grant asked me to call you and asked if you'd present yourself again at Carlisle Police Station.'

'Why? I already told you and Doctor Prince everything I know. I think I've done my bit.'

'We're grateful for your help, and also the time you've given up on our behalf. But that's not it. Wait up!' In the background, the noise of moving traffic obscures Openshaw's voice. Kylie comes back on the line. 'Have you heard about the latest murder yet?'

'There's been another one? No, like I said, I'm at work. After taking the morning off, I've had my hands full with—'

'There's been another victim found today.'

'In Newcastle?'

'Yes. Rather close to you. A preliminary identification of the victim is of a twenty-nine-year-old white male named Darren Sykes. We haven't been able to determine if he's the same as the Darren you mentioned last night, but Grant doesn't want to take any chances with your safety. He wants you to go to Carlisle, where you'll be given protection.'

'I don't need protecting.'

'Grant said you'd be against the idea, but Nate, it's only for a short time. Only until we're sure you aren't a potential victim. If the deceased and the boy saved alongside you turn out to be different people—'

'The Darren I knew would be about twenty-nine by now. He was one of the youngest children in the compound.' He has a flashback to the burning building, hugging the terrified boy in his arms, carrying him through billowing smoke and stinging sparks, passing him out of the window broken by Turrell. Stomach acid bubbles up his throat. He remembers his brother, Will, taking little Darren from him to safety, moments before their mother's frenzied attack on the special agent. 'If the victim is Darren, my brother's in more imminent danger than I am. You have to help me find Will and warn him. I'm pre-warned, and if I'm a target, I can look after myself. But Will might have no idea who could be coming for him.'

'We're working on finding him,' Kylie tells him, 'and as soon as we do, we'll have him in protective custody too.'

'Custody?'

'Figure of speech.'

'Yeah well, figure of speech or not, I'm not going to the nick.'

'It's for your safety, Nate!' Kylie pauses, listening again to Openshaw. She comes back on. 'OK. We can't make you go. But Grant asks that you don't go back to your home alone. Is there a friend or—'

'I don't have any friends.'

'Then book into a hotel for a couple of nights so that there are other people around you.'

'I'd prefer to spot any strangers coming. Look, it's pointless going on about it. I'm not hiding in a police station, and I'm not going to any bloody hotel either. If you're worried about me possibly being the next victim, then don't. The murderer will have to find me first.'

'He found Darren.'

'Perhaps. But was Darren already in hiding, the way I've been hiding these past two years? Look, Kylie, and you can tell Grant this too: I appreciate your concern, I do. But it's better spent on finding my brother, and stopping the murderer.' Before she can argue further, Freeman ends the call.

FOURTEEN

Heaton Interchange, Newcastle upon Tyne

'How were you able to identify the victim?' DCI Openshaw asks.

DS Rodgerson, an austere young man with the whites of his eyes as red as his ginger hair, gestures at a small stack of neatly folded clothing sitting on the lid of an oil drum. A pair of expensive training shoes tops it off. 'The victim was wearing a lightweight utility belt, for carrying a water bottle and iPod. It also had a pocket for his mobile and an ATM card. We got his name off the card, and double-checked his ID with his phone provider. Unless he nicked them off somebody else, we're reasonably certain we've got the right man. Besides that, I've had CSI print him and we're running them against our records, and also PNC'd him: he doesn't have a criminal record. I've had officers round at his address, just to confirm things. No family. He lived alone, but a neighbour gave a good description and said Darren was in training for next year's Northumberland Coastal Marathon.'

'He was out jogging when he was taken?'

'That's the general consensus. There was no sign of a struggle at his address, and, well, judging by his clothing, he was dressed for a run.'

'Any clues as to his route?'

The DS wearily shakes his head. 'Nah. He could've been anywhere in the toon. I doubt he'd've chosen to run around here at night though.' They currently stand in an abandoned locomotive shed alongside the Heaton Interchange, to the east of the town centre. It has long been the refuge of down-and-outs and graffiti taggers, surrounded by a prairie of weeds and the corroding husks of decommissioned train carriages. 'Sykes lived in Denton Burn, over on the west side; my guess is he was grabbed nearer there and brought here in a vehicle before *that* was done to him.'

Openshaw follows his gesture.

The naked corpse of Darren Sykes is strung up with chains, hanging like a marionette, a forgotten plaything. His legs are almost parallel to the oil-stained floor, while his upper torso tilts towards it. A steel bucket positioned under him has gathered the blood from his slashed throat. His hair is thick with blood clots, his face a scarlet mask. As before in the other murders, skin has been excised, both from Sykes's upper back, and from his thighs. Blood from the bucket has been used to daub Berith's sigil on the nearest wall, a drip trail between them confirming the artist's medium.

Staring at Sykes, Openshaw says, 'It'd depend on how far out from home his run took him.'

The DS concurs with a downturned mouth.

'You've got somebody checking CCTV and traffic cams to see if you can determine his route?' Openshaw poses a suggestion rather than a question. It's best not to piss off the local CID. Throwing his weight around or sounding as if he knows better could encourage a jurisdiction battle he can do without.

'Already on it, sir. We've officers looking at cameras nearest his home address, and also from his place of work at a DIY superstore in St James Retail Park, where he also could've set off on his run.'

'Good thinking. I'd appreciate it if you let me know if they find anything.' Openshaw hands Rodgerson his card, and is gratified when the DS tucks it safely in his wallet. Openshaw looks around. Where has *his* DS gone?

Kylie is in a huddle with other detectives near the entrance of the shed. As Openshaw starts towards her, she breaks away from the pack, lifting her phone to her ear. She moves outside. Reaching the door, he spots her pacing at the side of the building. She nods and gestures as she speaks. Openshaw waits for her to finish. She slips her phone away, frowning. Spotting him, she opens her mouth. He holds up a palm and approaches her.

'That was DI Brady,' she explains. 'He's still working on

getting a judge to have the adoption records reopened. We can't confirm if this is the same Darren that Nate Freeman knew yet.'

'And we're still waiting for the name of the other repatriated kid . . . Nate's brother.' Openshaw ruminates. 'They say Darren Sykes lived alone, but I'll ask the locals to check his background and if there are any parents or other relatives who can confirm if he was adopted. If he was one of the kids saved from the commune, I want to know how the previous victims are connected to him.'

Prior to the victim found in the Peak District, two other men had been discovered murdered, missing sections of their skin and with the Berith symbol painted near their corpses. The first, named Alan McKenzie, a married father of two, was a construction foreman and Londoner; the second, named John Richard Croft, was a single man employed as a live-in chef at a hotel outside Nuneaton in the Midlands. The third murder victim, decapitated alongside the ass at the Peak District farm, has since been identified as Paul Sutton. He was married with kids too, and worked as a letting assistant at an estate agency in Tamworth. Latterly there is Darren Sykes, who lived alone and worked at a DIY superstore. There is nothing beyond the obvious that connects the victims: they are all working class white males in their late twenties to early thirties. None of them had a criminal record. None of the previous three victims had any direct or fringe associations to any religious, political or social groups that the NCA can determine. The only definable pattern beyond those is that their murderer had begun in the south, gone westward and then tracked northeast towards his latest victim. Could his next move be to head west again, and go after his next victim, Nate Freeman?

Before he can voice any theories, Kylie continues. 'DI Brady was able to liaise with an FBI spokesperson, who has dropped a couple of bombshells into the mix.' She pauses, as if for dramatic effect, but perhaps she is trying to order her thoughts so that she misses nothing.

Openshaw raises his eyebrows in anticipation.

'Weyland Berith's dead,' she announces. 'But not through a lethal injection . . . unfortunately.'

'Murdered or natural causes?'

'He contracted an acute form of fulminant hepatitis, due to a

Hep B and D co-infection, and was verging on severe liver failure. He had emergency surgery, but while in hospital he had other life-threatening complications, sepsis and respiratory failure, and deteriorated fast. He died ten weeks ago.'

'We can scratch him off our suspect list then. What's the other bombshell?'

'The FBI is also investigating several murders that have similar MOs to ours. White male subjects, the flaying of skin, Goetic symbology found at the scene.'

'Goetic symbology, what's that?'

'According to DI Brady, it's one of the names used to describe the angelic symbols Nate told us about. He's got Emily Prince digging up more detail on it. Basically though, we're talking about the same thing, and the FBI confirmed that Berith's "seal" appears at each of the murders. The taskforce is currently sharing information with our US counterparts to get a more rounded view of the case. DI Brady said that the first US murder coincided with the day Weyland Berith died, and, interestingly, their murders ended shortly before the first victim here was killed.'

'So we've an international serial killer on the loose,' Openshaw muses. After concluding his murder spree in the US, had the killer flown in to one of the major London airports, then travelled up the country from there? Had the first three victims been slaughtered to draw out the killer's real targets? 'That could help us identify him in the short run: it's worth having our guys hook up with Homeland Security to identify anyone with a connection back to the Ohop Island community travelling from the States between that time.'

Kylie's shoulders hitch. 'Or there are two killers working independently but towards the same goal.'

'By that you mean there's a specific reason the killings are being carried out; they're not just the acts of a psychopath with a flair for the dramatic?' He smiles to show he's kidding. 'Yeah, the way I see it, there's a motive behind the way the murders have been staged. One, it's because each is part of a larger ritual; or two, the killings are deliberately staged to attract everyone's attention. Huh! No, let me rephrase that. They're deliberately staged to attract the attention of specific people. I'd be keen on learning if Darren Sykes has made any public reaction to the previous killings in the news.'

'The first deaths were to draw out those the murderer is really after?'

'That slip-up by DI Logan – allowing those kids to video the symbol at his crime scene – brought Nate Freeman out of hiding. Maybe it worked similarly on Darren Sykes, and will do the same with Nate's brother. Which makes it all the more important we have those adoption records opened and find Will before it's too late.'

FIFTEEN

Newcastle upon Tyne

Her fingers rattle the computer keys and files are opened, minimized or discarded with almost manic speed. Emily Prince is on a roll, searching only for what is pertinent and getting rid of everything else that'll clutter her screen and her mind. Finally she pushes back from her desk, exhaling as she stretches out her legs to get distance from it. She stares, evaluating, and then finally nods. Before plunging into her next task, she paces out of the small office, really a tiny spare bedroom in her flat. She requires coffee before forging on. She blasts water into her kettle and switches it on, and spoons granules into the largest mug she can find. She enjoys a nice smooth latte, but this job requires copious amounts of black coffee to keep her going. It's been a long day, and there are still hours ahead before she can even contemplate getting any real sleep.

While the kettle fizzes and pops, she thinks about Nate Freeman. After everything that happened to him as a child, it's no real surprise he's withdrawn; the ending to his police career would have been enough to send another person spiralling into the deepest depression. At first she'd found him robotic, soulless; but it was a defence mechanism, and it pleased her when his actual nature had later surfaced, and she had found him to be a good guy, as DCI Openshaw had promised. There was that one glitch where his intensity had momentarily thrown her, when he fervently wished he could have killed his father, but in hindsight who could blame him? That was only an expression of passion and, though heartfelt, she doubts he has the capacity to kill in cold blood. His reaction to the death of Jenny Onatade shows he values life more than he does vengeance.

The kettle steams to a boil, and she fills her mug almost to the brim. As an afterthought she piles in three large spoonfuls of sugar. She got no sleep last night, and only caught a nap on her settee this afternoon after returning from Haydon Bridge, before the doleful DI Jeff Brady pulled her from exhaustion with another urgent request. 'What can you tell me about Goetic symbology?' he'd asked.

'Ever heard of Aleister Crowley?' she replied without much thought.

'He was that Beast bloke, six-six-six or whatever?'

'I only mention Crowley because he's the one most often associated with Goetic magick. His writing and practice of the subject has made it into pop culture: books, movies, song lyrics; it gets everywhere. The Internet's awash with references to it, and if you're wondering if Berith's seal makes an appearance in Goetic symbology, the answer's yes. A quick Google search will give you everything you need to know about it.'

'Right then . . .' The DI sounded stuck for direction.

'But,' said Emily, knowing fine well she was deliberately adding to her workload, 'if I'm right, Crowley relied heavily on ancient grimoires when researching Goetia. From what I learned from Nate Freeman today, Weyland Berith's teachings were based on a more ancient text. If you want, I'll pull together a chrono-logical history of Goetia from the earliest days?'

'Uh yeah, if it's not too much to ask? This'll be two nights running that I've put you out.'

'Honestly, it's my pleasure. I can't complain when I'm being paid so well, and besides, I prefer to keep busy.'

It wasn't a false platitude. Taking work home isn't unusual for Emily. It helps fill her apartment with something other than the loneliness she'd endured since her husband walked out. There are only so many hours she can sit alone on her settee, bingeing on chocolate and Netflix, before a sense of solitude overtakes her and she seeks escape. By nature she is outdoorsy, and the walls close in on her too quickly unless she has something to concentrate on. To purge the claustrophobia anything will do; mostly she'll wander the bustling Quayside or the Metro Centre malls across the river in Gateshead. She prefers hills, lakes and forests, but being a social anthropologist, the busier locations on her doorstep give her ample opportunity to study her fellow human beings. On those occasions she rarely interacts in person, but it is enough to sense the vitality and movement around her, the opposite to being alone in her flat. For this evening she'd earlier contemplated window-shopping around Eldon Square, but the promise of an intense research session trumps the idea.

Armed with nuclear-strength coffee, she returns to her office. She settles at her desk, the mug cupped under her chin in both hands, and relishes the aroma before taking a sip. The temptation is there to go to the furthest lengths with a concise paper on ancient symbology and its relationship to Goetia, but that isn't what the NCA team wants. They require only bullet points, confirmation of Berith's inclusion in its practice, and a clue to direct them at the murderer. Emily opens and then discards many pages, but bookmarks others.

She concentrates on those sources referred to by Aleister Crowley when penning his most famous work on Goetic magick. Backtracking, she finds the fallen angel Berith in Johann Weyer's sixteenth century volume *Pseudomonarchia Daemonum*, and a century earlier in the anonymously written *Ars Goetia*, the first section of the *Lesser Key of Solomon*, in which Berith is described alongside other demons or fallen angels said to have been evoked and imprisoned by King Solomon in a bronze vessel sealed by magic symbols. In the *Ars Goetia*, the demonic spirits are ranked in an infernal hierarchy, and Solomon assigned to each a seal, or 'sign they must pay allegiance to': a quick image search shows various renditions of Berith's seal, an intricate design that reminds Emily of a deconstructed chandelier. These sources are well known across the Internet, but she needs something more historical and finds it in ancient Canaanite texts.

In ancient Israel he was worshipped as Ba'al Berith, translated as 'God of the Covenant' or El Berith, 'Lord of the Covenant'. People known as Shechemites, and also the 'Sons of Hamor', had entered into a covenant sealed by the sacrifice of a male ass to their deity. There are too many similarities to Nate Freeman's depiction of Weyland Berith's Children of Hamor and the inclusion of an ass's head at one of the crime scenes to be a coincidence.

Emily again sits back in contemplation. She tilts her mug to her lips, and finds it empty. She can't recall drinking the tarry brew, but instantly feels a need for more. An idea strikes her, but before she can go through with what's on her mind, she has to fortify herself. She visits the kitchen and gets her kettle boiling again. She spoons in an extra portion of coffee granules: her drink must be as dark as the corners of the web she is about to enter.

SIXTEEN

Kershope Forest

Bolting upright, Nate Freeman is off the bed and standing beside it before he's fully conscious. He has no idea what has startled him awake. With the heavy curtains drawn, the bedroom is in near darkness. His throat nips off the air in his lungs, and his heart beats wildly. For a moment he shivers with anticipation, as if something is about to leap on him out of the shadows. He tenses for an attack, and jerks in surprise when a fist hammers on wood a second time.

Somebody is intent on rousing him.

Tentatively he opens the bedroom door, and spies along the corridor that leads to the front porch. A car's headlights etch two silhouettes against the glass, before they blink out. He exhales.

'Nate? Hello? You home?'

Last night he'd written off DCI Openshaw's concern that he could be a potential victim of the murderer. 'I'm pre-warned,' he'd said, 'and if I'm a target, I can look after myself.' He feels stupid. If the murderer had found him, he'd have been caught in a deep sleep. It's fortunate it's the police at his door and not the murderer leaning over his bed.

'Uh, gimme a minute,' he croaks.

He palms on the light switch. Glances at his bedside clock. It is just after seven a.m. He should have risen an hour ago!

He stumbles to where he left his discarded clothing, pulls into jeans and a T-shirt. Barefoot he heads along the corridor, even as his old friend Grant beats a fist on the door once more.

'I'm coming. You don't have to knock the bloody door off its hinges!'

Opening the door a crack, he finds DCI Openshaw grinning at him. 'Good morning, Sleeping Beauty. Did we get you up?'

It is still dark, and will be for hours, but Freeman has a sense he's missed part of a day. 'It's a good job you did . . . I, uh, slept in.'

Saying so makes him feel odd. He never sleeps in. In fact, he rarely sleeps a full night; when he does, disturbing dreams leave him feeling unrested in the morning. 'What do you want? You'll have to make it quick, 'cause I need to get to work.'

'Mind if we come in? It's bloomin' freezing out here.' Openshaw's breath puffs with each exhalation. Beyond him, Kylie McMahon shivers, her hands thrust into the pockets of her anorak.

Freeman steps aside.

'Point me at the kettle,' Openshaw commands as they bustle inside from the cold. 'I'll get us all a brew going while you make yourself presentable.'

Freeman waves away the offer. 'I don't have time for a cuppa. If you want something, go ahead, but you'd better get it down you sharpish.'

'Chill out, Nate.' Openshaw indicates for Kylie to enter the sitting room, as if he wants to speak in private, but then Freeman hears the DS speaking and realizes she is making a phone call. 'You won't be going into work today,' Openshaw announces.

'I have to. I already took yesterday morning off, and I promised my boss I'd . . .' He notes Openshaw's smug smile. 'What?'

'I already squared things with your boss. You aren't going to work today, Nate, and maybe not for a week or two more.'

'What do you mean? I can't afford to take time off. I've bills that need paying and—'

'We'll keep you right for money. Not me personally, but I've got the NCA to agree to a consultant's fee for you. It'll easily match what you're getting from the Forestry Commission for sawing a few logs.'

Freeman shakes his head. 'No. I've done my bit and want nothing more to do with this crap. I've got to get to work.'

As he turns towards his bedroom, Openshaw grasps his

elbow. Freeman glares at him but his old friend doesn't let go.

'You wouldn't go into protective custody, so to keep you safe, this is the best alternative I could think of.'

With a twist of his elbow, Freeman draws out of Openshaw's grip. 'I don't need babysitting, Grant. Hell, you don't know if those murders have anything to do with—'

'We do.'

Freeman chews his bottom lip, staring into Openshaw's eyes. The DCI nods, regretful.

'I'm sorry, Nate. The latest victim is the same Darren you helped to escape all those years ago.'

Freeman pushes his hands through his tousled hair.

'We had the adoption files reopened; Darren Sykes was previously Darren Paul Wagner, and one of the children repatriated from the US after his parents died at Ohop Island.'

Standing with his fingers laced in his hair, Freeman says nothing. Tears prick his eyes. He can only picture the terrified little boy he'd carried to safety, not the man he's grown up to be. Little Darren's slaying is a kick in the teeth.

'You were in those files, Nathaniel Walker.'

'What about Will?'

Openshaw nods. 'William James Walker: Yes, we found out his new name too . . .'

Freeman drops his hands, clenches and unclenches them at his sides. 'Come on, Grant. Just tell me.'

'Your brother was initially fostered by a couple called Parkinson, and took their surname, but from what the social services could tell us, he didn't settle. The boy had . . . let's just call them *behavioural* problems. He moved around quite a lot, going from foster home to foster home, and as soon as he was old enough, he ran away.'

'So you've no idea who he is or where he is now?'

'I know where he was for five of the last seven years.' Openshaw gives another regretful shake of his head.

'Prison?'

'Yes. He did time for ABH: he got into a drunken fight and didn't know when to stop. Left his opponent with a broken jaw and an impacted eye socket. While inside, he couldn't behave, and got another two years added to his sentence after attacking a guard. The only thing saving him from a longer sentence was that the guard wrestled the weapon out of his hand before he got a chance to stab him with it.'

'Jesus . . .' Freeman tries to equate the violent inmate with his little brother, and doesn't like the conclusion he comes to. Even as a child Will had, in many ways, been Carl and Ellen Walker's son. It's little wonder that the police are treating him as their prime suspect.

'He was released two years ago?'

'Yes. That was when he dropped the name William Parkinson and assumed a new identity. For the past two years he's been living under the name William Ballard. Nate, his last known address was in London, not far from where the body of the first victim was found.'

'That doesn't mean he's responsible for any of the murders,' Freeman says without conviction.

'He disappeared from home at around the same time that Alan McKenzie's body was found. Plus, before McKenzie's murder, he used his original birth details to obtain an ESTA allowing travel to the US. While he was there, it coincides with the murders of other survivors from Ohop Island.'

Freeman hangs his head.

Openshaw says, 'I know it's difficult to take in, Nate, but while you've been looking for your brother, we think he's been doing the same with you. Only for a different reason entirely.'

Freeman's head snaps up. 'That's an assumption only. There's nothing in what you've said that proves Will's responsible for the murders.'

'Yeah. Everything's circumstantial, Nate, but pretty damning all the same. Look,' Openshaw gestures at Freeman's bare feet, 'why don't you go and finish dressing? I'll put the kettle on, and once you're ready we'll sit and talk a bit more.'

Unconsciously, Freeman glances at the front door, anticipating his brother suddenly pushing inside and waving a bloody knife at him. 'You think that Will could already be on his way here?'

'We're confident he hasn't been able to identify you or your address yet, but not confident enough to take any chances. Nate, look, I know you're against the idea, but I'd rather you work with rather than against me on this.'

'By hiding me in a police station? No thanks.'

'That's not the idea.'

Freeman pauses, waiting for an explanation. There's little hint in Openshaw's face. 'You want to use me as bait?'

'Ha! If only.' Openshaw holds up both hands. 'No, don't worry, I'm not thinking of using you to trap the killer.'

'You should. If he's after me, we could drop a hint where I'm at to the media, and let them lead him to me and you can grab him.' He smiled snarkily. 'That way you'll see the killer isn't my little brother.'

'I'd never get the authorization to do that, Nate.'

'But you would if you could.'

Openshaw smiles. 'Can't say I haven't thought about it.'

'OK. I suppose it's best we're straight with each other. So . . . say I do agree to work for you as a consultant, what's actually expected of me?'

'You can offer insight into the motivation of the killer. We'll partner you with another member of the team, that way you can each help watch the other's back.'

'Where at exactly? You're still trying to get me hidden away somewhere, Grant.'

'That's up to the two of you. As long as she's in agreement, we could have you working together out of a faculty building at Newcastle University.'

Freeman perks up; he stares at Openshaw. 'Are you talking about me working with Emily Prince?'

'You guys worked well yesterday, so why not? The benefit of the university is it has its own security system; the killer would be crazy to attempt to get at either of you there.' Openshaw halts, he studies the look on Freeman's face. A smile again blossoms on his. 'I see you aren't as averse to the idea as before. So you like Doctor Prince, huh?'

Freeman scowls, feeling colour creeping into his cheeks. 'I'll, uh, go get my boots on,' he says, and rushes for the bedroom.

Out of Freeman's sight and hearing, Openshaw stands in the corridor a moment longer, before entering the sitting room where Kylie McMahon raises an eyebrow. Openshaw winks and holds up both thumbs. 'Suggesting we pair Nate with Emily was dead on the button, Kylie. It seems the good doctor has left quite an impression on my old mate.'

'I just got off the phone with her; I think the feeling's mutual, sir. When I suggested she work with Nate she was all for it. In fact, she asked what the chance of us bringing him back to Newcastle was, because there's something important she wants us to look at.'

'What exactly?'

'She said you'd have to see it to decide if it's something we can use to identify and locate the killer.'

'What did you tell her?'

'That we'd be there within an hour or two?'

'I'd best go put the kettle on then,' he says, 'or who knows when we'll next get a brew.'

SEVENTEEN

The crescent blade of the *lunellum* glints under the harsh halogen light. With an expert eye it is checked for the tiniest defect, any nick or warping of the steel could cause imperfections in the surface of the parchment. Having a finite stock of base material, none of it can be wasted by the improper maintenance of his tools. The edge appears sharp and undamaged, but for good measure he works it with a type of sharpening iron found in most professional kitchens, wipes the microscopic residue off it with a chamois, and again tests the blade, this time with his thumb. A single hairline slit beads with tiny rubies, and he is satisfied. He returns and stands before his *herse*, the frame on which his material is fixed around its circumference with cords and pippins; periodically he must adjust the tension, keeping the material taut to prevent tearing. He begins working in shallow arcs, removing wafers of flesh with each stroke. He falls into a rhythm, lulled slightly by the metronomic action, but his feverish mind is never at peace.

The preparation of vellum has been refined over the centuries, but the process has barely changed in millennia. Modern scholars use the term 'membrane' to differentiate between the finest vellum and coarser or synthetic parchment, but he has no such hang-ups. Originally made exclusively from calfskin and called *vitulinum*, after Roman times the term 'vellum' has been adopted regardless of which animal hide is used, and it is the term he thinks of when preparing his writing surfaces. Before attaching it to the *herse* for stretching and scudding, he'd washed the skin in distilled water, followed by calcium hydroxide, then allowed it to soak in lime for a number of days to soften and remove the hair: the inner side he now works on is almost unblemished, while the outer dermis still bears signs of the once-living donor, a detail he took great pains to preserve when excising it.

He takes a step away from his task, reaching unconsciously to adjust the halogen light overhead, to illuminate the *herse* at an angle. He is satisfied. Through the almost translucent vellum, the original scarring appears as the finest of watermarks. On other frames, skins he's previously worked on are hung to dry in his temperature-controlled studio, waiting for a final clean and 'pouncing' with a flat pumice stone. In shallow vats, more recent skins soak in lime, awaiting his administration. Soon all will be processed into sheets, but there is still a quota to be met if he hopes to form a quire thick enough to meet his needs, still skins to be taken.

For some of those sheets, the donor doesn't matter, only that it be the skin of a Caucasian male – to retain uniformity – but others need to be specific. The donor hide on which he works now is from one of the first Children of Hamor taken, and shipped at great risk from the US, hidden among a consignment of animal pelts sent to a tannery in Scotland, from where it was brought to him by a young man sympathetic to his needs and also eager to please. Other skins had found their way across the Atlantic by different routes, and via different delivery men and women. Those skins collected in England he's seen to mostly alone, though he'd required the assistance of his zealous helpers when it came to setting the macabre scene at Cowley Dale Farm, and also when grabbing and transporting Darren Sykes to the railway yard in Newcastle. To preserve his anonymity and ensure the fulfilment of his destiny, a high level of secrecy is required, so he called on the assistance of the most devout of his followers. He accepts that involving them risked everything, but the necessity outweighs the risk.

Anthropodermic bibliopegy is the practice of binding books in human skin; even he doesn't know the correct name for the practice when an entire book – cover and interior – is produced from the flayed hide of men, and he doesn't care. All that matters is that he must complete it before 21.47 hours on Wednesday 21 December. Time moves swiftly when he has so much to do; an inexorable flood rushes against him so he must constantly push to meet the deadline. In pushing he's set in motion the events that will lead him to the specific donors he seeks. Deliberately he'd set the murder scenes in London and the Midlands to draw out his actual prey, but it wasn't until news of his grotesque human-ass hybrid leaked that things had moved swiftly in his favour. Darren Sykes, the fool, had immediately sprung to light, and it was fortunate he was still placed in northern England and in position to organize Sykes's kidnapping at such short notice. The ease in taking Sykes proved he was right to push his agenda, even if it threatens his freedom, because now his hunters must be on high alert. No doubt with the clues he'd laid, or inadvertently given them in the killings, they are already piecing together the motive behind the murders. But that is all part of his plan, because the police will then reach out to other Children of Hamor, locating them for him. He is confident they'll be under his knife soon, and his book ready for when the winter solstice occurs.

Content with the latest vellum, he jostles the *herse* aside, freeing up space under the work lights for the next. He fetches another trestle, intending fishing out one of the skins from its lime bath to dry, but decides it can wait until later. Time spent in his studio is important, but not as imperative as his search for the remaining Children. Setting down the *lunellum* on a soft cloth, he cleans off his hands on a towel and leaves his studio. Downstairs he pauses at the large window overlooking a usually verdant landscape, now crisp with frost. In the distance rolling hills melt into a haze of mist. There is a stark beauty to his surroundings, but it is lost to his gaze: in his mind he paints it with splashes of crimson. Turning his back on it, he sits at his desk. Lighting a cigarette that he nips between his teeth, he wakes up his computer, and begins keying access codes to a virtual gateway to hell.

EIGHTEEN

Newcastle upon Tyne

'Well?' asks Emily Prince. 'Do you think it deserves further investigation?'

Her three visitors are gathered behind her in her office-cum-spare bedroom, filling it to capacity and reminding her how tiny the place is. She wishes now that she'd arranged to meet at the university, rather than at her apartment. Nobody else seems to care about the squeeze; they've more important things on their minds. DCI Openshaw sucks air between his teeth. 'I'll liaise with the NCCU on it, but for now, if you show me how far you've got . . .'

Emily's eyes widen as she waits for an explanation: police acronyms are a foreign language to her.

'The National Cyber Crime Unit,' Openshaw clarifies. 'They assist us in identifying and pursuing people using the Internet for criminal means. They've some of the sharpest tech analysts anywhere: if there's anything in this lead you've given us, they'll find it.'

'That's good. I'm already uncomfortable going this far in; I'd rather it was done by someone with better safeguards in place.'

Openshaw bends over her shoulder and peers at her computer screen. Emily glances back at him; she can feel his breath rippling the small hairs on her neck.

'Here, sit down.' She offers the detective her chair. 'Just scroll through using the mouse, but I wouldn't advise clicking on anything.'

Openshaw takes a hasty step backwards, bumping Nate Freeman. He is no Luddite; he knows his way around a computer as well as most of his generation does, but there is something grubby about what is on the screen that he wants no part of. 'I'll defer to your superior knowledge on this kind of stuff.'

Emily dithers a moment. She has gone as deep as she is prepared to for now.

'Do you mind if I take a look?' As keen as ever, Kylie McMahon jostles past the men.

Sliding on to the chair, she reaches for the mouse without waiting for permission. Emily and Openshaw stand together, each looking over the sergeant's shoulders. Freeman lurks uncomfortably behind them. Emily can't help taking a glance at him, shooting him a quick smile. His features relax a little, and his lips quirk in response. It is the first greeting they've shared since he'd watched her drive away from Haydon Bridge. Immediately, Emily returns her attention to guide DS McMahon through what is on the screen, unaware Freeman's attention remains fully on her, and only partly because there is nothing he hasn't seen before on the computer.

Kylie pauses with a finger aimed at the screen. 'Is this the dark web, Emily?'

'Yes. Well, one tiny corner of it. Users don't always go for fancy graphics and plug-ins and all that stuff when they're trying to conceal their activity.'

The website looks circa the end of the last century, without finesse or distinction. It is a black message board, with lurid green type in oblong-shaped, orange-framed boxes: difficult on the eye. Basically, it is a rolling forum on which certain sick-minded individuals chat with others with equally disturbed minds, all under the anonymity of assumed names and obfuscated log-on details.

'Is it as much of a cesspit as I've heard?'

'Mostly,' Emily says. 'In the past I've deliberately shied away from it, but it was helpful when trying to find a way into the sects I infiltrated. I entered a couple of chat rooms, posing as somebody with an interest in their occult beliefs, gaining trust and acceptance before I ever turned up at any of their gatherings. For such secretive people, they were surprisingly open when it came to chitchat with those who'd found a way to them via the deep web. There's chatter on the normal web about the murders, but it's mostly by people with no clue about the connection to Berith. Here though, it's very different.'

Kylie scrolls down the page. Users submerged in a subculture of angel and demon worship dominate the discussion board. Some of those who've found their way to the forum have come via various online games featuring characters lifted from angel lore, or are fans of a TV series about two demon-slaying brothers. Others are practitioners of magic, most notably Goetia – be they followers of Aleister Crowley, or otherwise; there is no real way of telling how some have arrived there. Kylie ponders a moment, then looks up at Emily for guidance. 'It's all gobbledygook to me,' she admits.

'Some using the deep web tend to be paranoid by nature,' Emily explains, 'even here they don't like their discussions to be easily translated by anyone who isn't in their immediate circle. I'm confident I've already deciphered a few of their code words; your NCCU techs should be able to crack it fully and give full transcripts of what's being discussed. Here, look . . .' Emily reaches past the detective to take control of the mouse and scrolls back up the page. 'I've highlighted some of the more interesting discussions, with references to Beal and Bolfri, other names historically used to depict Berith, and also to the Red One. From what I've been able to figure out, there are users on here who seem to know more than they should about the murders. Some, I'd say, are followers of the killer.'

'It makes sense,' says Openshaw, 'because he must be getting help from somebody.'

Kylie chips in. 'There was definitely more than one person involved at Cowley Dale Farm, and here in Newcastle when Darren Sykes was snatched and killed.'

'What are the chances that the killer recruited his helpers via this forum?' Openshaw wonders aloud. 'Emily, is there some way to identify who each of these users are?'

'That's beyond me, I'm afraid. Your Cyber Crime guys might be able to dig deeper and identify the IP addresses, but users are notoriously careful when covering their digital trails.'

'You were able to access it, and I'm assuming you've done so anonymously.' Openshaw has an accusatory tone to his voice. 'Are these users getting on and covering their identities the same way you have?'

'I should explain myself.' Emily stares meaningfully at the DCI. 'Nothing I did in accessing this forum is illegal. Despite what I said earlier, and what your understanding of it might be, the deep web also has a legitimate side. It's not all about terrorists, drug dealers and paedophiles; you can also join online chess clubs, social networks and various fan clubs and affiliations. The dark web's a small part of the deep web, and has been decentralized, meaning the websites can't be accessed via regular Internet browsers. You can, however, download a free browser that allows you to enter what's basically a massive network of websites and communities existing outside mainstream Internet culture. Browsing the dark web isn't illegal, as long as you don't take an active part in any of the illegal actions, services or products you find there.' She smiles sweetly. 'Hence my warning not to click on anything.'

Openshaw chews his bottom lip. It takes him only a moment to decide. 'I'm tempted to have you engage with some of these nutjobs and see if you can get any positive leads on the killer. I'd bet some of them are in contact with him only at a distance, but if we're right about him having assistance at the murder sites, then some of these could also be complicit in the murders. No. Rather than risk giving away that we're on to them, let's just back off for now and I'll have the NCCU pick up where you left off. I'll need your login details and username for them . . . is that a problem, Emily?'

'No. I'm happy to give you them, and the list of codes I've already deciphered. It should give your tech guys somewhere to start. That way they'll sound more authentic and—'

'I could do it.'

They all turn and stare at the interruption. Freeman squirms under their scrutiny. 'I could do it,' he repeats. 'If it's one thing I can help with, it's sounding authentic to fellow Berith worshippers.'

'Except you're not a worshipper,' Openshaw states, but to all it sounds more like a question.

'I never was. I was forced into following my parents' beliefs, but even back then I knew it was a load of bollocks. I sussed out Weyland Berith as a sociopath, a narcissist, and a Machiavellian son-of-a-bitch long before I ever knew the meaning of the words. But that isn't to say I wasn't indoctrinated into the teachings and beliefs of his sect, the same as the other Children of Hamor. I'd probably be able to put these weirdoes right on a thing or two, and also separate the wheat from the chaff.' He gestured at the screen. 'I couldn't help reading over your shoulder, Kylie; for instance, that guy right there, *Dantalion666*, has no idea what he's talking about; he's only playing at being a believer.'

Openshaw shakes his head.

'Why not?' Freeman lowers his brows. 'Oh, right! You're worried I'll warn William off if I happen to come across him. Don't you trust me?'

'My reason has nothing to do with you alerting your brother. If it turns out he's involved in the murders, I trust you'll do everything you can to help catch him.'

'So what's the deal, Grant; either you want me to help or you don't? Which is it?'

'I just don't want to take any chances with this. Emily has given us the best lead we've had yet, and I want to make sure we make the most of it. Fair enough, Nate, you could dig around, sort the suspects from the time-wasters perhaps, but where could you go from there? It's as Emily said, they do their utmost to cover their tracks. Now, unless you're a secret computer hacker and have never told me, I don't see how you can lead us to them quicker than the experts at the NCCU can.'

'If nothing else, I could give you an idea on those the killer's involved with. I can help narrow things down so that your experts know who the hell to concentrate on.'

Again Openshaw shakes his head, but Kylie shifts in her seat, desperate to speak. 'You disagree, Detective Sergeant?'

'I don't see any harm in Nate digging around a bit.' Kylie indicates a gadget displayed at the right of the rolling message board. 'I've just noticed the number of users active on this forum and it amounts to thousands. If the NCCU haven't any idea who to start with, they could be at it for ages before they get to where Nate can pinpoint in a couple of hours.'

'Hmmm, maybe you've got a point. Listen up . . .' Openshaw directs his words at Freeman. 'We've to go and see where the local CID are with Sykes's murder. For now, you stay here with Doctor Prince, and . . . OK, see what you can do about identifying who, if anyone, is in contact with the killer.' He turns to Emily. 'If you're happy enough with that arrangement, could you then email the info through to Jeff Brady at GMP? I'll warn him that you'll be sending stuff over and have him liaise with NCCU.'

With no objection, Emily shows the detectives to the door. As Openshaw strides for his Audi A6, his coat flapping behind him, the two women exchange mutual smiles of understanding, and make brief goodbyes. When she returns to her office, Freeman stands from the computer, shuffling awkwardly.

'I hope you're really OK with this,' he says, indicating his presence with a wave at the screen. 'After what I said yesterday, well, I was worried I gave you the wrong impression of me.'

'Relax, Nate. Anyone in your shoes would be forgiven for making a similar threat. Given what I heard about your childhood and what your parents did to you, I think most people would feel this way. It's totally fine that you're here.'

'I'd no idea I'd be in your home . . .'

'Yeah, well, neither did I when DS McMahon called me this morning. In hindsight, perhaps it would've been more appropriate meeting at the university.'

'We can go to the university if you prefer?'

'Oh, I don't mean because of you. I mean rather than using my own computer to log on. I've only gone as far as opening the web page, but if we're going to dig deeper and get into any actual conversations, I'm going to have to register as a visitor. The rules of the deep web are that everything is kept ultra-secret and you must obfuscate your identity, but I don't trust the rule-makers. Not when they're the exact opposite by nature. It wouldn't surprise me if there's some kind of program in place backtracking logins to their IP addresses and identifying users that way.' Emily catches herself, realizing she is babbling. She exhales in laughter. 'You do realize we've both just been played?'

'Yeah.' He also chuckles, unconsciously rubbing the back of his neck. 'Grant knew you were reluctant to go any further with this, and that I hate the idea of being babysat, but somehow he manipulated us into doing exactly what he wanted. The fly bugger made it sound as if he was agreeing to our idea rather than the other way around.'

'Classic reverse psychology,' she agrees. 'And now here we are . . . about to do the last thing we originally wanted.' She didn't add that she was mildly pleased with the arrangement, but could tell that he was too.

'By that you don't mean working closely with me?'

'Sit down, Nate. I'm guessing you know your way around a computer . . .'

'I don't own one, but yeah, I've worked on them plenty. Can't say I've ever been on the dark web before; are there any other protocols I should be aware of, other than "not clicking on anything"?'

'We'll have to break my own advice. Click the login tab there, and I'll talk you through it from there.'

Freeman hovers the cursor over the tab, while looking up at her. 'Are you sure you want to do this?'

'If it helps catch a killer, we must.' She wavers a moment, but unless she clears the air they can't move on. 'Can I ask about your brother William? Is there *any* possibility that he's involved?'

'I hope not.'

'I got the impression he could be from DCI Openshaw. What will you do if something on here points at him as a suspect?'

'I honestly don't know. I've been searching for him for years; right now, if I find him, I'm unsure if I'll hug him or tackle him to the ground.'

This time, he doesn't mention hunting down and killing anyone. Emily feels no discomfort crouching alongside him, guiding him as he logs into the forum. More than once their shoulders brush; neither of them shies away.

NINETEEN

Sunderland

A police car is hidden at the end of his street, tucked in the mouth of a service alley. It is unmarked, but the array of stubby aerials on the boot gives the game away: under the front grille will be a blue light. Of late there'd been mutterings of anger about the flagrant disregard of the posted speed limits on the adjoining main road; the presence of the police can easily be explained as a speed trap, but Will Ballard is too paranoid to accept that. The police must've decided he was a person of interest by now, and it was only a matter of time before their suspicions were piqued enough to move on him. Taken into consideration, it is highly likely the squad car has been situated to keep a discreet eye on his comings and goings. It doesn't matter how circumspect their interest is at present, the last thing he wants is to give them reason to come barrelling into his home, because a search of his place will be his undoing.

If the cops inside the car had dressed down in civvies, he might not have noticed them, but their white shirts, black ties and epaulettes gave them away. Luck was with him. He'd spotted them before drawing their attention, and had immediately about-turned and retreated to his house, to spy out of an upper-storey window. From his vantage point he can make out the front end of the car's bonnet only, while he is invisible to them. His gaze tracks across the street to the facing terraced row of houses – unless they have closer surveillance set up on him from one of those neighbouring homes? He jerks back into the shadows, leaves the bedroom and rushes to his computer in the adjoining room. Rapidly he deletes his browser history: in future he must take care to purge it after every session.

It is cold outside, not as bitingly as at daybreak when frost had rimed everything. His jacket would've been sufficient for the short walk to where he'd left his van last night, but it is an inap-propriate disguise. He digs a hooded coat from a closet, and adds a scarf, beanie hat and tinted spectacles to the ensemble. Once camouflaged, going out the front door is still not a great idea if he is under direct surveillance. Instead, he heads through to his kitchen and the adjoining utility space, where a door allows access to the small walled yard at the rear. A gate opens into a narrow passage that in turn leads to the service alley where the cops lurk, but in the other direction he can circumvent his watchers. It is a squeeze getting past his neighbour's overflowing wheelie bins as he negotiates the passage, but he manages without making much noise. Once beyond the row of houses the passage makes a right turn, taking him behind the homes on the next block, and at its end he spills out on to a street almost a mirror image of his own, except for one major detail: it dead-ends at a large retaining wall. He must make his way to the parallel street before the next junction with the main road, but at least by then he'll be well out of view of those in the cop car. Muffled by the scarf, hood thrown up and the glasses hiding his eyes, he'll be unrecognizable at a distance, but he aids his disguise by slumping and shambling as he walks, taking a few inches off his height and camouflaging his athleticism.

Once on the main road, he takes care not to immediately approach his van. It is parked under trees, a sweep of common ground beyond, all bleached of colour by winter's touch. It's possible the police know it's his van, though he's taken pains to conceal the fact, using a former name when registering its ownership with DVLA. If the police had some way of opening his adoption records, then yes, they'd be able to piece together that William Walker, William Parkinson and William Ballard were one and the same, but then the ownership of the vehicle wouldn't be the main issue. In hindsight, the fact that the cops are watching him suggests they've already discovered his true identity. It was a concerning issue, but one possibly of his own making: wouldn't they already have grabbed him if they knew who he was? Perhaps their presence on his street is mundane and unrelated to him after all . . .

No. He must remain cautious.

He scuttles towards the van. It is a Ford Transit Connect, not overly large, but big enough to transport a body if that's the way an investigator's mind works. With a box compartment and blanked-out windows it could invite extra attention. The cold engine is sluggish, but takes with a billow of diesel fumes. A quick scan around assures him he isn't in immediate danger of being spotted, but the van faces the wrong direction. To avoid the police, he has no recourse but to pull a U-turn in the road. Luck is with him; none of those speeders come haring along while he manoeuvres the van around and takes off. He watches his wing mirrors until a bend in the road takes him around the common. He isn't being pursued. He exhales raggedly, only realizing then that his breath had caught in his chest.

It is time to move on. He can't do that without first removing the incriminating evidence from the loft in his apartment, and besides, if he is forced to leave them behind, a manhunt will be launched to catch him. His own agenda will be hindered if he's forced to run and hide, and he isn't certain he can replace what had already proven difficult and time-consuming to compile, possibly impossible to replicate if he is forced into hiding.

There are few surviving Children of Hamor; in fact, discounting himself, with the taking of Darren Sykes, it leaves only one other who'd been snatched from the hands of the sect by the FBI. He is so close to finding his brother. After their repatriation to the United Kingdom, he'd only seen Nate a handful of times before they were forcibly separated and sent to opposite ends of the nation. How could anyone blame him for being maladjusted when the last person he'd clung to after being dragged half a world away from home was subsequently hidden from him? His adolescence had been spent angry and rebellious, and hadn't been tempered by the intervention of his social workers, whose refusal to reunite him with his big brother had only made him angrier. Once beyond the control of his adoptive parents – a pair of wishy-washy liberals he'd loathed with a passion – and the social services, he'd fallen under the beady eye of law enforcement. Rage and bitterness marked his late teens and early twenties: it was inevitable his violent behaviour would lead him to prison. He can't recall what had incited him to violence that time; perhaps it was a triviality, a passing comment, or a brush of shoulders in the pub, but he'd unleashed with a ferocity that horrified a jury and left his victim disfigured for life. He hadn't helped his case when a fellow prisoner tried to shiv him, and he'd wrestled the homemade blade away from his attacker. The prison officers had come in hard and fast and decided that he was the aggressor: maybe he should've stabbed the fuckers and had done, then the extra two years he'd served would've been worth it.

Since his release from prison and the end of his parole term, he has lived a nomadic lifestyle, never staying long in one city, and often on opposite sides of the Atlantic. Without family, he feels equally adrift when it comes to setting down roots; having spent his childhood in the United States, he is unsure to which nation he owes his allegiance. He is a Brit by birth, a Yank by upbringing, and most lately neither . . . he is a fugitive. He has lived by obfuscation over a number of years, employing different names when required, and thinks that he will likely continue to do so. The house he currently resides in is as temporary as all the others he's lived in over the years, rented on a short lease term, but it isn't his only bolthole. There are other apartments and houses in other towns, also rented under bogus details, and he is confident the police haven't identified any of those yet. Yes, it is time to move on. He has helpers. One of them can return to his house on his behalf, collect what he requires and leave the rest behind, maybe set the place ablaze on exit to conceal any evidence he's been there. Yes, he decides, that is the order of play.

After Weyland Berith's recent death, another must be ready to take his place, and it is bare weeks until the time of transfiguration will occur. His brother Nate must be found and taken before then; Will can waste no time.

He presses down on the fuel pedal, and feels the van surge forward in response. He is still on the route around the moor, skeletal trees to one side, and a housing estate to the other. Some distance ahead is a bus, but otherwise he has the road to himself: he'll be out of town in minutes. He hits fifty miles per hour and doesn't slow, the van gaining speed as he heads for the freedom of the dual carriageway ahead; the posted speed limit is thirty. A marked police car peels out of an adjoining junction, its blue lights flashing. A second later, its sirens blare. Idiot! He has fled from one trap directly into another. Swearing under his breath, Will's hatred of the authorities takes control. He stamps down harder on the accelerator.

TWENTY

Newcastle upon Tyne

'This guy calling himself Nephilim's interesting.' Freeman taps a finger on a highlighted dialogue box, and the thread of comments added to it.

'Yes, that was one of the first messages I spotted referring to Weyland Berith's recent demise. I know it's difficult reading a tone of voice into it, but I got the impression he wasn't unhappy about the news the way the others are. In fact, if you look further down the page, you'll see he gets argumentative when the others grow sycophantic about Weyland. Also he says something very interesting.' Emily places her hand on his over the mouse. 'Here, let me show you . . . See here? He says: "You don't know the Red One the way I did. You've no idea what you're talking about, so shut your damn mouth, asshole." What does that tell you, Nate?'

'You mean he's implying that he once personally knew Weyland Berith; others on here have made the same claim.'

'You do know what a Nephilim is, don't you?' Emily asks.

'Of course I do; a Nephilim is the offspring of an angel and a human mother. Before you ask, I've no memory of Weyland Berith having any children. Could that be a possibility, though? That he has a son who is intent on avenging his father's death?'

'There's no mention of a child in any of the notes I've read on him, but there could be an illegitimate kid out there somewhere. It's something we should raise with Grant Openshaw.' Emily ponders the idea. 'Weyland Berith was an American, right? Check out the way Nephilim writes. Does "damn mouth" sound British to you? And look at how he spelled "asshole".'

'So he's more than likely an American, but I'd guess half the idiots on here are from across the pond.'

'Except that here he spells "jeopardise" with an S and not a Z,' she points out. 'Here he uses "colour" instead of "color", and "self-defence" also with the Brit spelling, with a C instead of an S.'

'So maybe he has his keyboard defaulted to British English.'

'It's doubtful. He writes quite formally, and pays attention to his grammar. I'm assuming he can spell the words correctly he's typing, and if American English is his native tongue, then he'd use American spellings . . . they'd get flagged up if his keyboard was defaulted to the UK versions.'

'So what you're implying is that he's a native Brit but spent enough time in the US to pick up certain turns of phrase? Maybe.'

'Were you schooled by your parents when you lived in the commune or by someone else?'

'By schooled, we didn't take normal lessons; any teaching we endured was in the form of verbally reciting scripture from the Book of Dead Names. When we made a mistake, a correction was beaten into us with a stick.'

Emily frowns, sympathetic to his pain. 'That's awful. But what I was trying to get at is I've listened to you speaking, Nate. How long is it since you returned to the UK, nineteen years? You don't have a regional accent; if anything I'd describe it as being mid-Atlantic. But you occasionally slip into British slang, probably picked up from when you were on the Force, but every now and then an Americanism pops up. It wouldn't surprise me if you admitted to being the one who'd typed those comments.'

Freeman scowls at the suggestion. But he understands what she means. He stares at the words on the screen. 'You think Nephilim could be my brother?'

'It's a possibility. But who could really say?'

'If it's Will or not, he should go on the list for the NCA.'

'Agreed. He seems too knowledgeable about the murders not to be a person of interest . . . especially when claiming to be the child of an angel.'

Emily has compiled a separate list on her tablet. She has double-checked the usernames of those they were most interested in, ensuring there is no confusion when the National Cyber Crime Unit takes over. She adds Nephilim, highlighting the name as a priority and making a notation that it could be William Ballard. Something on the main computer screen catches her eye. She sits back in surprise. 'Wait a minute,' she wheezes.

'What's up?'

'There,' Emily jabs at the thread they've been following. A new dialogue box has materialized, currently flashing orange. 'Someone's online right now typing a reply.'

They pause open-mouthed in anticipation. Expecting the murderer to make an announcement is too much to ask, but the type that finally appears makes them turn and stare at each other as they absorb the importance of the message. Input by someone claiming to be Baphomet, it reads:

Is that reward for information on the brother still good? I might have found him. If you've got the money, go to our private place. I'll be waiting.

'Are you kidding me?' Freeman shakes his head at the enormity. 'Are they talking about me?'

'If Baphomet's talking to Will, then yes, I'd say the latest message concerns you.'

Shaking his head again, Freeman pushes up out of his chair, causing Emily to follow suit. They face each other. 'I should leave,' he says.

'Why?'

He points at the screen. 'This guy claims to have found me. What if he means *here*?'

'We don't know that he means here at my apartment, how could he? Perhaps he only means he's found out who you are. And let's not be too hasty. We're assuming he's talking to Will. That might not be the case. Depending on who Nephilim is, he might be referring to having found your brother, not you. Maybe, they're talking about somebody else entirely, with nothing to do with either of you.'

'C'mon, Emily, what are the chances he means some other

brothers? We were the only brothers in the commune at Ohop Island.' He pauses. 'OK, I'll grant you we weren't the only siblings; there was a brother and sister too, but they were Americans. What are the odds they're talking about *that* brother. Whoever Nephilim is, they don't sound like a woman to me.'

'Baphomet typed *the* brother, not *your* brother. It suggests Nephilim could be someone else entirely, and not Will as we first thought.'

'We can't take that chance. I'd hate for you to get caught up in my trouble. If we're right and the killer is hunting down the surviving Children of Hamor, then I'm definitely on his radar. Have you seen what the demented son of a bitch does to his victims? I don't want you anywhere near somebody capable of that.'

'I should be flattered that you care so much about my welfare,' says Emily, setting her jaw, 'but I'm no shrinking violet, Nate. You forget; I've infiltrated other occult sects before, and I had to look out for myself. I didn't need a man to keep me safe.'

He holds up his hands. 'I wasn't suggesting you need protecting. I'd rather you weren't put in danger because of your association with me, that's all. I'm talking about getting out of here, so that you aren't in his way when the bastard comes after me.'

'I'm sorry, Nate, that sounds like a terrible plan to me. The other victims were targeted when they were alone. You should be with other people until he's caught so the killer doesn't find an opportunity to get you as well. Sit down and stay put. I'll call Grant and let him know what Baphomet and Nephilim are talking about; maybe he can get the Cyber Crime team directly on to them and hopefully locate them.'

Reluctantly Freeman sits again, chewing his bottom lip in contemplation. 'I suppose you're right, and I shouldn't be too hasty. Nephilim hasn't replied yet; maybe he won't for ages, until he's next online. What do you think they mean by our private place?'

'If you're thinking of an actual prearranged meeting place, think again. I reckon they've conversed before and have set up a gateway off this main page to one exclusive to its members.

Don't forget, there are everyday users on here – not all of them are Weyland Berith-worshippers – and, dark web or not, those who are involved won't speak openly about the murders on this forum.'

'I see, so this is just one tier of a shitty multi-layered cake?'

'You could put it that way, yes. Potential followers are possibly approached and groomed via sites like this; then when they've proven they're trustworthy, they get invited across to another exclusively used by the killer and his followers. That's probably where Baphomet's waiting for a reply.'

'Is there no way you could find your way into their private place? At least then we could confirm who they're actually talking about.'

Emily shakes her head. 'I wouldn't know how. Even if I did, I wouldn't dare, because they'd be alerted to my presence and I could blow the best lead we've got so far.'

She is right, of course, but Freeman is deflated. He stands again, but is at a loss where to move. He is a guest in her home; it isn't his place to wander around her private rooms, any more than she can invade the one on the dark web. Emily says, 'Why don't you go and make yourself comfortable in the lounge. We've done as much as we can here for now. I'll get the list of suspects over to DI Brady, and also phone Grant about Baphomet's latest message. I'm certain he'll prioritize the search then.'

'I should stay and watch the screen while you're busy,' says Freeman. 'In case Nephilim answers.'

'He might not respond here, but go straight to their private place. We'd have no way of knowing, Nate. I'll keep an eye out and give you a shout if anything comes up.'

'I'll wait. I want to speak with Grant; I've changed my mind about a police protection detail.' He spots her eyebrows rise in surprise. 'Not for me,' he says, 'and, no, I don't mean for you either, Emily. If Baphomet has discovered my identity, it could lead them back to my adoptive parents. I want them safely out of harm's way until this is over with.'

TWENTY-ONE

Sunderland

The police aren't for giving up the chase. Even after he's jumped three red lights, hurtling through gaps in screeching traffic, and driving the wrong way up a one-way street, where he'd forced a motorcyclist to mount the pavement and crash into a shop front, they have remained dogged. Will Ballard's only saving grace is that regular patrols are forbidden from conducting high-speed pursuits, allowed only to follow and report until highly trained officers can take over. He is never in fear of being run off the road by the more versatile patrol car, but has to be mindful of other patrols joining the chase, perhaps getting ahead of him and blocking the route or setting a 'Stinger' trap and shredding his tyres.

Sweat pours off him; the exertion involves a war with nervous anxiety for control of his body. He bounces and jostles in the driving seat, fights the steering as the van pitches and yaws like a cumbersome boat at each corner. The van creaks and moans, while he swears and hollers, but all sound is muffled in his hearing, even the constant wail of the siren behind. By contrast his binocular vision has grown sharp as he plunges into an endless high-definition tunnel, blinkered at the edges by a red haze. His mind, in perfect unison with his vision, is three steps ahead of every manoeuvre he makes, watching for, plotting and then commanding his escape route.

He has left the common far behind, avoiding the dual carriageway out of town, because he'd be too easily caught on a straight stretch of road. Instead he's bolted into the city, where there are more options to lose his pursuers in the cross streets and sprawling housing estates. The traffic calming measures on roads with a posted speed limit of 20 mph wreak as much havoc on the patrol car as they do his van, and he is also prepared to go where the cops are reluctant to follow. He ramps off speed bumps, takes shortcuts directly over mini-roundabouts, and also drives on footpaths where necessary. He finds a cycle track that cuts across a swathe of fallow ground, and doesn't pause. He spins the van on to the pavement, gets two wheels astride the track and hammers the throttle to the floor. The cop car streaks past, hurtling to cut him off by another route. Ballard almost cheers, but his voice catches in his throat as his tyres begin throwing up clods of dirt and frost-stiffened grass: for a moment it sounds as if the van is shaking apart around him. He slews to the right, gets the nearside tyres on the hardpack but the van fishtails wildly: he is forced to slow down or roll the van altogether. He thinks about spinning the van around and heading back the way he's just come, giving his pursuers the slip, but he spots more blue lights in his mirrors. A second patrol has joined the chase, blocking that route at the entrance to the cycle path. There are allotments to his right, and a deep ravine to his left through which a sluggish stream flows. No other option but to go on. He simply can't – won't – allow the police to catch him while Nate is still out there. He pushes on, scans ahead and to either side. Hundreds of metres beyond the allotments, the original patrol car parallels him, its blue lights flashing off the roofs of houses, the whistling in his ears obscuring the intermittent thin strain of its siren.

Originally pre-war council houses had filled the fallow ground, but they've been demolished a decade ago, and await an upturn in the economy for fresh social housing to be erected. He speeds by the burnt-out husk of a stolen car. There are the remnants of last month's bonfire night celebrations, burnt wood and singed metal scattered everywhere. A wheel clips a concrete post; thankfully it has already been uprooted from the earth. The van lurches, and the post flies up, colliding with the undercarriage, before it spins away, trailing a length of corroded barbed wire. Will struggles to control the van. He bites his bottom lip, drawing blood and a fresh curse. Against the odds, he wrestles the van back on track, but his vehicle has been fatally wounded. The steering wheel judders and there is a shriek of metal grinding on metal. He fights the steering again, tries to halt the relentless surge to the left, then as an afterthought hits the brakes. But already it is too late. The van is off the path and leaning towards the bank of the ravine. Will has no recourse except jump from the vehicle, or ride it down into the stream. He slaps at the door handle, and throws it wide, ready to jump . . . but is halted by the seatbelt.

A shout of alarm jumps to his throat as he claws to release the safety belt, but it is too late. He throws his crossed elbows in front of his face as the van tears a tight arch of avalanching dirt down into the ravine. The noise is as horrendous as the impact. The airbags inflate, metal crumples, glass implodes. Immediately filthy water rushes around him. For a moment, Will has no idea if he is up, down or sideways – everything is a chaos of noise and movement, but he has survived the wreck. He fights free of the deflating airbags, clawing again at the seatbelt clip, one part of him thankful it thwarted his attempt to loosen it seconds earlier, otherwise who knows how badly he'd have been hurt. He scrambles out of the door, his feet going up to his ankles in the churned earth. He aches in a dozen places, but miraculously has avoided any serious injury. The van has nose-dived into the stream, but it is barely a foot deep, and the banks of the ravine no more than a few metres high from top to bottom. He backs away, watching steam rising from the overheated engine where the stream has flooded in at impact. The van is dying, but he is alive! He kicks backwards, going up the embankment on his backside, digging in the heels of his palms for traction. All the while he thinks furiously about whether there is anything he should grab from the van that will incriminate him further than his stupidity already has in fleeing. There is a knife concealed under the driver's seat, another in the rear compartment, but they're only two pieces of dozens of other tools that will have scattered as the van crashed. He slaps a mucky hand to his shirt pocket, and is relieved he hasn't lost his mobile phone: more than ever now he must rely on his helpers to get him out of this shit.

No, before he relies on anyone else, he has to get moving. Those cops blocking the entrance to the cycle track must've witnessed the crash: they will be coming. Any minute now his original pursuers will arrive at the other end, and they'll decamp their vehicle too and come in on foot. If they've called in a dog handler, he's in big trouble. He has no idea when he lost his hat; there is glass in his hair, and his clothing is soaked. He struggles out of the sodden hooded coat as he tops the rise and stands momentarily on the path. Two hundred metres away, two figures chug down the path towards him, bulky in stab-proof vests and equipment belts. Will is winded from the collision, and his thighs have cramped up, but otherwise he seems reasonably uninjured and more mobile than the pair of coppers. He dashes for the allotments, chased by their thin commands for him to *stop*. As if!

He claps a palm to his chest as he hurdles the crumbling ruin of a wall, keeping his phone safe. Loose bricks threaten to twist his ankles as he dances across a weed-strewn expanse, and a wire fence further slows his passage. The chain-link had been erected at around about the same time the bulldozers had moved in, and hasn't fared well over the last decade: locals using the fallow ground as a shortcut to the allotments have buckled down most of it. He clambers over rusty wire, tearing down a support post that can't bear his weight. Then he is on a cinder path, running adjacent to vegetable plots now devoid of crops, pigeon lofts and chicken coops. His route takes him closer to the pair of coppers now running obliquely across the waste ground to cut him off.

He kicks open a tiny wooden gate and charges up a narrower path between two sheds with sagging roofs and skewed walls. He clambers over a stack of barrels and a roll of chicken wire, then has to scale a taller fence. Behind him the cops are hard on his trail. He is in a second plot of ground, this one used to grow crops. The air stinks of turnips left too long in the ground. His feet are already caked with dirt, and now he kicks through rotting vegetables. Tiny crystals of windscreen glass are shed from his hair with every lurching step.

He is blowing hard by the time he finds the next gate. He prides himself on keeping fit, but the shock of the crash has sapped him of strength, if not the determination to escape. He shoulders through the gate without slowing, stumbles out on to another cinder path that leads towards the nearby housing estate. With firmer ground underfoot, he pushes harder for freedom. The path is hemmed in on both sides by tall hawthorn hedges; here and there bramble snakes across it. A trailing branch snags his feet and brings him down. His elbows catch the brunt of the impact, sending twin jabs of pain all the way to his brain. He curses as he scrambles up and sets off running once more. Ten paces on, he feels a difference, but has taken another half-dozen steps before it makes sense and he skids to a halt. Back where he'd fallen, his phone has slipped from his shirt pocket. He can't see it anywhere, but the silhouetted figures of his two pursuers race up the path towards him. Can he run back, find his phone, and still make his escape from the coppers? He has to try, otherwise he has no easy way of reaching his helpers: now more than ever, he needs somebody to beat the cops to his house and remove the incriminating evidence. He runs back the way he's just come. Every step the grimly set faces of his pursuers come into sharper focus, one man slightly ahead of the other on the narrow footpath. Will can't see a Taser on the lead copper's belt, but he has pulled out his extendable truncheon and racked it open. His rictus grimace shows he means business.

There's the snag that had brought Will down. The phone has to be somewhere between him and it. Will casts around, snatching glances towards the approaching coppers, who again holler commands at him. There! His phone lies partly concealed beneath the discoloured grass at the edge of the path. Will snatches for it, even as the first copper looms less than a dozen feet distant. He is turning to run when the copper charges in and takes a swing at his legs with the baton. Will jerks out of range, but then the man's forward momentum throws them together. One-handed, the copper snatches at him, encumbered now by his extendable truncheon. Will yanks himself out of his grasp, only for the second copper to lunge in and grapple him around the waist. If he is taken down, and the two coppers get on top of him, he'll have no hope of escape. Bracing his feet, he forces down the copper's shoulders with one hand, even as he thrusts his phone in his trouser pocket. The first officer grabs at Will's shoulders, trying to get a grip, but Will yanks free, avoiding him. The man with his arms wrapped around his waist isn't for letting go though. Will punches down between the copper's shoulders, and feels him sink to his knees. It is actually a worse position for Will to be in. The copper only needs to force forward and Will can be pushed to the ground. Immediately Will goes on the offensive, throwing his weight over him and grappling the second copper. He kicks and flails his legs and slips from the kneeling cop's grasp; in the next instant he twists, and flips the upright copper off balance. With a shout he thrusts the cop on top of his colleague, even as he dances free of the jumble of limbs. He kicks out, catching the topmost copper in the ribs. Then uses the sole of his foot to stamp both men down in the cinders. Neither is seriously injured – their stab-proof vests have saved them from his kicks – but they are off balance and their confusion buys him seconds to flee. He races up the path, hoping that their brief fight hasn't allowed other pursuers to close in ahead.

TWENTY-TWO

Northumbria Police HQ, Wallsend

'Get Dr Prince on the phone straight away, Kylie.'

'Yes, boss.' Earlier DS McMahon had grown suspicious of DCI Openshaw's motive for involving her in the case: if he only required an assistant to field all his telephone calls, he could've chosen a constable for the task. Her suspicion was only fleeting, a blip in her self-confidence rather than anything Openshaw is responsible for. She has grown so used to Ray Logan dumping all the scut work on her that she'd briefly wondered if the DCI also saw her as a receptacle for the rubbish he didn't want to deal with. But no, the reality is he has delegated tasks to her because he trusts in her ability to get them done. She brings up Emily's number on her phone and hits the call icon.

The call is answered almost instantly. They are in a private office in Northumbria Police HQ at Wallsend, adjacent to the incident room into Darren Sykes's murder. Currently they have the office to themselves, so Kylie puts the call on speaker.

'I was just about to ring you!' Emily's voice is octaves higher than normal. 'We think we've found something important.'

'Wait one,' says Kylie, as she checks with the DCI for instruction. Instead he holds out a hand. This is a call he personally wishes to make, and rightly so.

'Emily? It's Grant Openshaw.'

'Great. I need to speak to you about—'

'Hold on a sec,' he cuts in. 'Is Nate there with you?'

'Yes. He's right here.'

'Good. Put him on, please.'

'But—'

'Whatever it is, we'll get to it in a moment, but there's something I need to tell Nate first.'

Emily must have handed over her phone, because Freeman speaks up. 'What's going on, Grant?'

'We have a rapidly developing incident in—'

'Concerning the killer?' Freeman jumps in.

'That's yet to be determined, but it does involve your brother.'

'Wait? What? You've found Will?'

'I'm waiting for confirmation, but I'm confident it's him. At least the van he was driving was registered in one of his previous names and, from what I've heard, his description matches what we have on file.'

'What's happening, Grant? Your tone of voice—'

'He's running from us, Nate. He led officers on a high-speed chase, then after crashing his van he made off. During the escape he injured two constables trying to detain him.'

'Shit,' Freeman rasps. 'That doesn't sound good.'

'No. It doesn't. Those aren't the actions of an innocent man.'

Kylie exchanges a glance with her boss at Freeman's silence.

Openshaw says, 'I know it isn't something you want to contemplate, Nate, but Will isn't fleeing us for no reason.'

'Maybe, like I did, he thinks that by coming forward he'll be treated as a suspect.'

'By running he isn't helping himself. Hell, he's piling up the charges as it is: dangerous driving, police assault . . . he's acting like he's got something to hide.' Openshaw chews his bottom lip, thinking. 'Nate, by telling you this, it might mean you having any further inclusion in the case rescinded.'

'Why?'

'You know why. If your brother's the killer, it compromises you as a reliable witness.'

'I choose to think he isn't the killer; you should give him – and me – the benefit of the doubt until you know otherwise.'

'Perhaps.' Surprisingly Openshaw looks to Kylie for a second opinion.

She says, 'I guess we should still involve Nate until something concrete's proven against Will. As it is, I tend to agree – he could be running because he's afraid of being treated like a murderer.'

Openshaw rocks his head in consideration. 'OK. For now we

keep things as they are. Emily, you said you'd something important to tell us.'

'Hold on a minute!' Freeman isn't finished yet. 'You said you've a developing situation. What exactly is going on?'

'Will's on foot,' says Openshaw, 'and won't get far. All available patrols have joined the chase, and we've a helicopter in the air. It won't be long till we have him.'

'Armed response?'

'Yeah, Nate, we've ARVs in the area. After the first arrest attempt, we can't take any chances. He's been deemed dangerous . . . if he's the killer, he's shown he has no qualms about using extreme violence.'

'For God's sake, make sure nobody has an itchy trigger finger. You don't want anyone making the wrong judgement and—'

'Nobody will shoot without express permission.'

'And who's gold command on this . . . you?'

'No, Nate, a Northumbria chief super's in command of the Sykes case. I only coordinate the CID resource seconded to the NCA.'

'Yeah, your remit's to support and advise, right? Well, advise gold command *not to shoot my brother*. I'm telling you, Grant, Will *isn't* your man.'

'You can't be certain of that.'

'No more than you can be that he's the killer. You just agreed to give me the benefit of the doubt – do the same for him, as well.'

Emily pipes up in the background. 'Nate, there's something you should consider. If Will's on the run, it could explain why there's no immediate reply to Baphomet's message.'

'What's that all about?' Openshaw asks, happy to change the subject.

'I'll let Emily bring you up to speed,' says Freeman, 'just remember what I asked, Grant. No shooting.'

Emily sets off at a rush. 'We've taken a close look at the forum I showed you earlier and have been able to identify a short list for your Cyber Crime guys to look at, but first they should concentrate on a particular discussion between two with the usernames Baphomet and Nephilim. Particular attention should be paid to finding Nephilim, as we thought at first it could be William Ballard, but who might actually be the murderer—'

'Whoa! Hold on a second, Emily. I'm not following. Kylie, how's your shorthand?'

Kylie already has a pen poised over a notebook. 'I've got it all, boss, but yeah, it'd maybe help if you slowed down a bit, Emily.'

'Sorry.' Emily takes a calming breath. 'OK, we've highlighted two users, Nephilim being the one that the Cyber Crime team should focus on.' She goes on to explain the angel/human hybrid connection of his name and how that could relate to someone believing themselves to be a direct descendant of Weyland Berith, and how he'd apparently offered a reward for information about *the* brother. 'We've concluded that Nephilim is a Brit who might've spent some time in the US, and could be Nate's brother, Will. However, if Will's currently on the run from the police, it's unlikely he'll be able to respond to Baphomet any time soon. Look, Grant, we might be totally off the mark with this, but it's the best lead we've been able to find. If Will and Nephilim aren't one and the same, it could be the killer, or it could be unrelated altogether.'

'Can you even be certain that Nephilim's a man?' Kylie wonders aloud.

'Going by his speech patterns, or more correctly the way he writes, it sounds more male to me than female, but I can't guarantee that. Nate said that there was also a brother and sister raised in the commune at Ohop Island alongside him and Will.'

'They're no longer in the equation,' Kylie informs her. 'The NCA and FBI are exchanging information on a similar set of crimes that took place in the US. The siblings Nate referred to have both been traced, and the brother identified as a victim.'

Emily doesn't reply. Kylie gains the impression she's offering her sympathy to Freeman over the latest shocking news. To get the doctor's mind back on track, Kylie asks, 'Emily, can you read us the exact wording of the message Baphomet sent?'

Emily does as asked, then explains her understanding of what the 'private place' might refer to.

'It's a tenuous link,' Kylie muses. The two idiots could be talking about *any* brother totally unrelated to their investigation, although the request for Nephilim to reply in private does make things sound suspicious. She checks with Openshaw, who has also mulled over the message.

He says, 'Send what you've got over to DI Brady, and I'll

give him a call and have him prioritize this. Nate, are you still there?'

'I'm here,' Freeman grunts from a distance.

'Good. Listen up, please. If this Baphomet character's talking about finding you, it's highly likely he's talking about discovering your home address. There's no way he could be aware that you're currently in Newcastle at Dr Prince's flat. Hang tight there, and I'll let you know as soon as possible what's happening down in Sunderland.'

'Hold on, my brother's in *Sunderland*? Why didn't you damn well say so? He's less than twenty miles away from here?'

'If you hadn't butted in before I'd've—'

'I should go there,' Freeman announces. 'I could help talk him into surrendering, then—'

'Nate, hold it right there! You're forgetting; Will's also only twenty miles away from where Darren Sykes was recently murdered. That's too much of a bloody coincidence for my liking. You showing up is the last thing I want, but possibly what he's hoping for.'

'If he is the killer, he isn't going to try to kill me there and then. The other murders have all been ritualistic: what purpose will it serve if he goes for my throat? Besides, there'll be armed officers at the scene who can arrest him before he can get near me. Grant, I want the opportunity to bring him in safely, and there's nothing you can say that'll change my mind.'

'I can have you bloody arrested for obstructing police business!'

'So arrest me. You can come find me in Sunderland.' With this, the call is terminated.

TWENTY-THREE

Sunderland

Without the use of blue lights or sirens, DCI Openshaw bulls a route to where the police cordon is tightening on William Ballard's last known location near Sunderland Royal Hospital. Getting out of Newcastle and over the iconic Tyne Bridge proves difficult, but once he's sped through Gateshead and on to the A184, he drives his Audi as if possessed by a demon. Alongside him, Kylie McMahon feels like a co-driver in a rally car, both fielding phone and radio messages while she snaps warnings of possible hazards ahead. Because neither of them is familiar with the locality, Kylie is patched into a police dispatcher in the comms room, who feeds them directions. Spotting the turning for the A19, she relays an instruction to turn right, which Openshaw does, taking the roundabout on two wheels. Behind them car horns blare at their recklessness, but Openshaw ignores them and floors the pedal. It is only a short run down the dual carriageway before Kylie points out a junction and the Audi sweeps into the suburbs of Sunderland and through a series of mini-roundabouts. At one of them, Openshaw leaves tyre tracks in the grass at the central island when he swerves to miss the back end of a bus too slow to clear enough space for them. He doesn't decelerate, he pushes faster, swerving past slower-moving traffic at every possible opportunity. Ahead blue lights dance where police cars sit astride the carriageways. A helicopter hangs in the pale grey sky, buzzing like an angry hornet as it seeks the fugitive. Onboard the craft, the crew will be utilizing their FLIR cameras in their search for Will Ballard, scanning the warren of streets adjacent to the hospital for his overheated signature.

Openshaw still fumes at Nate Freeman's pig-headedness, and fully expects to spot him haranguing the local coppers up ahead. Of course, there's no possible way that Nate could have beaten them to the scene, particularly when he isn't party to where the hunt is currently under way. Sunderland is a major conurbation, and there's little to no chance that Nate could foresee where his brother is hiding. Yet Openshaw also knows Nate is resourceful and will probably find his way. All he needs do is follow the blue lights and sirens and they'll lead him here. *If he shows up, I'll bloody show him!* He will have Nate in cuffs and into custody in quick time. Nate won't thank him, but he'll be safely tucked out of harm's way, and that is what's important to Openshaw. Nate's safety is only secondary to catching the killer, and if it turns out that Will Ballard is their man, he isn't going to let Nate get between them.

There is backed-up traffic between them and the roadblock,

but Openshaw doesn't slow. He mounts two wheels on the near-side pavement and drives along it until he's halted by a road sign only metres short of the next junction. They've elicited angry and confused glimpses from other motorists, and a uniformed officer is heading their way with a stern face and raised palm. Openshaw and Kylie are out of the car in an instant, and Openshaw marches towards the uniform with his warrant card held aloft. Immediately the constable's demeanour changes and he drops his officious look as he pushes back his flat cap.

'What's the latest on Ballard?' Openshaw demands without preamble.

The constable is a rotund youth, who resembles an overripe lemon in his high-visibility jacket worn over a bulky stab-proof vest. Judging by the pristine nature of his jacket and the high shine on his boots, he's relatively young in service, possibly a probationer being tutored by one of the other officers at the scene. It explains his confusion and the way he stammers out an unintelligible response.

Openshaw snorts and weaves around him, gesturing to another officer. Again a flash of his warrant card demands an immediate reaction, and a taller, older constable jogs over. The first cop reddens, and glances at Kylie, who squeezes him a supportive smile: they were all young in service once, and she can recall the confusion she felt when thrown in at the deep end with little experience and less of a clue as to how to handle a chaotic situation. There were still times, working alongside her boss, DI Ray Logan, when she had been left dazed and confused by his lack of direction at a crime scene.

'I, uh, was just told to stop anyone gannin' any further,' the youthful cop blusters in a thick accent. 'Ah dunno what's gahn on with . . .'

'Don't worry about it,' Kylie says, 'we've all been there.'

Openshaw is marching back. He doesn't even look at the red-faced probationer. He nods at Kylie to get back to his car. 'They're going to let us through.' Then he jerks a thumb at the young officer. 'Shift those cars over so we can get by.'

The constable stammers another response but rushes to comply. He begins going from car to car, issuing orders, and the nearest vehicles angle into the next lane, making a gap between them and the road sign. Back in the Audi, Openshaw squeezes through the gap, and then manoeuvres around the nearest police car and on to the adjoining street. He speeds between rows of cars parked nose to tail, barely slowing for the speed bumps. At the far end of the street, a police van sits astride the junction, and several cops are grouped alongside it, one of them with a German shepherd straining at its leash. The helicopter chatters overhead.

The Audi squeals to a halt, and again Openshaw is out in seconds and marching towards the nearest officers. Kylie follows, her head swivelling to take in as much as possible. Downwash from the rotor blades ruffles her red hair. She watches the helicopter swoop over the rooftops to the west. The other officers grow animated, and again Openshaw is rushing back towards her before she has any real clue of what's going on.

'Ballard's been sighted near a cemetery a couple of streets away.' Openshaw doesn't need to tell her to get back in the car. Kylie beats him to it. The police van is already rolling, its blue lights flashing. Openshaw starts the Audi, and swings past the larger vehicle on to a side street and races ahead. He's determined to be first on the scene when Ballard is located.

TWENTY-FOUR

Blowing like a racehorse, Will Ballard scurries under a canopy of branches hanging so low to the ground that they drag on his clothing and score tiny wounds in his scalp. The scrapes are minor discomforts he's willing to put up with for the sake of concealment. He can hear the rhythmic chop of rotor blades but can't yet see its source: if the police chopper has a thermal camera he will easily be spotted if he tries hiding somewhere with less cover. The conifer tree he's scrambled under has been shaped to blend in with others throughout the cemetery, and also with some of the larger memorials and tombs in this ancient corner of the burial ground. The density of its branches will help conceal his heat signature from the cops above, but won't help much against those on foot. He digs deeper under the foliage, and squirms around so he faces out, propping his elbows under him. He spits brown needles from his lips as he draws in one breath after another. His heart slams against his ribcage and his pulse beats behind his eyes. His vision is blurry and his body trembles.

He is fearful of capture, but is more angered by its prospect. It was stupidity making off from the police the way he did. He should have bluffed things out with the patrol officers, taken his ticket for speeding and then moved on to another of the identities he has carefully built over the last few years. But haring off and leading the police on a wild chase ensured a reaction exactly like this one, especially since he'd scuffled with those two constables back at the allotment. One thing cops never tolerate is violence aimed at any of them; it always guarantees a concerted response.

Urgent voices dance across the cemetery, but he's unable to pinpoint their sources from the way they echo off nearby headstones. Vehicles are approaching on the side streets, and in seconds they'll be within the boundary of the graveyard too. The helicopter is somewhere to his left, out of sight, but looming closer, judging by the deafening beat. He pushes backwards on his elbows, trying to get deeper beneath the boughs, but is halted by the thick knot of roots at the tree's base. He drags handfuls of fallen needles to pile in front of him, before realizing he's wasting his time. Sooner or later the search will converge on his location, and a tiny wall of needles isn't going to deter his determined hunters. He begins squirming forward, digging in with his elbows for traction. A high-pitched bark halts all movement. *They've got dogs!*

His hiding place might throw off a thermal camera, but not the sensitive nose of a police dog. Shit! A dog on his scent will lead his hunters directly to him and, caught under the canopy of branches, he'll have no hope of escape. Without further pause he breaks out from under the tree, scrambles up and races off, hoping it's in the opposite direction of the dog. His feet dig into spongy grass as he darts for the concealment of a huge mausoleum dedicated to a wealthy Victorian businessman. The marble edifice is pitted with more than a century's grime. It is tiered like a wedding cake, the lowest dais tall enough to hide behind if he goes to all fours. Being in that position is the last he wants if the dog finds him. He swings around behind it, vaults on to the first tier and braces his spine against the second. A screen of ancient yew trees, possibly hundreds of years old, forms a gnarled bulwark between him and the helicopter, but he can hear it hovering closer. He'll be spotted in no time. He bounds down from the mausoleum and over the final resting places of poorer people. In the shadow of a tall headstone, where frost still remains, he skids on the grass and goes down hard. Cursing, he scrambles for balance and darts to the right, weaving between markers skewed by age, and finds momentary shelter against the trunk of an overgrown yew tree. Its reddish bark is jagged under his touch as he pushes up against it, hoping somehow that he can blend with its uneven shape and throw off the pursuit. His breathing is more laboured than before, fear of discovery pinches his throat.

'Police! Stop right there!'

The curt shout comes from his left.

A tall police officer runs across the cemetery towards him, one palm held out.

Ballard ignores the command. He puts the tree between them and runs, his elbows pumping furiously. A stab-proof vest and equipment belt encumbers the officer. Ordinarily Ballard would easily outpace the copper, but the chase has been long and he has barely any breath left: his limbs are cramped and the effects of crashing his van are catching up; pain is everywhere. But he won't be stopped until he finds Nate. Gasping he keeps running, and he can't hear the pounding of the copper's footsteps for his own pulse in his skull. He glances briefly over his shoulder and wishes he hadn't. The officer is only metres behind him, his face set in a determined snarl. Ballard spits out a curse, tempted in that moment to slow and allow the copper to catch up. Not that he's for giving up, only that he should fight the man off while he still has some strength.

It's fortunate that he managed to make a phone call to one of his helpers earlier while hiding in a deserted park, and arranged for the loft in his apartment to be stripped of incriminating evidence: surely with the cops on to him their next stop will be to search his home. He wishes he'd grabbed one of his knives from his cache prior to leaving the house, or had the forethought to secure one from his van before it rolled into the ditch. With a blade in his hand he could stop the copper, and make an escape once he has caught his breath. Wishes though are for other people; he has to make his own luck. He puts another yew tree between them, using the distraction to race off obliquely across newer graves. He jumps one headstone to place a barrier of stone between them. The officer shouts at him to stop. As if he's going to!

Another shout.

There are two more constables racing through the grounds to intercept him. Ballard swerves to his right, and spots the boundary wall looming ahead. If he can scale it, cross the street, maybe he can again lose himself in the warren of terraced houses on the far side of the road. His mind made up, he rushes for the wall.

'Dog loose!'

He barely hears the distant shout. It is not solely for his ears. The dog handler has yelled a warning to his colleagues: a police dog is not selective when sicked and will bring down a running constable as readily as a fugitive. Ballard knows that the trio of pursuers is pulling to a halt behind him, but he has no such intention. He hurtles towards the wall, holding his breath in anticipation of teeth snapping into his flesh. He leaps and grabs at the top of the wall. Skin is rubbed off his fingertips, and leather from his shoes, as he digs for purchase and clambers higher. He throws a knee over the top, and makes the mistake of looking back.

An open maw lunges, and his concentration is centred on the large yellow canines streaking at him. He jerks away, and tumbles from his perch, falling on to the pavement on the adjacent street. The air erupts from his lungs in a shout of pain. Beyond the wall the dog barks furiously. He pushes up, stiff and sore, and catches brief views of the dog's muzzle snapping at the space he's just vacated. He's fortunate the dog is concentrating its efforts there; given seconds it will rethink its approach, back up a few steps and come sailing over the wall after him. Ballard isn't hanging around to give it the opportunity. He limps across the street, gaining speed with each hopping step, and searches for an escape route. He is faced by a long row of terraced houses, with no gaps between. The chopper hovers over the road, low enough for its downwash to buffer him. He knows it's only seconds away until the nearest trio of cops scramble over the wall in pursuit, with the dog leading the charge. He lurches away, hoping to find an open door, or a vehicle he can commandeer.

A police carrier van sweeps up the street in his wake, blue lights flashing. Ahead, another patrol car blocks the road. Two constables in high-visibility tunics are already out of the vehicle and jogging towards him. The carrier squeals to a halt and doors are being thrown open. Ballard doesn't check, he only keeps going, now gasping as much in desperation as for lack of oxygen. The constables move to block his path and he veers into the tiny garden at the front of a terraced house. He tries the front door and it's locked. He throws a shoulder against it but it isn't for budging. The cops shout commands, some of them conflicting. He ignores them, turns away and scrambles over a low wall into the adjoining garden. He again tries a door, and it's locked too. He slams his palms against the front window and it shudders in its frame. This is the type of street where once doors were left unlocked and neighbours came and went without knocking; housewives gossiped out of open windows or on their front stoops. It is a shocking indictment of modern society that residents now need to barricade themselves inside their homes . . . but who knows when a murder suspect might come banging on their doors seeking entrance? The irony makes him wheeze. He turns to face his pursuers.

He holds no fear of the regular divisional uniformed constables, even those scaling the cemetery's perimeter wall, bringing with them the German shepherd, because now it is once more leashed. Those from the van are a different entity: they are from the Tactical Support Group, specialists with tactical training to quell public disorder. They wear coveralls, protective equipment and helmets, and one carries a plastic shield employed in curtailing rioters. In effect, they are the heavy mob, called in when pinpointed controlled aggression is required. There'll be no way of fighting them, so he runs again, hurdling the small walls adjoining each property.

Other cars appear ahead – one is a marked police car, another a black Audi – and people swarm out to help stop him. Two constables already approach along the pavement, in position to block his progress through the front gardens. Ballard halts and puts his back to a door. A tall, silver-haired detective and a red-haired woman move adjacent to him, because they've already guessed he isn't going to try to plough through the two burly constables blocking his escape. The detectives could be the softer option, he thinks, until he spots the resolve in the man's eyes, and realizes he's no slouch. The woman doesn't seem fazed either; her hand dips into her pocket and pulls out a canister of incapacitant spray. Ballard has been on the receiving end of PAVA spray before, and doesn't relish being sprayed in the eyes again, but he's still not for giving up without a fight. He searches for a weapon.

The only thing to hand is a loose kerbstone he jostles out of the soil at the edge of a dirt plot devoid of flowering plants.

'Come another step closer and I'll smash your heads in!'

His warning falls on deaf ears.

The detectives crowd him, keeping him from darting across the road while the constables move in from one side and the Tactical Support Group stormtroopers the other.

'I'm warning you—' Ballard stamps, hefting the stone.

The dog goes crazy, straining at its leash, but until the others move aside it won't be loosed on him. It's unnecessary. The TSG are armed with Tasers. One way or the other, Ballard knows he's going down.

'Get the hell away from me!' Ballard hurtles forward, towards the tall detective, and swings for his head with the rock.

'No, Will, he's trying to save you . . . don't!'

The shout impinges on his desperation. It's a voice echoing from the past. Ballard's head twists as he seeks out the shouter. The rock misses its target and Ballard is tackled around his waist. The detective throws a shoulder into his midriff and forces him backwards and his heels catch on the low wall. They both hit the ground, crushing brown and stunted plants beneath their struggling bodies. They spill apart, and Ballard couldn't care less about the detective; he cranes, searching for the source of the voice. The red-haired cop sprays his face with incapacitant spray, and Ballard can see or hear nothing through his tears, streaming snot and saliva, and the thundering inside his skull.

TWENTY-FIVE

Emily Prince is hauling on his jacket, trying to halt his mad rush. Freeman glances at her apologetically, but pulls loose of her grasp.

'Wait,' she cautions him. 'Let the police finish doing their job first.'

'After Will's just gone for Grant with that rock . . . there's no way they'll go easy on him.'

'Perhaps he doesn't deserve to be treated with kid gloves.'

Freeman nods in agreement, shakes his head in the next second. William Ballard – *his brother* – had just attempted to smash in a detective chief inspector's skull with a kerbstone; it wasn't the normal response of an innocent man. It's obviously an act of denial, but Freeman is still prepared to give him the benefit of the doubt.

He continues forward. Emily grabs at him again. He's torn. He doesn't wish to annoy her, but he jerks loose a second time. He wishes now she hadn't accompanied him, because he doesn't want her to see him acting like this, but she'd argued she shouldn't be left alone if the police were chasing the wrong man; not if there was validity in the claim made by Baphomet that he knew where 'the brother' was. She'd had a point, and he hadn't objected when she'd followed him outside, only for him to stand with his palms held up in dismay. In his urgency he'd forgotten he'd travelled to Emily's apartment in Grant Openshaw's Audi . . . he had no immediate way of getting to Sunderland. Emily, though, had ushered him along the road to where her VW Golf was parked at the kerb. He'd instantly recognized the car as the one in which he'd watched her drive away from Haydon Bridge yesterday.

'I'll drive,' he'd announced, and reached for the keys.

'It's my car, and I'm the only one who's going to drive it.' Emily had stared at him, hard.

'OK. You drive. It's probably best . . . you probably know where we're going better than I do.'

Partly he'd expected her to drive slowly and carefully, obeying the posted speed limits, mostly in an effort at stalling so that Will's arrest was over and done with long before they could arrive at the scene, but she'd surprised him. She'd negotiated the roads with the confidence of a skilled rally driver, and made ground faster than he could have. Her local knowledge of short-cuts was an immense benefit. In a short time they had entered the outlying districts of Sunderland, and Freeman had spotted the police chopper hovering in the sky. He'd pointed it out, seconds before it dipped low and was concealed behind rows of rooftops and the crowns of distant trees. A cop car went hurtling past and, without instruction, Emily had fallen into its wake, because it was obvious the cop was racing to help close the cordon around Will Ballard.

The cop car, lights flashing and sirens wailing, had cut a swathe through the other road users, and Emily stuck close behind. They reached a road adjacent to an old burial ground within a few minutes, beaten to the spot by other police, and judging by the Audi abandoned in the road, by Grant Openshaw and Kylie McMahon. Ahead of them two uniformed cops had decamped their vehicle and they rushed to assist their colleagues, and the detectives weren't far behind them. Freeman spotted Grant, a tall figure in a flapping overcoat, and alongside him Kylie's red hair stood out like a flame. He'd scrambled out of the Golf the second Emily pulled it to a halt, even as the cops converged on a single point about fifty metres away. Freeman's gaze swung on to the figure bouncing on the balls of his feet in the front garden of a terraced house. He was as tall as Grant, but bulkier with muscle, with short dark hair and the beginnings of a beard and moustache. Freeman hadn't seen this adult version, but knew instinctively that he stared at his kid brother. He felt it like a dagger to his heart. He could barely breathe as he began to approach.

Will yelled at the police, brandishing a chunk of broken kerb-stone. He launched a mock attack, stamping a foot as if about to launch forward, but it didn't slow the cops. Grant lunged in, and Freeman realized what his old friend was up to: getting between Will and the TSG officers, shielding him in that moment, ensuring that his promise to Freeman to stop his brother being gunned down wouldn't be broken. But Will hadn't recognized the selfless act of the detective, and he swung at Grant's head with the rock.

'No, Will, he's trying to save you . . . *don't*!'

Despite the intervening distance, Freeman's shout had reached Will, and his head had snapped around, seeking its source. The rock missed its target, and in the next instant Grant had powered in and both men went down in a tangle. Kylie swooped in to assist her boss, a canister of incapacitant spray held out as if it were a gun. She didn't shirk from the task, going down on top of Will, aiming the spray directly in his face. Freeman rushed forward, even as the uniformed cops and TSG officers surged in to contain their prisoner. More than one of them had drawn their Tasers. That was when Emily tried to halt him.

Now she follows as Freeman runs to intervene.

There is a bunch of officers around his brother. Some assist Grant and Kylie to stand: Kylie has caught a backwash of her own PAVA, and her eyes and nose stream. She's familiar with the effects of the spray, and avoids wiping her face; doing so will only compound its potency. She bends with her hands on her thighs, spitting on the pavement. Will Ballard is being roughly handcuffed, his hands to the rear. He continues struggling, but it's a pointless fight that he can't win. As Freeman moves in on the scuffle, he realizes that Will is searching for him. He has heard and recognized the shout.

'Will, it's me, Nate! You have to stop struggling or—'

A TSG officer is in his path. The cop's astute enough to recognize the similarity between the prisoner and the man rushing to get involved, and comes to the wrong conclusion. He throws himself at Freeman, grappling to push him aside. Freeman rolls his shoulders with the motion, and the officer loses his grip and stumbles against him.

'I'm trying to help!' Freeman barks, but his words mean nothing to the cop at this moment. The guy grabs him, again tries to wrestle him. Freeman – stupidly – pushes back. A second TSG officer bounds at him. The burly cop grasps his jacket, yanks on it, and sticks out a leg to trip him. Freeman has been trained in the same close-quarters tactics. He merely hops over the extended leg, and now it's the cop who's off balance. A shove sends the cop down on his back in the street. It isn't Freeman's most expedient response. The first TSG officer and a uniformed bobby immediately beset him, bringing him down between them. One of them kneels on his back while the other wrestles to get his hands cuffed. Over their guttural commands and muttered curses, Freeman's aware of Emily as she exhorts them to take it easy on him. She has gone to her knees alongside them, and bleats directly into the face of the TSG officer. If she isn't careful, she'll be the next to be arrested. The bobby cautions and arrests Freeman, despite Emily's attempt at explaining he's not involved with their other prisoner. Freeman is rolled over, and the cops prepare to help him stand; he's destined for one of the police cars because Will is already being hustled to the secure cage in the TSG carrier van. Will's head is turned towards him, his bloodshot eyes out on stalks. Freeman's unsure if it's an effect of the PAVA or because he can't believe his brother is there. He opens his mouth to offer Will words of support, but none come.

Openshaw blocks Freeman's view. His face is flushed from his recent tussle with Will, and there's dirt on his coat and the knees of his trousers. He clenches his teeth as his eyes meet Freeman's. 'For Christ's sake, Nate! What did I tell you?'

'You knew I wouldn't stay away.'

'I also warned you that you'd be arrested.'

'Then you were right on both counts. What now?'

'I should have you locked up . . .' Openshaw shakes his head.

The arresting officers are thrown by the DCI's familiarity with their prisoner. They glance at each other, frowning, then at Openshaw. The TSG officer already knows who he is, the uniformed bobby has guessed. Rather than drag Freeman to a car, they hold him, awaiting instruction. Emily moves alongside Openshaw, about to plead for leniency, but Openshaw has already made up his mind.

'De-arrest him.' Openshaw's instruction is blunt, and brooks no argument.

Nevertheless, the constable is momentarily confused. 'Sir, he's been arrested for—'

Openshaw cuts him off. 'He's with me. Uncuff him.'

The TSG officer shrugs and says, 'You heard the boss.'

While the bobby does as instructed under the watchful gaze of the TSG officer, the second TSG officer rubs a sore spot on his lower back. He has taken off his helmet, giving him freedom to scowl at Freeman.

'Sorry for knocking you on your arse, mate,' says Freeman, 'but you wouldn't listen.'

'You said you were tryin' to help,' the other cop stabs a finger towards the carrier, 'for all we knew, you meant tryin' to help that fucker over there. Bit of a resemblance between the two of you, if you don't mind me sayin' so.'

Enlightening the cop that they're siblings might not be a good idea. Freeman only grimaces, and rubs at the indentations on his wrists where the cuffs have dug in. He's still getting the stink-eye from Openshaw. But Openshaw offers an explanation. 'Mr Freeman's a consultant engaged by the NCA to assist us in identifying a murder suspect. As is' – he nods at Emily – 'Doctor Prince. As I said, Freeman's with me, so you can stand down now.'

He receives muttered affirmations from the three cops, and they move away, the two TSG officers heading for the carrier. The uniformed constable joins a small cluster of colleagues in the vicinity of the garden where Will Ballard was taken down. Some of them will be required to pacify the inquisitiveness of people now appearing at their front doors and windows, now that the immediate danger has passed. The dog handler has retreated, backtracking towards where he's left his vehicle on the far side of the cemetery. His dog isn't eager to leave, though; it barks madly at missing out on the fun. The helicopter, too, has left the scene. The street still resembles a police vehicle parking lot, and already the local traffic is backing up, some of the drivers leaning out of their windows to see what the drama is. Before long, the press and camera crews will arrive, but they won't get the exclusive footage they hope for, it is already being filmed on half a dozen civilians' mobile phones. The police carrier starts up. Will and his escorts are dim shadows beyond nigh-on opaque windows. Will shoves his face hard to the glass.

Freeman jerks forward, but Openshaw palms him in the chest.

'Where do you think you're going?'

'I want to speak with Will before he's taken in.'

'There's no bloody chance of that happening, Nate.'

'Come on, Grant? Just let me see him; a minute, that's all I need.'

'No. You aren't getting near him. Not yet. Not until after he's been processed and interviewed.'

'I haven't laid eyes on him for twenty years . . .'

'Well, another couple of hours won't make a difference. You should be grateful I'm going to let you see him at all.'

Freeman nods into his chest. 'I am. I just thought . . .'

Openshaw turns and walks away to converse with Kylie McMahon. The detective sergeant is still spitting and sneezing, but is recovering from her exposure to the incapacitant spray. Both briefly glance in his direction, and then Kylie scowls at whatever Openshaw tells her. Freeman shuffles uncomfortably at her response.

Emily lays a hand on his forearm and Freeman blinks at her in apology.

'Are you OK?' she asks.

His wrists chafe from the rough application of the cuffs, but otherwise his aches and pains are nothing to those he's put himself through in penance over failing to save Jenny Onatade. Emily looks as flushed as Openshaw was a minute ago. 'I'm fine,' he says, 'but what about you? I'm sorry, Emily. I shouldn't have put you through that.'

A brief exhalation escapes her: it sounds scornful. 'No, you shouldn't have. But I chose to come with you, fully expecting you to act like a lunatic, so let's leave things at that.'

After a moment she smiles, and it dawns on him that she's pulling his leg. Her hand, he notes, never leaves his forearm. He can feel the warmth of it through the material of his jacket, and also its spread to his chest where heat blossoms. He has to clear his throat before he can speak. 'Thanks for, uh, backing me up.'

'I was unsure if I was doing the right thing,' she admits. 'What were you trying to do? Get yourself arrested so you'd be closer to your brother? You do realize they'd have kept you separated in different cells, don't you?'

'I wasn't trying to get arrested, I just needed to speak with him. To find out if . . .'

'You want to find out if he's the murderer? That's DCI Openshaw's job, not yours, Nate.'

'I know, but, well, maybe he'll say something to me he's unwilling to admit to Grant.'

Emily tilts her head on one side, studying him. 'It's years since you've seen him; you don't know him as an adult. If you think you can work out what's going on in his head better than the police can, you're deluded. Your take on his psyche will be based on your own emotions as much as his, and on your denial that he's involved in these killings. Nate, if you ask me, his actions have been pretty damn telling.'

Freeman shakes his head. 'I only saw a frightened person, fighting to escape, not to hurt anyone.'

'He almost smashed the DCI over the head with a brick!'

'That's my point. He could've, but he didn't.'

'Only because your shout distracted him.'

He thinks for a moment. 'Maybe,' he finally concurs, 'but I'm still not convinced he's the one we're looking for.'

Kylie approaches. She has a paper hankie wadded in one hand, and before she halts she dabs at the corners of her eyes with it. 'DCI Openshaw will be a few minutes yet, but once he's ready you should follow us to the nick. You won't be allowed in the interview, but he thinks having you there might come in handy.'

'Thanks,' he says.

'Don't thank me; if it were my decision, I'd send you both back to work on that website. I think you'll get more from it than speaking with your brother.'

'So you don't think Will's the one we're looking for either?'

'I didn't say that. A single person didn't commit those murders; Will had help and they need catching too, and I think you're on the right track.' She acknowledges Emily's input with a nod of respect, followed instantly by a frown. 'Did you send those angel names over to DI Brady yet?'

'I didn't really get the opportunity,' Emily admits with a glance at Freeman. He grimaces at the memory. No sooner had they spoken about doing so on the phone than he'd rushed from Emily's apartment on his way to Sunderland.

Kylie clucks her tongue, but then waves away any apology. 'I'll do it on the drive to the nick. Hmmm, the sooner Brady gets NCCU on things, the better. I suppose sending you back to work won't get us any further without the Cyber Crime Unit's assistance. You'd best jump in your car, DCI Openshaw won't hang around when we leave.'

She is correct. Openshaw doesn't give any concession as he pursues the carrier van to the police station: the van travels on blue lights to force a path through the stalled traffic. Unlike the DCI, Emily is unable to openly disregard the rules of the road and will soon fall behind, but for Freeman's insistence that she stick closely to the Audi. 'I don't think we need to fear the police pulling us over,' he smiles conspiratorially.

TWENTY-SIX

Southwick Police Station, Sunderland.

One police station is much the same as any other these days, Freeman muses, as he settles on the hard plastic chairs arranged in a single row along one wall. Modern police stations look like soulless office blocks, lacking the menace of the Victorian nicks he'd grown to adulthood seeing. He'd initially been surprised when Openshaw's prisoner wasn't taken to a central station in Sunderland, but instead across the River Wear to Southwick, but he concedes that it makes sense. This station has the facilities to accommodate Will, as well as the dozens of high-ranking police personnel destined to arrive here very soon. For now, Openshaw and the others have delivered their VIP prisoner through a secured gate to the station's custody facility, whereas Emily had no option but to try to find a vacant parking space. After circumnavigating the visitors' car park twice, with no luck, she'd dropped Freeman at the front door and gone off to find a roadside parking space. For company in the entrance foyer, Freeman has a surly youth who talks loudly into his mobile phone about the injustices some other youth called 'Macca' is currently enduring at the hands of fascist pigs. His words are pitched for the ears of the male receptionist seated behind safety glass at the desk; he is wasting his time, the police staffer has heard similar too many times to count and has tuned out the youth's whining complaints. The more he's ignored, the louder the youth gets. Freeman folds his arms and grits his teeth, resisting strangling him into blessed silence. The automatic doors occasionally make sucking noises, and each time it draws Freeman's gaze, hoping to see Emily. Apparently available parking spaces are at a premium in this neighbourhood.

Freeman has announced his presence to the receptionist, and waits to be summoned to the desk as eagerly as he does for Emily's return. The latter occurs first. She draws the attention of the youth as the doors whisk open, and his lascivious gaze lingers on her a moment longer than respect dictates. Freeman grunts as loudly as any of the youth's proclamations into his phone of police brutality have been, and catches a nervous glance in return. Freeman sets his snarl and glowering expression, and the youth abruptly decides he'd rather make his telephone call in private. He brushes past Emily in a hurry to escape outside, carefully avoiding staring at her. Emily's frown flickers and it's replaced by a smile that curls up one corner of her mouth. He grunt-coughs into his cupped palm, so it doesn't sound as if he was just engaged in a testosterone-fuelled challenge over a potential mate, but knows Emily can see right through him. Surprisingly she doesn't respond as she had last time he'd gone Neanderthal on her. She sits alongside him, and he has to shuffle his backside a little to give her some shoulder room. She could have chosen to sit in any other of the chairs, but she hasn't, and Freeman's relieved: it means he's been forgiven for dragging her into his sphere of trouble. He relaxes, and their knees touch, and neither flinches from the contact.

'Sorry I took forever finding a parking spot,' she explains needlessly. 'I had to circle the neighbourhood. And just when I thought I'd found a space nearby, these idiots in a van beat me to it. They didn't look the type to argue with, so I had to drive a few streets over and walk back.'

'Thanks,' he says by way of reply.

'Hmm?'

'For your support,' he explains. 'You know, for being here with me.'

'What other option have I got? It's not as if I can abandon you to walk all the way back to Cumbria.'

'Yeah' he agrees. 'Probably wasn't my finest idea leaving my car at home.'

'Thanks. I'm not that bad at driving, am I?'

'No, it's not that, it's just—'

'I'm only kidding, Nate. I know what you meant.' He has no way of getting home now Openshaw won't be returning to Carlisle. She shrugs. 'If it comes to it, I'll drive you back.'

'I couldn't put you to such inconvenience,' he says.

She holds up her palms. 'Like *this* is convenient?'

'Huh, yeah, you're right. Sorry.'

Her smile has returned. 'I'm not complaining. I'm being paid for my time. The thing is, in hindsight, it was quite thrilling taking part in a high-speed chase and arrest. It's more exciting than digging through fusty old documents in the university library, I'll tell you, and more fun when it comes to earning my consultancy fee.'

'There is that.' His lips quirk up at the memory. During the dash to Sunderland, his mind had been on the terrible prospect of his brother being gunned down, but occasionally he'd glanced across at Emily as she raced her car around slower-moving traffic, and noted her clenched jaw and the flashing of her eyes. 'First time we met, I wouldn't have taken you for an adrenalin junkie.'

'First time we met, you didn't even take me for a doctor,' she reminds him. 'It's my intention to shatter all your preconceived notions of me at least once a day from now on.'

Freeman doesn't answer. He feels warmth in his chest, and welcomes it. In a subtle way, she's admitted that she hopes to see more of him after they are done here.

'Thanks,' he repeats.

'For aiming to shatter your illusions?'

He doesn't answer, as it's unnecessary. He only chuckles, and is reminded that her daft humour had put him at ease when first they met at Haydon Bridge.

'How long do you think this is going to take?' she asks, meaning how long does it usually take to process a prisoner.

'It varies,' he admits. 'Depends on whether Will wants legal representation or not. If he wants somebody in the interview with him, we could be forced to wait until his solicitor arrives. Besides that, Grant will want all his ducks in a row too. He'll probably spend some time consulting with his superiors and with the CPS before interviewing Will.'

'So in the meantime we just have to *cool our heels*? Isn't that what they say across the pond?'

'You've been watching too many detective shows,' he says.

'Guilty as charged.'

Her words are poignant, and bring him back to the fact that his brother is currently locked up, suspected of several heinous murders. Will had been a moody, rough-and-tumble child, and apparently in adulthood wasn't averse to throwing around his fists, but Freeman can't quite equate the little brother he remembers with a sadistic, demented murderer. Then again, what if the apple didn't fall far from the tree? Their parents had both proved unhinged and ultimately murderous when fighting for their twisted beliefs. Their biological father, Carl Walker, had been elevated to Weyland Berith's second, and it stood to reason that once Weyland passed on, he'd be the next in line to house the fallen angel's spirit. But Dear Old Dad had been burnt up, consumed by the 'Cleansing Flame' he'd helped set to raise the compound on Ohop Island. With Nate – a heretic in his thoughts and actions – out of the loop, what if Will still believed he was one of the Children of Hamor, and the hereditary vessel of Berith's reincarnated spirit? Could Will be the one responsible for the slaying and butchering of all those victims, and building his own—

'Christ!' Freeman bolts out of the chair, eliciting a yelp of surprise from Emily. He turns to her, his face draining of colour. 'I should have thought of this before!'

She's stunned into silence by his sudden animation. Before she can string a question together, he spins to the counter and slaps his palms on the security screen. The police staffer jerks away in fright, afraid that Freeman is going to smash completely through the barrier.

'Whoa! Steady on, sir,' the man says. He stands from his chair, pushing it back on its castors to make some space between them. His fingers hover near to an emergency buzzer, primed to summon every copper in the nick to his assistance if things get further out of hand.

Freeman backs up a step, but is still as agitated as before. 'I need to speak with DCI Openshaw right now. Call him, tell him it's very important I speak with him and pertinent to his case.'

Emily has also stood. She's as confused as the man behind the counter. Freeman looks at her, shows the palm of his right hand. 'The skins,' he says, 'the *covenants* . . . I know what the killer wants them for.'

TWENTY-SEVEN

'What did you find out?' DCI Openshaw asks. He's standing in a corridor of Southwick Police Station, waiting for Kylie McMahon where she'd last seen him.

As she walks towards him, she gives a little tilt of her head. It isn't a full enough explanation, so she expounds. 'I checked with DI Brady, who liaised with his FBI contact. There's nothing tangible, sir. It was never recorded in the inventory of exhibits taken from the Ohop Island compound.'

'So it may never have existed in the first place?'

'Or it was burned during the fire,' Kylie suggests.

'You said there was nothing tangible?'

'That's right, sir. Although it was never seized in evidence, Weyland Berith referred directly to it on several occasions during subsequent interviews. In general he lamented its loss.'

Openshaw nods sharply. 'Then we can agree that Nate's possibly on to something.'

'It's a reasonable assumption; the killer isn't just taking flesh from his victims as trophies. Nate's idea that he's collecting these seals, these covenants, for a specific purpose makes a lot of sense.'

Again Openshaw nods, and turns on his heel. Kylie doesn't require instruction to follow him. Again he strides off, showing slight discomfort in his knee but not letting it slow him, and she settles into his slipstream.

Nate Freeman and Emily Prince have been moved inside the station to a vacant office. They're seated next to each other on chairs whose fabric seats have been worn thin by the backsides of many detectives. Kylie's aware that they're sitting closer to each other than necessary and wonders if their newfound familiarity is more than collegiality. She flicks a glance at DCI Openshaw and wonders about him too, if he's experienced anything remotely similar in regards to his proximity to his new DS. Who is she kidding?

Openshaw sits opposite Nate and Emily. There's a chair alongside his, so Kylie takes it. They are shoulder-to-shoulder, knee-to-knee. She can feel the heat radiating off him and is certain it's visible in her cheeks.

'Tell me more about this book,' DCI Openshaw says to Nate.

'The FBI does have the original then?' Nate counters.

'No, but DS McMahon checked. Weyland Berith spoke about it several times and – in the words of our Yank friends – *lamented its loss*. If it existed, then it was destroyed in the fire along with the rest of the cult's paraphernalia.'

'It existed. I saw it. On numerous occasions.'

'Like I said, tell me about it. It was some kind of bible, was it?'

'Not exactly, it was more of a grimoire.'

'A book of magic spells?' Grant sniffs, and to Kylie it sounds dismissive.

Nate bristles. 'Whether or not you believe in magic doesn't matter. It only matters that the bloody killer believes.'

'Yeah, yeah, I get that. I don't doubt you're on to something, Nate, it's just that I have a little trouble reconciling myself with all this *Da Vinci Code* stuff.' Openshaw spreads his feet, cupping his hands between his knees as he leans forward. 'So let's pretend that I know nothing, and you're going to explain it to me in layman's terms.'

Nate's mouth pinches, but his head drops and then lifts again, and the spark of anger has left him. 'I've explained before how I was designated one of the Children of Hamor, and was branded by my own father, promised to Berith.' He shifts uncomfortably, as if the scars on his back prickle. 'Along with the other Children, I was going to be sacrificed to help usher in His return, to allow the transmutation of Weyland Berith to risen angel on Earth. I know it sounds like mumbo-jumbo, but to Weyland, and to my parents, it was the absolute given truth: Berith's covenant with his followers.'

'I understand that, but what's the significance of this grimoire?'

'The Book of Dead Names,' Nate calls it. 'It contained a record of the angelic seals, and the ceremonies and incantations by which each could be summoned.' He lifts his hands to forestall Openshaw's disbelief. 'I witnessed several of these summoning rituals, and the sceptical part of me can now dismiss them, but back then, well—'

Kylie interjects. 'You're saying you witnessed the summoning of actual angels?'

'I witnessed people who believed they were possessed by and in communication with the fallen angels; is it any different to those fundamental Christians who profess to be possessed by demons and require exorcism?'

'Yeah, but they're obviously nutcases,' Openshaw intones.

Nate exhales slowly.

'Sorry. Go on,' says Openshaw.

'The book used by Weyland was very old and quite possibly unique. Allegedly the pages and cover were made from vellum. You know what vellum is, right?'

'It's a kind of ancient paper,' Openshaw answers.

'It predates the use of paper, it's a kind of parchment,' Nate corrects him. 'Vellum was originally manufactured from untanned skins.'

Openshaw's eyebrows knit together. He knows where Nate is leading. He glances across at Kylie, and she too has caught the as-yet-unspoken truth of what they are facing. She feels her stomach flip over.

'The Book of Dead Names was supposedly made from human skins, human vellum.' Nate lets the penny drop. 'I think our killer is trying to replace the original book with one of his own.'

'He's making pages from the excised flesh?' Openshaw asks for emphasis.

Nate gestures towards his back. 'All of the promised Children were scarred with individual seals, those of different angels. In order to summon Berith, certain of his vassals must first be summoned to assist in his transfiguration with His chosen avatar. I think our killer, whoever he is, has been harvesting the seals he requires to build his own copy of the Book of Dead Names, in order that the ritual to call Berith into him is successful.'

Openshaw thinks.

Kylie's mind is also working overtime.

'You said the seal you were marked with belongs to Berith. What you're implying,' she says, 'is that the killer won't stop until he has also excised your flesh; without it, everything else will have been for nothing?'

Nate nods. He leans forward, holding her gaze earnestly. 'His book is unfinished. I'm not the only surviving Child who is similarly scarred.' He turns his gaze on Openshaw. 'Have you checked Will's back? I can assure you he's marked the same way I am, and he carries the sigil of one of those vassals. I seriously doubt he's the one collecting the pages for a new grimoire if it means also peeling off his own hide.'

Openshaw's headshake is minuscule. He entwines his fingers, his knuckles turning white. He shakes his head again, slightly harder. 'I know what you're suggesting, Nate, that we've got the wrong man. But Will could still be involved. Whoever we're dealing with, there's something seriously wrong in his head, and by association those working with him must also have a few screws loose. Weyland Berith brainwashed his followers, including your parents, into believing in him, and in your own words carried out some pretty horrible crimes on his behalf. Whoever has picked up Weyland's mission since his death could have equal power over his followers, and they'll do anything on his behalf. Including sacrificing themselves, and allowing their own skin to be harvested.'

'No, I don't see it happening,' says Nate, and Kylie's in agreement.

To Openshaw she says, 'It's one thing having your skin removed during a surgical procedure under sanitary, operating theatre conditions, but if Will is the murderer, and also one whose seal is required for the book, then he isn't going to survive to go through with any transfiguration.'

'There won't be a damn *transfiguration*,' Openshaw counters. 'That's only what these fanatics believe, not what will actually happen.'

'I still stand by what I just said.' Kylie shrugs an apology, but it isn't what the DCI expects from her: he told her to call out bullshit when she hears it. 'I'm not suggesting Will isn't involved, just that he's not the one who thinks he's the next Berith. Maybe he is one of the helpers. Maybe he is willing to sacrifice himself to herald in Berith's return; some fanatics have done some pretty extreme things in the name of faith. I've heard of monks dousing themselves in petrol and setting themselves on fire.'

Nate says, 'If my brother's willing to die for the cause, why not stick his hand up and shout, "Here I am, come and get me"? If he has been working with the killer, then why hasn't his seal already been harvested?'

Openshaw doesn't have an answer, and neither has Kylie.

Until now, Emily has remained silent, absorbing the argument. She pats Nate gently on his knee, begging a moment, and bends forward at the waist to fully engage the detectives. 'Before we came here, we were following that conversation between those Berith followers on the deep web. If your tech guys are currently monitoring it, and there's been more activity, they'll be able to strike Will off the list as a possible identity of Nephilim. Being chased and then locked up by the cops gives him an alibi, doesn't it?' She smiles at her theory, earning her a frown from Openshaw.

He turns to Kylie.

'Can you check on that please?'

'Of course, sir.'

'And while you're at it,' he adds, 'ask the custody sergeant if Will had a mobile phone on him when he was brought in. I want it checked for any online activity, or any calls he might have made while he was on the run.'

Kylie begins to stand.

'Another thing,' Openshaw adds. 'Have Will's back checked and photographed. I want to see exactly which of those seals he carries and, more pertinently, if he's already had it surgically removed.'

TWENTY-EIGHT

William Ballard stands shivering. His reaction isn't to the cold, but to barely concealed shame. He is hemmed in by three burly coppers, and stripped to his waist. He's been told to turn around and stand still while a CSI takes photographs of the scar that rides high on his right scapula. The three cops mutter, calling him a 'Satanist', a 'sicko', and one even suggests he's a 'kiddie-fiddler'. All of the accusations levelled under their breaths are untrue and they make him burn. The crime scene investigator keeps his own opinion secret, but Will can hear his ragged breaths as he angles for a different shot, and can tell he's got an equally low opinion of him. He turns his head, trying to meet the photographer's eye, but can't see him.

'Eyes forward,' barks one of the constables, like he's some sort of drill sergeant.

Will exhales noisily but does as he's told. He resettles his feet, and senses the coppers stirring around him. 'Calm down, lads. I'm just making sure you get my good side.'

'Shut it,' snaps the wannabe drill sergeant, 'or you'll be back in your cell, and we'll be in there with you.'

Will's unafraid of the threat. It's bollocks anyway. Once upon a time, a deserving prisoner could expect a kicking, but that was then and this is the age of CCTV and 'human rights'. These days a copper in a custody suite will barely ruffle your hair for fear of a complaint of assault against them. That isn't to say they won't rough him up if he misbehaves and 'needs' to be carried back to his cell. He has been temporarily moved from his cell to the same room where he was earlier fingerprinted, photo-graphed and DNA swabbed. They are hoping he'll give them an excuse to haul him kicking and screaming back to lock-up, but he won't play their game.

Someone else enters the room. He can see her observing him in his periphery. He turns slightly for a closer look.

It's the woman detective sergeant, the ginger one who hit him with a mouthful of CS earlier. His nostrils still tingle at the memory of the debilitating spray. He doesn't hold it against her. In fact, without her intervention, things might have turned out much worse for him. He'd made a big mistake in picking up that stone, and if he'd actually clobbered the DCI with it, who knows what would've happened when some of the other cops were armed with deadlier weapons. Shot, even wounded, there'd be no possible way of completing his mission.

As the CSI bloke lowers his camera, and begins checking the digital images he's captured on its tiny screen, the detective steps forward, holding her phone, and snaps a photograph of his scar for her personal record.

'I don't want to see that shared on Instagram,' Will says. 'It's been a while since I worked out and I don't want to disappoint my female followers.'

She doesn't reply to his quip. Will rocks his head, easing an imaginary crick in his neck.

'What next?' he asks the 'drill sergeant'. 'I've got a tattoo of Donald Duck on my arse cheek – wanna photo that, too?'

'Put your shirt back on.' It's the detective sergeant who speaks. She isn't interested in listening to his bullshit, probably having heard similar – or worse – from every other arsehole she's locked up before.

One of the constables shoves his wadded shirt into Will's hands. He begins unfurling it. The detective says, 'Give him a little space.'

The CSI steps out of the room, followed by two of the constables. The 'drill sergeant' stays close, menacing Will with a face reminiscent of a closed fist. Will ignores him, while pulling on his shirt. He turns as he does so in order to face the detective. She returns his gaze coolly. Maybe she's too much of a professional to allow her hatred of him to show; instead she seems to study his features, judging if he's capable of the monstrous acts he's suspected of.

He holds up his hands. 'Guilty as charged,' he says. 'That is, of leaving the scene of a traffic accident and resisting arrest. Not whatever other bollocks I'm supposed to have done.'

'Save it for your interview, Will. You'll have plenty of opportunities to admit what you've done then.'

'So let's get it done, I'll admit what I did, and you can charge me and then I can get the fuck out of here.'

He isn't goading her out of badness; he's trying to ascertain what his chances of bail are. He knows why he's been brought to this station, and it isn't simply for failing to stop, or subsequently trying to scrap his way free. Those were just the accusations they used in order to get him here in cuffs. He has done some horrendous stuff, yes, but all that shit about him being a sicko and kiddie-fiddler, he's not having it. Despite being guilty of other violent crimes, he has never touched a child physically or sexually.

He wishes now that he hadn't run and fought; those were the actions of a guilty man. But he had to: it was imperative that the police didn't catch him and search his loft, because the evidence there against him is damning. He had to put a bit of space between him and the cops so he could call for help, and thankfully he'd managed. He hopes his instructions have been carried out to the letter and everything has been moved, and all that remains put to the torch. It's tempting to ask the detective sergeant if there have been any suspicious house fires reported, but that'll only make her home in on his address. Hopefully the two won't be connected, because he had rented his latest pad under one of his aliases.

He has listened keenly since his arrest. As well as the accusations levelled at him by his current jailers, he'd also heard the words 'murderer' and 'serial killer' bandied around. He'd also come to understand that the original chase was only initiated because he was foolishly speeding in a 30 mph zone. If only he'd pulled over, taken his ticket, and the inevitable telling off, he would have been on his way again in no time, able to continue his mission, instead of being stuck here for who-knows-how long. Without any evidence of his other crimes, there's still enough to hold him overnight as a flight risk so he can be put before a magistrate tomorrow. He can forget about being granted bail.

Something else: when the DS spoke to him a moment ago, it was with unexpected familiarity. He'd been booked into custody as William Ballard, but she'd used the shortened form of his name. It reminds him of the shout he'd heard just before he'd been taken down and hustled, eyes streaming and snot flowing, to the police van: '*No, Will, he's trying to save you . . .don't!*'

He'd searched for the source of the voice, but by then the DS had bathed him in incapacitant spray and there was no chance of seeing anything. Bodies jostling him were wavy, indistinct figures, and his senses were so overwhelmed that even his hearing was muffled. But had he heard those following words? '*Will . . . Nate! You . . . stop struggling or . . .*' He was unsure at the time if he'd heard correctly, or if his brain had merely formed recognizable sounds out of the jumbled cacophony going on around him. Searching through tears for the source of the voice had been unhelpful. He's more certain now that he'd heard his name shouted correctly – considering the DS has also used his shortened nickname – but what of that of his brother? Had Nate been there? His brother? The very person he's been hunting with absolutely no luck, despite the overt attempts at drawing him out. The voice hadn't struck a chord with him. How could it? The last he'd spoken to Nate was when they were boys, and more than two decades have passed since. They've probably grown up in totally different corners of the country, had unique influences on their dialects and accents since then, but still . . . there was something familiar in that voice.

The temptation to have the DS clarify things is strong, but he doesn't ask. He has his shirt buttoned up, but takes his time rolling up the sleeves. His outer clothing has been seized for evidence, along with his shoes and belt. He's surprised that he's been left with the jeans, socks and shirt he stands up in, because if there was the least inkling he was a murderer, they'd have taken the lot and given him a paper suit to wear. The thought gives him hope that there's a way out of here yet. He says, 'Come on, detective, what's keeping you? I don't want a brief, I just want to admit my crimes and get this over with.'

'What's the rush?' she responds. 'Aren't you enjoying our hospitality? Shame, because you'd better get used to it.'

'So I crashed my van and did a bunk,' he says, 'what's the big deal? It's my van and I didn't damage anything else. It's not as if I was pissed up or something.'

She stares at him.

He stares back, but without animosity.

She lowers her brows and says, 'You've a long way to go to prove you're not a monster.'

Will shakes his head. 'The onus isn't on me. You're the ones who must prove I am. Good luck with that, Miss Marple.'

She sniffs at his remark, and says to the 'drill sergeant', 'Put him back in his cell.'

The constable grabs Will's elbow. 'C'mon, you,' he growls.

'I can bloody well walk.'

The copper's grip tightens, and his uniformed pals loom in the doorway. They're itching to pounce. Will smiles genially and says, 'Then again, these socks are a bit slippy on this concrete, so thanks for the support, boss.'

The constable guides him through the open door, and the others form a wedge as he's led down the corridor to the cells. The DS observes him until he's back at the cell and he's shoved inside. He spins abruptly, and the three uniformed coppers brace to halt him. He slams his palms on the doorframe, and can't see her, but he knows the DS is still in hearing range. 'I'll do you a deal, detective. Let me see my brother Nate, and I'll tell you everything I've been up to.'

'Don't hold your breath for any deal,' she replies.

'But that was Nathanial Walker I heard?' he pushes.

'Can't say I know who that is,' she says, but she's lying, and she knows he knows it. She hurries away before she can be pressed for more.

Will backs from the door, holding his hands up, surrendering to the constables who are preparing to rush him further inside. He sits on the blue plastic-covered mattress on its solid concrete base. He smiles, and the cops fume, but he's now under the watchful gaze of the custody sergeant's cameras. The door is slammed resolutely. His smile doesn't slip, it grows wider. Nate was at the scene of his arrest. It's obvious that Nate is working with the police, which means the efforts to draw him out have been successful after all. Having raised his head above the parapet, it means that Nate can be got at, and Will's mission is still in line for success. He just needs to get out of here. He knows the hopes for success are on a clock, counting down. He finds it unbearable to be sitting here locked up while precious seconds are ticking away.

He expands his thoughts beyond the steel door, along the corridor past the custody sergeant's desk, to the next airlock-style doors that separate the rest of the station from the cellblock. He imagines he can sense his older brother out there, separated from him by less than fifty metres. It's the closest they've been since the day they were parted by a court ruling, and taken in secret to different foster homes. Soon, he thinks, they will be much closer. He lies back and settles into the mattress, his smile flickering, before it dissolves entirely. Any notion of a fond family reunion is buried beneath what must then happen, and the images he conjures are horrific.

TWENTY-NINE

'It's the seal of Samyaza,' Nate confirms with barely a glance at Kylie's phone screen. He obviously recalls the seal their father branded on his brother's back. 'He's sometimes referred to as Azza or Ouza, if you want a name that's a bit easier to remember.'

Nate halts in thought. He turns to Emily for confirmation, to ensure she still feels included. 'Samyaza was purportedly the leader of the band of fallen angels known as the Grigori, or Watchers. You know their story, right?'

'Yeah,' Emily says. 'I certainly do. But you go ahead and explain for the others' sake.'

Nate ponders how much he should admit to the detectives, and can't see how he can clam up without it growing apparent he's hiding something important. Before he can come to a conclusion, Emily steps in and takes the reins. 'It's said that the Grigori became consumed with lust for mortal women, and they rebelled against heaven in order to have sex. It was through this consummation of their sinful desires that half-breed children were born, giants called the Nephilim.'

'Aah, the codename used by one of the suspects we're monitoring on the dark web,' Grant clarifies.

'I'm glad you're able to keep up,' says Nate.

'I must admit, with all these outlandish names, it can get a bit confusing: why didn't those angels take simpler names like Bill or Ben?' Grant's double meaning isn't lost on any of the others. Nate shakes his head: DCI Openshaw obviously meant *Will* or Ben?

'It doesn't mean that my brother and Nephilim on the web are the same person.'

Grant doesn't reply; he has made his point already.

'Let's wait and see what your Cyber Crime Unit finds out before making further judgement, eh?' suggests Emily.

Nate glances at her, surprised by her directness. It shouldn't surprise him, really; she is a civilian and not under similar constraints as Nate. He too is a civilian these days, but Grant Openshaw was once his boss and the dynamic between them is proving difficult to shake. In some respects, the institutionalizing he'd undergone in the police force wasn't far removed from when he was a member of the Berith cult: he could argue that mainly it was a difference in terminology, but the hierarchy was pretty much the same, and you didn't argue with your superiors.

Kylie produces a second mobile phone.

'That's Will's?' Grant asks.

Kylie nods. 'I loaned it from the custody sergeant.'

This is not proper procedure, and they all know it. Any property seized from a detainee brought into a police station must be recorded, bagged and tagged, and any movement of the property logged and signed for. The phone isn't in an evidence bag, so in effect they could be accused of breaking the chain of evidence; sure as hell, if there is anything pertinent to their case in the phone's memory, Kylie and Grant will ensure that the paper trail reflects that everything had been above-board while handling it.

'I haven't gone through it yet, but I don't think we'll find anything obvious in the camera roll,' Kylie says, 'though, this killer wouldn't be the first to record his handiwork for posterity.'

'Will isn't your killer,' Nate says.

'Just saying,' Kylie replies as she sifts through very few photographs: there's nothing obvious in them that pertains to their case. She switches apps. 'I'm more interested in the recent calls.'

'It's only a bunch of random telephone numbers. They tell us nothing,' Nate says, but knows fine well that there's more to the list than he makes out. For starters, the timings of the calls can corroborate either Will's innocence, or his guilt. From what he can see on the screen, Will made several calls to different numbers while on the run and trying to evade the police earlier. He could have simply been reaching out for help from friends, or there was something more sinister behind his calls.

Kylie uses her own phone to take a snapshot of the recent calls displayed on Will's screen. Some detective will be tasked with looking more deeply into Will's phone, if or when he is charged, but for now, his most recent calls are enough to get started with.

'Get that list to Jeff Brady and have him identify the owners of those phone numbers,' Grant suggests, though it's apparent Kylie is already on it by the way she has switched to composing a message. Her fingers and thumbs move too fast for Nate to follow.

'Is that even legal?' asks Emily in a hushed voice meant only for Nate's ears.

'Sometimes needs must,' Grant replies for him, and he sends Kylie away, to return the phone to the custody sergeant. 'Right now,' he says to Emily, 'we haven't time for serving IPA notices, we can dot the i's and cross the t's later if need be.'

The Investigatory Powers Act (IPA) 2016 relates to the acquisition of communications data, but whether or not she's aware of that, Emily doesn't let on. In an ideal world, cops must cover all aspects of legislation, ticking all the relevant boxes as they conduct an investigation, but it is apparent to most – Emily included – that the world is far from ideal. She aims a shrug at the chief inspector.

'Do you get to interview him?' Nate wonders.

'No, his interview will be conducted by local CID,' Grant

replies. He's not happy at the idea, but they mustn't forget that DCI Openshaw's presence here is only a matter of courtesy, that his role is to advise and coordinate, not stick his nose in where it isn't wanted.

'How are they playing this, Grant? Are they treating him as a murder suspect or—'

'For now all they have him on is a charge of dangerous driving, and leaving the scene of an accident, and they'll be hard put to make the latter stick – he didn't cause damage to any other vehicle or property, and no person was harmed, so . . .'

'They aren't going with charges of resisting arrest or police assault then?' Nate says, and sneers, because they know that few courts will countenance any such charge. 'The way things are looking, they'll have nothing to stick on him and will have to let him go.'

'I've already requested that he isn't bailed, on the strength that he's a flight risk. His actions earlier kind of prove my point. He'll be held here over the rest of the weekend and put in front of a magistrate on Monday, plenty of time for us to come up with proof of his involvement—'

'Or of his innocence,' Nate stipulates.

'Yes, or his innocence in regard to these murders.'

'What about CID up the road in Newcastle?' asks Emily. 'Haven't they got a stake in this? Won't they want Will interviewed about the Darren Sykes murder?'

'Why should they?' asks Nate. 'There's absolutely no reason to tie Will to the murder of Sykes.'

'Not that they know of yet,' she agrees. 'But what if there's anything in what we found on the dark web, and he is Nephilim or Baphomet? Shouldn't they be made aware that it's an avenue we're investigating?'

'Not if I can help it,' says Nate under his breath.

'I'll coordinate with Newcastle CID,' Grant promises then, as a concession to Nate, adds, 'but only once we know we've something solid to give them. I won't get to interview Will here, but that isn't to say that I won't if he's asked about Sykes's murder.'

'Would it not serve you to name him as a suspect?' Emily prompts. 'I mean, he is, right? Why not use that to your advantage and it will allow you to speak directly with him.'

The colour drains from Nate's face at Emily's sudden turna-round. He thought she was his ally not . . . no, she's correct. Naming Will as a suspect will put him directly under the juris-diction of the taskforce, and DCI Grant Openshaw. The sooner that Grant can clear Will of any wrongdoing, the better.

'I don't need to,' Grant says, 'seeing as I've already asked that he's treated as a potential victim. Refusing his bail is all part of the process of squirrelling him out of harm's way.'

No sooner are the words out of his mouth than Kylie returns. Her face is florid, and it has little to do with her usual complexion. She has jogged back from the custody suite. She pants, 'Boss. They're moving him out.'

'What? Who's moving him?' demands Grant, and lunges for the door as if with the intention of cutting off the guilty party.

'They're taking him to a more secure facility than this one,' says Kylie, following Grant out of the door. 'Apparently the order came down the chain from the chief super . . .' Their voices fade as the door closes behind them.

Nate and Emily exchange glances.

'What's that all about?' Emily wonders.

'I don't know, but I don't like the sound of things. Maybe we should—'

'No, we have to stay put, Nate. If we go wandering around the station, we could get in trouble.'

'Not if we stick close to Grant's heels. Come on.'

Emily dithers a few seconds longer, until Nate stretches out his hand. She looks at it a second longer, then accepts it, and allows herself to be hauled out of the room by him. Her palm is soft and warm, and he can feel her racing heart as a soft buzzing through his skin – or perhaps it's psychosomatic. Maybe she took his hand so she has a good excuse to explain why she is being dragged through the nick if challenged.

At the end of the corridor, a door is sucking shut, pulled to by the passage of Grant and Kylie through the airlock-type set-up designed to foil any escape attempt from the custody suite. They'll need either an electronic key fob, or the code on the lock to admit them further. 'Hurry,' says Nate, almost tugging her arm out of its socket in his urgency.

He snatches for the handle of the outer of two steel doors, but it's too late. It has already closed tight and the magnetic lock engaged. A small, almost impregnable window allows a view inside the airlock. Already his old boss has gone through it, and Kylie is about to. Nate bangs his fist on the door. She turns at the sound, flashing him a warning look to go back to the meeting room, and allows the door to close behind her.

He slaps the door in annoyance.

Being kept out of the loop is akin to being refused admission to his personal party. He turns to Emily, about to apologize for the curses that must've slipped from him a moment ago. She says, 'Shit, shite and sugar,' and it raises a chuckle from him. He again checks through the window, but Kylie hasn't had second thoughts and returned to let them inside.

'What now?' Emily prompts.

'We could wait here until somebody comes and try slipping inside with them, but the chances of that happening without us being slung out are close to zero. Let's just go back where we were and hope that Grant doesn't forget about us before he buggers off with the others.'

'Maybe you should have a little more faith in him.'

'I'm under no illusion, Emily. Grant's using me to get what he wants, end of story. As soon as he has something definitive to pin on my brother, he'll drop me and leave me sitting twiddling my thumbs.'

'I don't believe that, Nate. Bringing us along, including us as much as he has, he has actually stuck out his neck for us. If he was going to drop you, why bring you here when he could have had you chased off after Will was arrested?'

'I don't know. Maybe you're right, but—'

'You don't trust your superiors any more. I get it. It's unsurprising that you'd have issues after the way you were treated following the death of Jenny Onatade. Back then Grant was your immediate line manager, right? Did he fail to support you then?'

'I don't recall having much face-to-face time with him after the shooting.'

'Was that his doing or yours?'

Nate grunts in concession. They've reached the meeting room as they've walked. They don't enter. When Will is moved it won't be via this corridor, but Nate knows that the thoroughfare will grow busy with coppers involved in his case as they abandon the custody area in search of their vehicles back to their respective stations. Nate doesn't want to miss when it happens by being shut inside the room. He sets his back to the door, stalling Emily from entering. 'OK,' he says, 'let's wait here a minute and give Grant the benefit of the doubt.'

'Yes, let's.' She aims a smile at him then a playful punch to his gut. Yes, it tells him, she can see right through his ploy. He smiles too, and it's with that stupid smile he'd worn when told he'd be working with Emily again after thinking he'd blown his chance at Haydon Bridge.

Behind them the airlock sucks open.

Grant marches towards them, his coat flaring, his eyebrows beetling. Two steps behind, Kylie hurries to keep up.

Nate opens his mouth to speak, but Grant practically brushes past.

Kylie, her face flushed so that the freckles on her nose appear three-dimensional, jabs a thumb at her boss, and says, 'If you're coming with us you'd best get to your vehicle now. He isn't going to hang around.'

Nate looks at Emily. He's unsure if he was right about Grant dropping him now that he's no longer useful, or if his old pal has prompted Kylie to galvanize them. It doesn't really matter; if it's the former, at least Kylie still believes he has some worth and they'll be kept in the loop.

'This way,' says Emily, and Nate follows, hauled along the corridor similarly to how he'd led her only minutes ago.

THIRTY

The cops are obviously intent on getting a charge with more weight than dangerous driving imposed on him. After thinking he was possibly on the cusp of being released on bail, or at worst held over the remainder of the weekend until the magistrate's court opened on Monday morning, it appeared that the coppers had other ideas. This was not the doing of the tall, silver-haired detective whom he'd almost crowned with the kerbstone, but by the newer arrivals who'd turned up at the nick in the past half-hour. From what he'd

gathered from the conversation drifting from the custody desk
to his cell, these detectives were investigating Darren Sykes's
murder, and wanted to interview him back on their home turf.
It made sense to them to transport him to Newcastle, rather than
have everyone involved running back and forward along the A1.
Whoever was in charge of this remote station seemed happy to
hand over his prisoner to his big city neighbours. Several times
the hatch had been lowered on his cell door and accusatory faces
had peered in at him: an orange-haired copper had eyed him for
several long seconds, chewing on his tongue, his eyes like slits
of ice. Going by the manner in which the detective had viewed
him, he'd already been judged and found guilty of Sykes's
murder, and that guy would do anything to prove it.

He had considered calling out and demanding to speak with
the other red-head, the woman who'd taken a great interest in
the seal burnt into his shoulder, or, better still, with her boss, and
confess his crimes to them instead. After confessing he could
say goodbye to ever finishing his mission, but at least he felt that
they might understand his motives, seeing as they were consulting
with his brother. Nobody had confirmed that Nate was involved,
but Will was confident that it had been Nate who'd yelled out
to him during his arrest, and who was now feeding information
concerning the covenant seared into their hides to the cops.
Learning that Nate had taken the side of the cops over his blood
family had come as no surprise: back on Ohop Island, he'd helped
the big Fed lead the Children of Hamor to freedom through the
blazing compound, and had been more upset afterwards about
Milo Turrell's murder at their mother's hand than by their mom's
subsequent slaying. A streak of morality ran through Nate as
wide as the immoral one that compelled Will to deem anyone in
authority as the enemy: perhaps the indoctrination they'd been
subject to by their parents had impacted on Will more than it
had on Nate, purely down to Nate being older and therefore less
malleable in the face of their preaching.

He hadn't shouted. He'd remained silent, listening, trying to
overhear the plans made for him. The carrot-haired detective had
returned, and this time squinted at him through the open-door
hatch. 'You sure you don't want a brief?' the detective had asked.

Earlier, Will had turned down legal representation. That was
when he'd still hoped to convince his interviewers that he was

no more dangerous than somebody prone to panic and flee when they saw a blue light. Since learning that he was definitely under suspicion for Darren Sykes's killing, things had changed. 'Yeah, mate; I've changed my mind. I'd like representation – the duty solicitor will do.'

'We'll have a brief waiting for when we get back to Newcastle.'

'What do you mean? Why am I being moved to Newcastle?'

'You know why.' The detective lowered his voice to a whisper, ensuring it wouldn't be picked up by the CCTV system. 'Some off-the-record advice for you. Don't give us any shit on the way there and you'll maybe arrive in one piece.'

Before Will could reply to the threat, the detective slammed the hatch.

Will had lain back on the blue vinyl mattress. His hands were folded at his midriff.

He'd lain this way for several minutes. Now he hears the shuffle of feet outside his door. Slowly he rises up, and stands with his hands out at his sides, presenting no form of threat. It makes no difference. The cops charge inside his cell, treating him exactly as if he is a killer prone to savaging his victims, and peeling their hide from their living bodies. They make a wedge, two burly cops at the front hefting Plexiglass shields. They ram into Will, forcing him backwards so that he is crushed against the cell wall, barely able to breathe, let alone fight back. As they hold him in place, other cops take control of his arms. Rigid cuffs secure his hands to the rear, and he is practically picked up and carried from the cell. He is rushed down the corridor, and he notes how little notice the custody sergeant takes of his maltreatment. He recalls being bundled through a heavy door into a waiting room before being processed and placed in a cell. This time there is no waiting. The back door is thrown open and he's forced outside, and already a prisoner transport van has been backed up to within a metre of the door. The van doors stand open, and hands reach down to take control of him. He's bum-rushed and forced into some kind of narrow cubicle. He is over-whelmed for the few seconds it takes for his new captors to push his feet inside the small cubicle and force the door shut. He lifts his head, blinking in dismay, but already his guards have backed off, and he can't see them clearly through the semi-opaque plastic door. He sucks in a breath. Exhales it raggedly. He feels sore, but can't tell if it's from his most recent manhandling or from crashing his van and scuffling with the police earlier. He wants to spit out phlegm, but it'd mean doing it on his own thighs or on the door that's only bare inches from his nose: he has no intention of watching the glacial flow of saliva dripping to the floor during the journey north.

Don't give us any shit on the way there and you'll maybe arrive in one piece. It seems as if the ginger cop's advice might well be worth heeding. He can guess how he'd have been treated if he'd resisted, and it doesn't give him a warm fuzzy sensation.

He has no option but to sit. The cubicle confines him; the manner in which the cuffs have been fitted means he must bend forward at the waist to relieve the gnawing ache in his shoulders. His head feels heavier than one of those old-time leather medicine balls. Heavier still feels his heart.

His mission has ended. There is no possible way of completing it, not now that he is banged up, and is certain to stay that way for the foreseeable future. His mission has a tight deadline and the winter solstice is looming. He has helpers, assistants loyal to the cause, loyal to him, but without him they are directionless, unable to complete what must be done in time. Sickened at the realization, he allows the saliva to dribble out between his lips, aiming so that it drips between his knees and on to the floor of the van.

Doors slam, and the engine starts. Words are muffled. The automatic gate whirs open. Then the van is moving. His left side squeezes against the cubicle wall as the van ascends the slight ramp to ground level. Then the van straightens out and he tilts marginally the opposite way. The door's only semi-opaque. It allows light and shadow to be seen, but that's all. A solid door, offering no view at all, would probably set off claustrophobic attacks in detainees, making them more unmanageable. *Be thankful for small mercies*, he tells himself, knowing full well that if he had been fully enclosed by steel, he would probably lose it.

The van stops and starts at road ends and crossings. When it is moving, it's at a steady clip, but not excessively fast. It tells him that it is – for the time being, at least – sticking to town and minor roads, rather than joining the motorway north. His local knowledge is good enough to suspect that they are heading for the Tyne tunnel, so probably aiming for one of the city centre police stations rather than another outpost like at Southwick. There's a spell where the van rolls unimpeded for several minutes, as if they are travelling along a dual carriageway, and he tries orienting his location but is unsuccessful. He has no idea if the van is alone or travelling in convoy. He can't hear the driver or his pal talking, but occasionally the volume on the transport van's radio is high enough to hear it, though usually it's a babble unrelated to his situation.

Without warning his right shoulder is thrown against the cubicle wall. The van brakes so hard that he feels the chassis of the vehicle torque beneath him, or it's him twisting in his seat, he can't be sure. He is expelled from the wall to thump heavily against the opposite one and then he tips forward and his face contacts the door. His cheek sticks to the tacky plastic, and it feels as if he leaves behind a layer of skin when the van's movement abruptly throws his weight backwards and his skull cracks off the wall behind him. His cuffed wrists are abraded.

The van has come to a sharp halt. It feels as if the world is tilted to the left, but Will understands it's because the van has been forced into a dip at the side of the road. There's shouting from without, and more noise; somebody repeatedly slams something heavy against the van.

His guards – not coppers, but security guards – are stunned into silence. The banging continues, growing louder, and then there's a sharper crack. It sounds like somebody has taken a baseball bat to the windscreen. Will straightens, his pulse quickening. His breath catches in his chest.

There's the sound of an engine, but it isn't from a car or other vehicle, more like . . . what, a generator? Something else kicks to life, shrieking mechanically.

The body of the large transporter van shudders. He can feel it through the soles of his feet and his backside. His teeth chatter in time with the rattle. He straightens, tensing his shoulders. There's no play in his cuffs whatsoever. He relaxes again, as best he can, while the shudder grows harder, and louder. The back door falls off, its hinges shorn by whatever mechanical saw was used. Voices urge each other into action. He feels the van rock as somebody clambers inside. Another person joins the first, and they rush along the narrow confines of the van, and through the Plexiglass he watches their dim shapes as they first test the locks, and then use a hammer to smash open a lock.

Will rears backwards as the door is tugged open. He looks up at the figures looming over him, but they wear hoodies and scarves around their faces and they also sport goggles. Nothing about their body shapes help identify them to him.

Are they friends or foes?

He doesn't know.

They grab him, and yank him out of the cubicle.

He is again bum-rushed, and this time is passed down into the waiting hands of others. He can smell over-heated metal, and also body odour: one of his saviours stinks – or maybe this is simply a transfer from one form of captivity to a second – and Will assumes it's probably the first time this man has been involved in breaking out a prisoner. It's probably a first for the others, too, but they are cooler under pressure than their sweaty pal is. Admittedly, this is a first for him as well, and his nerves are buzzing. He wonders if he is stinking as badly as the sweating man; he never had the opportunity of showering after being on the run earlier.

He is shoved inside another van. This one isn't equipped to carry prisoners, it isn't even equipped to carry passengers, and he is pushed into a corner, up against a wooden partition separating the cab from the storage space in the back. When he was processed at Southwick Police Station, his trainers were taken from him, as was his belt and several other small items with which he could either harm himself or others, or use in an escape attempt. His bare feet absorb the cold stickiness of the van floor, the sensation riding up through him in a tremor that reaches his shoulders. He shivers, moans, and is immediately warned to stay silent. Some of the masked figures climb in the back with him. One of them holds a sawn-off shotgun, another a baseball bat. One of them has already thrown the grinder used to cut off the transporter van doors back into the van. It lies a few feet from Will, hot and smelly. The rest of the break-out party get in the cab and, even as the passenger door is closing, the van takes off, the tyres spinning on tarmac in the driver's haste to leave.

Will briefly wonders if the security guards survived the assault on their van unharmed. He didn't hear the shotgun, but there'd been plenty of bangs and clatters that could've been them being beaten with the baseball bat. He doesn't really care about their fates, only that their treatment might give a clue as to what is next for him. Are these people, he thinks again, friends or foes?

THIRTY-ONE

A184, Wearside

Nate had forgotten how cold the evenings had become, but it was December after all. He stands outside Emily's car, arms folded tightly across his chest, trembling because of the plummeting temperature. His breath steams with every exhalation. Emily has exited her car as well, but stands with one hand on the steering wheel, as if the car has a mind of its own and will take off if not kept hold of.

They've been forced to halt several hundred metres back from where the transport van was forced off the road into the shallow drainage ditch alongside a dual carriageway. Between their car and the van there are several marked police cars, also the unmarked vehicles that Grant and Kylie, and the Newcastle CID teams were travelling in. There are more police vehicles arriving by the minute, with several behind Emily's, penning them in. Nate has to avert his gaze, sometimes even squeeze tight his eyelids, because the disturbing strobing effect of blue lights is enough to set off some kind of neurological fit.

Uniformed officers swarm around the van. Some are inside securing any evidence that might come to light. One constable has been given the onerous duty of protecting the door that has been cut off at its hinges and now lies at the side of the carriageway.

Nate shivers harder.

This time it isn't from the cold, but from a wave of adrenalin washing through his body.

He has mixed feelings about Will's escape. He'd feel more at ease if it's confirmed that this was a jailbreak and not abduction: not that he hopes his brother is the killer, but the latter, if he's innocent, will definitely end with Will's slaughter. From what he has gleaned already from the cops, they fully believe it's the former, and also that the killer's helpers had acted to spring their soon-to-be-reborn god from jail. Admittedly, the way in which the operation was put together, and launched at the most opportune moment, made it clear that the people responsible were organized, daring and no slouches. The same must be said for the helpers assisting the killer in his hunt and taking of the Children of Hamor.

A repeated tap on the roof of the car draws Nate's attention.

Emily is deep in thought, unaware she's tapping out the rhythm.

Another police car comes to a stop a few metres behind them and the uniformed officers decamp. They rush past without a word, summoned no doubt to perform a task as boring as guarding an inanimate door. Their arrival disrupts Emily's thought train. She stops tapping, looks over at Nate.

'I think I saw the ones responsible for this,' she announces.

'How could you have?' Nate corrects himself. 'When?'

'Earlier,' she replies, 'when I was scouting a parking place. Remember I told you about some ruffians in a van taking my spot?'

He does. She'd mentioned that she got bad vibes from them so hadn't challenged them over the space. At the time he'd barely given her announcement any consideration: he had been too busy playing the white knight and chasing off the youth who'd ogled her.

'How'd they know where he'd been taken?' Nate wonders aloud.

'We found him by following all the police activity. I'm betting he called them when he was on the run, and they did the exact same thing and were following when he was taken to Southwick. While we were inside, they must've planned busting him out.'

'What were the chances they'd have the equipment and manpower . . .'

'There was nothing stopping them calling in others with the right tools.'

Again, he has to accept that Emily is probably right.

She'd make a good detective, he thinks. *Personally, I'm not proving my own detective skills.*

To be fair on himself, he hadn't been thinking about who, what or when, his thoughts had been more about how his little brother was deep in the shit now, whether or not he proved to be the killer. He doesn't want to believe that Will is responsible for the awful murders, but his jailbreak only helps convince most of the others around them of his guilt, and maybe it's time he accepts the obvious too.

'Can you describe the van, or those inside?'

'Yeah,' she says, 'I can describe both. Because of the way they acted, they've kind of stuck in my memory.'

'Then we should let Grant know.'

It's not the first time that the mention of the DCI's name appears to summon him. They see him striding towards his car, his unbuttoned coat flaring open and displaying his shirt and tie despite the iciness; behind him, barely a step out of sync, Kylie follows. She has a mobile phone plastered to her ear.

Emily waves to attract their attention, but it appears that the detectives are too preoccupied to notice. Grant piles into the driving seat and the engine barks to life before Kylie can even get in the Audi. Emily shouts, waving again, and Kylie glances at her, but without responding: the red-headed detective pulls open the front passenger door and slides in alongside her boss. Emily, who has yet to relinquish a hold on the steering wheel, uses the heel of her hand to depress the horn. It sounds like a strangled goose to Nate. But the sound is obtrusive enough to turn a few heads in their direction. Nate signals a uniformed cop: this man will have no idea who Nate is, but he starts towards him nonetheless.

'Can I help you, sir?' asks the cop, formally.

'I urgently need to speak with one of the investigating officers,' Nate says, 'Preferably DCI Openshaw, the one driving that Audi.' He points directly at Grant's car. 'We have information about who attacked the transport van and broke Ballard out.'

'Pardon? Can I ask who you are, sir, it's just . . . uh, are you job?'

'Kind of,' says Nate. 'I'm retired police, but currently working as a consultant with the NCA taskforce.'

The constable eyes him a moment, chewing his bottom lip. Probably he's deciphering the acronym, probably he's unaware that the National Crime Agency is involved. They haven't time for him to mull things over.

Nate snaps, 'We need to speak to DCI Openshaw before he leaves the scene.'

The constable holds up a finger. 'Wait one,' he instructs, and strides towards the Audi. Before he reaches it, Grant hits the throttle. The car is in reverse gear, so powers backwards through a gap between parked vehicles: the uniformed cop is forced to dance aside to avoid being run over. He doesn't get an opportunity to pass on Nate's words to the DCI but that's OK. Grant brings the Audi to a stop alongside Emily. Nate swerves around her car to join her.

'The people that did this—'

Before Emily can expound, Grant cuts in. 'I haven't time for hanging around, the van used in the breakout has been found less than a mile away. It's on fire.'

Skin crawls at the nape of Nate's neck. 'With Will and the others inside?'

'No,' says Grant 'as far as can be seen, the van's been abandoned and torched.'

His skin still crawls, but Nate also feels a sense of mild relief: his brother is still alive. For the time being, at least.

About two hundred metres behind them there's a junction. Grant's car is in the wrong carriageway, but all the traffic has come to a halt, and there's a clear path along the hard shoulder: apparently he intends reversing back along it to take a shortcut to wherever the getaway van has been found. 'There's nothing more you can do for now. Why not go on back to Emily's place and I'll be in touch.'

He makes it sound like a suggestion, but Nate understands it's an instruction.

'We can follow you,' he says.

'You don't have the same dispensation to break the rules as us,' says Grant, and with that he powers off, using his mirrors to guide him. The shoulder isn't as wide as on a motorway, but he has no problem negotiating a path back to the slip road.

'Well that's that then,' Emily sighs, exasperated. 'I guess our usefulness has ended for now.'

'Remember back at the nick how I said we'd be dropped at the first opportunity?'

'Yeah, well, you can boast how you told me so, if you wish, but it won't change things.' Her lip twitches: Nate's unsure if she's pulling his leg again.

'Grant's gone to where the van's been set alight. I don't know what he intends to find there – it's not as if Will or his buddies will be standing around the fire toasting marshmallows.'

'Maybe there are witnesses and they saw whichever replacement vehicle they switched to.'

'Yeah, it's unlikely they took off on foot.' Having a standby vehicle to switch to proves they're organized and they didn't just blag their way through the jailbreak before. Nate exhales at the thought, his breath forming a steaming shroud. 'We can speculate that Will called in backup from some pals, but it's looking more as if they aren't just a couple of random guys, but people he's been working with.'

'You're talking about a team of experienced criminals, like the killer is suspected of working with. Yeah, Nate, it's looking more and more likely that you're right.'

He exhales again.

Emily takes a seat in her car.

Nate waits another few seconds, staring again at the transport van, but it tells him nothing new. He waves over the uniformed constable he'd pressed to help them before. He speaks briefly with him then takes his seat. Emily understands what he was up to without explanation, following the cop's instruction to pull out and follow him past the crime scene. He guides them through the cluster of vehicles, and once beyond the scene he steps aside and gestures to leave. The carriageway ahead is empty of traffic, allowing them a free run until the next junction. Overhead signs indicate they are on the A184, one of the major roads that will take them into Newcastle not via the tunnel but over the world-famous Tyne Bridge. Once over the river they'll be within spitting distance of Emily's apartment.

'Maybe you should drop me at a hotel,' Nate suggests.

Eyes firmly on the road, she shakes her head. 'Grant said he'll be in touch with us at my place.'

'It could be hours till he's done, d'you really want me making the place untidy all that time?'

'I'm not worried about taking you home now that it's night-time. I think you've proven you're not someone to take advantage of a single girl and ravish me in my own home. I think I'm safe enough . . . right?'

'Uh, well, I, uh . . .' Nate feels heat rising from the back of his neck.

Emily glances over, and he catches a twinkle of humour in her eye. She's taking delight in his discomfort.

'I have an inkling that however I answer it could be the *wrong* answer,' he says, and smiles at the grin that breaks out on her face.

'You needn't worry, Nate, you're safe too. I'm not going to throw myself at you either.'

'That's a shame,' he says, only partly joking.

'There's no time for fooling about, Romeo. We've still got work to do. I'd like to see what Baphomet and Nephilim have been up to.'

THIRTY-TWO

DCI Grant Openshaw curses under his breath and shakes his head at the blazing van. It sits at the dead end of a cul-de-sac in an industrial estate, surrounded by buildings that have seen little industry in the past decade or more. This late in the evening the estate is deserted, apart from rats, pigeons and the occasional down-and-out. It is probably equally deserted through the day. There's nothing he can learn from the burning wreck for now, and all he's doing is wincing from the painful heat, and breathing noxious smoke. Kylie McMahon has more sense, and has chosen to stand clear of the fire while she exchanges calls with DI Jeff Brady. Grant walks towards her, smelling the acrid smoke wafting off his coat, and deciding the stink is prob-ably clinging to his hair too. It has been a long day; he could do with a shower and shave, and something to eat, but he has a more urgent need for a stiff drink to assuage both his thirst and his disappointment.

He had William Ballard in a jail cell, and if it had been his decision alone, Ballard would still be in the same cell. Things had been taken out of his hands though – his role was as an advisor, and his advice had been duly noted, and then promptly ignored. Now his prime suspect was in the wind, and Grant expected that his could be one of the heads to roll because of the mess up. None of them could have foreseen the ambush of the transport vehicle, but why the hell hadn't Will's escort comprised more than a couple of minimum-wage security guards? At the very least, a police escort should've been arranged prior to the van leaving Southwick Police Station. Grant had assumed that Newcastle CID would've ensured their prisoner was thoroughly guarded before allowing the transporter to leave the station, but apparently that had not been the case.

One of the first rules of detective work is to assume nothing.

You know better than to assume, you deserve your frigging head to roll, Grant admonishes himself.

Kylie has ended her call by the time he reaches her. She greets him with her lips pressed tightly together. She's as disappointed as he is, but for other reasons.

Grant doesn't waste time relaying the obvious. Will has been spirited away, there are no eyewitnesses, and it will take time for CCTV or other evidence to be gathered and scrutinized that might identify the second getaway vehicle. Patrols are circling the vicinity, and setting up roadblocks, but Grant suspects that Will is already well beyond the cordon. The police helicopter that had been used in the earlier chase has been drafted in to make a wider search, but with no description to go on, the crew have no idea who they are searching for; they'll be more useful only if and when a getaway vehicle is identified. This isn't Grant's crime scene. The locals will have to handle it, and he'll trust them to conduct door-to-door enquiries, and to collect all the available street, closed-circuit TV and dash cameras in the area and plot the comings and goings of the gang. Any ID is probably hours at least in the making.

'Let's get out of here, Sergeant,' he suggests, using Kylie's rank for the first time in hours.

She nods, but says nothing.

They get in Grant's Audi.

'I take it Jeff has nothing new for us?' he asks.

'Nothing immediately useful, but you'll want to hear it all the same, boss.'

He drives, seeking the nearest route across the Tyne.

'First off, he's been back in touch with the FBI, who have named Will Ballard as a person of interest in their investigation. They've confirmed that – according to flight records – he visited the States and left to return to England shortly after the final murder. They've concluded that Will is his father's son, so to speak, and that the apple hasn't fallen far from the tree. The biological father, Carl Walker, was one of the sect leaders, and it isn't much of a stretch to believe that Will, being young and impressionable at the time, embraced the insanity of his teachings and has been planning this murder spree for years. If Nate's right, and the killer is harvesting those covenant symbols from his victims, with the intention of making a copy of their grimoire, then it's probably Will Ballard who's behind it. They say that the recent death of Weyland Berith probably kick-started Will on this murderous path, now that their god-angel-thingee will be seeking a new avatar on earth.' She shrugs an apology at how wild it all sounds, but the speculation from the FBI isn't anything new to Grant, not after hearing the similar theory from Nate earlier. The only difference really is in their prime suspects; Nate is praying that Will isn't the killer, but Grant knows that even his old friend isn't convinced of his innocence.

Grant takes a turn on to a feeder road, taking them back to the A184 but beyond where the transport van was attacked.

Kylie isn't finished briefing him. Apparently DI Brady had more to say on the subject of their fugitive. 'Fire crews were called to a house fire very close to where police first gave chase to William Ballard earlier. The fire was concentrated in a converted loft, deliberately started to burn evidence and tools pertaining to the murders we are investigating. A quick check of the electoral roll confirms that the house was rented under one of the previous pseudonyms used by our William. He was a busy lad while on the run: not only did he ring his pals to alert them to his possible capture, he must've also asked them to go and destroy the proof of his crimes. The arsonist didn't do the best of jobs, though, and the fire was extinguished before it got a real hold.'

'Do we have the address?'

'Yeah, I asked DI Brady to text it to me.'

'Stick it in the satnav, will you? I want to see what has survived the flames.'

He drives in silence, mulling things over, while Kylie too catches some time to calm her brain. She settles in the passenger seat, eyes closed, mouth in a deep pout. He darts an appreciative glance at her profile more than once, but concentrates on the directions he's given. The recorded voice emanating from the satnav is robotic, a facsimile of a posh female, and pronounces street names totally unlike a local would. Nonetheless, she doesn't steer him wrong, and within twenty minutes, Grant guides his Audi along a narrow street with blocks of terraced houses on each side. Regular side roads cut towards where a more modern ring road circles the neighbourhood. A cordon has been erected on the main street, limiting access to one of the side roads. Before they reach the bored bobby controlling the perimeter, Grant has his warrant card out, and flashes them through. The copper lifts the blue and white tape to arm's length, allowing Grant to drive underneath. The fire engines have already left the scene, but the fire chief and his vehicle are still in evidence. As Grant parks near the kerb, the change in motion causes Kylie to stir: her gaze is starry, and he suspects that she has snoozed for the last few minutes of the journey.

'We're here?' she asks unnecessarily.

'It appears so.'

The fire has been extinguished but smoke still plumes from the broken windows of a house, and from under the tiles on the roof. Some detritus, originally pulled burning from the house by the fire crew, is piled unceremoniously in the gutters, now wetted down but still smoking. A crime scene investigator crouches at the edge of the pile, using an extendable grabber tool to pick anything interesting from the damp ashes. As at the other crime scenes, there are several uniformed cops present. Also two women in sharp trouser suits are probably local CID. There's a CSI vehicle, a converted SUV with its rear hatch open, and another couple of investigators stand near it, deep in conversation. Also there's a small police van, with extra decal warning that dogs are onboard. Right now, the signage is untrue, as the handler and his springer spaniel are performing a grid search extending from the front of the smoking terraced house, to the nearby ring road.

They are currently at the head of a service alley towards the end of the street, the energetic dog nosing through some wind-blown litter for clues. There are several residents in the street, mostly keeping to their open front doors or leaning from upper-storey windows for a better view of the drama. Constables move from door to door, seeking witnesses. There are lots of nosy people but as many with shaking heads.

The two detectives approach and again Grant flashes his ID.

'We've been expecting you, boss,' says a forty-something woman, whose lined and haunted face suggests she carries a piece of all the victims she's ever dealt with in her soul. By contrast, her thirty-something partner's face is pinched, her eyebrows forming an arrowhead pointing to her narrow nose. She has eyes so dark they look black, with barely any hint of sclera. She inclines her head at Kylie, and Grant doesn't miss the sniff of disdain that follows.

The older detective makes the introductions. 'I'm DI Janice Cooper. This is DS Anne Southwaite.'

'DCI Openshaw,' Grant says, and makes a backhanded gesture, which glances off Kylie's shoulder because she has crowded in so close. 'Detective Sergeant Kylie McMahon, on special assignment to the NCA taskforce,' he announces, using her entire title so there's no misunderstanding that might lead to a jurisdiction struggle. The pinched-faced detective visibly grimaces, understanding she has been put firmly in her place.

'What do we know?' Grant asks, with a nod at the smouldering house.

It's the DI who answers. 'From what we've been able to figure out, the fire was set deliberately in an effort at destroying evidence.'

'The arsonist wasn't completely successful, though?'

'No. They hurried the job, probably out of fear of discovery. From what we could tell, stuff was torn down off walls, and probably carried away in bags. A computer was trashed, but has mostly survived the fire. The weirdest stuff we found was upstairs in that attic room there.'

Grant follows the stab of her finger and spots a dormer-type window jutting from the roof. The glass is blackened with smoke.

'Weirdest stuff?' Kylie prompts over his shoulder.

'Black magic stuff,' DI Cooper says, her world-weary eyes suddenly widening for emphasis. 'Satanic symbols and God knows what else.'

DS Southwaite makes a strange hissing noise, perhaps because her superior used her Lord's name alongside that of the devil. Or maybe it's her dislike of what they found that has left a nasty taste in her mouth: it helps explain her sour expression.

Grant wants to correct the DI, to inform her that the symbols aren't Satanic, but based on a much older belief system. He's heard too much from Nate Freeman and Doctor Prince about angels and Berith to go back to thinking of the covenant seals in any other fashion. Now isn't the time for sharing their know-ledge, and besides, he needs to see what they're talking about to make certain that the stuff the arsonist missed has anything to do with his case.

'What say we take another look?' Grant phrases his words in a manner that refusal is out of the question.

'Of course, boss. Anne, go fetch the fire chief, eh?'

The DS agrees, the angles in her features losing some of their sharpness. And she heads off in search of the chief. For now, the FC has control of the scene, and could refuse admittance until he's confident that the fire is completely extinguished and the building safe from collapse. Grant thinks he spotted the chief's white helmet near to the converted SUV a moment ago, but now there's no sign of it.

Grant, Kylie and DI Cooper approach the house. The smell of petrol is rank in the air. The accelerant should have ensured that the fire burned fast and hot, so they were fortunate that it had been discovered early enough for the fire crews to extinguish it before the entire terraced row of houses was gutted.

DS Southwaite appears from within the house. She is grimacing once more, but this time from the stench. Her eyes are pinched and watering. The fire chief must be inside as she gestures them forward.

'There's no need for either of you to come inside again, we'll find our own way up,' Grant announces, and the two locals appear pleased to hear it. DI Cooper waves over one of the CSI techs and within minutes Grant and Kylie have been issued with paper facemasks, eye protection, nitrile gloves and plastic overshoes – the latter are as much to save their shoes as prevent them from disturbing any evidence. The carpets inside are sodden with water, petrol and ashes.

'We'll wait, if you need anything else,' says DI Cooper.

'Thanks, uh, Janice,' says Grant, recalling her forename. 'But we've got it from here. Please feel free to get on with your own workload or you'll be at it all night.'

'No rest for the wicked,' she quotes, and then lowers her head when realizing how out of turn her words might prove. She adds, 'Aye,' in acknowledgement of her possible faux pas.

Grant's keen on seeing what's in William Ballard's attic. He smiles a brief goodbye and then turns sharply and enters the house, with Kylie close on his heels.

Minor damage has been caused by the invasion of water flooding down from above. Apart from sodden walls, the house looks untouched by the fire there. The white helmet of the fire chief stands out in the torchlight of a CSI tech: the two are in consultation. A glance from the chief catches Grant's eye, and they communicate without speaking. He aims a finger upward, and the chief simply nods permission to continue.

They go up, each stair squelching underfoot. The power is obviously off, and there hasn't been time since the fire was extinguished for alternative lighting to be set up. Kylie pulls out a torch and flicks it on. She offers it to Grant, but he's happier that she holds it. She illuminates their path, aiming the torch over his shoulder.

The upper floors are blackened. There's an awful stink, a concoction of chemicals, accelerant, burnt plastics and melted upholstery, and the rancid smell from everything drawn from the fabric of the building by the hose water. The stench catches and burns their throats. Thank god for the masks, or they'd probably be unable to withstand the toxic atmosphere. Discounting the effects of the fire and its extinguishing, there's nothing remarkable about the first floor. They find a carpeted hallway, bordered on each side with bedrooms and a fully equipped shower room. A quick bob of the head through each open door shows that William Ballard kept a basic home. The rooms hold little by way of personal items and, if he is right, Grant thinks the house has been rented furnished, and the furniture has been in situ for a couple of decades at least. It appears that somebody has already gone from room to room, emptying drawers and trinket boxes of anything incriminating: Grant thinks that the CSI team would benefit from being as thorough as Ballard's helpers. He finds the short staircase up to the attic.

Before proceeding he looks at Kylie. She's as eager as he is to see what might have been missed, and if there's enough to deduce if this was the lair of a serial killing maniac. She stabs the torchlight overhead, tracing the doorframe to the attic. It's as if there's some kind of tangible darkness beyond the touch of the beam, a swirling, sentient, and supremely evil murk that will prevent them accessing the converted roof space. As she tilts the torch, it grows apparent that some smoke still hangs among the rafters, giving the semblance of something alive shifting about. Up there, breathing will be challenging. Clearing his throat, Grant adjusts his facemask, but goes up. These stairs are soaking wet, a slip hazard. He reaches back and Kylie gratefully accepts his hand. Together they climb the stairs, each supporting the other.

The open door spills them on to a landing barely a metre across. A second doorway bars their passage. Grant swipes at the smoke lingering in the air, but it doesn't help clear it. Kylie points the torch at the door and he sees the brass door handle. It's ancient, worn and dented with age: possibly it holds the fingerprints of the arsonist. Grant uses the back of his forearm to force the door inward. It swings away easily, and they are engulfed in a river of bitter-smelling smoke. Despite his eye protectors, Grant's eyes sting and tears wash down his cheeks. Kylie mutters and curses, and for a moment he loses the benefit of her torchlight as she throws her arm across her face, trying to avoid being choked. Coughing they both push inside the attic.

There's nothing much to see, but it's enough.

The attic space runs the length of the house, the sloping roof forming its walls. A large dormer window has been added to allow natural light inside during the day, and for the room to be ventilated at night, and it also adds a slight box-like area to the otherwise tightly pitched walls. The space under the window has been used as some kind of workspace in the past. A trellis table – blackened now – looks like it was the nucleus for where the fire started. Nothing identifiable has survived the flames there. A couple of other tall trellises stand at the far end, looking almost like looms. Cords hang from the burnt wood, but there's no sign of whatever they were attached to. Forensics will confirm what it was that William Ballard had hung out to dry on the looms, but Grant can guess. He turns and finds Kylie sweeping the walls with the torch beam.

The fire, short in duration, but intensely hot due to the presence of accelerants, has scorched the walls, but not enough to show that several posters or pieces of artwork had been hung there. There's still evidence of tacky dough, used to fix the papers to the walls. Where they were ripped down before the fire took hold, they have left behind ripped corners of paper, which have survived the fire, though singed. Next to those, there's more evidence that Will had been thumb-tacking stuff to the walls, forming a collage of madness, no doubt. There is evidence of photographs, and newspaper clippings and articles printed off a computer having been hung there: it doesn't take much to decide that the stuff on the walls could incriminate him in the murders as easily as if they'd found the murder weapons.

Kylie stabs the torch beam about and then lingers on one spot where she has torn free a larger scrap of paper.

'Does that look familiar?' she asks, as Grant leans in to inspect shiny daubs on the wall.

It is a fragment of a painted symbol, and it has survived the flames. He almost feels like an expert in this esoteric stuff now.

'Does your torch have UV?'

Kylie obviously understands where his thoughts are going. She shouts down the stairs and within a half-minute a CSI tech arrives in the doorway to hand over another torch. Kylie fiddles with it, and it goes through several flashing sequences, before settling on one in particular. She sends the almost invisible beam at an angle to the walls. The place is practically covered in symbolism, many of them smeared, singed or with a layer of smoke residue: an effort has been made to conceal them, but under ultraviolet light they fluoresce, as blood often does in that spectrum.

'I'd say Will has a lot to explain,' he says.

'Yes,' Kylie agrees, 'and Nate is going to be destroyed when he hears about this.'

'Or worse still . . .' Grant crouches and picks at an object that has slipped between the floorboards. It takes a sharp tug to release it. It probably holds DNA evidence that ties it to one or more of the previous victims, so Grant takes care not to touch the strangely curved moon blade.

THIRTY-THREE

Newcastle upon Tyne

It feels like an age since Grant and Kylie woke him in the early hours. There was a point or two on the drive back to Emily's place when Nate had given in to fatigue and closed his eyes. He'd slept for several seconds or more, waking with a sense of startlement and mild panic each time. It was fortunate that Emily was behind the wheel and not him, otherwise they'd have never made it safely back over the Tyne. He didn't admit to falling asleep, but Emily had sussed he was tired, and didn't comment. He caught her smiling at him one time he'd resurfaced, probably he'd snored or made another weird noise as he clawed back to wakefulness: she didn't say so, but he thought she'd found it endearing.

Since arriving back at her flat, he'd drunk enough industrial-strength coffee to keep him awake for an entire month, and now his brain buzzes with caffeine overload, and his fingers tremble.

'Better?' asks Emily as she again tops up his cup from a jug.

'I've a bladder the size of a melon,' he admits.

'You know where the bathroom is.'

He does. He has used it before, and will likely have to make an emergency visit in the next minute.

She says, 'I've put out fresh towels if you'd like to shower, and, well, there's a few bits and pieces of clothing my ex left behind. I'm sure I can find you something fresh for you to wear.'

His clothing isn't dirty, and there's no way he's going to wear another man's underpants. 'I'll make these do.'

'Your choice,' she says.

He wonders if he smells bad. He possibly does, but it's most likely of strong coffee rather than of body odour. Emily has produced various titbits to snack on – crisps and biscuits and a pack of iced lemon cakes – but he hasn't started on them yet. His need to stay awake was more pressing than eating, but now it is his need to empty his bladder that pushes to the fore. He stands, wincing at aches in his muscles. His job is physical and he often punishes himself in laborious acts of contrition; lazing in chairs and car seats has played havoc on his body. He takes marionette-type steps before he regains full control, and makes his way to the bathroom.

For the briefest of moments he considers leaving open the door, wondering if Emily will take the opportunity to come check him out and from there . . . no, that's as far as he will allow the fantasy to go. He finds her attractive, and yes, he'd love to take things further with her, but he has no right to expect more than simple hospitality from her. Thinking in any other terms could make things awkward, or worse, uncomfortable, for her, and he has no intention of alienating her. He closes the door and pushes across the privacy bolt. After he's done and flushes the toilet, he goes to the sink and turns on the taps. He runs water until it meets the overflow. He strips out of his shirt. Stands a moment, staring into a mirror. His face in reflection is drawn, almost haggard. He understands he isn't only tired after a long day, he isn't as conflicted as before, and the realization that his brother could be the killer has sucked the vitality out of him. It is difficult finding an appropriate word to describe how beyond disappointed he feels.

He lathers up and washes his face, neck and upper torso. More suds are added and he uses them as an impromptu shaving foam. Emily has left out a razor: it is pink, with a sleek shank, and normally used on more delicate skin than his coarse chin hair, but it does its job. He shaves, feeling a slight sense of relief when he doesn't peel back a layer to reveal a face more tired and haggard than before. The wash and shave refreshes him more than he'd have believed possible. Rinsing off the soap, he turns to his hair, and some of Emily's products to shampoo and then condition: both times he empties and refills the sink to rinse his hair. He swills the sink, cleans it with a wad of toilet tissue and then flushes it. Done, he steps back.

The temptation to check is too powerful. He twists, aiming his shoulder at the mirror while he cranes to see his scarred flesh. In the past, he has fantasized that the symbol pulsates, barely able to contain the evil imprisoned within it. He has dreamed that it pulses red hot, and that visible light could be seen emanating from it. Of course, it is nonsense: the scar is ugly, risen and pink in places, but mostly it is off-white scar tissue against his marginally darker skin. He turns from the reflection, reaching for one of the towels Emily has supplied. It is a huge bath sheet, fluffy, and smells freshly laundered. He drapes it over his shoulders, less to soak up the moisture than to conceal his scar.

Emily is quiet. He strains to hear, but all that comes to him is traffic noise from nearby, and the lightest of tapping noises: fingertips on a computer keyboard?

He suspects that her urge to deep dive into the deep web has been too much to resist. He wants to learn if there's been any more conversation or activity logged between Baphomet and Nephilim, and if what's happened will clarify if Will is devil or angel.

The thought draws a grunt of irony from him. Considering the original identity of Berith, and the reason behind all these horrific murders, to him the term *angel* has lost any connection it had to goodness and light.

He shrugs back into his shirt. He thought earlier that his clothing was still clean, but putting it on top of his freshly washed body, he can feel that the cloth is a little coarse and smells mildly of tobacco smoke. He can't imagine how, other than that a heavy smoker must've used one of the chairs he'd spent time in before him. Not to worry, the odour of shampoo and soap overwhelms the slight unpleasant smell from his shirt. He looks again in the mirror. Finger-combs his dark hair off his forehead. He looks presentable, he supposes.

Before sliding open the privacy bolt, he takes a steadying breath. He steps into cool air. It isn't unusual. The bathroom was small and filling with steam, so was bound to be a warmer space. There's a cool breeze. He doesn't recall the apartment being draughty before; in fact it had been mildly stuffy, especially when four of them had been crammed around Emily's computer. Perhaps she's thrown open a window to air the place out? It's a bit contradictory, seeing as when they entered she'd immediately turned up the central heating to take the December chill out of their bones.

He heads to her tiny bedroom-cum-office, expecting she'll be beavering over her computer.

She isn't there, and the screensaver swirls like a multi-coloured squid on a black background. She hasn't worked on the computer in the last few minutes, if at all.

The tapping noise he'd heard is coming from another room.

There aren't too many choices in the small apartment. He returns to the kitchen where they'd downed their coffees. The tapping grows louder, but he can tell now it isn't her fingernails on keys, the sound is far too rhythmical. He steps into the kitchen. Emily isn't there. The ticking sound draws him to an extractor fan that Emily must've turned on to rid the kitchen of the strong coffee aroma. A pull cord with a plastic end dangles down, knocking against the wall: *tick . . . tack . . . tick*. Contrasting airflows move it. Air sucked into the extractor vent vies with the breeze that Nate first noticed on leaving the bathroom. He follows it to its source. The front door stands open a few inches.

'Emily?'

He expects the door to swing inward and Emily to come back inside, explaining how she'd stepped outside for some fresh air.

The door moves fractionally, pushed and pulled by the breeze.

'Emily,' he calls, louder this time.

He strides towards the door, unsure why but his heart has quickened as if instinct has already told him what has happened.

'Doctor Prince?' he tries, and gets no reply.

He stops in the hallway, one hand reaching for the door.

The rug is slightly askew, as if rucked up by somebody's heel when they were twisting around.

Alone, the dishevelled rug isn't great evidence, but to Nate, it's enough to suggest wrongdoing. He yanks open the door and steps outside.

Not far away there are late-night revellers in the bars on the Quayside, and from the front door Nate can hear them babbling, trying to make themselves heard over a thumping bass soundtrack. Nearer by, Emily's riverside neighbours are either asleep, or have given into the inevitable and joined the other drinkers enjoying an early prelude to the upcoming festive season. The traffic sound continues from adjacent streets but there's no hint of voices or footfalls nearby.

Emily's apartment is on the first floor, situated above a boutique shop that closed hours ago. A shared set of stairs allows access to hers and an adjoining property. Nate goes down them three steps at a time, and lurches out on to the street. He immediately checks for her car: the VW Golf is exactly where she parked it on their return, its windscreen already filmed with a layer of frost. She hasn't gone to fetch something from her car, but has she gone to collect something else? Maybe she grew hungry while he washed, and the snacks weren't enough to satisfy her; perhaps she'd gone to collect an order from a nearby take-away or something? It was unlikely.

Nate spins around, checking for movement. There's none.

Emily hasn't gone to collect an order.

She has been abducted. To hope for anything otherwise is a fool's dream.

'Emily!'

The night is crisp, but Nate is abruptly overheated. Blood rushes to his face and to his fingertips, leaving his exposed skin tingling.

He charges across the road, on to the pavement that skirts the river. For a second he hopes that Emily escaped her abductors and jumped for her life into the Tyne. It would be a desperate move for anyone in these low temperatures, but he shouldn't rule it out. She isn't wallowing in the river. It was a ridiculous thought, but he'd followed the urge to check, the way he had when first plunging downstairs.

Earlier, he'd asked Openshaw to ensure that his adoptive parents were protected, safe from abduction or other harm. He should've demanded a similar level of protection for Emily. He'd thought his presence was enough, and a selfish part of him had hoped to keep her to himself, to show he was safe and reliable. He'd been too sure of himself though, believing he'd be capable of protecting her when he obviously wasn't. She isn't downstairs fetching something from her car, nor collecting a food order, nor taking a midnight swim in icy water. She is *gone*. Snatched. Taken.

'Emily!' he shouts at the top of his voice.

Shouting for her is pointless.

She must've been taken shortly after he entered the bathroom, when he was making enough noise while washing to cover any sound she or her abductor made. If she'd been forced downstairs and into a vehicle, she could be miles away by now.

He was employed as an armed response police officer once,

trusted to carry a gun. He had been vetted and deemed sane and responsible, capable of making on-the-spot life and death decisions. Most of the time the psychological evaluation has proven true, but that isn't to say that panic is an alien concept. For a few protracted seconds he dances back and forth, throwing his hands in the air in silent question, and then shouting for Emily again, before he thinks more rationally. Nothing he is doing is going to help, and it isn't going to bring Emily safely back to him.

He hurtles back up the stairs, taking them four at a time. He darts inside her apartment, this time seeking any clue he might have missed before. There's the rucked rug. He also spots dark smudges on the floor, caused by rubber-soled footwear. The smudges point in different directions, some overlay others. They are further signs of a brief struggle: Emily must've been lured to the front door and, when answering it, been immediately grabbed, perhaps subdued somehow to silence her, and then bundled physically outside and down the stairs.

He must check the rest of the apartment before doing anything else. He'd look like a crazy man if somehow he'd misread the situation, and Emily's door simply hadn't closed correctly when they'd entered; that it was they who'd rucked the rug and made the smudges on the floor on entering. For all he knew she was in her master bedroom, changing her clothes perhaps, or readying to use the shower after he's finished in the bathroom. He has been in all the other rooms in the house, but has respectfully kept his distance from her private bedroom – he has hoped that when he ever does enter that room it will be at Emily's invitation – so he's uneasy about going inside now.

He taps the door. 'Emily?'

No answer.

The silence feels like a dead weight across the nape of his neck.

'Emily, are you OK?'

What if she has slipped and banged her head, or something else equally as unlikely, and is lying there unconscious and in need of help.

'Emily, I'm coming in, OK?'

He turns the handle and the door swings inwards silently. He steps into the room. The carpet is plush and barely worn. The curtains are open. The lights are switched off. Emily isn't here. She hasn't been in the bedroom since their return. He has to ensure that she isn't lying at the far side of the bed. He takes a cursory look. The floor is empty . . . as he knew it would be.

He lunges away and returns to the kitchen.

Nothing there tells him anything more than before.

He goes back to the spare room.

Her computer's screen server still dances, whirling colours.

He hits the mouse pad.

The screen jumps to life, but it is hopeless to think he can do anything with it. He can probably dig out the hyperlinks from her browsing history, but he hasn't got access to the log in details she used to enter the deep web, or more specifically to the private chatroom she'd discovered where the followers of Berith congregated.

Besides, he hasn't time to waste trying.

He leaves the computer alone, and digs out his phone.

All day long he has had the ringer on silent. He has missed a number of calls and text messages, most of them from his work colleague and would-be pal, Jim Powell, so he ignores them. There are two missed calls from unknown numbers – probably scammers – and another from his adoptive parents. He should speak with them, they are probably horrified by what is going on and need reassurance that he is OK, but again, he can't waste what precious time he has. DCI Openshaw has had them safely squirrelled away for now, so he's happy that his mom and dad are both safe, while Emily is the one in imminent danger.

He checks his historical calls, and finds the one he's looking for. It was from Emily, from back when they'd arranged their meeting at Haydon Bridge. She'd called him, and he'd texted back a message to meet on the bridge, the town's major landmark. He hadn't saved her number in his contacts at the time, so is relieved to find it now.

He's tempted to call her, but if her abductors hear the phone ringing they'll probably take it from her. Best he wait and, if she is able to access her phone, allow her to call him when it's safe to do so. If that fails to transpire, he'll have Openshaw put a trace on the phone, and pray it leads the police to her.

He looks for Openshaw's number in his contacts. He doesn't

have it. But DS McMahon called him, so her number is in his recent call list. He hits her number.

'Nate?' she says, the instant she answers. 'Is everything OK? We are only a couple of minutes away now if—'

'They've got her, Kylie!' he butts in, even as he lunges for the front door again. 'They've got her.'

'Who has got her . . . what?'

It should be obvious who he's talking about but, to be fair, his announcement has come out of the blue, and probably falling on ears that have been bombarded with details day and night since she joined the NCA taskforce. 'Emily. Doctor Prince. They came here to her apartment and snatched her from under my nose!'

'What do you mean? Did you see them, Nate? Are *you* hurt?'

'Forget about me! Emily's gone. She has been taken by the sick bastard!'

DCI Openshaw can be heard over Kylie's phone.

'Nate. Listen to me. It's very important. You say Emily has been taken: why? When it's you they want, why take Emily? What use is she to them?'

'They've taken her to lure me to them.'

'Exactly,' Grant says. 'Which is why you must do the exact opposite to what they expect. Lock the door, barricade yourself inside and do not open up for anyone but us. Do you hear me?'

Nate's feet have propelled him outside once more. They have taken him down the stairs and on to the road adjacent to the river. At Grant's instruction he turned around to look back up at Emily's apartment. Grant's right. Emily isn't one of the chosen, she isn't one of the Children of Hamor, and as far as he knows, her skin is unblemished when it comes to ancient Canaanite religious symbology, so it would be pointless harvesting it for vellum. This has to be about using Emily as bait to draw him into a trap. He should get indoors and lock the door as instructed, not parade around in the open like this.

He doesn't retreat.

He moves further into the road, almost to the opposite side and the edge of the quay.

He throws his hands in the air.

'Here I am, you bastards. Let Emily go and come and get me.'

'Nate? What do you think you're doing?' Kylie McMahon's

voice is strident through her phone. Nate momentarily forgot he was holding it, and had a line open.

'They want me, they should come and get me,' he shouts, loud enough for Kylie and Grant to hear, but also so her abductor could hear if he's in earshot. 'Let Emily go, you bastard! She's innocent in all this, and is useless to you. Let her go, God damn you!'

From further up the Quayside, voices lift in response to his shouts, but it is the drunken tittering of revellers.

One thing is for certain, Emily's abductors wouldn't have dragged her to where the bars and clubs were in full swing. Nate runs several metres, and finds a narrow service alley alongside the apartment block. From the darkness of the alley, he thinks he can hear a scuffle of feet. But then again it could be . . . he has again forgotten he's holding the phone. Tinny voices shout his name.

'I'm here.'

'Nate, don't do anything stupid,' Grant snaps. 'We are only another two minutes out. Whatever you have in mind, wait for us to get there. Wait until we can back you up.'

'I think I know where they have taken her, Grant. Sorry, but I can't spare you two minutes,' he states, and darts into the alley.

THIRTY-FOUR

Following his success at arresting William Ballard earlier, it feels to Grant as if he has been trying to catch up since. It's like he's on the back foot, lurching from one crime scene to the next, always a whisper's distance behind the action, always a heart's beat late. It's the same again as he powers his Audi the wrong way up a one-way street and brings it to a juddering halt on the cobblestoned road alongside the River Tyne. He knows from the last time they were at Emily Prince's apartment that he's chosen the quickest route, but it won't help to block her abductors' escape route. They are long gone, and Emily with them. He has no idea where Nate is, or what the bloody hell he hopes to achieve from running about hollering challenges at invisible enemies.

He gets out of his car, stands with one hand on the open door. From several hundred metres away, he can hear the sounds of drunken partying. He identifies Emily's apartment. Her VW Golf is parked in a designated space on the Quayside. He can't see hide nor hair of Nate.

After abandoning his urgent call, Nate has been silent, but that is mostly because Kylie has given up trying to get a response from him, and called 999 to pick up the local switchboard. As pinpointed with the details as possible, she'd called in the situation and asked for police back-up. There'd been a short spell of confusion while she explained who she was, and more pointedly who Doctor Prince was, and the case she was assisting them on before the controller understood the urgency of her call and mounted a response not unlike the Charge of the Light Brigade. Now sirens wail, closing in from all quarters, even from across the river in Gateshead.

There's a streak of motion, a high-pitched shriek.

Grant spins towards the mouth of the narrow service alley, already disregarding the cat that bursts from cover and runs screeching to hide under a parked car. It isn't Grant and Kylie's presence that has disturbed the cat, but he can guess who is responsible. He rushes to the alley, spreads his arms like a goalkeeper readying for a penalty shot and asks the obvious, 'Nate, are you in there?'

There's no immediate reply.

But he hears a scuffling noise, and recognizes it as a shoulder rubbing against a brick wall. In the darkness a deeper shadow stirs, growing denser as it moves up the alley towards him. Grant shifts his stance, hands forming a barrier between them. He believes it is Nate, but it might not be.

Before his defence is tested, Grant relaxes. The figure isn't as black now, and he recognizes Nate's features as they morph from the shadows. Over the last few days, he has watched Nate take on various expressions, ranging from happiness, through confusion, and doubt, to outrage and everything in between. This face, though, is the one Grant recalls from after Nate failed to save Jenny Onatade from her murderous husband. Back then Nate blamed himself for failing to take the shot in time that would have spared the poor woman: what did he blame this time for his failure to save Emily?

Nate barely stops at the end of the alley. He barges into Grant, and Grant is momentarily surprised by the impact of their bodies. He stands taller and outweighs Nate, but for a second there he was not exactly an immovable object in the face of an unstoppable force. He is forced to chase Nate a few steps towards Emily's apartment, before Nate comes to his senses and recognizes him. Kylie, Grant notes, has drawn her extendable baton, and he's unsure if she means to use it on Nate, or if she'd half expected Emily's abductors to flee the alley with Nate in dogged pursuit. She wavers a moment, looks at her baton, and then lowers it, concealing it behind her hip. Nate hasn't missed the fact she's armed though. He clenches his teeth, aims a sharp nod at the alley. 'You're going to want to check I haven't murdered Emily and dumped her body down there.'

'Don't be daft,' Grant tells him, but to be honest, now that Nate's put the idea in his head, maybe they should check, to cover all bases. He looks at Kylie and can tell that she isn't totally in Nate's supporters' camp on this one, and her wariness is understandable. She doesn't know Nate the way that Grant does, and all she can be certain of is that the man's prone to irrationality at times: maybe he has turned psycho like his brother, murdered Emily and concocted a story about an abduction to cover his tracks.

Yes, it's a totally ridiculous hypothesis, but they must remember the rules of detection: assume nothing; believe nothing; challenge/ check everything. Nevertheless, he surreptitiously shakes his head, forcing her to stand down, but makes a mental note to have the alley searched by the responding officers. Not that he expects to find Emily there, but maybe her abductors did use it as a getaway and there's some kind of evidence to be found.

Nate continues towards the stairs to Emily's apartment.

Grant and Kylie rush after him, wondering what he's up to. They both have a thousand questions for him, but for now he's in charge and they can only follow. Grant mounts the stairs. It has been a long day, and the air is verging on frigid: ice has found its way into his damaged knees. He limps up after Nate, taking one painful step at a time. He recalls warning Kylie about his dodgy knees, and is thankful she falls back, allowing him to make the climb unpressured. She uses the opportunity to check around Emily's parked car, but as Nate had – unknown to her – investigated the car earlier, she finds nothing out of sorts either.

Nate waits for Grant in the open doorway.

He indicates the floor immediately inside the threshold. 'Look,' he says.

The rug is rucked up and there are a number of smudges on the parquet flooring. They are like the rubber-sole residue left on the floors of squash courts and dance floors. It appears that a short and probably swift altercation occurred after Emily answered her door, before she was subdued and dragged outside and into a waiting vehicle.

'There are no other signs of violence inside?' he asks.

'Come check,' says Nate, and before Grant can assure him he'll take his word for it – which he shouldn't – Nate takes off inside the apartment. Grant follows.

The apartment is as Grant remembers from earlier in the day. Nothing is out of place. The screensaver swirls on Emily's computer, suggesting it has gone unused for several minutes at least, and in the kitchen there's evidence that Emily and Nate had attempted to assuage their thirst with strong coffee, if not their hunger, because most of the snacks are unopened.

'I was dead on my feet,' Nate explains. 'I drank a shit-load of coffee, then Emily let me use her bathroom to freshen up. I was in there when she was taken.'

'And you're positive she was grabbed? She just didn't—'

'Didn't what, Grant? Go for a pleasant midnight stroll along the riverside?'

'We have to consider it, as unlikely as it is.'

Nate rocks his head.

'I know, but I have to check,' says Grant.

'Same as Kylie has to consider me a suspect, I suppose,' says Nate.

'I've never thought of you as a suspect.' Kylie has made it upstairs and entered the apartment. 'But it's like the boss says, we have to double-check everything. You were in the job, you know the score.'

'I know, I know. I get it. It's just that by following protocol we're wasting time. They have Emily, but it's me they really want. We need to plan a swap.'

'Are you serious?' Grant asks.

'Deadly.'

'It's not going to happen,' Grant goes on, 'so you may as well forget about sacrificing yourself.'

'I've no intention of sacrificing myself. I'm more capable of fighting back than Emily is.'

'Drop the idea,' says Grant. 'There's no way on earth that I'm going to be party to it. Even if I was in agreement, which I bloody am not, I haven't the level of authorization to allow it.'

'You're not my superior any more,' Nate reminds him, 'I don't *require* your authorization.'

'Do you want me to cuff you and throw you in a cell till this is over with?'

'You can quit with the lame threats, Grant. We both know you aren't going to do it. And this thing about not being in agreement with me . . . I think you're lying.'

On a personal level, Nate's probably right about him, and dangling Nate as bait to not only bargain for Emily's safety, but to also draw the murderer into a trap is a plausible idea. But as a DCI he can't possibly agree to it. Not only would he be risking both Nate and Emily's lives, but his reputation, career and life will be destroyed if anything goes wrong.

Responding officers begin filling the street outside. Grant says, 'We'd better go and try coordinating a search, otherwise it's going to turn into chaos out there. Nate, I'm going to have a constable take a statement from you. Keep it pertinent to what happened, and don't be tempted to extrapolate. We know what *we* think happened here, and we are probably right, but until we know for sure, I'd rather not have everyone believing the murderer has her.'

'Why not?' Nate asks, confused.

'Because we can't be certain that's the case,' Grant explains.

'Come on, who else would have grabbed her?'

Instead of replying, Grant offers a scenario. 'Once they hear a consultant has been snatched, it will be two minutes before the media start looking at who else is helping with this case: do you really want your name and face splashed all over the TV and newspapers? They'll have a bloody field day if they find out that you and the Nathaniel Freeman that kicked off the race riots in London are one and the same.'

Nate's eyes grow cloudy. Suggesting that he was responsible

for the riots is a cheap shot, but Grant doesn't care. It has the desired response, taking some of the heat out of him. The last time that Nate had come under the media spotlight, he'd run and hid in the woods, hopefully concern about it happening again will keep him sufficiently cowed for Grant to get on with his job without worrying his old friend is going to go maverick.

'All this police activity is bound to attract the media,' Kylie injects, in support of her boss's tactic of controlling Nate. 'You should probably wait inside, out of sight.'

Nate nods. His eyes are still dimmed. He chews his inner cheek, thinking. 'You're probably right,' he finally acquiesces, 'except for one thing. It's not the media I should hide from, it's from whoever grabbed Emily. There's only one reason they took her, and it's to draw me out. Well, you ask me, they've stuck around to watch, to check that their plan worked, and right now you can bet your asses I'm being watched.'

All three turn in unison, first towards where the partying is going on further up the Quayside, but it's doubtful that the murderer or one of his lackeys is mixing with that noisy crowd, so they look across the river instead. It's not so distant to the Gateshead side that somebody across there couldn't observe the street outside Emily's apartment even during the night. In the time since Emily was taken, Nate has given his hunters plenty of opportunities to photograph or video-record him while he flapped around shouting pointless challenges.

'I wanted them to see me,' Nate admits, 'to come and try taking me and letting Emily go. But that is never going to happen. Even if I let them take me, they will keep Emily, so they can use the threat of harming her to control me.'

'Glad to hear you're coming around to my way of thinking,' says Grant.

Grant can't tell if Nate's expression's a grimace or a sneer.

As Nate returns to the apartment, Grant accompanies him. Nate mentions the possibility of tracing Emily's mobile phone, and Grant agrees they should do it. He also calls over a uniformed constable and asks that the man take Nate's statement as a matter of urgency: to get the ball rolling on triangulating the phone's location, he needs to coordinate with the local force.

Officers are inside the apartment, searching. It's standard practice: to ensure the missing person hasn't been harmed there and concealed somewhere out of sight. Grant makes a mental note to have Kylie dispatch some searchers to the nearby service alley . . . to write off the possibility of Nate being the perpetrator of Emily's disappearance, of course.

'You going to be OK?' Grant asks as they stand in the kitchen.

'Not till we have Emily back safely.'

'You like her, eh?'

'Whether or not I like her isn't important. She's one of us, and trusted us to keep her safe.'

'You're right. I promise you, I'll do everything in my power to find her and bring her home.' He squeezes Nate's shoulder. 'This should never have happened, Nate. And before you try shouldering any more of the blame, don't. We've all been taken by surprise at how organized this killer is, and at how many people he has willing to help him. We've known for a while now that he isn't working alone, but . . . I dunno . . . he seems to have an army at his beck and call.'

'Not an army,' Nate reminds him. 'It's a sect, or a cult, call it what you will. He doesn't have infinite numbers, but every last one of them is a *believer*. That's right, the belief in Berith didn't die back on Ohop Island when the compound was burned down and Weyland Berith was taken into custody. While Weyland lived, he still had his followers, and now that he's gone they've switched their allegiances to the avatar preparing to accept his spirit at the time of the winter solstice. If their belief is anything as powerful as my parents' was towards Weyland, they'll do *anything* for him, and damn the consequences. Yeah, that includes attacking a prison transport vehicle, or snatching a consultant from her home to use as leverage. We've been hunting one killer when really we're up against many.'

'The winter solstice,' Grant says, echoing Nate's words as if he'd heard nothing of the rest.

'Wednesday the twenty-first of December,' Nate informs him.

'Only a couple of weeks away.'

'Only ten days, and' – Nate checks the time on a digital display on Emily's microwave oven – 'sixteen minutes. This year's winter solstice occurs at 21.47, to be precise. This will be the exact time that the rite of conjoining will happen, supposing that the killer has harvested all the covenants by then and his grimoire is complete.'

Grant's hand reaches for his shoulder again, but his fingertips fall short, as if he can feel the evil emanating from the covenant seal through Nate's shirt. He says, 'Best we don't let any of them get their hands on yours then. Stay here for now, Nate, keep your head down, and let me do my job without having to worry about you getting grabbed.'

THIRTY-FIVE

There's little else to do except follow orders, or at least appear to do so. It is torturous to Nate, but he can't give any hint that he's going to do anything except go along with DCI Openshaw's instructions, so he returns inside the apartment, waiting to be joined by the constable tasked with recording his statement.

He isn't alone inside. There are still a couple of uniformed officers trudging around, and from their lack of enthusiasm he doubts they're keen on going back out in the cold any time soon. In the front foyer, a CSI tech is finishing up checking the area for evidence. He has dusted down the door's handle and the front panels, checking for fingerprints, and has taken high-resolution photographs of the scuff images on the floor – from what Nate has already seen, there're no full shoe prints, no visible tread pattern to match against a perpetrator's shoe. A tiny vacuum cleaner has been used to collect any shedded hairs, skin, or other trace residue left behind after the scuffle. Other processes have likely been used to check for bodily fluids – saliva and blood in this case – that might have been expelled by either the victim or victimizer. Nate knows all of these things, because once upon a time he would've been involved in the protecting of such evidence at too many violent crime scenes to vividly remember.

By the time the constable from downstairs appears, the searchers have finished and reluctantly left, and the CSI tech has turned his attention to the landing outside the apartment. Nate has settled again in the kitchen, sitting in the same chair he'd used earlier while drinking gallons of coffee. His stomach flips and nausea rushes up his throat, a flood of bile. He chokes it down and pushes aside the snacks laid on by Emily, not because they repulse him, but because they're a weird reminder of how empty her apartment feels without her personal presence. Without asking permission, the constable settles on the chair that Emily had earlier pulled out from under her kitchen table but barely spent any time in. He lays out his notebook and a stack of official statement forms on the tabletop, then scratches in his chest pocket for a pen: by now Nate expected that statement recording would have joined the digital revolution, and his version of events would be recorded on an electronic tablet, or on video on the officer's bodycam.

He keeps his statement to the bare facts, and the officer finishes up by asking Nate to read over the statement and then sign it as a true record of the facts. Nate does so, and scrawls his name. His fingers still quake but he's happy enough that his signature is legible. The initial flood of endorphins has subsided since discovering Emily's abduction, but a fresh trickle has begun, in anticipation of what's to come.

He sees the constable out, and finally has the apartment to himself again. He wonders if Grant and DS McMahon are still outside, coordinating pointless door-to-door enquiries and a wider search for any CCTV footage: these days people have doorbell cameras, so there's the possibility that there is some fuzzy but distant image of her abductors to be had, but he doubts it will help.

He returns to the spare bedroom, and again looks at the computer. One of the constables searching the room must have hit the mouse as the screen has been recently brought to life. It has the factory set background, but Emily has somewhat personalized the screen by bringing her favourite apps to the front. If he counted them there'd be nearly twenty different apps she uses on a regular basis, but he isn't interested in any of them. He brings up her search engine, and opens it, set on a message stating that the page she was last on is no longer available. He grunts, and aims the mouse at the top of the screen on the history tab.

Apparently she hadn't taken even a peek at the computer since their return from Sunderland. The last hyperlink visited is made up of a series of numbers and characters, and he knows for sure that it's to the chatroom where Baphomet and Nephilim hang out.

He clicks on the hyperlink, but is immediately scuppered from going further when he is presented with a different screen than expected: he has no idea how Emily circumvented this page to the chatroom. He tries previous hyperlinks in her history, but with no luck. He can't use her computer to call out the murderous bastard as he'd hoped, but he isn't at a dead end yet.

He takes out his mobile phone and checks his call register again. He had asked Grant to have Emily's phone triangulated, but it is too soon for the DCI to get any results. He wonders if Emily's abductors have searched her and discovered her phone. If that is the case then more than likely they will have ditched it, or at the very least switched it off. It isn't enough to switch off the phone to render it invisible, because inbuilt features allow a modern smartphone to be found even with the power off. If they have disassembled the phone components and randomly scattered them along their escape route, then he's fucked. He can only hope that they recognize the phone as a tool by which to reach him without risking a face-to-face confrontation, and so they haven't yet destroyed or got rid of it.

Ringing Emily's number to talk directly with her abductors is tempting, but that might spook them and cause them to panic, and what if they harm her as a result? Instead, he decides to be more nuanced, and only sends a text message to her phone. The message is short and pointed: *Contact Nate.*

He returns to the front door and peers outside. There's still police activity out there. He thinks he can probably slip past them unnoticed, if not for the duo of constables that stand guard at the foot of the stairs. He assumes that Grant has allocated him protection, should Emily's abductors still be hanging around and make a second attempt at snatching their main target. Nate appreciates the gesture, but having the coppers hanging around is the last thing he wants. He closes and locks the door. He has residue on his fingertips from when the door was dusted for prints. He wipes his hands on his jeans as he paces down the hall, seeking Emily's bedroom. Earlier he'd deliberately avoided the room, and had to force himself to enter when first checking she hadn't collapsed inside, but this time he has no qualms about going in.

He doesn't expect to find her ex's clothes still hanging in her closet alongside hers, and instead seeks secondary storage where she might have shoved them after he ran out on her. There's a small door in the wall, set low. He suspects it gives access to a crawl space under the eaves and he isn't wrong. Immediately inside the crawl space, there's a basket hamper. He drags it out and flips the lid and finds folded clothing inside. He digs through, discarding trousers and shirts, until he finds a pale blue sweater. He worms into it. The sweater is a size too small for him and has a faint damp odour to it, but it doesn't matter. He hopes to find a jacket to replace his with, but after digging to the bottom there isn't one. He bundles his thin cotton jacket into a tight roll, and stuffs it through his belt, and tugs the bottom of the sweater over it. He does find a hat. Nate isn't a stranger to wearing baseball caps, but this one is more like a fisherman's hat: all it is missing is some fishing hooks and flies stuck in the rim. Pulled low, it will help disguise his features, but Nate's aware that coppers are drawn to persons that deliberately hide their faces. He puts on the hat, but pulls it no lower than anyone else would to keep the frost away. Checking out his reflection in a vanity mirror, he's satisfied that he looks a different person to the one who was running about flapping his arms on the Quayside. He ensures his mobile is in the breast pocket of his shirt, with the ringer switched off for the moment, and then returns to the bathroom.

The small room still retains some residual warmth from when he'd cleaned up earlier. There's a thin layer of condensation on the window. He has to pop open the window and crane to look outside. Emily's bathroom, he knows from his earlier recce down the service alley, overlooks a goods delivery yard. There's no obligation to provide a rear fire escape, but Emily's landlord hasn't scrimped and scraped. The bathroom window, pushed open to its extreme, can be released with the flick of a recessed button in the frame, allowing its removal, making room for a person to escape.

He stands a moment on the fire escape, checking that the police have left the yard. Kylie, he hopes, will have ensured the service alley was searched and discounted at first order. After a few seconds of silence, he descends the metal stairs, taking his time, and making as little noise as possible. He pads across the yard, and into a narrower alley running parallel to the discount store served by the goods yard, emerging on to the next street over. There is a police presence there, but they are spread thinly and doing the rounds of knocking on doors and questioning people who – Nate suspects – have nothing of value to say. There are people out on the streets too, returning home after partying on the Quayside, or maybe moving on to destinations that remain open well into the small hours. Nate affects a purposeful stride, and heads away, hoping that his departure has gone unnoticed. Once he makes a couple of turns and cuts across a couple of blocks, hope grows to confidence. He isn't cold. The sweater and shirt are ample to keep the frosty air from his outdoors-conditioned body, but he unfurls his rolled jacket and dons it. He tosses the fisherman's hat in a waste bin.

He doesn't know Newcastle well, but he has enough of a sense of direction to head towards the railway station. It could be too late to catch a train back to Carlisle, but fleeing home isn't his purpose for seeking the station: it's a landmark, one at which he can be easily found by an out-of-towner. This late in the evening, the station might not be that busy, but there will be enough people around that Emily's abductors will be wary of attempting another snatch, especially when Nate might fight back and be vocal enough to attract the attention of witnesses, and maybe alert the British Transport Police officers on duty.

Several times he checks the mobile for a reply, but there's none. Either Emily's phone has been shattered and the parts scattered, or it hasn't been discovered on her person yet. He fears the former, as much as he hopes for the latter. No, that isn't exactly true. If and when they do find her mobile, it might encourage them to hurt her for not coming clean. If anyone lays a hand on her he'll . . .

He's unsure what he should swear to here, because he has already been remiss in protecting her, and failure has become a fucking facet of his life. First time he failed to save Special Agent Milo from his demented mother, and without any doubt whatsoever it was because he'd watched his mother slit open the heroic agent's throat that he'd paused in horror the moment that Jenny Onatade's husband threatened to similarly cut her. His latest failure is different; a killer didn't faze him with a blade at Emily's throat, he simply wasn't there when she needed him most. Earlier, Emily had mildly rebuked him for his suggestion that she needed a manly bodyguard, and she had gone on to prove that she was tough and fearless under certain circumstances. But even as she'd scolded him, he thought he had detected a flicker of trepidation, as if there had been some event in her past that warned that it didn't hurt to have him watching her back. Without agreeing to it, she'd accepted his protection, yet the first time she'd needed it he'd let her down.

Stop it, Nate!

Doubt is smothering him; next it will fully subdue him. If he allows the black dog to get its teeth in, it will drag him broken and ashamed back to his bolthole in Kershope Forest.

The railway station comes into sight. A tall wall, a bulwark almost, conceals the platforms and lines from passers-by on the street. Taxicabs stand idling, waiting for the next train to disgorge its passengers: this late in the evening it must be the last hurrah. Soon the drivers will leave to wait at other locations to scoop up drinkers leaving the bars and clubs instead. For no other reason than he has hidden his identity from others on the walk here, he averts his gaze, so as not to attract any of the taxi drivers. He makes for the entrance to the station. A middle-aged couple huddles immediately outside the door, drawing on cigarettes, taking them down to their stumps: they've gasped their way through a long rail journey, Nate assumes, and are feeding their habits before hailing one of the taxis. He stands a few feet away from them, and for all intents and purposes could be mistaken for somebody who has just arrived in town and is contemplating their next move. He takes out his phone and checks for an answer. There is none.

Grant is going to be pissed when he learns that he has given his protection team the slip, and has sneaked here to the station to try setting up an exchange of hostages. Maybe he has already been found missing from Emily's apartment and it has set off an alarm and there's a concerted effort to track him. To stop his phone from being located, he should turn it off and separate the parts; even then he's unsure if it will make the technology untraceable. But then he might miss a return call from Emily's abductors, meaning that sneaking out of the apartment, evading the cops, and more importantly the killer, and coming here will have been pointless.

The smokers stub out their cigarettes underfoot. They move away, towing an acerbic cloud past Nate. He wrinkles his nose at the smell, though not totally in distaste: he's tempted to beg a cigarette from the couple; a nicotine kick will help calm him, and maybe relieve his jitters.

His actions are risky, and could get him flayed alive, but his shaking isn't caused through personal fear. At first it was through worry for Emily, and then through frustration and anger, but lastly it has been solely through the mounting flood of endorphins coursing through his body. There had been times during his police career when he'd felt the prolonged effects of adrenalin, usually through anticipation of trouble ahead. It was the same now, only magnified tenfold, but instead of calming down the effects, he should welcome them. In its simplest form, the effect of adrenalin on the human body is widely known as 'fight or flight', and it is what feeds the natural instinct to survive, a throwback to when man was predated upon by sabre-toothed cats and other prehistoric monsters. In his case, Nate's putting himself directly into the jaws of his hunter, taking away his option for either response, but if it helps free Emily, so be it. Besides, once he knows she's out of harm's way, let anyone confuse him for a willing sacrifice and they'll learn how wrong they are.

He again looks at his phone.

It vibrates in his hand; the movement is startling and he almost casts it away. Shock over, he lifts it up to better see the screen and is disappointed to see that the number calling isn't Emily's. At first he thinks it could be Grant or Kylie ringing, either to check on his welfare or to bollock him for ducking out of Emily's apartment on this hare-brained rescue attempt. No, it isn't either police officer calling, because their numbers are also in his call list. Maybe the call is from another officer, maybe the one he'd given his statement to, wishing to follow up on a point or two.

He stares at the vibrating phone.

On a normal day he rarely receives calls, maybe he'll get one from a telemarketing company, or scammer, but most usually it's from his co-worker, Jim Powell, urging Nate to join him for a pint at the local pub. Unless he has changed his number since yesterday morning, then it isn't Powell calling.

The phone continues to vibrate.

Nate takes a surreptitious check around. The smoking couple has disappeared and none of the taxi drivers is interested in him. He hits the answer button, holds the phone to his ear and waits.

THIRTY-SIX

While training and then practising as a social anthropologist Emily Prince had studied both the best and worst of the human species. On the latter subject she had seen how even intelligent, genuinely decent people could be reprogrammed or coerced into acts that would normally be alien and despicable to them. She didn't have to look much further than Nazi Germany to see how ordinary people could be swayed by an enigmatic leader, to carry out acts of murder and extreme depravity on an unbelievably horrific scale. She doubted that more than a handful of those responsible for the Holocaust began the process with genocide in mind, and most gradually morphed into monsters a tiny step at a time with each order they obeyed. The very same was probably true of Weyland Berith's followers, or more currently the followers of whomever was in line to absorb the angelic spirit they believed had resided within him. She imagined that some of them had been lonely and lost individuals who'd been seeking a tribe to belong to, who had been reeled in and recruited through the appeal of the dark fantasy that the Berith cult was built upon. What had probably begun as a way for them to hang out with others of a similar disposition had likely grown daily, weekly, yearly into a complete lifestyle based on the indoctrination and dogma of their leader and his lieutenants. From experience she knew that many cults employed brainwashing techniques in order to fully control their members: at first it was all about reward, soon the carrot was replaced by the stick, and often it ended with complete control through blackmail and intimidation. People forced to perform minor illegal acts could soon be manipulated into carrying out more serious offences through fear of their previous misdemeanours coming to light. Their descent into depravity was a self-propagating phenomenon.

So, originally these people could have been decent, law-abiding individuals, and it was purely the bullying and strong-arm tactics of their nefarious leaders that had led them to forcefully drag her from her home and into the back of a car against her will, so perhaps she shouldn't hold it personally against them. Like hell, she won't! She has no pity for their situation when her own plight exponentially trumps theirs. Whether these were once good people forced to perform evil deeds, abducting her is still fucking evil! Especially when the end result could find her skinned alive, beheaded or gutted like some of their previous victims.

Initially the shock of being grabbed had cowed her – that time that she was attacked when attempting to interview a violent criminal had left its traumatic hooks in her. As the couple had scrambled to each get a hold on her, she should've screamed for Nate to help her. But as it had when that awful prisoner had lunged at her, her body had frozen as solidly as the thoughts in her mind; her throat had constricted and – rather than emitting an anguished scream, she'd barely been able to squeak. The tiny noise of alarm wouldn't have carried beyond the hall, let alone to the back of her apartment and through the bathroom door to Nate's ears. For seconds she had been unable to muster a defence, and the only resistance she'd offered was to sink her weight, and drag the doormat with her to the threshold before she was bodily yanked out on to the landing and down the stairs. Her throat had stayed pinched, making breathing difficult, and darkness had edged her vision. By the time they had manhandled her down to the riverside, and a car had swept towards them, the couple had full control of Emily's arms and head. One of them clenched her hair in a grasp that threatened not only to rip her hair out by its roots, but with a swift wrench could snap her neck. She was shoved face first into the car – it was a large thing, perhaps some kind of people-carrier, and it had had some of the rear seats removed. She was crushed under the man holding her hair, while the other person – a woman – released her arms to close the doors. A third abductor was the driver, and there was a fourth, another woman, who encouraged haste. Before Emily could find her voice, she felt the car reversing, and then it shot away from the Tyne to who-knew-where.

When she has a big man sitting on top of her, his palm forcing her head flat into the rough carpet, there is no need for a blindfold or even a gag. She can't see much beyond the man's shoes. Her mouth has been mashed against the floor most of the journey, and for every time it has been freed for a few seconds, she has spent the time trying to breathe or spitting dirt, lint and dog hairs out of her mouth. Her cheek has been rubbed raw too, and she's certain that it is going to scab from being abraded so much . . . supposing she lives long enough for the healing process to begin.

She hasn't a clue how long it is since the two presented at her front door, holding up what she mistakenly took to be police warrant cards, in order to lure her out. The bastards had dropped names, DCI Openshaw and DS McMahon, lending to the ruse, and she'd genuinely believed that they were detectives sent by Grant to update them after Will Ballard's escape. Since opening the door, and being grabbed and forced to their getaway car, an hour could have passed, or many hours. Hell, the way the nightmare played on her mind, she could have been a hostage for days already, her situation felt that interminable. Of course, she is thinking illogically. It isn't days, or even several hours, it's unlikely to be more than one or two. However much time has passed, there's been ample to leave Newcastle and drive a fair distance away. Even if Will Ballard had based himself in Sunderland, and that the murder of Darren Sykes had happened in her hometown, it doesn't mean that the killer has stayed local. More likely he's fled the scene, and left the dirty work of abduction to these brainwashed minions. Alternatively they could have been driving around, awaiting further instructions, and travelled no further than the city limits: there is no way of confirming where she is while flat on the floor of the car.

Finally there's a noticeable lessening of pressure on her ribs, and her guard even releases her head so that she can breathe a little easier. She's tempted to try rolling on to her back and sitting up, but that is tempting a second squashing from her large abductor. She stays face down, only allowing her head to rise a few centimetres. She looks around, but it's too dark in the back to see anything. Her hearing seems more acute than ever, as does her other senses: she can feel a hand worming under her, checking her pockets for items.

'Do you have a phone?' It's a woman that speaks, and not the one who'd assisted the big man. It's the one from the front who had earlier advised them to hurry.

Emily does have her mobile on her. If she denies it, and they find it, perhaps she'll be punished for lying.

'Front left pocket,' she says, her voice brittle.

The hand searching her switches position, and digs for her phone. Earlier, at the scene of Will Ballard's arrest, she'd witnessed how quickly she could become embroiled in a scuffle. So after last using it, Emily had secured her phone in her front jeans pocket, rather than risk losing it from its usual place in a hip pocket where it could easily fall out. She'd forgotten that her phone was there, but even if it had come to mind, there hadn't been an opportunity to use it. She lifts her pelvis, arching her back, allowing her searcher to free the phone.

Once the woman has it, she sinks down under the palm of the big man, his hand having transferred to her backside: there's nothing sexual about his touch, not like when she was assaulted by the prisoner; simply it was the perfunctory act of somebody experienced in handling captives, but she shivers all the same.

Her phone gets passed forward.

'You gotta be kiddin' me,' says the woman up front in an accent.

'Looks as if we might just have won the lottery,' says the first woman.

'You can say that again,' agrees the second woman.

Emily has no idea what has excited them so much.

The big man offers a clue. 'You gonna call him back, Zandra?'

Apparently somebody has tried calling her phone, and it is obvious to Emily that it would've been one of Nate's first reactions after finding her missing.

'Not yet,' says the woman named Zandra. 'I'd let him do it himself when we get back, but won't it be neat if we take him the prize?'

Him. The killer. It's obvious to Emily who Zandra is referring to. She can't think of a single other reason why she has been forcefully abducted, other than to be used by the killer as bait to lure Nate to his death.

'You don't need me,' she croaks.

'Be quiet.' The big man leans down on her, crushing the wind from her lungs.

Emily croaks again. 'You have my phone and a way of contacting him. You don't need me any more.'

'You were told to be quiet.' The big man cuffs her head, bouncing her chin off the floor.

'Steady on, Robin,' says the woman in the back. 'We were warned not to harm her.'

'Didn't harm her,' grunts Robin. 'Just makin' sure she knows the rules.' He crouches, aiming a locally accented whisper at Emily. 'Quiet means quiet, y'kna, hinny?'

His words send a shiver of terror through her. Hinny is a Geordie term of affection, derived from honey, but it's also the name given to the offspring of a male horse and a female donkey: from the research she'd conducted for DI Jeff Brady, she knows all about the ass's decapitated head placed on the shoulders of a previous victim, and fears a similar fate. She fights down the terror, determined not to show weakness to her captors.

'This is wrong,' she says defiantly.

'Fuck sake, what about bein' quiet don't you understand?' the man growls.

Emily tenses for another cuff of his big palm, but it doesn't happen. She senses as much as feels that the woman beside him has taken hold of his wrist and drawn it away. The woman's action is a chink that Emily can perhaps work on, widening it ever further until she's convinced to be an ally against the other abductors.

'This is wrong,' Emily repeats, 'and you all know it. You do understand that you're all going to prison for kidnapping, don't you?'

When none of them answers, she goes on, 'Even if none of you actually harm me, you will still be charged as accomplices of the murderer and will go to prison. Is that what you want? Do you want to spend the rest of your days behind bars?'

'If I must, I must,' says the big man, sounding exactly like a brainwashed automaton from a sci-fi movie.

The woman in the back doesn't appear to be as keen on going to prison. She shuffles around, and it's probably more about gathering her thoughts than it is finding a more comfortable position. She croaks, 'You do understand that there's more chance of getting out of this unharmed if you keep your mouth shut like you've been told. Keep talking and see what happens.'

The woman's voice wavers towards the end, as if she isn't prepared to be the one to carry out the prophecy. Emily doesn't miss it, and again wonders if she should be the one to pick at.

'You don't sound as if you enjoy violence,' she says, 'so why are you helping a killer?'

The big man clamps his hand over the back of her skull and forces Emily down.

At first she thinks it's because she pushed too far, but no. Within seconds she notices a riot of darting shadows and lights in the back of the car, a strobing effect of black and blue, and then the source of the emergency lights sweeps past. She hasn't a clue if the lights were from a police, ambulance or fire service vehicle, but the appearance of it has thrown momentary concern at her abductors. Even as the emergency vehicle continues away, the pressure on her doesn't lessen, while there's a babble of four voices as her captors rush to express their worries. Emily is reminded that these are possibly originally decent people forced into depravity and fearful of the consequences.

'You see?' she demands. 'The next time you might not be as lucky, and you will get stopped.'

'Shut up!' A fist digs into her side with enough force to make her squirm. The hand is too small to be that of the big man. That's OK; it adds to the fact that her anxiety is getting at the woman, and helping to soften her resolve.

Sadly, she might need more time to work on the woman than she has left, because from the shift in atmosphere, and the way in which they all talk now in hushed whispers, she senses that they are approaching the car's destination: hopefully it won't be her final stop.

THIRTY-SEVEN

Central Station, Neville Street

'Talk about an ambush,' Nate says into his phone.

'You're bloody lucky you haven't been the victim of a real ambush,' DCI Openshaw replies. Apparently Grant has guessed that Nate might not reply if he saw either his or Kylie McMahon's number on the screen, so had chosen to make contact on another phone. 'What the hell are you thinking, Nate? I'm trying to protect you and you're only making things very difficult for me.'

'I've told you before, I don't need your protection, Grant. It's Emily who needs protecting and this is the best way I can think of.'

'By sacrificing yourself?'

'We've gone over this already too. I've no intention of sacrificing myself. As soon as Emily is safe, I'll show that I'm not going to go quietly.'

'Nate, you're delusional, mate. If you think they're going to let her go, and then allow you an opportunity to escape, think again.'

'They aren't dealing with a frightened woman this time, or an unsuspecting jogger they ambushed in the dark,' Nate says.

'That's exactly why they'll be more cautious. Nate, they'll probably immobilize, if not kill you outright, the instant they have you.'

'That's a wild assumption,' says Nate.

'It's an assumption based on facts. All the previous victims have been jumped, usually beaten unconscious, and then taken to a prearranged location to be skinned and displayed. You don't think a similar fate has been planned for when they get their hands on you?'

'Before I'm killed they'll want to get Will first. I'm not being conceited when I say that I'm literally the icing on the cake for them. Without my seal their grimoire is incomplete, and will be useless to the rite. Without harvesting Will's seal, it's pointless for them having mine.'

'Need I remind you that they might already have Will?'

'I don't think it was the killer who took him.'

'Fair enough, I'm kind of leaning towards it being some of his own pals who broke him out. See, it's likely that he's the killer, and he's got his minions prepped to take his seal the moment they have you.'

'William isn't the killer.'

'You keep saying that, but each time you say it you sound less certain. If you'd seen what I did at his apartment, and know what I found there, then you'd have no doubt of his guilt.'

'I'm guessing you found something tying him to the Berith cult.'

'It was more than that, Nate. I found physical evidence of his involvement.'

'As in?'

'I shouldn't really say . . .'

'But you're going to have to.'

'Yes.' Grant changes tack. 'What do you know about processing hides for vellum?'

'I'd guess that the hide is cleaned, stretched and dried, maybe subjected to a chemical process?'

'Do you know what a *lunellum* is?'

'Something to do with the moon?'

'It's a moon-shaped blade used to scrape the hides clean.'

'Yeah, now that you mention it, I remember seeing several of them when I was a child back on Ohop Island.'

'At his apartment, his pals tried removing and then burning the evidence, but missed Will's *lunellum*. I'm waiting on forensics, but I'm confident that they'll find damning DNA evidence on the blade. You said the killer's making a grimoire out of the victim's skins . . . why else would Will have a *lunellum* unless he's processing it into vellum?'

Nate has no answer, so stays silent.

'Got you worried, have I?' There's nothing smug about Grant's words; if anything he sounds regretful about having to slap Nate with the horrible truth.

'If Will's the killer, it actually helps me,' Nate says.

'How?'

'Because I don't think he will have me killed straight away. After all these years, he'll want to speak with me. Either to gloat or to maybe even try explaining himself.'

'Now who is making assumptions?'

'Twenty-odd years have passed since he's seen me. It stands to reason that he'll have lots of questions he wants answers to.'

'You don't think he can ask them while he's skinning you alive?'

The scenario Grant paints is so vivid that Nate imagines his blood in vivid splashes: instead of terrifying him it elicits a short, sharp bark of incredulity.

'You sound as if you aren't taking this seriously,' Grant says.

'Of course I am,' Nate replies. 'I just have no intention of letting things get that far.'

'It'll be out of your hands, Nate. You can't control the situation, not when dealing with these maniacs. Don't forget, it won't only be your brother that you have to contend with, his followers have shown themselves to be as deviant, capable and dangerous as he is.'

A voice draws Nate's attention for only the briefest of moments. It's only an announcement made over a tannoy in the station behind him. He swaps the phone to his opposite side. Despite the chill, his right palm and right ear have grown warm and sticky. He says, 'Will's followers might not follow him if they learn of another more fitting receptacle for Berith's spirit.'

There's a second of silence before Grant snaps, 'You can't be bloody serious?'

'Why not? If we were still active members of the cult, I'd be next in line, being as I'm the first son of Weyland Berith's closest disciples.' Nate snorts. 'Don't worry, Grant, I'm not serious about claiming the crown, but they needn't know that. I can probably stall them long enough to free Emily and find a safe way out for us.'

'Abso-fucking-lutely not,' Grant almost shouts. There's another voice in the background, but this time it is on the DCI's end. The voice is barely audible, but for two words: Neville Street.

Nate peers across the road. He needn't double-check the street sign on a building opposite him, as it had already impinged on him, but yes, Newcastle's Central Station is located on Neville Street.

'Are you tracking my phone?' he demands.

'What did you expect, Nate, after trying to give your protection detail the slip?'

'I expected you to try tracing Emily's phone!'

'You don't think I can do both?'

'That's not the point. Don't waste time worrying about me. The priority right now is Emily.'

'So let me concentrate on finding her. You were brought in as a consultant, and are therefore under my supervision. I've a duty of care towards you, and I can't protect you when you're off haring around the bloody city like this. What are you doing at the station, Nate? And don't try bluffing, I heard those tannoy announcements earlier, and guessed where you were before DS McMahon was able to confirm it. What's your plan? Catch the train back to Carlisle, then try luring Will and his helpers to a showdown in the woods?'

'That idea was never on my mind, but now that you mention it . . .'

'Don't you bloody dare. I'm sending a car to pick you up. Stay right there, Nate, or so help me I'll—'

'There's nothing you can threaten me with that's more frightening than having my skin flayed from me, and right now I'm not letting even that slow me. Sorry, Grant, but don't bother sending a car, 'cause I won't be here when it arrives.'

'That's not acceptable, Nate. Now stay put or—'

Nate hits the end call button.

It's tempting to turn off the phone, but he knows that even triangulating the area in which his phone can be found will be vague enough, especially when a bobby sent to pick him up hasn't direct access to the computer screen showing its location. He strides across Neville Street, and stands in the doorway of a shop that had closed hours earlier. He doesn't have to run and hide; it's better that he avoids any suspicious behaviour and hides in plain sight.

It's only minutes before a police car approaches along the street, slowing as it passes the parked taxis. The constable in the car searches for Nate, but has nothing but a brief description to go on. There are several men in the vicinity, most of them drivers standing around chatting, and they draw the cop's attention. Nate remains undetected in the shadowed doorway. The constable parks his vehicle and heads inside the station. Nate again crosses the street, back to where he had stood near to the smoking couple. He can see the police officer, who makes a cursory check of the entranceway before keying his radio and reporting back to his controller. He's obviously told to continue his search as he heads into the station and on to the nearest platform, where Nate can no longer see him.

His phone vibrates again.

This time it isn't an unknown number.

Emily is calling.

No, of course it's not Emily.

It's Emily's abductors.

THIRTY-EIGHT

Leazes Park, Newcastle upon Tyne

There were times as a child when Nate had believed that there was truth in Weyland Berith's claim to being the avatar of the Canaanite angel, Ba'al Berith, but his belief, even then, had easily been eroded. It didn't take long to figure that Weyland was seriously deluded – though not as madly as those closest to him, namely Nate and Will's parents – and his claims of divinity were about playing the part and holding power and control over his sycophantic followers. Emily would probably agree that most cult leaders were intelligent psychopaths, who got off as much on the power they wielded as from the sexual favours they demanded, the riches they stole, or the worship bestowed upon them. Weyland was no more a heavenly creature than Nate, and it doesn't matter how much magic is believed to be contained in this latest claimant to the title's grimoire, they won't become one either.

It's hard for Nate to believe that anybody can put any faith in ancient magic these days. How can they believe that their soul will meld with that of an angelic being, making them one, and bestowing on them power rivalling that of a god? They must be as deluded as Weyland was, and every bit as batshit insane.

Come the winter solstice, there is not going to be any metaphysical bonding of human and divine beings, but does it matter? As long as the killer believes in this bullshit then Emily, William – it's still difficult for him to separate his little brother from the probability he's the killer – and Nate are still at risk. The grimoire will be as much use as a fake prop in a B-horror movie, and even to the killer it will be useless unless complete: he will endeavour to collect all the covenants from all the Children of Hamor, Nate's certain, to ensure that his followers fully buy into the dark fantasy he is selling them.

For now, it appears that his followers have complete faith in whatever lies he is peddling, and that they will be *favoured* once they assist his earthly avatar to align with the divine Berith.

Whatever has earned their complete devotion, it is complete bullshit, Nate knows, but sadly, bullshit often trumps sense. These people, given an order by their leader, will happily skin him alive. They will happily behead Emily, and offer up her decapitated skull, the way in which the Shechemites had offered up the head of an ass to Ba'al Berith in ancient times.

So why go through with his crazy plan and hand himself over to these nutjobs? Grant Openshaw's right, it won't be only William, or whomever the killer is, he'll have to contend with. He's afraid. Who in their right minds wouldn't be? But he isn't prepared to give in to his fear when there's a slim chance he can free Emily, and escape with her. Grant argued that he has a duty of care towards Nate; well, the same can be said of Nate's duty to Emily. The way he sees it is that she was under his protection and he failed her. This is about redemption, doing the right thing, saving her from certain death. An image of Special Agent Milo Turrell flashes through his memories: the agent is shouting, his lips moving, but he is soundless. And yet Nate hears the *thwuck* as his mother's knife buries deep into the agent's throat; hears the *slushk* as it parts his skin, hears the *burrrabbblle* of blood gushing out and spattering the floor and window frame.

The memory sickens him, but it is only the first in a parade of images and sounds that assail him: he sees the Onatade tragedy play out again, Henry opening his wife's throat a second before Nate can shoot; he imagines the murders of Darren Sykes and the other victims, pictures their deaths as if he's a silent observer, while he hears their cries of torment as their skin is sliced from their bodies, hears the dribbling of spilled blood and emptied bladders.

The images are atrocious, the soundtrack worse, but rather than send him scurrying back to the relative safety of Emily's apartment, they have the opposite effect. Each cut of a knife, each droplet of shed blood, angers Nate, and the angrier he grows, the more determined he becomes that he is going to put a stop to this horror. He failed to shoot Henry Onatade in time, pity he doesn't have access to his MP5 Carbine now because he'll happily drop as many of the killer's followers that stand between him and Emily.

He walks.

He has spoken with her abductors on his phone, and the instructions he was given were clear, concise and brooked no deviation.

He was given a location to meet, a timescale of less than thirty minutes to reach it, and a warning that even the faintest sniff of a cop will have dire consequences for Emily.

It's crazy that her abductors haven't yet rid themselves of her phone, and that his instructions didn't include dumping his phone the second after they ended the call. Nate's no idiot: once they have him, they will strip him of his phone and probably the other items carried in his pockets – wallet, change, half a roll of mints – so the longer he keeps control of it, the better. What was it that Grant exclaimed when asked why he wasn't tracing Emily's phone? *'You don't think I can do both?'* Nate hopes that after losing his hunters back at the railway station, a fresh attempt has been made at locating his phone. For a while he's carried it in his hand, but there's no expectation that Emily's abductors will call again, and if Grant or Kylie does then he can't answer. He ducks into the doorway of a shop and stuffs the phone deep down in the front of his jeans, ensuring that it is as snug to his groin as is comfortable. In his day-to-day duties as a copper, Nate had regularly conducted body searches of suspicious individuals. It was especially important that anyone detained was checked for weapons, illegal substances, syringes, and any other item that might prove harmful to the suspect or to the arresting officers. As experienced as he had become, there were times when even he had missed a concealed item, and it was through the human reticence to touch the intimate areas of another person without prior permission or encouragement. Most hidden weapons and contraband smuggled into prisons tend to be concealed in or around the genitals and anus. Nate trusts that he will be searched, but he will also wager his pension that the searcher goes nowhere near his man-bits.

He has been directed north, to skirt the town centre via St James' Boulevard to the grounds of Newcastle United Football Club, and then beyond. His instructions specifically direct him into Leazes Park, and on to the trails surrounding the lake with an island at its heart. He is not much more than a hard stone's throw from the Royal Victoria Infirmary and potentially hundreds of witnesses, but because of the trees and shrubbery around the lake, he could be miles outside the city in the countryside.

He has arrived as instructed, within the timescale set by the woman on the other end of the phone. He stands on an intersection of paths, adjacent to a Victorian-era lodge, converted these days to a quirky themed café, now securely locked up for the night. He can smell the lake water, which isn't unpleasant, and also the aroma from an overflowing rubbish bin, which is. His sense of smell is working on overdrive, but is probably the least sensitive of his senses just now: his vision, hearing, touch are all acute to the approaching danger, and his taste is almost overpowered by the acidic bile that bubbles in his trachea.

He stands there for minutes.

He has been warned not to do anything except wait.

Really he should have made a brief exploration of his surroundings so he has a better understanding of them, but in hindsight he probably hasn't missed much. The park is shut, the lights around the lake doused, but there is still enough ambient light to see by, and besides, the streetlamps on the roads surrounding the park cast their glow deep inside. From his place near to the lake, he can make out the looming football stadium to one side, and a walkway going towards the infirmary on the other. Directly beyond the lodge there is a pay-and-display car park, empty of vehicles at this late hour. He assumes that Emily's captors will use the car park, and is tempted to relocate to it, but stays put. He was told where to wait and it's important he's seen to obey: they're more likely to expect him to be on his worst behaviour if he acts obstructive from the start.

A chill settles over him.

He can feel hoarfrost in his hair, and wonders now why he didn't keep hold of the hat he'd liberated from the hamper in Emily's apartment. He's grateful for the extra sweater as it helps keep in the warmth where his own jacket is unzipped. He leaves the jacket open on purpose: he needs freedom of movement more than he does an extra layer against the cold.

His mobile phone is hot against his crotch. Maybe he should have switched it off, rather than allow it to overheat. He imagines the battery discharging and burning his flesh. It is a concern but he's willing to chance it. He wonders if Grant has tried calling him again, if there are a number of missed calls now listed in the app. He's pretty confident that his old supervisor will have doubled down on locating the phone now that Nate has definitely gone off the reservation. He counts on it.

Footsteps approach.

They are heavy and confident.

He turns and faces a duo of men approaching from the depths of Leazes Park. He keeps his hands by his sides, palms open to show he is unarmed. The men halt ten metres away, one middle-aged, the other little more than a teenager. They stare at him like he's an extraterrestrial being that has just beamed down from a flying saucer. These men had not expected him to be here, and he realizes that they are not the people he is expecting. He raises a hand and waves dismissively. They begin walking again, their faces averted, and he guesses that they'd hoped to keep their rendezvous in the park a secret. They pick up speed, their shoes rapping on the tarmac. The sound echoes off the nearby trees and is echoed by the quacking of fowl on the lake, partially tamed ducks that have forgone flying south for winter.

He waits again.

At a guess he'd say that he was forced to march here at speed so he would have no opportunity to form a contingency or to reach out for help. On the other hand, time was on their side, and making him wait was probably another deliberate move to keep him under control. Right then, he supposes that he is being observed, that Emily's captors are conducting reconnaissance of the area to ensure that he has obeyed instructions. For a moment he worries that they might have spotted the two men and formed an opinion that they are undercover cops. No, it is unlikely. More likely they are forcing him to sweat until they are good and ready to move.

Sirens sound and blue lights dance, but they're only from an ambulance darting along the nearby road. They soon diminish as the ambulance makes a couple of turns.

Nate scans around him.

The ducks on the lake have fallen silent, subdued rather than alarmed by the sirens. From a distance he hears high-pitched laughter as a bunch of young women share a humorous story. The sound of traffic is constant, even at this late hour. He looks through a gap in the bushes towards the car park. It still appears empty: does a barrier secure the car park during the hours of darkness? He takes a few steps towards the path leading to the hospital, altering his vantage point, and now sees a vehicle has crept undetected into the park. It has its lights off, but he can still make out the shapes of figures seated in the front and back. He watches, and it's another thirty or more seconds before the front passenger door opens and the internal light glows. The passenger slips out, and at the same time a second person gets out the back: the latter has to literally unfold their frame, they are so tall and bulky. The other back door opens and another, lithe figure dashes away; there one second, gone the next. Most likely they have the task of circumnavigating Nate and guarding the approaches from the lakeside.

Nate ensures they see him the moment that the two from the front of the car approach from the side of the lodge. Again he displays his empty palms, this time spreading his arms wider too. The couple is a woman and man, and if they are crazy cultists there's nothing to set them apart from any other regular Joe he might pass in the street. He keeps his eyes fixed on the woman, avoiding eye contact with the giant at her side but fully aware of his presence. The man breathes heavily, and his fingers curl open and shut, as if he's tempted to spring on Nate and crush him with his boxing-glove-sized hands. When he'd argued with Grant that they wouldn't find him a willing sacrifice, he hadn't expected to have to fight a brute as big as a grizzly bear.

The duo moves in unison.

Nate keeps his gaze trained as they approach, and the more he stares the more certain he grows that the woman's face is familiar. He just can't pinpoint where, or how recently he's seen it. Considering that most of his last few days have been taken up in police stations or in the company of coppers, he is concerned that the woman must be an insider and the realization makes his blood boil.

'I've done as you said,' Nate begins, 'now where's Emily?'

'Hush now,' says the woman in reply.

Her voice instantly takes the heat out of him, not by any calming effect but because he's surprised by her accent.

He swallows, and it's a struggle because of how tight his windpipe has become.

The woman stops, but waves the big man forward.

'Arms in the air,' the man orders.

'You won't find anything,' Nate says, barely concerned by the big man's looming approach. He tries to see past him, intent on scrutinizing the woman's face again.

She stares back at him. Her eyes reflect the glow of distant streetlamps but are devoid of warmth. Her teeth are set in a grimace, forming tight folds in the skin to each side of her nostrils. The left side of her face is puckered and shiny in places. She has deliberately pulled back her hair and pushed it under a beanie hat to make her less identifiable, but he knows her.

He steps towards her, one hand reaching in question.

'Robin,' the woman snaps curtly.

The big man swipes at him, knocks his hand aside, and half spins Nate around.

'Hey!' Nate says. 'There's no need for the rough stuff. I told you I'd come quietly if you released Emily.'

'Shut your mouth, and don't move.'

As expected, the big man called Robin pats him down, and takes away his wallet. Maybe the big fella worked the doors or mall security before turning his hand to henchman, because he conducts a more thorough search than most untrained people would. However, other than a quick pat of his pockets, he barely touches Nate below the waistband or above the knee.

'Where's your phone?' Robin demands as he flicks through the contents of Nate's wallet.

'I threw it in the lake.'

'Bollocks.'

Nate opens his hands.

'Turn out your pockets.'

'Sure.' Nate does as asked, and drops a few coins and a partially eaten roll of mints on the floor. He pulls the inner material out, leaves them hanging like a bloodhound's ears.

'You threw your cell in the lake?' The woman sounds incredulous, and probably rightly so.

'I didn't want to hold on to something that might compromise Emily's safety. You know the cops can trace phones, right?'

She nods, a barely perceptible jerk of her chin.

Nate says, 'I got rid of mine so that you know you can trust me to uphold our bargain. What about you, can I trust you to uphold yours?'

'Emily is safe.'

'No. Before I come with you, I need proof that she's free, proof that she's alive.'

'You're just gunna have to tack oor word for it, man,' says Robin. He grabs Nate's wrist.

'Hands off!' Nate twists his arm, at the same time using a pivot on a heel to employ the entirety of his bodyweight to help get free of the grip. Robin chases him, hand groping to regain a hold.

Nate skips aside nimbly, leaving the big man off balance.

When Robin turns to confront him, there's a promise of brutal violence in his eyes.

Nate's fists rise.

'Try touching me again, I swear I'll break your nose.'

'Ya little shit,' Robin barks and lunges in.

Nate jabs with his left hand, stopping Robin sharp in his tracks, and in perfect range for a snapping right. His fist smashes into the bridge of the big man's nose. Robin rocks back on his heels, legs stiff, his eyes unfocused. As he finally coughs in shock, blood floods from both nostrils.

'Don't say I didn't warn you.' Nate doesn't lower his fists, but neither does he try hurting Robin again.

Robin cups his face with his hands. Blood dribbles between his fingers. He looks across at the woman as he backs away. Judging by his reaction, Robin's probably the type that uses his size to intimidate and doesn't have to get physical very often. By comparison, Nate is experienced in dealing with violent individuals: he holds no fear of a big shambling punk like Robin. 'That's right, keep backing off,' he says directly to him, 'you aren't dealing with a defenceless woman this time.'

'Neither are you,' says the woman, and Nate snaps his attention to her and is shocked at who greets him. Hers is a face he hasn't seen since they were kids. He'd always believed she'd perished in the fire, but apparently she survived and grew to adulthood. She has slipped a weapon from her pocket: it glints as she aims its point at his stomach. As dismissive as he's just been towards Robin, he can't afford to underestimate the efficacy of a knife in her hand. Confidence radiates from her: by all accounts Cassandra has grown adept with a blade since escaping Ohop Island.

'You won't need that yet,' he assures her, and opens his hands to placate her. 'All you need to do is prove to me that Emily has been released unharmed and I'll go with you.'

'As my big buddy just said, you're gonna have to take my word for it.'

Nate shakes his head. 'Nope. That isn't good enough, Cassandra.'

She snorts. 'So you do recognize me?'

'You know I recognized you the instant I laid eyes on you.'

'It has been such a long time,' she says, 'but I have to admit, even if I didn't know who you were already, I would've recognized you in a crowd.'

'I guess with you being around my brother so much, I'd look familiar to you, regardless of how many years have passed.'

'Are you talking about William?' She laughs, but it's a nasty sound. 'Jeez, he used to follow me everywhere like a lovesick puppy! Do you remember how he tried to defend me from that stinking Fed?'

'You were our friend,' Nate says.

'No, that's untrue. We were never friends. We were thrown together because we were chosen. We were the Children of Hamor, we were *promised*.'

'I see you still believe that bullshit as much as you did back then.'

'My faith is strong.'

'Have you already had your covenant excised from your back, or are you just going to lie down and let it be cut from you once you hand me over? You're going to die, don't you get it?'

'I'm going to be raised up to sit on Berith's right hand.'

'You're being played for a fool by a madman, Cassandra.'

She points the knife at his chest. 'You are the fool, Nathaniel. I must say, you come across as much as a lovesick puppy as William ever did. Who is this Emily Prince to you that you'd willingly exchange your life for hers?'

'She's an innocent in all this, and I won't be exchanging places until I know she has been safely released.'

'So you say.'

There's a split-second where Nate understands his mistake. He has kept Cassandra talking, while keeping an eye on Robin – since having his nose broken, the big man has shown no enthusiasm for another fight. He has forgotten that a third person alighted the car. He turns, his right hand coming up to ward off a blow, but it's too late.

Something solid caroms off the side of his head.

Maybe if Robin was the one clubbing him, he'd be unconscious after the first strike of the club, but it's a much smaller person who hits him, a woman weighing less than fifty-five kilos: she strikes him another four times and even then Nate resists the darkness. However, now that he is being beaten down, Robin rallies from tending to his nose and rushes in, pounding Nate across the nape with the weight of a meaty forearm. Nate sprawls on the path, and Robin and the woman continue raining blows down on him. Even Cassandra moves in, but thankfully she has stowed away her knife. She produces plastic cable ties, and while her friends hold him down, she secures his wrists and ankles.

Nate's oblivious to further ignominious treatment as he's carted back to the waiting car – Robin grasping his jacket collar one-handed while tending his bleeding nose with the other, the women each grasping an ankle – and dumped inside next to Emily's unmoving body.

THIRTY-NINE

Forth Banks Police Station
Central Newcastle

There are times during any rapidly developing incident where those expected to be in control can only stand a moment, blink in astonishment and shake their heads. It's only once evidence and information are collated and absorbed, that some sort of counter-action can be launched. Often, when so many high-ranking officers converge in one place, the response is hampered by the natural reaction of people waiting for answers they don't possess but hope somebody more informed in the room does. There's often stalling tactics employed by those who should be in the know while they try to get their heads together, and often they need a metaphorical kick in the pants by the most superior ranks in the room demanding immediate action.

On those occasions it is as if the world is also kick-started, and sharp minds get to work once more. DCI Grant Openshaw is as easily mired as anyone else, so he too gives a mental jerk in response as those in the major incident room erupt into action, galvanized by a single bark from the chief constable. He doesn't stay in the room, he's not the designated gold commander and, being as he is NCA rather than Northumberland police, nobody challenges his exit. Kylie McMahon follows, and the way in which she repeatedly exhales in a staccato rhythm suggests she's relieved to be out of there.

Grant's happy to leave. He has briefed the room with what is going on with Nate Freeman, and his report went down like the proverbial lead balloon. With a gruesome murder, a prisoner escape, and the probable kidnapping of Emily Prince to contend with, the last thing the locals need is a loose cannon taking matters into their own hands. Grant promised he would deal with Nate. To that end, Grant also assured them that the majority of resources he needs access to are already available to him via those seconded to the NCA taskforce at Greater Manchester Police HQ.

Techs from the National Cyber Crime Unit are deep-diving the deep web, chasing the crumbs scattered behind Baphomet and Nephilim, with the aim of identifying the players. Once they have IP addresses, it is believed that physical, real-world addresses will follow.

In the meantime, Jeff Brady and Kylie McMahon double-team on trying to discover exact locations for Emily and Nate's phones. Minutes ago, both phones had apparently converged in Leazes Park for the briefest time, before they were again on the move. With modern technology there isn't the same need to ping a signal off nearby cell towers in order to triangulate a locale, when smartphones are tethered to global positioning satellites and can be pinpointed down to a few square metres. That said, the technology can still prove glitchy at inopportune times, and a signal can become disrupted, and DI Brady is also often a beat or two behind with his reports. Under the circumstances, Grant believes he can muster a response to throw a tightening ring around Emily and Nate's position, and stop their abductors, but he can't be certain that it will save their lives. Say, for instance, that their abductors are tech-wise and have deliberately placed the phones together and are now randomly driving them around while their owners have been spirited elsewhere in a different vehicle. Hell, Grant would've sneaked the phones into somebody else's car, and let some innocent person drive around with them, oblivious, and maybe that's what they've done too. Chasing the phones might prove to be a wild-goose chase but there's no way they can risk ignoring them.

Several times now, Grant has rebuffed Nate's idea to use him as bait. But that was before the pig-headed fool went and handed himself over. The scenario is entirely different now, and there's benefit in allowing events to play out a while longer. The last thing he wants is for either Emily or Nate to be harmed, but their current situation is out of his hands, so why not try to turn it to his advantage? The very instant the phones come to a halt, he'll personally lead the charge to liberate the captives. When it happens, they will likely be in the hands of the murderer, and Grant fully intends being there to arrest that sick bastard.

Outside in the car park, Grant stops to get his bearings. His Audi is parked adjacent to the old red-brick building, in the lea of one of many arches upholding a railway line. There are marked police vehicles on each side, parked snug enough that it will prove difficult getting in without leaving a mark on their paintwork. He curses in annoyance, but won't be deterred. He's none too gentle about the way he slides down the narrow gap and yanks open the driver's door. It dints the wing of the police van squeezing it. He catches a grimace from Kylie, who takes greater care about opening the door on her side. It's Grant's turn to exhale in staccato bursts: he has no right to be mad at the inconsiderate parking of the van, and deliberately leaving his mark on its paintwork is a childish act. Yet he can't help feeling that Emily and Nate might urgently need his help, and he can't afford to mess around while space is made for him to manoeuvre. He sticks one long leg inside the car, puffing and grunting as he squeezes the rest of his body inside. It's a struggle drawing his right foot through the narrow gap, and his knee reminds him that it isn't as stable as it once was. He hisses in pain.

'Hopefully this will lighten your mood,' says Kylie.

'What is it?' he asks, squinting at her phone.

She has been toggling between screens and there have been times where he's been unsure what exactly he was supposed to look at. She indicates a message overlaid over the top of the GPS map she and Jeff Brady have been scrutinizing.

She explains. 'Your NCCU guys have traced Baphomet to what amounts to a digital dead-letter drop. He – yes, it has been confirmed that Baphomet is a male – has taken great care to cover his tracks on this occasion, but from his activities on the original site it has proven simple enough to reverse his digital movements from other times before he got himself involved in this Berith carry-on. They've traced him to an IP address registered to a Blake Drummond.' She pauses, allowing the name to sink in.

'Doesn't mean anything to me,' he admits.

'It won't, but ask any copper in Carlisle and they'll probably tell you who Drummond is: he's one of the civvies that works on the front desk at Carlisle nick. It's apparent now that when he got online with Nephilim, he was talking about Nate, after Nate showed up at Carlisle nick and more or less blew his cover. The fact that he said he had information about *the brother* suggests that Nephilim isn't William Ballard, but somebody else entirely. We might have to start thinking differently, boss, and treat Will not as a suspect, or an escaped prisoner, but another abductee and potentially the latest murder victim.'

'And this news is supposed to lighten my mood?' he asks.

'We can have Drummond arrested and interviewed, press the bastard for information on Nephilim. I might be overstating his involvement, but I think Drummond has probably been digging around for more information and it was him who directed the killer's people to Doctor Prince's address. They probably went there with the intention of grabbing Nate, but were forced to take her instead when she answered the door. They were probably worried she'd kick up a stink if they tried getting past her to Nate.'

Never assume, never speculate, but he has to admit she is probably right. It jars with what was discovered at the house William Ballard had rented in Sunderland, but unless that *lunellum* comes back from forensics and is covered in the victims' DNA, he should give Will the benefit of the doubt.

Grant starts the car and pulls forward. There's not much room at the front to turn, with more police vehicles hemming in his Audi. He takes more care than before, and this time negotiates

the available space without causing further damage. An electronic
gate shudders open as he drives forward and trips a sensor.
'Wouldn't mind heading across to Carlisle and being the one to
put the thumbscrews on Blake Drummond,' he says, though he
knows he hasn't the time nor inclination to abandon the immediate hunt of Nate and Emily's phones. 'Maybe Jeff can travel
up to Carlisle, to make sure that he's asked the right questions.
Does he need to be on the other end of the phone to you all
night?'

His latter words are delivered with his tongue firmly in his
cheek. Jeff Brady, despite having the looks of a grumpy bulldog,
can be quite the charmer. Over the last forty-eight hours he has
had the pleasure of both Emily and Kylie's attention, and Grant
bets that the old devil has flirted shamelessly the entire time.

Sending DI Jeff Brady up the M6 perhaps isn't the best use
of Grant's resources. Jeff has proved to be a huge help during
this case, and is better suited continuing to helm the numerous
enquiries that Grant has had Kylie send him and is bound to
again before this is over. He isn't certain that he could've achieved
half of what he has done until now if not for Jeff's assistance,
and what would he have done without Kylie's help? He'd touched
lucky when her lazy-arsed superior, Ray Logan, seconded the
DS to him.

As if sensing she was the object of his thoughts, Kylie looks
across at him. He returns the look.

'What?' he asks.

'Do you want me to ask Jeff to do the interview or not?' she
prompts.

'No, I'm sure Carlisle CID can handle it. Jeff can coordinate
from his end, so that everyone's up to speed on what Drummond's
done.'

'Boss,' she says.

She types a message, rather than speaks directly with Jeff. It's so
she doesn't lose attention from the map she's still scrutinizing.

'It looks as if they're travelling west,' she says after another
minute. 'Interestingly they're not far from Nuns Moor, where
Darren Sykes was ambushed and taken.'

'It's doubtful that it's their destination this time. Don't forget,
after he was grabbed, they took Sykes to that disused railway
building.'

Kylie nods several times, and another minute or so passes. 'You were right, Boss. They've gone past the Moor and are heading out towards the A1. You ask me, they're going to go north, otherwise they'd have taken a different route to the dual carriageway.'

'How the bloody hell do I get to the A1 from here?' Grant asks. After leaving the nick, he turned left, under the railway, and – unbeknown to him – on to Scotswood Road, another route out of the town that more or less hugs the banks of the Tyne until it meets the A1.

'From what I can tell,' says Kylie, nipping and stretching the map with her fingertips, 'if you stay on this road, we'll meet the dual carriageway, and then can go north. It puts us about a quarter-hour behind them, but there's nothing else for it. Unless you want me to ask for the locals to pitch in and—'

He holds up a hand to stall her. He doesn't want any marked vehicles getting too close.

She understands, and doesn't push it. Instead she continues watching the map, and after less than a minute this time, she grunts at the inevitability of it and says, 'They're at the Kenton Bar Interchange, but they haven't taken the A1, they've crossed the roundabout and are heading out towards the airport.'

'It's doubtful they plan on putting Nate and Emily on an airplane.' Even as the words leave his lips, he realizes how ridiculous and naïve they must sound. He's only vocalizing his thought processes but still, he's quick to add, 'but I assume there are loads of buildings and warehouses out that way they can choose from.'

'Are you certain you don't want me to mobilize the locals, Boss?'

'Let's see where they're going first, and if they meet up with the killer. I don't want to blow the opportunity of getting our hands on him if—'

'At the expense of Nate or Emily's safety?' Kylie butts in.

'Of course not.'

'I only bring it up because that's the first question we're going to be asked if anything goes wrong.'

He pushes the Audi to greater speed. Thankfully, this late in the evening, traffic is light. He only has to overtake one car as he heads for the dual carriageway. On the A1 in particular there's more traffic, mainly overnight delivery vehicles and taxis, but he commandeers the outside lane and powers along at over a hundred miles per hour. Kylie's estimate that they'd be fifteen minutes behind the abductors gets cut second by second.

'They're past the airport and continuing into the countryside above someplace called Pont-e-land,' Kylie says, stumbling slightly over the pronunciation of the town. She uses her fingers to stretch the map, zooming in for greater clarity. 'Yeah, they're passing a place called Smallburn.'

'Can you see anywhere ahead of them where they might be going?'

'The only place of note is a zoological garden, but I doubt that's it. Next stop's a little village called Ogle, then, well, more countryside.'

'In hindsight, I suppose it makes more sense than hiding out in a warehouse near the airport. They'll probably want a secluded place where there's no chance of being disturbed.'

'That hasn't always been the case,' Kylie reminds him. 'Sykes was taken and subsequently murdered in the heart of a city.'

'True. But from what I've come to believe, Nate is a far bigger prize than Darren Sykes was. After the trouble they've gone to in order to capture him, I think that the killer will take things in a more leisurely way and take Nate's suffering to new heights. For that reason he'll have planned ahead, and found somewhere remote where he can take his time.'

'You're probably right. There are any number of farms out there. Maybe they've accessed one already like they did at Cowley Dale Farm.'

'No mention of a donkey sanctuary on there?' he asks, only partially joking.

'The map isn't that detailed, but I can search for—'

'I wasn't being serious,' Grant tells her, 'but now that I think about it . . .'

Grant takes the slip road off the dual carriageway, following signs for the airport. He wonders how far behind they are now. But it is unimportant: as long as he arrives in time before the cutting and slicing begin. He's fearful of giving the game away by sending patrol cars screaming towards Ogle. There's still the possibility that the killer isn't in situ yet, and the last thing he wants is to blow everything by grabbing his accomplices without putting the cuffs on him too. Still, it's going to get a bit remote out there, and available officers will probably be few and far between: maybe it's time to begin assembling a response team and have them travel out to a staging area, perhaps on the fringe of Ponteland.

As they pass the airport, and negotiate some roundabouts, Grant voices the idea. Kylie's first response is to exhale in relief: maybe she feared he was leading them to career suicide and she'd been hoping he'd change his mind before things went wrong.

'Remember I asked you to shout up if you think I'm making the wrong decision,' he says.

'Don't worry, I will.'

He takes her words as confirmation that, even if his plan wasn't originally protocol, he isn't acting too maverick for his own good. Not yet.

FORTY

Lying in the bed of the car, Nate feels the warmth radiating off Emily. Her back is to his, and he can feel her shivering, a faint tremor that he's in fear of catching, as if it is some type of transferable virus. His hands have been cinched together with cable ties, and he assumes hers have too. He has reached out, tried to find her fingers, but without contorting his spine he's been unable to find them. Emily hasn't responded to being pushed or prodded, and at first he thought her dead, but now merely feigning unconsciousness. She has probably been gagged. After he was dumped in on top of her, the big man, Robin, and the girl who'd sneaked up and struck him over the head, had each set about trussing him more securely, and that included the addition of some electrical tape that they'd wound around his face, sorely parting his lips, to help keep him quiet. The gag is ineffective. If he wants to, he's certain he can shout, probably even form words because his tongue isn't constrained, but that isn't the purpose of the gag: it is a psychological tool, to debase and to cow him into obedience. He assumes that Emily is similarly wrapped, and she is staying silent out of fear of retribution.

There's no way to know where they're being taken. Nobody in the car has spoken lately, except for Robin, who, once Nate was at their mercy, crouched low and whispered how he was sucker-punched and, if it weren't for instructions to bring him in alive, he'd have ripped Nate's head clean off. The guy is not only a bully and a coward, he is seriously deluded about his fighting prowess, too.

Somewhere along the journey, Cassandra had demanded that Nate be searched once more, to ensure he wasn't wearing a wire or bug. His captors must have watched too many cop shows on TV, because they instantly pulled open his jacket and yanked up his sweater and shirt to check for wires duct-taped to his torso. They missed his phone entirely, instead sharing the satisfaction and wonder when disclosing the vivid scar on his back: if there'd been any doubt they had the right man, his covenant brand confirmed it.

It surprised him that the covenant should hold such awe for them, they must have seen those carried by the other victims, not to mention the one that Nate knew was seared into Cassandra's own flesh. It made him think about Cassandra, and how the girl he'd last seen rush away into the burning compound had survived. She'd boasted to Special Agent Turrell that the fire cleansed; well, apparently it had tickled the side of her face, but it had not been enough to purify her of madness. She had been totally suckered into believing the lies preached to them twenty-odd years ago, and had continued to be fooled to this day. He'd like to ask how she'd escaped the compound from under the noses of law enforcement, how she'd survived and grown to adulthood without her true identity being discovered, and how ultimately she'd come here to the UK to do the murderous bidding of a maniac. Not under these circumstances, though. His questions could possibly stir old enmity, and encourage her to have him punished. Robin said they were under instructions not to kill him, but nothing had been said about not smashing him to a senseless pulp. He needs his wits and his limbs intact for when – if – an opportunity to free Emily arises.

Thankfully they missed his phone, so it's still secretly beaming out a locational signal, but the same can't be said of Emily's. Somewhere, a few minutes and miles back, Cassandra had broken her phone into several parts and strewn them along the verges.

She used a different phone to call in a situation report, and an estimated time of arrival at their final destination. They were merely ten minutes out. It is never a great feeling having fore-knowledge that the remaining duration of your life can be counted in less than a couple handfuls of minutes. On the flip side, it helps build the determination to fight back and not surrender to the inevitable.

Nate's almost fit for exploding, except there's the small matter of the cable ties on his wrists and ankles holding him back. Then there's also the fact he hopes to arrive at their final destination, to come face to face with the killer, and prove to himself, as well as anyone else, that his little brother isn't the monster responsible for murdering the other survivors from Ohop Island.

He still entertains a niggling concern that William *might be* the killer, but when he thinks back to how dismissive Cassandra was about him, he doubts that Will's the one to have groomed her from adolescence to adulthood in the madness of the Berith cult. What was it she called him – a lovesick puppy, and never her friend? They'd only been thrown together because they'd been chosen . . . we were the Children of Hamor, we were *promised*.

Her words assure him that the one guiding these brainwashed idiots is somebody else entirely; he just hasn't a clue who it might be. He tries thinking back, ordering the faces of the chil-dren saved from the fire by Agent Turrell, matching them to the known victims of the would-be-Berith to date, and understands that only he, Will and Cassandra have survived until now. Correction, following Will being snatched from the clutches of the police, there's been no clue to his fate; for all Nate can tell, maybe he and Cassandra are the last living of the children. It's grown apparent that the cult has stretched feelers out to all corners, has ensnared the disenfranchised and the lost and drawn them into its stinking embrace. He only has to recall that there are the likes of Robin and the woman, and their driver, to assume that these are new recruits, and if the number of weirdos following the lore on the deep web is anything to go by, then the killer could be one of many risen in the past couple of decades who might entertain a claim to the red throne.

His attention is snatched from whom the killer is, to where he awaits. The car has gone off road. They're no longer on smooth tarmac, but a bumpy track, deeply grooved in places. The car rocks and bounces, throwing all inside around. Nate and Emily are forced together, and again he tries to find her fingers, to give them a reassuring squeeze. He's surprised to find Emily groping for him, perhaps to offer similar support. They entwine their fingers for the briefest of times, before the jouncing of the car tears them apart.

Robin, clumsy and too large to be one of those crouching in the back with them, curses as his head is continuously banged against the roof. He shifts, kneeling on Nate, and it's as if he deliberately bears all his weight into Nate's kidneys. Nate groans in agony, but it's not simply from the downward force: being shifted around has displaced his concealed phone. It digs mercilessly into his genitals. He tries shifting, at the same time desperate not to give away what is troubling him. Robin enjoys his discomfort, and ensures that he digs his knees deeper into Nate's back. He uses a bloody palm to ram Nate's face into the floor of the car, and twines his fingers in his hair so he can scrub his cheek back and forth. Nate loses an outer layer of skin. His cheek burns. He swears at the bully, but it only galvanizes him. Robin lifts and bangs Nate's face repeatedly against the floor until a snappy command from Cassandra halts him. He lowers Nate's head, but doesn't release the grasp on his hair: his act of defiance is as much about showing Cassandra she can only boss him around so far, but mainly it's to show Nate he made a mistake in taking him on.

The car continues to judder, and then it's as if even the bumpy track is a distant memory. It sounds as if the car struggles to proceed, and Nate understands why: they have left the road and are crossing a field of deep grass. The field is a large one, several acres at least, and it's minutes before the tyres find better purchase. Gravel tinkles off the car's underside. They are back on a trail of sorts.

There's a shift of atmosphere inside the car. It's easy to imagine them all leaning forward to see what is about to appear in the car's headlights. Robin releases some of the pressure on Nate, but it's probably a subconscious act rather than deliberate. The four Berith followers talk, but it is mostly indecipherable chatter, with each yapping over the top of the others. While they're distracted, Nate worms his hips aside, lessening the spearing of his phone into his pubis. The relief is massive.

The car slows to almost a crawl.

Then it stops.

Nate cranes to see, but he's too low down in the car. Through the windows all he can make out is the night sky, a slightly lighter darkness than the car's interior, and maybe the impression of tree limbs, skeletal and empty of foliage. The front passenger door opens and Cassandra gets out.

He hears a low murmur of discourse, and assumes a guard has met them. There's the briefest of metallic shrieks, and within seconds Cassandra gets back inside the car and it begins crawling again. She thanks the guard, and Nate can only assume he has opened a gate for them to proceed.

A short drive follows, and it's probably hundreds of metres that are traversed rather than miles. The car comes to a crunching halt. Cassandra's door swings open again, and this time the interior light comes on – she must have earlier switched it off so their position wasn't illuminated from the distant road. Nate wonders if they'd traversed the field and most recent road without headlights, explaining why the car had been driven so slowly. By turning back on the dome light, it hinted that they were now in an enclosed space and invisible from passers-by.

'Get them out and bring them,' Cassandra orders.

There's no doubt to whom she is referring. Robin immediately leans close and says, 'Give me any trouble and see what ya get.' The back hatch is opened by somebody, and Robin is first to scramble out. He stretches and rolls his neck: he never once releases his hold on Nate. He drags his prisoner out. Nate plays at being cowed. He slumps against Robin, forcing the big man to exert his strength to keep him standing. He sneaks looks, checking on Emily. The woman, and possibly it is the driver, both manhandle her out of the car, using the rear passenger door rather than the boot. Emily might be acting, too, because she slumps between them, and they each have to throw an arm under one armpit, and drag her on the toes of her trainers through what Nate can now tell is a large industrial shed. A tractor sits abandoned in one corner; nearer by there's a van, also abandoned. The shed is cavernous, it echoes with their steps, an empty space of tin sheets and metal girders. Double doors through which they must have driven are now closed.

'How much of that shit did you give her?' the woman asks, and her male companion smirks.

'Kept her quiet, didn't it?' he says, telling Nate he is wrong. She isn't acting, Emily truly is doped. Surprisingly he hasn't been given a shot of whatever they'd used to knock her out.

Robin drags Nate aloft.

'Stand up, will ya, man!'

Nate continues to lower his centre of gravity. Robin is going to be made to work.

'What the hell's that?' It's another voice, male, probably another of Berith's followers who has met them in the huge shed. It is probably he who has closed the doors now they are inside. Within seconds he has proved he is more security conscious than any of the others.

Cassandra croaks in her West Coast accent, 'Like, you've gotta be kiddin' me?'

Even Nate's unsure what has caused such surprise, but his confusion only lasts a split-second, until he follows their gazes below his waistline. A faint blue glow emanates from the material at his crotch. The pressure exerted on him has forced his phone to awaken, and the screen to come to glowing life. In the darkness of the agricultural shed, his jeans look lit with blue fire.

Cassandra aims a crooked finger. 'Is that your cell phone in your shorts?'

Well, Nate thinks, putting his own American twang on it, *I sure ain't pleased to see you.* He doesn't voice his words: it isn't as if he can pretend otherwise.

Cassandra shudders in place.

'He could be leading the damn cops here! Robin, how did you miss something as obvious as a goddamn cell phone stuffed in his shorts?'

'Don't blame me, Zandra.' Robin warbles something more about having had his nose broken and—

The newcomer lunges forward and drags at Nate's waistband, trying to tear open his jeans. Nate gives no resistance: the last thing he wants is for his jeans to be yanked down around his ankles, stymieing any hope of rescuing Emily. The guy isn't as averse to digging deeper than Robin had, and he forces his hand inside Nate's pants and grasps the phone. He pulls it free and immediately checks the screen.

'Don't know who from but he has missed calls,' he announces.
'Give me that.'

Cassandra practically snatches the phone out of the other's
hand. She checks the screen and then glares at Nate. 'Who are
these calls from?'

Nate mutters around his gag.

'Let him speak,' she tells Robin, and the big man drags the
electrical tape down under Nate's chin.

'Well?' Cassandra demands.

'I'm not a psychic,' says Nate.

She aims the screen at him so that he can see the list of
numbers.

He knows fine well that the numbers are Grant and Kylie's.

'Probably some asshole trying to scam me,' he ventures. 'As
you can see, I didn't answer them.'

'Liar.'

Cassandra scrolls down the list, showing where he had indeed
spoken with them both, most recently a little more than an hour
ago while hiding outside the railway station.

'Ah, yes, I remember now. It was some guy asking if I'd been
in an accident that wasn't my fault. I told him no but the son of
a bitch is persistent.'

Cassandra snorts, disbelieving everything, but that's to be
expected. All he cares about is that he distracts her from the
truth.

'You said you'd thrown this in the lake at the park.'

'Yeah. My bad.'

She appears on the verge of throwing the phone down and
stamping it underfoot, but she catches the eye of the newcomer.
Already her driver has left, helping the other woman to carry
Emily through a small access door at the rear of the shed. 'Take
this, and get it as far away from here as you can, as fast as you
can.'

He pauses, as if unsure he wants to miss the rest of the show.
But after a second's thought he holds out his palm to take the
phone. He has probably sussed that the phone might already be
leading their enemies to this place, and he prefers not to be
around when they arrive: apparently his worship of Berith doesn't
trump saving his own skin.

He leaves via a smaller access hatch in one of the huge front doors. Metallic noises follow as he locks the hatch behind him. After more seconds pass, a motorcycle engine growls to life, and the man sets off on his mission to lead any would-be rescuers on a wild-goose chase.

Nate stands in the darkness of the shed, with Robin clutching him at his collar, and at his cinched wrists. Cassandra stands before him, and she shudders once more. He's unsure if he's the cause of such revulsion or it's the fact she has been made a fool of through the ineptitude of those she's allied with. She points a finger at his chest, and says, 'If you've been followed, then may God take pity on you.'

'Whose god would that be, Cassandra?' he answers.

She sneers, and turns her back on him.

Robin reminds him he's not to be underestimated again, shaking Nate so violently that his feet leave the ground. 'Anythin' else hidden in ya knickers?' the big man demands.

'There's nothing down there for you, big fella,' Nate says.

'With room enough to hide a phone, I bet you're a dickless muthafucka.' Robin snickers at his wisdom.

'Talk about an oxymoron,' says Nate.

'Who are you callin' a moron?'

He again shakes Nate, and bullies him across the floor of the shed towards the door through which Cassandra is about to exit. She checks on their progress, ushering Robin to greater speed with the snap of her fingers. She doesn't wait, stepping through the door without another backwards look.

For the moment, Nate is alone with Robin.

The big man makes the mistake of releasing his wrists in order to reach and stop the door from swinging shut. Robin's grasp is only tenuous on his collar.

The temptation to spin and break his grip is strong.

He has the knowledge and ability to snap the cable ties, so can be free of them in seconds. In the instant afterwards, Robin will be upon him. Nate's confident that he can take the big man out, but not if Robin's given a chance to pile into him before he's ready. The big sap can still knock his head off if his weight is behind his fists. And besides, freeing himself isn't his priority.

After previously acting recalcitrant and sarcastic, he behaves, allowing Robin to manoeuvre him through the doorway, and even waits for the big man to regain his hold on his wrists, before moving on.

Once outside, the world opens up to a sky filled with a billion twinkling points of light. Woodland forms a bulwark on one horizon, and low rolling hills another. Predominantly the landscape to the south and east is aflame with town and city lights. He's somewhere rural, not a million miles from Newcastle or its neighbours, but there's no hint at his exact location. He can still hear the wasp's buzz of the motorcycle that bears his mobile phone away, and also the faintest rumble of traffic from a further distance. Nearer by, the sounds are of Emily's captors pushing her to walk towards a farmhouse. Emily takes staggering steps, and again is practically picked up and carried.

The house is large, a manse almost. It has been built from stones from Hadrian's Wall, he assumes, as many homes in the vicinity have. He knows that there's a village thereabout that is named Wall, for the very reason it was allegedly erected from stone reclaimed from the Roman fortification. Even in the darkness, the building has a yellow-luminescence to it. Most of the rooms inside are unlighted, but a single bulb burns over the front door. Nate expects Emily to be taken there, but before reaching the house, she's turned away and propelled towards the deep gloom of the woodland.

A person sits astride a quad bike. A trailer has been hooked to the four-wheeler, and Emily is forced to climb on to it. Her captors also get on and sit with her squeezed between them. Cassandra, her voice low enough to be out of Nate's earshot, waves the quad-bike driver away, and he takes off at a steady trundle along what Nate now sees is a rutted track. The track takes a long curve through an open pasture: for a second, Nate considers breaking free of Robin and running to cut off the four-wheeler, to grab Emily from her captors and dash with her into the cover of the woods. He discards the idea almost immediately, recalling that Cassandra carries a knife, and it's probable that Emily's guards are similarly armed. While he runs, puffing and panting after the quad bike, chased by a baying Robin, they could cut her throat long before he reaches them.

He's made to wait until the quad bike returns. It is several minutes of worry, while he frets over where Emily has been taken, and into whose hands she's been delivered. He is forced to climb aboard the trailer and made to sit. Robin releases him, but only so that he can accept the knife offered to him by Cassandra: she has no intention of sitting in the rear; she clambers up and sits in the pillion seat of the quad bike. Robin shows Nate the knife, holding the point dangerously close to his left eyeball.

'Fuck with me again and I swear I'll blind you,' Robin growls.

Nate doesn't take the threat seriously; he doubts that Robin has the stomach to stick a knife in his eye, but he doesn't want to test his theory. He sits, hands clasped and hidden behind him, and begins flexing and bending his wrists.

FORTY-ONE

'Bloody hell,' DCI Openshaw groans, and begins swiping his shoe back and forth on a tuft of grass.

Kylie McMahon stifles a smile.

'Bloody cows,' Grant goes on.

'You're in their domain now,' Kylie reminds him.

'You'd think they'd have more consideration than to shit all over the place, then.'

The conversation sounds inane, but its real purpose is to momentarily cover his concern for Nate and Emily's welfare. He searches the wide expanse of field: in the starlight, the grass looks spiky and stiff. Despite the crusted muck on the ground, there is no hint of cows or any other livestock. At this time of the year, they are probably kept in barns.

'Look,' he says, pointing.

Cutting through the otherwise silvery pasture, there are darker ribbons. It doesn't take great tracking skills to deduce that several vehicles have recently taken short cuts across the field.

Earlier, Grant had experienced a pang of panic when Kylie reported that the signal from Emily Prince's phone had died. After thinking things through, he wasn't as worried. Her abductors had probably had control of her phone from the beginning, and had used it to lure Nate into their trap, and had subsequently destroyed it to avoid it being tracked. Grant hoped that Nate had been more resourceful, and had some kind of plan in mind when submitting to capture. It seemed he had: Nate's phone continued to beam out its location, and they'd followed it this far before the signal suddenly grew erratic and began darting away. Neither Grant nor Kylie has been fooled into thinking that Nate still has control of his phone, but they have assumed that it has been discovered and that some-body is now trying to lay down a false trail to draw away any pursuit. Had they not got so close to their quarry, they might have followed the phone's signal, but it is clear to them that there was a reason the signal had halted for minutes at a distant farm hidden by the terrain on the opposite side of the field. The prisoners had been dropped off, Nate's phone likely found at that time, and it has been sent one way while he has been taken another.

'Time to call in the troops?' Kylie asks.

'I'd say so.' Grant hurries to get back in his Audi. Kylie is a few seconds behind as she toggles her phone from the GPS screen to her call list. On the way out she had requested that officers were put on stand-by but hadn't yet had any confirmation a team has assembled. Like any major constabulary, Northumbria has a specialist Tactical Support Group, as well as armed response officers. As Grant starts the Audi and finds a gap he can fit it through into the field, she requests them specifically.

The temptation to streak to the rescue is powerful, but it will ruin any chance they have at stealth. He takes it easy, driving with his lights extinguished, and follows the crushed-down grass across the frosty pasture. The terrain is rutted, and several times the low-profile tyres struggle to find purchase; rather than become bogged down, Grant drops a gear and keeps pushing on. It seems an age before they make it across to a defined track. Probably a few miles' diversion would have brought them to this place on better roads, but it doesn't matter now, they've made it and are closing in, Grant thinks, on the murderer. Correction: murderers, because it is obvious now that his disciples take part in the abductions and killings, as well as the one that literally takes his pound of flesh. Yes, they must be cautious, and take as much care around any of his helpers as they do when ultimately crossing blades with this wannabe angel.

Grant halts the car.

He grips the steering wheel, staring into the darkness ahead.

Mist rises from the icy ground, coils of it floating like oil on water.

'Are we waiting for back-up?' Kylie ventures after a few seconds.

'We should,' he says.

But with that he pops his door and steps out.

He stares again for a short time, then leans down and peers earnestly at her.

'Sergeant McMahon,' he says, all officious, 'I want you to wait here and coordinate with the task force when they arrive. I'm going to go on ahead.'

'You're going on foot, boss?'

'I have to. For all we know, they have guards posted. We can't drive in or they'll hear us coming.'

'I'd prefer to come with you.'

'I know, but I—'

'I don't require protecting, sir.'

'No, I know. It's not that, it's . . .'

Actually, he does fear for her safety, and despite being a modern copper, one who values his female colleagues as readily as he does any man, he can't help feeling protective of her. These criminals have already proven they can be violent, and equally willing to resort to it, regardless of the sex of their victim. He doesn't want to be responsible for getting her hurt, or worse, if he can help it.

'I can't be positive where they've taken Nate and Emily. I'm only going to go and take a look. There's less chance of being spotted if there's only one of us. Besides . . .' he offers a lopsided smile, and all trace of officiousness fades from him, 'if I'm captured, I'll need you to come and save my arse.'

'Give me your phone.'

'What?'

'Don't ask.' Kylie holds out her hand, and after a moment he drops his mobile phone into it. She fiddles around, and he has no idea what she's up to until she hands it back. 'I've downloaded an app. I've paired our phones so that I can easily trace yours – that way I know where to lead the charge when the taskforce gets here.'

'You can do that, huh?'

'Yes, boss. We moved on from pairing with tin cans and string a couple decades ago.' She smiles to show she's kidding before sobering. 'As long as there's a decent signal, that is.'

'You don't need a warrant for that?'

'Nope. Only your consent.'

'OK,' he says, enunciating both letters slowly, briefly wondering why the police have to jump through legal hoops when tracing a phone, when everyone else, it seemed, was at it through a bloody app. 'I give consent.'

He moves off, at first following the path. Gravel crunches underfoot, betraying his location, so he sidesteps into the grass at its edge, then after further consideration moves towards a boundary marked by bushes and, beyond them, the beginning of what is obviously a fair-sized wood.

He glances back, checking on Kylie.

Already the Audi is wreathed in mist and indistinguishable from the night. He can't worry about Kylie, no, he needn't; she's a detective sergeant, very capable of looking after herself.

After a while, he second-guesses why he chose to stop the car so far away from the last blip shown on Kylie's map. He must have been at least a mile off when he left the car, and the going isn't easy, trying to move through overgrown, coarse grass, now stiff and brittle with frost. Half the time he makes more racket than if he'd carried on along the gravel path, kicking it up in waves as he progressed. He's exaggerating, but to his ears every footstep does crunch, and it's a struggle at times to extricate his shoes from the grip of the turf. The cold too is playing havoc with his knees.

He smells cigarette smoke before spotting the smoker.

The smoker guards a metal five-bar gate.

It's a single man, not much older than his early twenties. He's dressed appropriately for the weather and the terrain, in wellington boots, jeans and a quilted, rainproof jacket. He has a green baseball cap, sporting the logo of a company famous for their tractors. He wears the cap back to front with the peak resting on his jacket collar. The young man wears glasses, and a moustache as fine as silk on his top lip, with similar gossamer hair sprouting from his chin. Grant eyes him, thinking that the young man was the opposite image of a Berith disciple to what he'd conjured in his mind.

The young man puffs down his cigarette then tosses the stump aside. It is still lit, the ember glowing brightly against the frosted grass. He has no idea he's observed. He turns his back to Grant and peers off into the distance, and from the droop of his shoulders he appears pissed off that he's missing the party. Grant considers grabbing the youth, and forcing answers from him, because he fully believes this lad lives at the farm, and he's loaned it to the killer for the duration needed to skin Nate Freeman's hide.

He doesn't though, because while he wastes time with the kid, the killer could be at work with his knife.

Sticking to the woods, he skirts the young farmer's position, and after negotiating a low wire fence, he carries on towards the farm he'd seen marked on Kylie's map. Once he is at a safe distance, he takes out his phone and sends the DS a message warning her of the gate guard's presence.

NOTED, she sends in reply.

He's happy to note that she is safe and able to respond.

He goes on, moving with more urgency now that there's little possibility of being heard. It's long minutes before he reaches the far end of the woods and looks down on the farm from up on a hillside. His trek through the woods has taken him off line, putting him hundreds of metres to the west of the farmhouse – a huge thing it is – and at first he curses his bad luck. However sound carries to him, and he realizes that it isn't from the farm, but rather from over his left shoulder. He hears the grumble of an engine and voices, several different voices, both male and female, raised in argument.

A look again at the farmhouse tells him that it is probably deserted. Other than a porch light, no others are on; all the rooms are in darkness. There's nobody at the front of the house, and he can't see around the back. To one side there is a cluster of smaller sheds, and there's also a huge one big enough to hide a fleet of cars: he assumes that's where the abductors have left their car, out of sight.

The voices settle down, the momentary dispute at an end. A man's laughter rings out and it's unlikely that it is Nate.

Again Grant types a message, this time for Kylie to direct some of the responding Tactical Support Group officers to the farmhouse, but the majority to the west. Without waiting for her response this time, he begins a slow trot along the edge of the woods. His shoes are wholly inadequate footwear for the terrain, and in no time at all are filled with crumbly frozen dirt and blades of grass: it's as uncomfortable as hell, but he grits his teeth and keeps going.

The woodland thins out. He spots where an old track has been beaten down to bare earth, and joins it. It is formed of twin ribbons of earth, with a grassy hump at its centre. Kicking free some of the grit from his shoes doesn't really help; it still feels as if he's trampling broken glass and drawing pins. It doesn't allow it to slow him down though; neither does he pay any attention to the niggling agony in his knees. He knows, from past experience, that when he needs them, his knees won't fail him.

Voices grow louder, and there's a huge bang, as if a thrown object has caromed off a solid object. He jerks at the sound, and squats to the ground, his fingers grasping frozen grass for support. He stares, but the night denies him a clear view yet. He gets a sense of figures moving about, and beyond them a huge, looming presence that draws his gaze skyward. It blocks the starlight.

The track leads directly to where there's obviously another building. The engine he heard earlier chugs to life once more, and a dim light probes the mist at ground level. Grant lunges off the path and goes down on his belly in the longer grass about five metres away. He squirms around so that he can observe the approaching vehicle. He had no time to lose: from the gloom the light brightens, and he sees it is from a single headlamp on a quad bike. A man drives the quad with a skill gained from experience, and Grant assumes that this man, like the gate guard, is at home on this farm and the wider acreage belonging to it. The quad flies by, and directly behind it an empty trailer bounces and shudders along now that it is empty of cargo: the trailer was probably most recently used to transport people, rather than feed for livestock, Grant guesses.

Once the quad and trailer disappear downhill, Grant rises up and presses forward, moving with more urgency again.

A large structure appears from the mist. He has never seen one of these structures in real life before, only on television. He's aware that they were built almost as fortified stables and cattle pens, to deter theft of a farmer's livestock during a turbulent period in history when raids from reivers were not uncommon. It's a bastle house, originally with an upper floor gained by a ladder that could be pulled up if danger threatened, from where the farmer would keep guard over his beasts, while the animals were bedded on the ground floor. The walls are sturdy, probably more than a metre thick, and the only windows are narrow and double as arrow slits. If it once had a slate roof, it has collapsed, but otherwise the building has survived for centuries. Often picturesque ruins like this might be converted to luxurious accommodation for the high-end glamping set, but the developers have missed this one.

Grant sneaks closer, then drops to one aching knee at the edge of a dry-stone wall, about fifteen metres away. He blends in with the mist and the icy stone, unnoticed.

A single doorway gives access to the bastle house.

It isn't so much guarded as there's a small group of people crowding the doorway, mainly younger men but also a couple of women. Again, none of these people fit the image he's conjured of religious cult-freaks, but he's been a copper long enough to know that few really conform to the image of a murderer either. He wonders if any of the group is the killer, and instinctively he searches for William Ballard among them. No. He has to stop thinking of Will as his main suspect, it was confirmed to him that the *lunellum* found at Will's burned-out home was devoid of forensic evidence, and that Nephilim and Baphomet had been referring to Nate during their online discourse.

A woman appears to be the one in charge. She is maybe thirty years old, a few years older than the majority, and carries herself with a bearing of somebody used to being in control. Even from the distance between them, Grant can tell she's suffered a burn to one side of her head at some point, and she's made an attempt at concealing her resulting disfigurement under a hat. When she presents the other side of her face, she can be described as attractive, but in the same way that he thinks vipers are quite nice to look at but best kept at a safe distance. All this time he's believed the killer to be a male, but what if . . .? No, he decides, because, although she likes to think she's in charge, he can tell there are some there who would beg to differ. It's doubtful any follower of Berith will act insubordinate to his chosen earthly host. The killer is either inside the bastle house or he is still to arrive at the gathering.

An engine roars, as if some road hog is revving up for a race. The sound attracts attention, some of those at the front of the house moving several paces from the building and looking downhill.

Grant checks too, wondering how close the Tactical Support Group is. Earlier he asked for DS McMahon to have them gather on the outskirts of Ponteland, but they'd travelled some distance since then. After he left her at his car, some time has passed, but long enough for the TSG to reposition here? She is supposed to help coordinate the response, and wait for his signal before sending them in, so surely it isn't them making the racket?

Some of the group look a bit perplexed, but aren't overly concerned. Perhaps it is the guy on the quad bike who's responsible for the noise. They move back to crowd the doorway once more.

Grant needs to see inside.

He's positive he'll find Nate and Emily within, but he needs to know their current state of being. If either is carrying as much as a single scratch, he'll have Kylie send in the heavy mob.

The engine sounds grow louder.

A vehicle approaches at speed, again drawing some of the group away from the building. Questions are cast back and forth but nobody has any idea who is approaching: Grant notes the first hint of concern in the timbre of some voices. One of the men is holding a walkie-talkie. He bleats questions, but there's no reply. Now concern morphs into mild panic. Apparently the smoking youth at the gate has fallen silent.

The burned woman snaps orders.

The group spreads out, a couple of the men moving down the slope, as if to confront whoever's approaching at speed across the fields. After ensuring they've done as instructed, the woman darts inside. Grant hears voices from within, and understands that there are more of Berith's followers in there.

He rises up, and it's lucky that he does. One of those from the front of the building is peering directly at him, a quizzical expression on his face. Apparently, those who have gathered are not all known to one another personally. There's a moment or two while the man stares, deciding whether or not Grant is one of them. Without pause, Grant raises his hand and beckons him.

The man approaches.

Grant turns to peer downhill, a disarming move. The man also checks downslope, but continues walking. He's almost on Grant when he turns, his mouth opening in question.

It is not strictly police procedure, but a certain amount of

Grant's personal wellbeing is at risk. He turns sharply towards him, and jabs the point of his elbow directly into the flexed jaw. The man sits down hard on his backside, and Grant swarms over the low wall and finishes with a right cross to the other side of his jaw: unconscious, the man sprawls on the road. Grant quickly grabs him under his armpits and drags him around the wall and props him hidden in its lea.

He checks the man is breathing and, confident that he'll live, he leans in and whispers: 'Don't move. You, my boy, are under arrest.'

He scrambles over the wall again and sprints across the track towards the single entrance. All thought of pain or discomfort in his knees is instantly forgotten, now that he's fully energized by adrenalin. He makes it to the bastle house. The door is thick and sturdy even after several centuries have passed; thrown shut, with a retaining bar slotted in place, it could prove almost impregnable: luckily the door stands ajar.

Grant peeks around the doorjamb.

There are possibly a dozen people inside, but with the low lighting coming from a single lamp, he can't make out friend from foe. He needs a closer look, to pinpoint where Nate and Emily are being held, but his way is blocked by a huge guy as tall as Grant, but almost twice as wide. He must find another way inside.

GREEN LIGHT. He quickly sends Kylie McMahon a message, a prearranged signal meaning go, go, go!

The intention of a bastle house is to keep out raiders, but that was their purpose back in the sixteenth century. The place is in disrepair, the roof already a memory, and though it hasn't been remodelled as a high-end holiday retreat, Grant discovers that some work has been done on it. Where once a rope ladder would've served the farmer to reach his living quarters, in a later, less turbulent period somebody had added stone stairs and widened one of the arrow slots to accommodate human passage. Grant climbs the stairs, and pokes his head through the narrow doorway.

He now has the advantage of height, and also a better angle on the proceedings.

He only briefly runs his gaze over the gathered disciples, before switching his attention to the figure commanding their attention.

There's nothing remarkable about the man's attire, no blood-red armour and flaming crown as he's learned Ba'al Berith is sometimes depicted in. He wears a black winter coat and jeans, and plain brown boots. His only concessions to the unusual are the ski mask concealing his features, and the straight blade he holds aloft.

He is the killer.

No ifs, no buts, no maybes . . .

There's no sign of Emily, but Nate Freeman's strung up before him, his clothing sliced open to display the covenant sigil on his back.

The blade the killer holds is not a *lunellum*, or any kind of ceremonial dagger, and rather than a weapon it is obviously a surgical tool, and he's poised to flay the flesh from Nate while his eager disciples watch.

Grant can't tell who the killer is, but he has only one suspect. 'Ballard, no! Don't do it!' he hollers, and springs down into the bastle house, intent on fighting off the entire crowd if he must.

At the sound of his yell, everyone turns towards him, including the killer.

Aiming the bladed tool at him, he shouts, 'Whoever that is, keep him back and allow me to finish.'

'I'm Detective Chief Inspector Openshaw,' Grant shouts in response, because if he lives through this, the question of whether he identified himself will become an issue in court; he's also supposed to tell them all he's arresting them and caution them under the Police and Criminal Evidence Act, but to hell with the red tape. He's not going to give any reason for them to laugh and spit in his face.

Several disciples block Grant's passage, and he suspects that to stop him they're willing to pay the price with their lives. He doesn't want to kill anyone, but if needs must: he crouches and hefts a broken piece of rock, recalling how William Ballard came close to crushing his skull with a stone once, and begins laying about him.

Unbeknown to him, the people sent to investigate the approaching vehicle shout warnings and run, and a huge van skids to a halt directly outside the bastle house. Doors fly open and men in boiler suits, stab-proof vests and protective helmets pile out: some of them are armed.

FORTY-TWO

t is hard to say if the shivering inside is down to a lack of nourishment over the past twenty-four hours, or if she's buzzing in anticipation of the end game. Kylie McMahon is in contact with the sergeant leading the Tactical Support Group. Moments ago, DCI Openshaw sent her the green light signal, and she'd relayed it to Sergeant Caraway, and he'd reassured her that he and a dozen jack-booted storm troopers were en route. With the best will in the world, it will take more than ten minutes for the TSG to make it to her location, so who the hell is it cutting sharply across the field in a huge van, with its headlights blazing? For a second she fears that she has been spotted, and the van is hurtling towards the Audi, but that isn't it. The van forgoes the tracks already marked through the frosty grass and cuts its own passage. Kylie would say that it's going to ignore the track she's on completely, and head directly to where Grant reported a youth standing guard at a locked gate.

One thing clear is that those in the van are not police, or any other branch of law enforcement, but she can't say if they are friends or enemies. They can be neither.

When he took off on his reconnaissance, DCI Openshaw had had the good presence to leave the keys in his Audi, so that she could switch on its heater to save from freezing. It was his personal car, not one of the CID pool cars often available at police stations, but under the circumstances she will risk a reprimand for commandeering it. As the van roars across the field at a tangent, she scrambles across into the driving seat. She must make rapid adjustments of the seat and mirrors, because DCI Openshaw is much taller, and at first she can barely reach the pedals. The engine comes alive and she sets off, the tyres spinning on the frozen ground before finding traction and throwing the car forward. Kylie presses down steadily on the accelerator, and the car responds with a surge. Once moving, it doesn't stop.

Ahead, the van continues its wild swerve across the field, and then a five-bar gate materializes out of the mist. A youth, chewing on the filter of a smouldering cigarette, holds up a palm, commanding the van to stop. He is no match for the hurtling vehicle and knows his limitations: he leaps headfirst into the couch grass at the far end of the gate. The van crashes through it, ripping the gate off its hinges, and throwing it over its roof. The twisted heap of bars rolls a few times, then is lost in the mist.

Taking note of the van driver's approach, Kylie doesn't slow down. She follows the van through the open gateway, only a short distance behind it. The van roars on, belching diesel fumes, its lights blazing a path. There's nothing subtle about their approach, it's all about shock and awe. Whoever these people are, she doesn't believe they're on friendly terms with Nate and Emily's abductors, but the enemy of an enemy is not always a friend.

A farm appears out of the darkness. It's so huge it looks like a farmhouse on steroids. Storage barns and tin-roofed sheds add to its considerable footprint. The van initially heads towards the farm, but those inside must've received similar intelligence to Kylie, as they ignore the obvious location and instead swerve uphill, heading up a beaten trail towards a wooded skyline. Kylie pushes the Audi in swift pursuit.

A third vehicle joins the mad race uphill, this time a quad bike dragging a trailer. The trailer bounces around so much it is ready for parting company with the bike. A man aboard the quad bike grits his teeth, and swerves it towards the Audi. Kylie isn't that concerned, the quad bike is no match for the large car, but then she sees him lift something from the seat behind him and her blood runs icy in her veins.

He can't realize that she's a police officer; more likely he believes she's another of those about to wreck whatever's going on over the crest of the hill. Kylie neither has the time nor inclination to try convincing him of his mistake, and she can hardly scratch about looking for her warrant card while trying to defend her life.

The quad-bike driver rides single-handed, while at the same time aiming the business end of a shotgun at her. He barks something, probably commanding her to halt. Kylie has no intention of stopping; she yanks the steering wheel, and the car slews sideways.

The gunman matches the move, and then once safe from a collision he rests the barrel over his extended left forearm and fires. Pellets punch into the door, thankfully forward of Kylie's leg, but she feels them rattling and ricocheting in the footwell: some strike her with enough force to sting, but not draw blood.

She snaps a look at the driver, and notes that the shotgun is double-barrelled. He jostles the gun, trying to get a clear bead on her. Kylie swerves aside and, as he follows, she again yanks the steering towards him, and this time contacts the front left wheel of the quad. The bike's knocked flying. The trailer jack-knifes, slamming down hard on the driver, and then the quad bike and trailer tumble. They cast off broken pieces, one of them its driver.

It's a terrible thing that has occurred, one that might haunt Kylie for the remainder of her life, but thinking of the circum-stances, she believes it is justified. The driver is possibly dead. At the very least he will be severely injured. But right now, he no longer matters.

Her duel with the quad bike has stolen some of the Audi's momentum. The van has already disappeared over the crest of a hill, and is out of sight, but she can still gauge its location by its blazing lights dancing off the woods. She pushes the Audi up and over the hill and leaves the woodland behind. A short distance ahead is another building, this one an almost solid block of stone with barely any points of ingress. People scatter near the van, even as she watches others piling out. The latter wear boiler suits and protective vests, and some wear crash helmets, and are not unlike a paramilitary or law enforcement strike force, except they wear no identifying decal. Some carry pistols, one has a shotgun, but the majority wields wooden staves. Instinctively she recog-nizes that these newcomers are the same criminal outfit to earlier break out William Ballard. In fact . . . unless she's mistaken, one of those rushing towards the only visible doorway into the building is Nate Freeman's wayward brother.

FORTY-THREE

B elieving she could work at her female captor's humanity had proved to be a mistake for Emily, and she'd been forced to rethink her escape plan.

The woman hadn't initially appeared as brainwashed as the woman with the burned face, called Zandra. Emily had hoped to work on the small acts of mercy that the other woman had shown, with the intention of getting her to realize the error of following Zandra's, and therefore the killer's, orders.

By the time they arrived at their destination, she'd counted on the woman perhaps aiding in her escape, or – at the very least – turning a blind eye long enough to allow Emily to slip away.

But this was all before Nate Freeman was dumped unconscious in the bed of the car. From what she had overheard, he had been foolish enough to believe that by surrendering, he'd pay for Emily's freedom. When she heard how Nate had hurt Robin, so it was over to her female captor to beat him senseless, she'd understood that there was little pity in that bitch's soul. She'd bragged about hammering him with an extendable truncheon she carried.

Instead of whispering to the braggart, she'd changed tack completely and fallen into almost catatonic silence. It was best that the woman got no hint whatsoever that Emily was planning to break free, and take Nate with her.

Even when she'd felt Nate rouse and grope for her fingers, she'd refused to take them, because she didn't want to jeopardize her act. It pained her, because Nate was offering support, and maybe equally seeking it in return. She longed to reach for him, but she had to keep up the sham.

When they arrived at the agricultural shed, she'd pretended to faint altogether, forcing the woman and the driver to manhandle her to the waiting quad bike for final transportation here to this ruined building. While they brought in Nate, and he was strung up over an exposed beam, Emily had been dumped in the dust and rubble. The driver had squinted at her, and unless she was mistaken, had mouthed the word '*sorry*', and then he'd slipped away, lost among others in the room, leaving Emily under the sole guard of the woman. Emily gave her no trouble. She just sat, head down, hands folded and, unbeknown to anyone in the place, she began working on her bindings, cutting at the tough plastic with a piece of broken slate dug from the dirt at her side.

The arrival of the man in the ski mask sent a thrum of anticipation through the others in the room, and more than once she heard his name uttered in tones approaching awe, and the excitement grew exponentially when he displayed a wickedly sharp surgical tool and used it to slice through several layers of Nate's clothing, exposing the scar on his back.

In the present, she's fully aware that the madman will begin slicing before she can help free Nate, pushing her to work harder at her bindings.

They snap apart, her hands are free. Emily finally peers up, judging the woman standing a few feet away from her. The bitch's attention is rapt on what's happening with Nate, but Emily's a bit fearful to stand, because the woman might hear before she can make it upright, and beat her senseless with the truncheon she carries, as she did Nate.

Then DCI Openshaw crowds an opening in the wall, and his presence ignites bedlam. Emily claws up to her feet, and in the next instant is running full tilt across the rubble, chasing her captor who has gone to help subdue Grant. The tall policeman swings a rock the size of a grapefruit, knocking down a couple of the bad guys and then smashing the cheek of another. She takes strength from his actions, and grabs the shoulder of the woman. She yanks her round, and hard against her own forehead. Usually head butts do not feature in a woman's fighting repertoire, and Emily's is dealt more by chance than design, but she can't knock its efficacy. The woman reels, blinking in startlement, and that's only before the pain and shock settles in and she moans and folds at the waist, cupping her face in both hands.

Recalling how she'd once considered these normal people forced into performing evil acts by a manipulative leader, she almost leaves the woman to her discomfort and bleeding nose; but no, she hurt Nate. Her punishment simply isn't enough. Emily balls her fist and slams it into the side of the woman's head. The woman cries out, tries to bat Emily away, but only invites another punch. This one strikes her in the temple. The woman rolls on her side, whimpering in fear, and finally Emily steps away. Around her a battle rages, and she jumps to join in.

FORTY-FOUR

Nate awaits the kiss of cold steel in his flesh. It's not that he's willing, only that some of his resolve to fight was stripped from him when faced with the person responsible for harvesting the covenant sigils from the other Children of Hamor, and also those innocents killed solely in order to draw out Nate and Darren Sykes. He had more or less swallowed the bitter pill that his brother might be the one responsible, and if it were William now holding the scalpel a few inches from his bared back, then he'd fight with all his might. Yet, here he is, stunned momentarily into docility by the identity of the ski-masked killer.

How can this be possible?

Actually, thinking about how Cassandra survived, and grew to adulthood under the tutelage of one she could accept as the next Berith after Weyland's recent death, maybe his identity is inevitable.

Nate watched his mother murder Special Agent Milo Turrell, even as she was blasted to hell by the agent's dying response, but he had not personally witnessed the passing of any other of the adult worshippers in the compound. The flames, the smoke, the running battles, all had helped ignite chaos, and it was only in the days and weeks that followed where Nate had tried making any sense of everything that had happened. As far as he'd been led to believe, some had died during the raid, choosing to resist rather than submit to the Feds, and more had perished in the conflagration lit by his father, Carl Walker. Back then it was understood that his father, as demented as his mother Ellen, died due to the 'Cleansing Flame', and Nate had no reason to disbelieve. And yet, Cassandra too was believed to have burned, and the only evidence that the flames had touched her was in the disfigurement to her face. It isn't such a stretch to believe that others originally thought charred to ashes in the burnt-out wreckage had found safe passage through the firestorm and escaped.

This killer covers his face, not simply to hide his identity, but to conceal from view the horrific wounds he suffered before finding his way from the blaze. Neither the scars nor the ski mask fool Nate, though. It is more than two decades since the 'promise' was hacked into his hide, but that depravity has been difficult to forget.

The killer . . . the same maniac that took his knife to Nate once before is his father, Carl Walker.

Understanding has stunned Nate, and ironically taken away some of the fire from his belly.

He hangs there, his cinched wrists over a crossbeam, a victim of karma, waiting for the steel to begin slicing.

'Ballard, no! Don't do it!' he hears, and he wants to correct the shouter, because his brother has no part in this.

Walker snaps at his followers to keep back the mistaken invader and allow him to finish.

And the next words act almost like a jolt of electricity to snap Nate out of his funk.

'I'm Detective Chief Inspector Openshaw.'

Nate twists to stare at his old friend. Grant stands on the sill of a window, several feet above and to his right. The DCI has his jaw set in determination, and his long coat seems to flare out behind him, giving him the look of a caped vigilante in a comic book. In the next instant, Grant springs down, and scoops up a broken stone. As Walker's followers surge toward the DCI, Grant smacks the first couple with the rock and they drop unconscious at his feet. A third person he strikes turns away, holding the bleeding furrow where his cheekbone existed a second before: Grant pushes through the gap he's made, beating at others while reaching for Nate.

After arriving at the shed and being transferred to the quad bike and trailer to be brought here, Nate has continuously worked on the cable ties binding his wrists. He has flexed and twisted and flexed his wrists over again, and now there is a little room between the stretched plastic and his rubbed raw skin. He doesn't try anything trickier than relaxing his hands, and allowing his body weight to drop sharply. His hope is that his hands simply pop free from the circlets of tough plastic. Sadly, he hasn't worked on his bindings long enough, and they won't release their grip on him so easily. He rises up and then drops, kicking out fully with his feet so that his entire weight is on the ties. His skin tears, blood pours, but he still hangs there, a flesh and bone pendulum.

Somebody leaps on him, grappling him around his waist, but they aren't attempting to subdue him, they lend their weight to his.

It isn't Grant; he is being forced backwards by Robin, who has one huge hand around the DCI's throat, his other hand cocked to deliver a smashing blow to his face.

Emily Prince, awake now, and as full of vim as any person he's ever seen, screeches in defiance as Carl Walker looms over them with his scalpel poised to slice.

'Remember when you said if you ever got the chance to kill *him* . . .' she shouts at Nate, and doesn't need to finish her statement.

Nate roars, and twists at the same instant he again plummets, and combined with Emily's bodyweight working on it, one of the cable ties snaps with an audible *crack*! The two tumble to the rubble-strewn floor, entwined for a moment. The irony isn't lost on him: he sacrificed his freedom with a view to rescuing her, but in the end it is down to Emily to free them. He suspects she was play-acting, deliberately swooning, lulling her captors into a false sense of security, before breaking loose and jumping to his aid. As they each scramble up, holding on to each other for support, he spots blood on her forehead, and on her knuckles, but none of it is hers. She has fought like crazy, now it's his turn.

He seeks his father.

He can't see him.

All around there's chaos. People shout and feet scuff the ground, kicking up dust in the ruin. Somebody knocks over the single lamp, plunging them into almost total darkness.

Nate reaches for Emily's hand, and it slips into his.

They don't abandon the fight.

Nate tugs her along with him, aiming for where he last watched Robin charge Grant against the wall.

He crashes into Robin's broad back, and his vision is adapting to the gloom enough for him to aim a perfect kick up between the angle made by the big man's thighs. His foot finds Robin's testicles, and the giant moans and sags, his knees giving way. Beyond him, Grant whacks down the stone in his hand, beating a painful lesson into the big man's skull. Emily also lends a hand, and between the three of them they drag and throw Robin down, and the man can do nothing to resist, so they leave him to cower.

The shouting changes volume, louder now than before, and with an added panic-stricken bleat to it. Some of those trying to escape out through the door are forced back inside, and Nate is stunned by the appearance of a helmeted figure, beating them back with a length of wood. Outside, a shotgun booms, followed by the firecracker retorts of several handguns: somebody screams, another cries out, running and wailing.

'What the bloody hell's going on?' Grant demands. Instinct has told him, as it has Nate, that an attack is under way but not from any expected party – the TSG, for all they are some of the toughest units of the police force, trained to quell violent disorder, don't attack with deadly force from the get-go. Nate and his friends are at equal peril as any of the Berith followers in the bastle house.

'This way,' Grant says, and pulls at them, 'follow me.'

He leads them back to the enlarged window. If there was ever a ladder or steps inside the building, they have disintegrated. But the window is only at shoulder height, so easily reached. Between Nate and Grant they lift up Emily, and she crouches in the opening, her arms extended for them to clutch at. She assists them to swing up and scramble through the opening, and then follows them down some stone steps.

Inside the bastle house a fight rages. Outside it's more of a chase, with people fleeing while others pursue. Those captured are dealt with severely and with bruising finality. Four or five times guns fire, and on at least two occasions, fleeing people are dropped.

The three of them stick together, and Grant leads them away from the bastle house, towards a low wall on the opposite side of the track. A large panel van sits across the track, blocking their view downhill, but sticking out just beyond it, Grant spots the familiar sight of his Audi car. His breath catches as he snatches glances around, seeking Kylie.

As if summoned from thin air, Kylie stumbles towards them. She looks unhurt, but she is not in charge of her own volition: a man wearing a boiler suit and stab-proof vest grasps her collar, and thrusts her before him. In his left hand he holds a pistol. Grant starts towards them, but Nate grabs his arm and draws him back. He recognizes his brother instantly.

'Here,' the man says, and pushes Kylie forward, 'she tried arresting me. I think she's got the wrong end of the stick.'

Nate asks, 'What's going on, Will? What's all of this about?'

Will's gang chase the final few Berith minions around, beating them into surrender, or delivering more final judgement at the ends of their guns. Nobody has made a single move to harm Nate, Emily or the cops. The way in which Will has treated Kylie, rather than resisting arrest, he'd ensured she was protected.

'Don't you get it, Nate?' Will asks. 'I'm not the bad guy here. For years I've been hunting our dear old dad. I never believed he died in that fire, and I never stopped hating him for what he did to us as kids, or for what he still intends to do. I recruited these others to help me, and we've been following his trail across in the States, to England, and finally to here. You know he's building a grimoire from the skins of his victims, and needs stopping. Keep out of our way, and let us do what needs to be done to end this once and for all.'

'I'll help you stop him,' Nate says earnestly.

'I can't let you do that,' Grant Openshaw butts in, reminding them that he's a detective with a different agenda than theirs.

'I don't see how you'll stop *me*,' Will answers, and holds up the pistol.

There's little fear that he will shoot any of them, he's already shown his aversion to hurting Kylie, but it's unwise to test him.

'There's a taskforce en route,' says Grant, and Will nods: Grant means it as a warning; William Ballard takes it as a heads up.

'Another time then,' he says, and salutes Nate with a snap up and down of the pistol. 'You make sure you watch your back, big bro.'

'Yeah,' Nate agrees, 'you, too . . . literally.'

FORTY-FIVE

Kershope Forest

N ate Freeman chops wood.
He has built a sizable pile that he stacks in a bunker
alongside his home. Last December proved to be a chilly
month, and this next one is forecasted to be colder again. Already
the pond next to his house has a thin coating of ice at its edges,
and the reeds there have gone stiff and brittle.

It's nearing a year since the rescue of Nate and Emily Prince,
and the routing of Berith's followers at the Northumbrian bastle
house, twelve months that has seen much activity concerning the
NCA's ongoing hunt for Carl Walker and Cassandra Jarvis. They
weren't the only cult members to escape into the night, but by
far they top the priority list of suspects. Throughout the past year,
Nate has kept in touch with Grant Openshaw, receiving regular
updates concerning the DCI's search for the murderer and his
closest disciple. After fleeing the scene, there has been no sight-
ings of either Walker or Cassandra, and Grant has admitted to
fearing that they managed to slip out of the country somehow,
and are now lying low in a country that doesn't enjoy an extradi-
tion treaty with the UK or US.

Nate's doubtful, and rightly so.

A man called Rory Jacobs was murdered several weeks
following their disappearance. He wasn't skinned, but he was
partially decapitated, and his tongue was wrenched out of the
gaping wound that was his neck: Rory's maiming was recognizable as a punishment to snitches by some South American cartels,
and had nothing to do with the symbology of Berith or any other
fallen angel. However, it was a gruesome enough murder to catch
the NCA's attention, and Dr Emily Prince, still engaged on a
consultancy basis, pointed out that she recognized him. The last
time she'd laid eyes on him, he'd mouthed 'sorry' to her before
slipping away, while those loyal to Carl Walker were otherwise
distracted with Nate's impending mutilation. Rory Jacobs was

the driver who had transported both Nate and her to the bastle house, an inside man and the only person who could have possibly alerted and coordinated the attack by Will Ballard's vigilante group.

Nate is convinced that Jacobs's betrayal was discovered and Walker sought him out and murdered him, or he had Cassandra find and punish him, because he recalls how she'd appeared confident of her ability with a knife when capturing him. He wonders if the crazy woman has studied at his father's elbow all these years, and has finessed her skills with a skinning knife and *lunellum* too.

Apparently, the dozen-or-so followers that gathered at the bastle house are only a fraction of the followers Walker has gained through the deep web. Throughout the country, and further afield in the US, Carl Walker, aka Nephilim, has built a network of worshippers believing him to be the true heir and soon-to-be earthly embodiment of their angelic master. People like Blake Drummond, the civilian worker at Carlisle nick who fed him intelligence, and people like Robin Ashton, who provided muscle, and then there are dozens more willing to harbour and protect him from the police. Nate suspects that his father has been moving constantly from one safe house to another, keeping ahead of law enforcement, and also Will Ballard's people, who've proved more dogged even than Grant Openshaw. Every few months a new suspect has turned up beaten, and delivered trussed in a leather sack to a police station, along with a video-recorded confession and supporting evidence to show their involvement in the murders of the Children of Hamor and the others used by Carl Walker to draw out his sons and Darren Sykes. It seems as if Will's network is equally far spread, and to date he too has evaded capture. It should rankle an ex-cop, but Nate can't help being secretly pleased by his kid brother's resourcefulness, and he silently roots for his continued evasion of the law.

Nate hews through another log, splitting it in two. He tosses a smaller chunk of wood on the pile, before positioning the log and splitting it again. A year ago he chopped firewood as an act of contrition, atonement for failing to save Jenny Onatade, and had welcomed the burning in his muscles and hands. This time the cutting serves a different purpose.

He piles more logs, and then collects smaller splinters to use as kindling.

He swings and leaves the head of the axe buried in the chopping block, and pulls a tarp over the bunker to ensure it is fully weatherproof: not only is a cold spell forecasted, it is to be accompanied by freezing rain.

He goes indoors, where the stove is already burning brightly. His home is cosy, comfortable, nothing like the Spartan cell it was before it was softened with Emily's influence. She still keeps her apartment in Newcastle for when she's at work at the university, but weekends she spends here with him. During her frequent stays, she has introduced cushions and other soft furnishings, and even a potted plant or two, and it's a reflection on how far he's come in recovering from post-traumatic stress that he doesn't object to a little comfort.

It's enough that his mother's slaying of Special Agent Milo Turrell ignited his PTSD, and affected him throughout his adolescence and into adulthood; there's no way he's going to allow his father to continue triggering him the rest of his days. Last year's winter solstice came and went without incident, but another one looms. Walker's studio was discovered in the farm below the bastle house, complete with trestles and *herses*, and the vats, chemicals and powders used to transform hide to vellum; but the book itself was missing. He has it, but the grimoire being assembled by Carl Walker is incomplete, and until their father catches up with Nate and Will again, there's no possibility of it ever being completed. But that isn't to say that some of Walker's other followers haven't done the unimaginable and promised their own offspring as a fresh batch of Children of Hamor: marked with a covenant sigil, they can be harvested and a new book built from suppler vellum than either brother could provide. Should this happen, then Walker can forget about Nate and Will, and even his right-hand woman, Cassandra, can keep her hide intact.

Nate doesn't see that happening, though, and knows that his father hasn't finished with him yet.

But that's OK, because the feeling is mutual.

Periodically, he's received anonymous intelligence – though he knows it's from William – about their father's next possible move. Nate has been preparing for him and the day has arrived.

Outside, while chopping, he'd been fed updates through the

tiny radio earpiece he wears. He had waited, ensuring that he was visible and recognizable, even as night settled over the forest and the stars sparkled between high cirrus clouds. Only once he was sure that Walker couldn't resist coming for him had he come inside.

'He's here?'

'Yeah,' says Nate. He touches her cheek and Emily cups her fingers over his.

'Be careful.'

'I will. Stay here, eh? No heroics this time.'

Emily smiles. She has often joked with him about how she had to save his arse at the bastle house.

'Don't worry, I'll make sure she doesn't leave the house.' DS Kylie McMahon has proven an invaluable asset to DCI Openshaw, who has since requested her long-term secondment to the NCA taskforce. Their relationship isn't as openly affectionate as Nate and Emily's but the respect between them is equally strong. Emily's convinced that they'd like to take things further, but for now they are professionals and duty trumps happiness: Nate thinks hers is a romantic view and they're probably sleeping together behind closed doors.

A voice speaks in Nate's earpiece.

'Roger that,' he affirms.

He turns away from Emily and Kylie, and goes back out the door and approaches the bunker.

Somebody steps out of the shadows to greet him. A knife glimmers in their hand.

'Hello, Cassandra,' Nate says. 'I see my father has you doing his dirty work again.'

As she had last year, Cassandra wears a beanie hat, pulled low to cover her disfigurement. The hair sticking out from under it is longer and darker than her natural blonde, dyed to assist a disguise: probably when she is in public, she wears a wig, and glasses, and maybe strategic make-up to help conceal her scars. She holds up the knife so it's obvious she means business.

Nate reaches and tugs loose the axe.

Cassandra doesn't advance, but neither does she retreat.

'Drop the knife,' he warns.

She drops it, but it has nothing to do with his command.

Carl Walker rises up behind her, feeding one arm around her

middle, and he places the tip of a dagger to the side of her neck. Walker has forgone his ski mask, baring a face with the texture of a relief map. It is hairless but for patches of grey over the gristly nubs of each ear. One side of his mouth is nipped up towards an eye that is milk-pale. Despite this, and the decades since he last saw his face, Nate recognizes his father. He tightens his grip on his axe.

'Put down the hatchet, Nathaniel.'

'No.'

'Then Cassandra's death will be on your conscience.'

'Kill her. I don't care about her.'

'Don't lie. You care. I can see it in you, your humanity . . . your *weakness*. You were always so compassionate, so protective of the other *promised*; I doubt you'll sacrifice another Child of Hamor, despite what Zandra has done in my name.'

'Your name?'

'Berith.'

'Your name is Carl Walker.'

'You can call me Father.'

Nate shakes his head slowly. 'You were dead to me for twenty years; you should've stayed dead, *Carl*.'

'But I'm not dead.' He gives a mocking laugh and speaks like the villain from an old-time horror movie. '*I'm alive!* And I've come because we have unfinished business.'

'Of course we have. I'm your eldest son and first in line should anything happen to you before—'

'I'm his heir now,' Cassandra butts in.

'That's good. You're welcome to the honour. Pity you won't live to inherit Weyland's craziness,' Nate says, 'let alone his.'

Cassandra stares at him, chewing her lip with an eye-tooth. She looks as if she's come to terms with her lot, and that she's willing to die to ensure Walker gets what he wants. Either that or she has no fear of the knife being used on her.

Walker takes the dagger from her neck for a fraction of a second. He jabs it towards Nate before returning it to her throat. 'Drop the damn axe.'

'No.'

Cassandra hisses, and rears from the dagger's tip: a single droplet of blood appears and then runs down her throat to her collar.

'He will murder you,' Nate warns her. 'He must, to harvest your sigil.'

Her shake of denial carries no power.

'Your death will be pointless,' Nate goes on. 'He's not getting my skin, and he won't get Will's either. He won't complete the grimoire or complete the rite of transmutation.'

'I'll reap you all,' Walker snaps, and Nate's aware of the flash of alarm that goes through Cassandra. They've planned their approach, Nate realizes, and he can guess the bullshit sworn to her by his crazy father. Walker has likely promised that using her as a hostage is only an act, and that she's valuable to him and will be raised to sit at his right hand once he attains his rightful divinity. It's the same kind of crap Weyland used to promise both Nate's parents to buy their devotion. She'd bought his lies, as she has for decades, but now a worm of doubt has crept in: the prick of his dagger at her jugular vein has exposed his lie.

'Carl, please be careful,' she whispers.

Walker ignores her.

'You see, even *Zandra* knows you're just plain old *Carl*. You aren't special, any more than Weyland was before you. You're a murderous piece of shit, that's all, but that ends now.'

Walker's smile hasn't slipped.

'Carl?' Cassandra whines.

'You're nothing to him,' Nate tells her.

'I'm his wife,' she replies, and Nate's skin prickles at the announcement. However, she isn't attempting to convince him, but the man she's served and hoped to serve for many years to come.

'Jesus,' says Nate, deliberately invoking Christ's name, 'you sure know how to pick the craziest bitches, Carl. I can't decide who is madder, dear old Mom, or poor deluded Zandra here.'

Walker again aims the knife at Nate. 'You should show her pity. Put down the axe, Nate, or I will slit the throat of this poor deluded creature.'

'OK,' says Nate. 'I'll put down the axe, but only once you let her go.'

'See, I knew you couldn't allow her to be harmed. See, Zandra, didn't I tell you—'

'You're clear,' says Nate, and takes a deep step to one side.

Walker frowns, turning slightly to follow him, watching as Nate allows the axe to swing down to his side.

'Armed police! Armed police! Put down your weapon and let the woman go!' DCI Openshaw, a veteran of SCO19, and current Authorized Firearms Officer, fills the gap vacated by Nate. He points a Glock 17 pistol directly at Walker. 'Drop the knife or I will shoot!'

Walker snarls, and Cassandra yelps in terror. She squirms and jabs sideways with her elbow, trying to escape. Walker's dagger begins to slide into her flesh, and Nate is momentarily caught again in the nightmare loop of his mother's slaying of Special Agent Turrell, of Henry Onatade's murder of his wife, but this time it spurs his response rather than freezes it. He hauls up the axe, even as Openshaw fires. The bullet strikes Walker's upper left shoulder, not fatally, but it forces him to release Cassandra's waist. She folds. Almost as if consciously ducking the axe whistling over her head, and her flesh is plucked free of the dagger. The axe blade chunks into Walker's right elbow, smashing it, and the dagger flies from his spasming fingers.

Cassandra collapses to a crouch, both palms wrapped around her throat. Behind her, Walker screams in fury.

Nate lunges forward, bringing the axe up and down in a short arc: he has reversed the axe, so that it's the blunt back edge that cracks Walker's forehead.

Stunned, his entire nervous system shocked, Walker sits down hard on the ground. Both arms hang uselessly at his sides.

Nate raises his axe.

He's tempted to end things fully but, unlike his kin, he isn't totally demented. He covers him while Grant kicks away the dagger, and then forces his prisoner over on to his belly. Nate kneels down to help fit the handcuffs over Walker's wrists while Grant secures his weapon. All the while, Grant speaks rapidly, 'I'm arresting you on suspicion of murder . . . you do not have to say anything, but it may harm your defence . . . anything you do say may be given in evidence . . .' and if he doesn't complete the entire caution, nobody there's going to dispute it after the fact. Walker has passed out in pain from his injuries, and Cassandra currently kneels in the dirt, trying to staunch the blood pouring from her throat.

DS McMahon and Emily rush forward, and Nate can't say

he's annoyed that they ignored his instruction to keep Emily
inside and out of harm's way. Kylie makes a perfunctory arrest
of Cassandra, while Emily slaps a cloth over the woman's wound
to save her from bleeding to death. Emily looks at him and Nate
nods at her. Moments ago, Walker had gloated that his humanity
was Nate's weakness, and that he was too compassionate, and
maybe he was right: despite everything the crazy bitch has done,
he doesn't wish Cassandra dead.

After . . .

Jim Powell's persistence pays off when Nate finally agrees to
a couple of pints down at their local. The pub is rather busy
when Nate arrives, and he isn't stupid enough to believe that
this is a normal Wednesday evening, not even when it's a 'Pie
and peas' night, or it's hosting a round-robin darts tournament.
There are a dozen vehicles or more in the car park, including a
minibus chartered from nearby Carlisle, when normally there are
three at most, and one of them is usually the bartender's. Jim
Powell has played his part well, cajoling Nate into accepting his
invitation to the pub, going to fetch him from his house deep in
Kershope Forest, with a promise to drop him home again in a
couple of hours, so he needn't worry about drinking and driving.
If he has to be honest, things have changed for Nate since his
father's arrest, subsequent trial and conviction, and the continuous
burden of his guilt has been shed: he actually does fancy a pint
or two in good company.

Powell enters the pub first, both thumbs sticking up and wearing
a Jack-o'-lantern grin, and his appearance is probably a prearranged signal to herald Nate's arrival. Even as he steps indoors,
cheering rises, and a round of 'For he's a jolly good fellow' is
belted out by the three dozen or more people packed into the
bar. Before now, Nate would've turned on his heel and headed
in the opposite direction. Many of the faces are vaguely familiar,
some of them his workmates, some from the nick in Carlisle,
and he spots faces that have become known to him more recently

from his father's trial: they are the families of Carl Walker's victims, who believe they owe Nate a huge debt for getting justice for their murdered loved ones. His adoptive parents are there, accompanied by an aunt, and a female cousin whose name Nate can't recall. He grins stupidly and steps into the crowd. Handshakes pump his arm, more than once his hair is ruffled, and he loses track of who's who and who says what within the space of half a minute. He gravitates finally towards faces truly recognizable to him even as Jim Powell thrusts a pint of frothing beer at him.

'Get your laughing gear round that, mate,' Powell says.

Emily touches a fingertip to her lips. 'Ahem, get it round me first.'

'I thought you were staying over at Newcastle till the weekend?' Nate says to her a moment before he presses a kiss on her mouth.

'You didn't suspect this was going to happen, at all?' she counters as they draw apart.

'Well,' he says, 'maybe . . .'

'There are no flies on you, eh?' says Powell.

'Did you really think I was going to come here and sit opposite your ugly mug all night?'

Powell laughs at the good-natured insult. 'Aye, I shoulda known better, eh?'

Nate grasps Powell's shoulder and gives it a squeeze of camaraderie. 'I don't know why you didn't give up on me ages ago, but I'm thankful you didn't.'

'Hey, don't get all maudlin on me or you'll have me crying into my beer, and it's already as weak as piss.'

They leave things at that, and Powell wanders off among the throng of well-wishers, sharing jokes with some of their co-workers.

Emily pecks Nate on the lips again, then nods at him to join her and the other faces he knows so well. Grant Openshaw and Kylie McMahon have both travelled from their respective patches to join in with the celebrations. Several empty glasses already decorate the small table they've claimed. The DCI stands and leans across the table. Nate accepts Grant's outstretched hand, and then feels Kylie's fingers squeeze his wrist too. He smiles down at the DS, whose cheeks are glowing pink as a result of the alcohol she's imbibed. Nate sits, and so does Emily. The four are comfortable in each other's presence, close friends now rather than associates in the hunt for a madman. They sit and chat, and drink, and before he knows it, Nate's head is swimming and his bladder bursting: it has been years since he's touched alcohol and it shows. He stands, and endures a joke about being an amateur, and heads for the toilet.

His hand is shaken, and his back patted several times as he negotiates his way between tables and past the bar. The toilets are in a separate part of the building, through an exit from the barroom and down a short passage that is accessible from outside. Somebody blocks it midway, resting their back on the wall, while they bend over the screen of a phone. As Nate comes to a halt, his brother turns towards him.

'I didn't expect you to be here,' says Nate.

'Hopefully nobody else does either.'

'Yeah. You're risking a lot turning up like this,' Nate tells him. 'There are at least half a dozen cops in that bar who'll arrest you on sight.'

Will Ballard shrugs and moves towards him, pushing away his phone in his pocket. 'It's a risk I'm willing to take. I couldn't stay away, not if it means missing your big moment.'

Nate shrugs. 'People want to thank me for catching our dad and Cassandra. I'm nodding and smiling in all the right places but, to be honest, I don't feel their thanks are necessary.'

'You've brought them justice, resolution, peace of mind' Will reminds him.

Nate waves a finger between them. 'We did, Will. If you and your friends hadn't turned up when you did, who knows how things might've ended at the bastle house?'

'You and your team would've done all right without us,' says Will.

Nate shakes his head.

'You should've killed him when you had the chance, you know,' says Will after a moment.

'Maybe.'

'There's no maybe about it. While he's alive, whether behind bars or not, he'll have his supporters, the way that Weyland did before he died. While Father lives, they'll cling to the hope he'll still transcend and become Ba'al Berith, and it might encourage them to take things into their own hands to speed things up.'

Now it's Will who waves a finger between them. '*We* are still Children of Hamor, we are still "the promised" to them, marked by *his covenant*, and they might come after us again. I'm not worried about them getting me. I've got my back-up team watching out for me, Nate, but what about you? Once all these folks bugger off home, you'll be on your own.'

'I won't be alone. I have Emily now and . . .'

'Your copper pals? You can't count on Openshaw or McMahon to stick around to look out for you. Their part in this is finished, they're going to move on to other cases—'

Nate holds up a palm, halting him. 'I wasn't going to mention either of them, I was going to say I've got my brother back. You're like the bloody Scarlet Pimpernel, but I know if I need help, I only need to reach out and you'll come.'

Will nods and purses his mouth, and Nate sees his eyes begin to sparkle with tears.

Nate says, 'It's the same for you, little bro, if you ever need me—'

'We are brothers, it goes without saying.' Will grabs him in a hug and, after only a second, Nate returns the embrace.